WHEN GIRLFRIENDS STEP UP

SAVANNAH PAGE

OTHER TITLES BY SAVANNAH PAGE

Everything the Heart Wants

A Sister's Place

Bumped to Berlin

WHEN GIRLFRIENDS SERIES

When Girlfriends Break Hearts

When Girlfriends Step Up

When Girlfriends Make Choices

When Girlfriends Chase Dreams

When Girlfriends Take Chances

When Girlfriends Let Go

When Girlfriends Find Love

WHEN GIRLFRIENDS STEP UP

Published by Pearls and Pages

ISBN-13: 978-1479310142
ISBN-10: 147931014X

Information about the author and her upcoming books can be found online at
www.savannahpage.com

For Heather, a sister who has always believed in me, always encouraged me, and always let me keep on telling stories in the late hours, even when Mom and Dad told us we better keep quiet and get to sleep. I love you. And thank you for being more than a sister.

PROLOGUE

A *n Unexpected Life.*
      Little Surprises.
Reflections of...

I set down my aqua-stained brush and stare long and hard at my nearly finished watercolor project. What am I supposed to name this piece of art that I've spent the last month trying to perfect? What suitable name can I give a painting that tells the story of the most traumatic, yet exciting moments in my life?

Usually I don't decide on a title for my paintings or sketches until they're complete, and even then I may not arrive at a title. So many projects have gone unnamed—shelved into one of my many hobby portfolios.

But this particular painting demands a title. It's being created during a pivotal time in my life, and it means a great deal to me. Its bursts of yellow and orange represent merriment and hope, while the trickles of blue represent the opposing sentiments: gloom and doubt. The sharp brush strokes tell the moments of fear and panic, while the soft and lengthy strokes are reminders of patience, love, and comfort. The spots of remaining white suggest the unknown or even the moments yet to be lived, and every fraction of paint smattering tells some piece of the story—my story.

The sound of my ringing cell phone snaps me out of my daze and I notice it's my good friend and roommate, Lara Kearns.

"Hey, girl," I answer.

"Hi, Robin," Lara says. "I'm at the store and I can't decide between strawberry cheesecake or cherry cheesecake ice cream."

"Well you got chocolate, right?" A girl cannot live on bread alone, but she can certainly make a go at it with chocolate.

"Of course," she says. "But I wanted to get something fruitier, too. Which one do you think the girls would like better?"

The girls. My close group of girlfriends who've been with me since college—going on eight years—are getting together tonight for a birthday party of sorts. And whenever the six of us get together, regardless of the reason, there are most likely plentiful amounts of sweets, cocktails, and food over which our mouths water (and quite possibly our thighs fear). Tonight isn't going to be any different from any other celebratory night. Well, maybe a tiny bit different. All right, maybe very different since our group of six became seven...or I guess you could say six-and-a-half.

"All right, Robin, I'll probably be home in an hour," Lara says, after we decide that both strawberry cheesecake and cherry cheesecake flavors will suffice. "Traffic's murder. New Years traffic should be over with by now." She huffs loudly into the receiver. "It's the third and a Thursday, for goodness sake! God, sometimes I hate Seattle."

"Oh, you love this city," I tell her. "Drive safe and I'll see you when you get here. And don't forget the pink candles!"

I click off the phone and stare a while longer at my painting. It seems nearly finished; it certainly evokes the complex little details of my life this past year... Complex details...

Life can be a strange thing. A *complex* and strange thing, for sure. See, it all started last March, when I did the most stupid, most thoughtless, most repulsive thing one girlfriend could do to another. I slept with one of my best mate's boyfriends. It was only one night. One very foolish mistake. One very forgettable evening filled with too much alcohol and too little common sense and self-respect. But all it takes is one time. One mistake. One betrayal.

Sophie Wharton is one of my best friends. We met our freshman year at the University of Washington and over the years practically became sisters. Why I decided to do the unforgivable one drunken night and sleep with Brandon, her boyfriend of three years, I'll never know. But by the grace of God Sophie found it in her heart to forgive me; to pick up the pieces of our broken friendship and form a stronger bond. We're better friends now than we've ever been. What tore us apart for two months, once the cat was let out of the bag, ended up bringing us together in ways we never could have imagined.

Forgiveness didn't come easy, of course. There was quite an icy wall between Sophie and myself last spring. I can't blame Sophie for having shut me out, though. I probably would have done the exact same thing if I had found out one of my best friends had broken a golden rule.

While Sophie and I were facing the worst possible situation in our friendship, I counted every one of my lucky stars that I still had a solid friend in Lara. She encouraged both Sophie and me to make amends—because friendship between women isn't the type of relationship that you can turn your back on, or pretend never existed. Years upon years of trust, love, care, and compassion for one another amount to *something*, and should be just the ingredients necessary to leap over gigantic hurdles.

As it turns out, my friendship with Sophie *was* special and very important, and it wasn't something that either of us wanted to lose. And thank God! Those two months without Sophie around were painful. And not just because I missed having her as part of my life, but because our problem had grown into a monster, tearing down each and every friendship that the six of us girls had with each other.

Claire Linley, whom I had also met my freshman year at U Dub, alongside Sophie during our orientation camp, felt like she had to literally choose sides, despite her close friendship with both me and

Sophie. However, she's always been closest to Sophie, especially since they became roommates once Sophie moved out of Brandon's apartment. Claire hated the entire ordeal; the situation, unfortunately, sort of dictated the wobbly ride and the choosing of sides, so to speak.

Emily Saunders, my out-and-about girlfriend, has always been the one with a strong sense of self, always has some wise or helpful input, and is simply there for you in some capacity when you need her, regardless of the situation. Emily was off in Ghana during the disaster—she's always traveling somewhere—but she remained a good friend, offering sage advice via email, throughout. Of course, the natural strain the affair had on all us girls couldn't be avoided, no matter how physically far Emily was.

The character of all characters in my group of friends, Jackie Anderson, didn't know what side of the fence to jump on during the Sophie versus Robin saga last spring. But she's usually too busy jumping some guy to know up from down. I love Jackie—we all do—but she's definitely our "fly by the seat of your pants" girlfriend. Often she has enough chaos ensuing in her own life that anything earth-shattering within our group of girls is tepid news to her. However, she was also irked by the whole chaotic mess I had created.

Which brings me back to Lara. Dear Lara was the only girlfriend I actually confided in initially about the mistake with Brandon. So naturally she had a huge secret to keep for me, and while I hated putting her in that position, I needed a BFF to whom I could tell such a story. She hated riding the fence, but she kept the secret that I had slept with Brandon...she kept it simply because I had asked.

That put her in quite the predicament, as one can imagine, since she also had a duty to Sophie to be a good friend. To tell or not to tell... It was a really rough time in all of our lives to say the least. Having Lara as my closest confidant, however, was probably the only thing that kept my head above water.

Perhaps you could say that of all the girls, I share the closest bond with Lara. I've felt a strong bond with her ever since I met her at my freshman orientation camp. She was a camp counselor for Claire, Sophie, and I, and she has a natural maternal sense about her that I've always appreciated and found comforting. Lara and I just "got" each other from the get-go. Maybe the fact that we were both from fragmented homes was the foundation for developing a close friendship. Two college girls breaking out on their own in need of support and comfort from someone... Neither of us had a picture perfect home life growing up.

Lara grew up with a single mom after her dad had passed away when she was a young child; and my parents divorced when I was in middle school, leaving me with a single mom who became increasingly forlorn as the years of her "unmarried with kids" status added up. Maybe Lara and I "got" each other because we could relate to one another's upbringing as single-parent children and the challenges that can pose. Like the lack of self-esteem or self-worth that can develop when a young girl doesn't have a strong—or any—male role model in her life to love her and encourage her. Or the fear of not being wanted because Dad left and never looked back. The fear of uncertainty because Mom has made her social life a priority, and you're just in the way most of the time. The constant questioning of the meaning of "love" and whether two people can really find it and keep it, because you know your parents couldn't. Whether by choice or universal forces, your parents have been split apart and you're the innocent bystander left wondering what life is all about. Left asking yourself why things happen the way they do and if you'll have the same bout of bad fortune.

I'll be the first to admit that my confidence isn't exactly up to snuff. It's better now. After this ride of a year I think it's a lot better, but sometimes I still feel like that shy girl in the corner who's laughed at by the other kids, ignored by the boys, and whose parents shake their heads in disappointment. I don't know if my self-esteem walked out when my dad did, or if that's just a cheap excuse for my lack of confidence. I can't necessarily blame my parents for my deficiencies, because I do think that at some point we must take responsibility for ourselves and our choices. Do I think my parents' split plays a role in who I am as a twenty-five-year-old woman today? To some degree, absolutely. But there comes a time when you need to step it up, become a woman, and write (or paint) your own history. I'm doing that now, and it's an interesting story to craft, let me tell you.

Now, Lara understands these shortcomings of mine and why I sometimes attribute them to living life as a single-parent child. Lara accepts me for who I am, and promises she'll always be there for me. She always knows what to say to pick me up. She's encouraging and supportive. She, well, "gets" me. Actually, each and every one of my girlfriends—even Jackie, though she can act a little jealous of my close relationship with Lara from time to time—is supportive and encouraging. We help pick each other up when we're down, and we also bring each other down to Earth when we might get a little too full of ourselves. It's a give and take with all of us, but for some reason—a mutual home life or what have you—Lara and I really have this give and take thing down pat. She's my Lucy Ricardo and I'm her Ethel Mertz...or the other way around.

But now, nearly a year later, things are back to where they once were. Or, at least they're back to a *version* of the way they once were. We're all the best of friends again, the way it's supposed to be. Actually, I'd have to say things are better than they've ever been. Life is exciting and definitely filled with the unexpected. Life is good. I'm finally at a place where I am happy. My self-esteem is slowly but surely improving. I'm not boasting a wild amount of confidence, but I think it's safe to say that I feel pretty damn good about where I am, who I am, and what my life is becoming. God, when I think back to where I was last March and where I am now, ten months later...I've made leaps and bounds!

Naturally, I had to endure a lot of hell to get to this point, and that's the story I hope my nearly finished painting tells. The past year was amazing, but frightening. It was a year that I don't think I could have survived had it not been for my best girlfriends.

The faintest of whines mixed with gurgles sounds from my one-way monitor that I've set on the dining table near my watercolors.

That monitor has become my second cell phone—always on, always within reach.

"Coming, Rose," I call out to the bundle of joy that turned our group of six into a group of six-and-a-half. Today is Rose's one-month birthday, and she still needs her sponge bath before I doll her up for her party. "Mama's coming."

While I feed Rose, I'll leave you with my painting. I'll let it tell you my story...

1

It was a beautiful spring Sunday in Seattle. The May sun was shining, the sky a vibrant blue, and all of the flowers in full bloom; the grass, trees, and shrubs were a radiant green, and the fragrant aromas of gardenia and honeysuckle hung in the air. Yet while the great outdoors was singing its cheerful spring song, a dark and heavy cloud had settled in my apartment, and bad news and awkward vibes were raining down. Torrentially. Luckily the storm itself hadn't lasted too long, but the ominous cloud still loomed overhead. Bad news likes to hang around like that.

For the past several hours I'd been both making amends with my long-time friend, Sophie Wharton (the storm that had settled), and explaining my latest conundrum (that ominous cloud of bad news). Sophie had unexpectedly arrived at my doorstep earlier that afternoon in an effort to repair the friendship both of us had been giving quite a beating since my sleeping with her boyfriend, Brandon. (Yes, I know. Horrible. *Really* horrible stuff.) I was completely taken aback by her visit, because we weren't supposed to get together to talk about the elephant in the room until later that week. But Sophie didn't want another lost minute between us, and, at that time, I couldn't have needed a friend more.

You see, for the past week...week-and-a-half or so...I'd had the dreadfully awful, sneaking suspicion that I was pregnant (now enter the latest conundrum). Going on two months without a period, a girl knows something's not right. Especially when the nasty little visitor normally arrives as scheduled month in and month out. Two months—no visitor. Serious problem.

And as daunting a situation it might be to find yourself in when you're not married or in a committed relationship, or when you're a single girl, or when your boyfriend will most likely high-tail it on out when he hears the news, it doesn't get much worse than my case. I'm unlucky in love (something that my best friend Lara Kearns and I sadly have in common, which we often lament together), and I'd made a really bad decision one night. So not only was I a single girl who might have been knocked up, but I was a single girl possibly carrying the baby not of an ex-boyfriend, not even of some John Doe I slipped up with from a bar. No. I could very well have been pregnant with the baby of one of my best friend's ex-boyfriends.

Six pregnancy tests later, each one as positive as jolly Mister Rogers, the guessing game was over. I, Robin Sinclair, was going to be a mother.

"I still can't believe this," Sophie said, pacing my cramped living room. "I still can*not* believe this." The shocking news of my pregnancy was still as true now as it had been just two hours ago when I sprang the news on Sophie.

I sat on the sofa, clutching one of the light yellow pillows that one of my best friends, Claire Linley, had made for me as a housewarming present when I moved into this apartment four years ago.

God, those were the easy times. All any of us had to worry about back then was passing our mid-terms...or if that guy from the party last night would call us like he said he would...

"Maybe the test gave you a false reading," Sophie said, stopping abruptly in the center of the living room. "Those things can be faulty, right?" Her face read of hope. Mine, however, had panic and fear written all over it. I know it did because the churning in my gut and the dryness of my mouth told me that I was making the face of a panicked pig going to slaughter. And the worst thing was that in a few months time I probably would actually *look* like a panicked pig going to slaughter. I let out a groan and pulled the pillow in tighter to my chest.

"Where's the kit box?" Sophie walked towards the kitchen.

"There are three of them," I said, no life behind my words.

With all three boxes in hand Sophie started to read over each set of instructions. She looked determined. That was Sophie—always taking (and needing) control. This was one particular thing, however, over which she would have no control. Neither would I.

"Honestly, Robin," she said, not looking up from the instruction sheets. "These home kit thingies can be faulty. I've read many stories about girls who take these tests and get false positives. It happens *a lot*. Just pick up a copy of *Cosmo* and those kinds of stories are all *over* the place. Or tune in to MTV."

"Oh forget it," I said, a hint of life coming back into my voice. "I've taken six tests, Sophie. *Six*. Every single one of them is positive. Who am I kidding?" She looked over at me. "I'm pregnant."

Sophie took a seat next to me. "I took four of those stupid tests before you got here," I said. "All of them positive. And you saw for yourself those last two. Positive, positive."

It hadn't taken long to break the news of my possible pregnancy to Sophie when she arrived that afternoon to make amends. A girl can't keep that kind of news to herself, even if the woman with whom she was sharing such news played a difficult role in the whole ordeal. Once the initial shock subsided, Sophie did what I least expected she would do in such a desperately pathetic situation. Instead of running out of my apartment, screaming profanities and calling me every whorish name in the book, she embraced me in a tight hug and promised that everything would work out fine. Then she handed me one of her homemade cupcakes she'd brought over. "Comfort food," she'd said, as I picked at the sweet frosting.

Then, finally, came the sudden moment of shock for Sophie: One of her best friends was *pregnant* with her *ex-boyfriend's* baby. Damn. She looked fearful for a while, scratching her head and pacing the floor, as if trying to figure out a solution to a problem that had no solution. Then a calm settled once again, and good ol' Sophie came around. Before I knew it she was whisking me back to the local drug store to pick up another home pregnancy kit because "there is just no way this is possible, Robin. We need to make sure!"

"I'm pregnant, Sophie," I said, resting my head on her shoulder, limply holding the two most recently positive test strips. "I know it." I waved around the strips. "You know it. Now what the hell am I going to do?"

After a brief moment of silence, Sophie said, "*We* are going to take care of this. *We* are going to figure this out." She ran her fingers along my back, giving me some relaxing chills. "Robin? I have to ask something."

"Yeah?"

"Are you positive it's Brandon's baby?"

"As positive as all those damn tests, Sophie." I sighed heavily, tossing the strips aside. "You know me. Unlucky in love. I've been closed for business for a long time. The only misstep was that night with Brandon." I stopped speaking, not wanting to inflict any more harm on Sophie. Having had a one-night stand with Brandon was enough damage; I didn't need to draw her a picture of the night's events.

"Well then, there's just one thing we have to do for starters," she said, still running her fingers along my back. "We have to tell him."

I shot my head up and quickly denied her suggestion. There was no way in hell I was going to tell Brandon. He was no more a part of my life than he was of Sophie's. Well, present bun-in-the-oven excluded. But still. He and Sophie had been broken up for about two months, and it wasn't like I had anything more than a one-night stand with him; no way either of us needed, or wanted, to bring him back into our lives.

Sophie figured differently.

"He *is* the father, Robin. As much of a dickwad as he is, he still deserves to know that he has a child." She shook her head, looking a bit astonished. "I still can't believe any of this is happening... You think I'd be raging furious, huh?" She stifled a small chuckle. "Whatever." She shook her head again. "That's neither here nor there. The point is, you're pregnant with his baby and he deserves to know about it. And *you* deserve support from him above all."

"Oh, I don't want anything from him," I said. "He's already given me enough. I don't want him to be a part of any of this."

"Robin." Sophie looked me sharply in the eyes. "Robin, you've told me more than once that you hate your father for not being a part of your life. For choosing to walk out on you and your mom and your siblings. Do you honestly want to deprive your baby of a father? Even if it is...Brandon." She squished up her face at the mention of his name.

Sophie had a point. I was always quick to blame my father for many of my male- and confidence-related problems. I've never gotten over his behavior and abandonment. Was I willing to purposely set up the same scenario for my own baby?

"No," I said defiantly, quickly rethinking my stance on the subject. True, I detest my father for leaving and not being a part of my life, but would I rather he had stuck around and made the rest of our lives miserable? Of course not. Would I rather have a loving and doting father who's actually *there* for me? Obviously. That wasn't the choice, though.

"Now, given the choice between a father who stays 'for the kids' and is a complete a-hole all the time, or a father who does the courtesy of taking his deadbeat self elsewhere..." I looked just as sharply into Sophie's eyes. "I suppose if Brandon were man enough to want to help me out, then perhaps he could play some role in this. But if he's going to be a complete jerk then I'd much rather have him play *no* part in my baby's life. None."

Sophie nodded in understanding, then said, "Well whether you want money for an abortion or child support to help care for the baby—"

"No," I cut her off. "I'm keeping it."

"Are you sure?"

The thought of terminating my pregnancy had never crossed my mind. The contrary, actually. One of the first things that popped into my head once I was convinced that I was pregnant (aside from the initial panic) was the health of the baby. Was it all right? Was it growing like it should be? How developed was it? Did it already have a heartbeat I could hear? Was it a boy or a girl? And would this baby —my baby—accept being the child of a single parent? Could I provide everything he or she needed to be a healthy and happy child? Thoughts of whether or not I would keep my baby never entered my head.

"Yes," I said matter-of-factly. "I am definitely keeping this baby. I couldn't give it up. I know I couldn't do something like that."

Sophie said she understood, and insisted that it was all the more reason to tell Brandon that I was expecting.

"He's going to have to help pay for the baby. At *least*," she said. "He's half as much in this as you are. It's only fair. And I'm not saying he has to pay up just because I think he's a scumbag and deserves everything he's got coming to him."

"I'm not trying to punish Brandon by keeping the baby, Sophie," I said.

"I'm not saying that," she said quickly. "No, no, no. This is *your* baby, but it's also a shared responsibility. He has to help, Robin. It's not fair for you to have to go at this alone. He has to know."

I nodded my head. As much as I didn't like what she was saying, she was making a lot of sense.

"And you won't be alone in this," she added. "Brandon may come through and really step it up! A total shocker if so." She mumbled the last part ironically. "He may surprise us all. And don't think for one minute that I—that all us girls—aren't going to be there for you, too. We're your family, Robin." She gave my shoulder a squeeze. "You know it's not right that Brandon sits around clueless. He *does* have the right to at least *know* that he has a baby on the way."

So it was decided. Somehow, someway, Brandon would find out that he was going to be a dad, and by some magical grace he was going to have to play a role in all of this. Agree to be a dad? Agree to split everything right down the middle? Responsibilities, finances, visitation? I knew being biological parents together to a child was the absolute furthest I wanted to take my relationship with Brandon. I didn't really know him, I certainly didn't love him, and it just wasn't an option to try to strike something up with him. What, say, "Hey, Sophie. Brandon and I are going to hook up since we have this kid together and all."? No. Out of the question! I wanted to spend my life with a man I loved, and I wanted my baby to have a father who loved him or her. One broken home in my memory was enough.

The baby—my baby—hadn't arrived yet, and Brandon was still clueless about the news, yet my life was already in the process of changing dramatically. It was changing physically, mentally, financially; in every possible way this baby of mine was going to change my life. I wasn't ready, but did I have a choice? The moment I learned I was pregnant, I knew it meant I was going to be a mother. Period. My baby wasn't going anywhere. Whether or not Brandon wanted to help, I was going to keep my baby, raise it, and love it unconditionally. The journey, though... God help me it was going to be a rough trip.

"Is there anything that you absolutely cannot stand eating?" Sophie asked that evening, skimming through the list of recommended take out eateries she'd pulled up on her iPhone. "Any foods you get sick over? Or how about cravings? Do you have those yet?"

I reached for my new book, *You're Going to Be a Mother,* which I had picked up at one of my favorite local bookstores when I first had a hint that I might be pregnant. Once I missed my period for a second month in a row I didn't run out and buy a home pregnancy test. Rather, I bought a book about what to expect if a baby really is on its way. It was much easier reading about the signs of pregnancy than actually seeing the big plus sign staring at me, via a pee-covered stick, over the bathroom sink.

"This book has everything in it," I said, and tossed my baby bible her way. "Everything from cravings and morning sickness, to preg-

nancy and post-delivery hemorrhoids. It's kind of disturbing sometimes. Did you know that morning sickness can come at any time, by
the way? Why the heck do they call it morning sickness when you
can get it any hour of the day?"

Sophie made a twisted face and started to flip through the pages.
"You don't waste time, hon," she said. "This is an in-depth preggo
guide. When did you get this? This morning when you got those
tests?"

"A couple weeks ago. At Randy's."

"Oh my—Robin!" Her exclamation made me jump. "I saw you
shopping there. Like a week-and-a-half ago."

I hadn't seen her; I was certain of that. Had I, I can only imagine
what an awkward situation that would have been.

*Hi, nice to run into you unexpectedly. Haven't talked to you in nearly
two months. And you probably hate me. So...uh...want to talk about how I
screwed up our friendship by screwing your boyfriend?*

Yeah, not so smooth.

"Well, anyhow," Sophie said, holding up the book. "So this is
what you picked up? God, Robin, I can't believe you've had to go
through all of this alone. Does Lara even know?"

I hadn't told Lara that I thought I might be pregnant, because up
until that morning, when the pile of positive preggo strips confirmed
the little bundle, I was in denial. No use in spreading a rumor that
might not be true.

After I rattled off the list of foods that had mysteriously started to
make me gag recently (hardboiled eggs, fried chicken, French fries,
fried onions, fried anything, tomato sauce, pineapple, and, oddly
enough, cinnamon), Sophie quickly narrowed down our dining
choices to Mexican or seafood.

"I don't think I can do fish," I said, recalling skimming over the
book's section of recommended foods to avoid during pregnancy.
"Gee, I wonder what Japanese women do?" There was a thought. "I
bet they eat fish anyway."

"We're not going to second-guess this book, missy," Sophie
protested, still looking through it. "This book says no fish, then no

fish for you. It's Mexican then. Pineapple-free. No fried food. No fear of tomato sauce, just don't get any enchiladas. Oh wait! It says here that—here, I'll read it." She looked like a little girl on Christmas morning, delighted over the plethora of gifts stuffed under the tree. It was endearing to see how excited she was about this whole situation. I started to feel a little more upbeat about everything. There was still a gnawing pang in my gut that held every possible worry about being pregnant, single, and without much of a plan. But there was comfort, friendship, and a baby with whom I was actually starting to feel a connection. A bond and a growing love, however small. I smiled as Sophie started to read excitedly.

"It says, 'Come the second trimester, your morning sickness will fade and you will once again be able to eat the foods that made you nauseous those first few months.'" She looked up at me, a huge grin on her face. "That's great news!" Then she read on. "'During that second trimester, not only will you be able to enjoy some of the foods you may have been missing out on, but you'll discover newfound cravings. The quantities you will want of these cravings may surprise you, but have no fear—this is completely normal. It is also normal to put on a decent amount of weight at this point.'" She stopped reading and closed the book. My groaning said it all.

Great, soon I was going to become huge!

"We'll just save that reading for another time," she said. She returned her attention to her cell phone, in search of a dinner option that I could handle. "One step at a time. Right now we need to concentrate on getting us some dinner, because afterward we've got to put together a game plan."

Brandon. How were we going to pull this one off?

"I think we should wait until after I go to the doctor," I told Sophie, as I stretched out on the sofa, unbuttoning my jeans. The baby book said I wouldn't start showing or really gaining weight for another few weeks. But it doesn't take a rocket scientist to know that a bowl

of pinto beans and a large helping of salsa loaded with onions and garlic could make a girl need to undo her pants and lie around, bloated and immobilized.

"That's a stupid idea," she said. She was back to reading through the baby book, seated nearby on the floor.

"I think it's brilliant. Let's see how long we can go before telling Brandon. Come on," I kidded, giving her head a loving little shove. It felt so good to have Sophie back. Even through all of this madness, she was right there beside me, guarding my back—best friends despite all that had happened. Even despite the current situation.

"Robin, Brandon needs to know. Let's get that out of the way. And speaking of a doctor's appointment, we need to get that figured out, too."

"How do you suggest we tell Brandon?" I asked. "Just call him up? Say, 'Hey, Brandon. Not that I meant to ever talk to you again but, uh, I'm having your baby. Thought you should know.'?"

"I didn't say it'd be easy," she said. "And I don't really know how to do this either, but that's what we need to figure out. Look, I've still got his phone number. We know where he lives. It's not like finding him is going to be a problem. We just need to figure out when...and how."

"Yeah," I said. "The *difficult* stuff. I don't want to do this. Let's forget about it all. I'm sure Brandon doesn't want anything to do with me or the baby anyway. Why borrow trouble? And besides, I have a decent job. I can manage on my own. "

That wasn't a lie. I had a secure and well-paying job as a graphic designer with Forster & Banks, a small yet distinguished publishing company in town, in the lively and peculiar Seattle neighborhood of Fremont. I had churned out plenty of fine book covers and was actually up for a pay raise in the next month or two. I didn't need some guy's pity pocket change to help me take care of my baby.

"It's the principle," she said. "It's his responsibility. Whether you want anything from him or not, we can figure that out later. For now we've got to let him know. Get this out of the way."

So just like that we started to work on our plan for delivering the

news to Brandon; and we even made a list of a few obstetricians I could make an appointment with the following morning. We worked right up until a must-see rerun of *Beverly Hills: 90210* came on. Sophie insisted we turn off the melodramatic soap and finish our plan, but I told her that I was the one with raging hormones in a delicate predicament. Pregnant chick: Score 1. Play on, Walsh family.

2

"Thank you very much. Please call me back at your earliest convenience," I said into my cell phone, reciting my phone number once again to a doctor's voicemail, one of the three physicians Sophie and I had found online the night before.

I glanced at my watch. Ten after nine. "Dammit." Normally I was never late to work, but I was eager to make an appointment with an obstetrician. The more that Sophie read from the book *You're Going to Be a Mother*, the more nervous we became and the more set we were on making my first doctor's appointment a priority.

I headed out to my Nissan Sentra without so much as giving myself a once-over before locking up. If I had corn flakes stuck to my front teeth, or toothpaste around the edges of my lips, or a few too many hairs out of place, I wouldn't have known. With that possible pay raise coming my way in the very near future, I didn't want to be any later than I already was for work. Besides, there was talk about a possible new project manager position opening up next spring for an up-and-coming chick lit author from the firm's very own hometown of Seattle. I didn't get the last PM position that I fiercely wanted; all the more reason I was revved up to nab this one.

I started to make a beeline for my office the moment I stepped through the front doors. "Hi, Bobby," I said briskly with my eyes cast down at the floor, buzzing right on past him in the hall.

"Hey..." replied Bobby Holman, a fellow graphic designer, his voice trailing as I put swift distance between us.

"Morning," I then said to my fellow officemate, Janet. As expected, and by the looks of her lipstick-stained coffee mug, Janet had arrived promptly, and then some. She had a hot, steaming, and *full* mug of black coffee. A full mug at nearly a quarter to ten meant she was already on her second helping. Which certainly meant she had been in the office awhile.

Dammit. Now she's one up on me today. I'll be furious if she gets that promotion instead of me...

Bobby's voice broke my train of thought as I tucked my knock-off Dooney and Bourke bag into my bottom desk drawer.

"Huh, what?" I was as discombobulated as I had been since, well, yesterday.

"Everything all right?" he asked in a low voice. He approached my desk, not paying an ounce of attention to Janet, who was leaning back her swivel chair in an ever so obvious manner and tilting her head our way.

Eavesdropper.

"Huh?" Still out of it.

"Everything all right?" Bobby rested both palms on the edges of the front of my desk after setting down a piping mug of coffee for me. Coffee with a spoonful of cream and one cube of sugar—he knew precisely how I took my morning java. Charming? Or matter of habit after working together for nearly three years? No, couldn't be. Charming, maybe? I stopped pondering mind before it wandered down another path of random thought.

"Thanks," I said. "I, uh..." I caught the scent of his cologne. I had been trying to figure out what brand it was for the longest time. Whenever I walked by the fragrance section of Nordstrom's I'd sometimes think I smelled Bobby's choice of cologne. But I could never quite peg it. Silly me. I guess I could have asked him. But wouldn't that look a bit presumptuous? It's not like I should have been interested in the brand of cologne he wore. It's not like I needed a come-on with him or wanted to flirt. That's a silly notion. I wasn't into Bobby that way anyhow... Besides, he had a girlfriend, and it seemed serious. At least that's what the picture of the two of them in Trafalgar Square, which had been sitting on his desk since he started working for Forster & Banks a few years ago, seemed to suggest. Take a girl to London, it must be serious. Must be real love.

"Robin?" Bobby said. "Is everything all right with you? Did you get into a fender bender or something?"

"Huh? Oh! I'm fine," I said, finally gathering my bearings and making a mental note to stop all other mental notes. "Absolutely fine. No problems."

"You're certain? You look a bit pale."

"Oh that...no. Do I?" I was tripping over my words. "No, I...uh... just had to deal with the doctor's office this morning. That's all. Running late because of..." I caught Janet's stare, which she quickly cut short, going right back to whatever über productive thing she was working on. "...Because of...yeah, dealing with the doctor's office." I grabbed a click pen and starting clicking it for no particular reason, smiling up at Bobby. "That's all." I was about to flash him a toothy grin but decided against it. Corn flakes could have taken up residence. I reminded myself to run to the bathroom to check my appearance once Bobby left.

"Well, I'm glad you're okay," he said, giving two knocks on my desk before turning on his heels. "What Forster & Banks would do if Robin Sinclair weren't working her magic I don't know." He gave me a playful wink before he left the office, leaving me alone with my horrible officemate.

"Good morning, Janet," I said again, trying to sound as kosher as possible. I took a sip of my coffee. Bobby had prepared it perfectly.

"Morning," she said, just as kosher.

Janet Horn and I never saw eye-to-eye. She came into the firm a few months after I had been hired on full-time following my stint as an intern my last semester at U Dub. She moved into my office space —the only available desk at the time—and came on board as if she had some royal prerogative. She had mentioned it to me on more than a few occasions that she was only at our small firm to get a shoo-in to the "bigger and better firms out there"—her words entirely.

Forster & Banks would just as soon be forgotten whenever Miss Janet got the call from some big shot over in New York, London, or where have you. Her brazen determination to climb the ranks and hold out for a golden offer elsewhere spilled into her everyday interactions with fellow "minions" like me and Bobby. Unless you were Forster & Banks's Board of Directors, you got the cold and determined shoulder from Janet Horn. But Janet did do one thing that I could respect: She worked her butt off. I think getting the hell out of Dodge was what helped keep her so driven. I say, let her go to New York or some big shot city. I'd be quite content with landing the PM job with the firm that's been my happy home for the past three-and-a-half years. I had no plans to move away from Seattle, and certainly no plans of seeking employment elsewhere. With a baby on the way such thoughts were absurd.

Baby. I'm going to have a baby.

I'd forgotten for the past few minutes that I was actually going to have a baby.

"Do you have those mock-ups ready?" Janet asked, breaking my train of thought. I really needed to get into the motion of the workday.

"Mock-ups? Yeah, they're done." At least one thing was going right so far that morning.

"Can I have them?" she asked bluntly.

I moved small stacks of papers around my desk, searching for the early sketches she wanted of a project we were working on together. Normally I didn't team up with someone on a book cover design, but the request to have "two minds on this one!" came from the top. We had to collaborate together, and where the design went from there neither of us knew.

I bet Janet wishes she knew. I bet she wishes she was a corporate bigwig. Ah, who am I kidding? She wouldn't want to stick around to become a bigwig of some tiny firm like this.

Janet cleared her throat only as an audible sign of annoyance with my disorganized habits.

"As soon as I find them I'll give them to you," I said, hoping my nervousness wasn't obvious by the timid tone of my voice.

She rolled her eyes and resumed her work. "Just make sure I have them before lunch. *I* don't want to look bad by turning them in *late.*"

Late. The one word that was quickly summing up my existence. Two months late. Pregnant. Nearly an hour late to work. Mock-ups late. Fired?

Suddenly my cell phone rang and I claimed it from my purse as quickly as I could, paranoid I would further tip Janet's anger scale. I didn't recognize the phone number, but then it dawned on me that I had left my number with various doctor's offices that morning.

I answered the call, trying to keep my volume to a minimum. It was, as assumed, one of the obstetricians calling me back with appointment information.

"Uh, I don't know," I said to the nurse who was asking how far along in my pregnancy I thought I was. The last thing I'd want to have happen was let Janet figure out that I was knocked up. I knew exactly how far along I was, though. I'm unlucky in love, so that one-night stand was without a shadow of a doubt the "lucky" date. Yet saying things like "ten weeks" or "two cycles ago" would be a giant announcement that I was expecting. Especially when eavesdropping Janet already knew I had been calling the doctor that morning.

I lied, telling the nurse that I wasn't sure, then she started estimating on her end and I gave her a sharp, "That's probably it!" when she neared my number. A few more questions about a healthcare provider, whether I had been pregnant before, if I was seeing any "signs of a possible period," and if I had taken a home

24

pregnancy test (Hah! Try six!), and I started thinking, *Is this ever going to end? Janet and the whole freaking office are bound to find out now.*

It was finally settled, and with as much discretion as I could muster. The following Thursday I was to have my first checkup, which included an ultrasound.

Ultrasound? Like a baby picture? Baby's first picture?

I kept thinking about this as the nurse confirmed my appointment and information. I couldn't shake the thought from my mind as I began to set about my day's workload.

I'm seriously having a baby. It's official. A baby.

As lunchtime neared, and after I found my mock-ups and shared them with Janet, I scribbled *Need Girl Night* on a bright pink Post-It note, with a little star above the 'i.' The baby was official. The first doctor's appointment was official. It was high time to break the news to my girlfriends. Oh, yeah, and Brandon. Minor annoying detail there.

"Another challenge; one step at a time," I mumbled to myself, causing Janet to turn in my direction. She asked me what I was talking about and I didn't dignify her with a response. It was none of her damned business. I was going to have a baby. I was going to be a mother. And I was also going to get that PM position. I just had to!

I looked up from my computer screen, tearing my eyes away from the practically blank digital canvas I was working on for a new mystery novel, and checked the time. It was near closing time for the day and I wasn't anywhere near where I wanted to be on this darn cover. My creative juices weren't flowing very well; it was difficult to think of an appropriate image for a book filled with neighborhood robberies and a high stakes kidnapping when I had my first ultrasound on the brain.

What would the baby look like? Would I already be able to see its little hands? Its little feet? What about its face? Could I tell if it was going to look like me? Or like Brandon... Would it be a little boy? Or a little girl?

Enough was enough. Another thirty minutes or even an hour at my current project wasn't going to make the slightest bit of difference. I would come in early the next morning and get a jumpstart on it. Until then, I needed to round up my girlfriends and set up a get-together. And I deserved to go home. It had been a rough day, having already thrown up twice—once after a turkey sandwich for lunch and once after I mistakenly had a bite of an oatmeal raisin cookie from the break room. Cinnamon was still off-limits, at least until my second trimester rolled around, at which point my morning, afternoon, and all-times-of-the-day sickness would pass. That is if that baby book knew what it was talking about.

"Going home?" Janet asked, while I started to power down my computer. "Already?"

Oh she could get on my nerves. I calmly replied with, "Got done what I needed to for today." She looked at me skeptically and went back to her business.

Before gathering my belongings I typed on my cell phone: *Must do girls nite!! Dinner+drinks Thur at my place?* I scrolled through my directory and selected "Claire," "Jackie," and "Lara," then hit send. Hopefully all of the girls could make it. I had some *big* news to share. The thought of having to wait a couple of days until Thursday night was driving me bonkers.

"Have a nice night, Janet," I said, toting my stuff out of the office as I began dialing Sophie's cell number.

Janet made some response, but I was distracted by Sophie's chipper answer.

"Hey, Sophie," I said. "Guess what?"

"You got your raise?" Sophie's voice was full of excitement.

"Yeah, I wish. That's not until the next month or so. Still a ways off. But I *did* get myself a doctor's appointment." I tossed my purse and files into the back of my car, then quickly surveyed the parking lot beforehand to make sure no one could overhear my baby-bundle news. "And guess what? I'm getting my first ultrasound then!"

"Oh my God! Like, baby's first picture?"

"Yup," I said, smiling ear to ear. "I'm so excited."

"I was going to ask how you're feeling about all of this. This is some heavy stuff. But it sounds like you're really positive about it. Like you're happy."

"Well, 'happy' might be a little bit of an overstatement right now. I mean, I guess yeah, in a sense, I'm happy. This is a pretty crazy thing happening to my body. To my life. Getting to see this little guy's picture—"

"It's a boy?" Sophie shrieked.

"I don't know yet. I was just saying—guy, girl—whatever."

"Ah, okay."

"Anyway," I said, "It is exciting and crazy what's happening, but I'm still really...scared. I guess it's still surreal right now. Maybe it'll become more real when I actually see the little guy. Or girl."

I didn't know if it was the pregnant woman hormones that made me feel elated one minute, and scared to death the next about the pregnancy, or if it was the simple fact that I was going to be a single mom. And I had big baby-daddy problems ahead of me. One moment I'd be happy over this big life change and the chance to really do something special, like raise my very own baby, and the next I'd think about the whole mess of a situation and how none of it was ideal. It was an emotional roller coaster, and I was ready to get off and leave the park. Too bad I had another seven months to go.

"The appointment is next week, on Thursday," I told an eager Sophie. "You want to come?"

"I was going to ask if I could, but that day's no good. I've got a *huge* order that night. There's no way I could ask Katie to let me off the hook."

Sophie worked for a bakery and catering company called *Katie's Kitchen* over in Belltown, a bit of a ways from where I worked, across Lake Union. She had big dreams of some day owning her own bakery and café. And last I heard she was heavily pursuing them, trying to get a business license and all that stuff figured out. I hoped she did open her own shop up. She had the determination and ethics it would take to run a successful bakery in the competitive culinary capital of Seattle. And she made a mean pastry. And her cupcakes! I could be on my deathbed from eating too many sweets, and if she walked in with one of her vanilla-raspberry swirl cupcakes, I'd willingly die one happy woman.

"I wish I could go with you, Robin," she said. "I can't get out of it at all. I bet Lara will be free. You should definitely call her."

Before Sophie could inevitably ask when I'd share the baby news with Lara, I said, "That's another thing. I texted the girls that we need a girls' night. Wanted to see if you were free this Thursday? After work? Dinner, drinks, whatever—my place? Figured I'd spring the news then."

"Count me in! And I'm sure Claire can make it without a problem, too," she said. "I'm pretty certain she doesn't have anything going on this whole weekend, in fact." Sophie was still temporarily living with Claire and Claire's long-term boyfriend, Conner, since Sophie had moved out of Brandon's apartment when they broke up. I thought Claire and Sophie hung out together all the time before, but now that they were roommates it was rare to see them apart. If they did have to separate, they were at least woven into each other's planner somehow each day.

"Oh and I'll see you in a few, right?" I asked. "You're still up for coming over tonight and helping me figure out the, uh, *situation*?"

"Thirty minutes sound good?" Sophie asked, ready to get back to our plans of telling Brandon the news.

"See you then!"

During my drive home, while getting three ebullient texts, all from my friends letting me know that they were certainly game for a girls' night, I started to reflect on how I would approach Brandon with the news that I was carrying his child. Sophie would be meeting me at my apartment any moment to help me figure out just that, but I had no idea where to start, and we hadn't gotten very far in our plans the previous night.

What would I do? Pick up the phone, dial his number, and then once he answered just sit there, mouth agape, speechless? Or randomly show up on his doorstep and say, "Hey, guess what?" And what if he wasn't home? What if he didn't pick up the phone when, or *if*, I called? Would I gather enough courage to attempt a second time? A third? Would I *ever* be able to reach him? And how would he react if I *did* get the chance to tell him?

At that moment, I thought I felt a tickle in my tummy, as if the baby was giving me a little sign that he or she was really there. It was probably silly, since my baby book said I wouldn't be able to feel any movement until my fourth month or so. And even then it might only be very light and unnoticeable.

"Probably just nervousness," I said to myself, as I turned into my neighborhood. "Probably butterflies."

Sophie poured me another glass of cold, refreshing water as I dug into my Caesar salad.

"Thanks for grabbing dinner on your way," I mumbled through my mouthful of lettuce, parmesan cheese, and croutons. She told me not to worry about it, that I needed proper nutrition and strength since everything I did was for two now.

Sophie took another bite of her salad while fanning through the pages of the baby book, then suddenly said, "Oh! That reminds me." She pulled some items from her oversized bag. "I picked up some stuff for you today while I was out at the market getting some ingredients for work. Here." She produced a bag of tea leaves, some dried Chukar cherries, a bag of mixed nuts and dried fruits, and a small bag of organic, gluten-free cookies.

I couldn't help but chuckle over the healthy options Sophie scored for me. "Gluten-free and organic?" I asked her, looking bemusedly over the ingredients listed on the back of the brown, paper bag-like packaging. "Does it say somewhere in that book I can't eat any gluten? Or that I'm restricted to eating cage-free only eggs or roam-free bird eggs or whatever the heck they are?"

She playfully rolled her eyes and explained, "They just looked good. Figured you could try them out. They won't do you any harm. But this other stuff is really good for you. And beneficial for the baby. Like this." She held up the bag of tea. "This is *decaf* tea, Robin. You can't drink caffeine while you're pregnant, so try this."

"What?" I think I had heard somewhere long ago that pregnant women couldn't consume caffeine, but I'd never paid much attention to it. Back then, it wasn't like I was going to get pregnant any time soon and needed to heed anti-caffeine warnings.

"Why not?" I asked, snagging the bag of less-than-appealing tea from her hands. "Why on Earth not? I'm still supposed to go to work, right? I'm still supposed to wake up in the morning and function, aren't I?"

"Chill!" She snatched back the bag of tea. "The *book* says you need to stay away from caffeine. It's not healthy for the baby. The book says that it can stimulate the baby, like it stimulates you."

"Well I hardly doubt one tiny cup of coffee is really going to stimulate the baby. It hardly stimulates me."

She gave me a childish headshake. "Baby comes first. No caffeine."

At first I conceded reluctantly, but the more I got to thinking about how this baby was relying on me for every single thing, the more comfortable I became with readjusting my life to suit the baby's important needs. It wasn't that I was *going* to be a mom. I was *already* a mom. Everything I ate, drank, and did would directly affect my baby.

So long, caffeine. Hello...decaf tea and...I guess I'll give these gluten-free things a go. Why not?

"It's time we get down to business," Sophie said, after we polished off a shared piece of apple pie she'd picked up while down at Pike Place Market that afternoon. "Time to talk shop and deal with Brandon."

I could do the decaf tea. I could manage staying away from the foods that made me sick. I imagined I could handle the plethora of unknown cravings that were headed my way. I was even convincing myself that I could deal with the whole "giving birth thing." But contacting Brandon? Hell no.

After nearly an hour of urging and finally insisting that I, as Sophie said, "grow a pair and pick up the damn phone," I held my cell phone in one hand, my thumb poised over the first digit of Brandon's number, and Sophie's cell phone in the other, Brandon's number burning into my eyes.

"I'm here for you," Sophie whispered. "I can take over at any point in the conversation if you'd like."

"I can't," I said, thrusting her phone back at her. "I can't do it." Tears started to form, and I felt like running off to bed, drawing the curtains, and calling it a night at, what? A quarter to eight? I took off my black, plastic-rimmed, cat-eye glasses and rubbed away the tears.

"Robin," Sophie comforted, pulling me closer to her on my living room sofa. "If you want I can do it for you."

Why would she want to do that? How could she do that? How could one of my best friends call up *her* ex-boyfriend and tell him that he was going to be the father of her *friend's* baby?

"I can do it," she repeated. "If you honestly feel that you can't do this, I can do it for you."

The offer was tempting. Very tempting. But could I let her do it? And beyond that, why would Sophie offer? Did she really have the guts to call Brandon up and tell him this?

"I don't understand how you could even think of doing this for me," I said. "Of all people, you seriously would do this? For me?"

"Robin, listen." Her voice was still, staid, and her face was glowing with compassion. She took my hands in hers once I'd readjusted my glasses and wiped away the remaining teardrops. "Listen to me. I can't imagine how difficult this is for you. You're so brave to carry on like you're doing. To choose to have this baby and raise it on your own if you have to. It's very admirable." She cracked a smile. "And the most important thing through all of this is that your baby is brought into this world showered with love...brought into a happy home. You can and you want to give that to your baby. And you want to give it a good life. The best life you can provide."

I nodded. "I do. I really do."

"Part of providing your baby with the best life it can have is starting out doing the right thing. It means telling the baby's father that he's going to have a child." She gripped my hands tighter and shook them as she said, "You *can* do this. And we can do it together if that's what it takes."

"He's going to hate me," I said. "He probably won't even believe me."

"Don't think about that—"

"I don't know how you can be so calm about this, Sophie," I interrupted. "How are you so calm? Why aren't you mad about this?" I gave a lighthearted guffaw, letting her know that while I was surprised she wasn't a raving lunatic about the situation, I wanted her to remain calm and supportive.

Her face turned down slightly, and she looked away to the corner. She seemed to wander somewhere for a moment, before coming back and saying, "Since Pamela died...I guess I've been given a new lease on how I look at life. Sounds goofy." She smiled weakly. "Losing her all of the sudden...it kind of put everything into perspective for me, I suppose you could say. We may not have been the closest of friends or anything. Not like we hung out outside of yoga class, but I still loved her. Still looked up to her. And I still miss her. It's not easy to all of a sudden lose someone, and when you do you kind of...well, like I said, you kind of see things a little more clearly or positively or something."

Pamela, Sophie's yoga teacher, had suddenly passed away from cancer a few short weeks ago. It was after Pamela's funeral, in fact, when Sophie unexpectedly showed up on my front doorstep, telling me she was sorry for cutting me out of her life, and that she forgave me for sleeping with Brandon. Pamela's passing made Sophie realize that life is simply too short to spend it toiling over troubles and matters that can be solved with forgiveness, kindness, an open heart, and an understanding that sometimes mistakes are made. And those mistakes can be forgiven and forgotten.

"You've been given the precious gift of this baby," Sophie said, "and it doesn't matter how or why it was conceived. The baby's here and it deserves your love. If this were me, Pamela would have said something like, 'When one door closes, a big window opens.' This baby is a gift, and you're going to be all right. More than all right." She gave me a squeeze, then added, "This baby's going to get all the love it deserves and much more. From you. From me. From all of us! Now come on, this is a new and exciting time in your life, Robin. It might seem rather daunting right now, but I say we get the crappy stuff out of the way and make the most of the best parts."

She fetched our cell phones, leapt off the sofa, and grabbed a fresh glass of water for me. "Drink up and I'll call Brandon for you."

"Seriously?"

"Dead serious."

"What about our plan?" I wiped the water from my lips. "We can't just call him! A plan, Sophie. A plan!"

"Look, he didn't have a plan when he knocked you up. Pamela certainly didn't plan for a short life. Neither of us planned you'd become preggers...screw plans; I'm calling Brandon now. More waiting like this and neither of us will have the nerve to tell him."

She hit the call button to Brandon's number on her phone, and I held my breath. Would he answer? Would he honestly pick up the phone from the all-too-familiar number of his ex-girlfriend? No way!

Sophie hung up. "Voicemail."

I picked up my cell phone and said, "Give me the number. I'll call him. Maybe he'll pick up from a different number." I don't know where I found the courage but I started dialing and then—

Ringing. More ringing. And finally voicemail.

"Voicemail," I mouthed to Sophie, just as the operator signaled for the beep.

I hesitated for a brief moment, then from somewhere foreign the words came spewing forth: "Hey, Brandon. It's Robin here. I know you're thinking—why am I calling? There's something I need to speak with you about. It's, well, kind of serious and we should talk." I gave him my number before hanging up, staying calm, cool, collected throughout the entire message, save for my shaking feet.

"I did it!" I shouted. "I called him!" Sophie looked bewildered. "I did it, and it feels great!"

The problem was, of course, the impending return call. Or worse, if I had to call him back. I may have gathered up the nerve to call him once, prepared to share the news, but actually telling him the news was going to be an entirely different story.

3

It was Thursday morning. Girls' night was planned for that evening, I had already made quite a deal of progress on the mystery novel cover, and there was still no word from Brandon. The anticipation of his return call, or my imminent second attempt at reaching him, was killing me. I hated playing the waiting game, and more than once the day before I'd considered calling him again. *Maybe this time he'll pick up,* I kept thinking. But I chickened out each time.

As if that anticipation wasn't painful enough, my caffeine withdrawal was starting up. I wasn't the most chipper of characters around the office, and I felt I could fall asleep at the drop of a hat. The decaf tea Sophie had picked up, which I brought in to work with me the very next day, tasted all right, but it lacked the whole caffeine factor, which was practically the sole reason I ever drank tea or coffee.

Bobby offered me a mug of my long-lost morning beverage, and it pained me to turn it down. Not only because I was craving it, but because I was worried it would sound off pregnancy alarm bells. I knew that at some point I'd have to make it clear at work that I was pregnant and would even—*gulp*—eventually need to take some maternity time off. But I wanted to delay the inevitable for as long as humanly possible. Maybe when my water broke...

On my way home from work that night I decided to swing by Chester Grey's Art Supply shop. I needed a release from all of the stress, and my initial stalling on the mystery novel cover could probably have been attributed to my lack of inspiration and the temporary withdrawal from the creative world I often enjoyed slipping into. I hadn't picked up my paintbrush and dabbled in watercoloring, nor had I brought out my sketchbook, since I discovered I was, in fact, pregnant. Normally I found a way to sketch or paint three or four days a week, even if it was just a little doodle here or there. I was starting to feel naked or barren because I hadn't recently escaped into my personal artistic frame.

Not that the creative muse was speaking to me lately. If I wasn't busying my mind with book cover art, or trying to make sure my slate was as clean as possible at work in hopes of earning that raise or snagging that project manager position, I was fretting over Brandon ignoring my call. And I was wondering if I was doing everything right, pregnancy-wise. *Make sure you're at work on time. Oh, and don't drink that coffee! Wait, I'm getting a call. Is it Brandon? Oh, no. Don't let your dramatic personal life sneak into your work life. Mock-ups? What? Sure thing, definitely! Wait! Get those eight hours of sleep and meet those deadlines.* Life had quickly become a marathon. It was exhausting. No 10k or half-marathon I ran during my track and field days in college could have prepared me for this race.

"You think two bags of tortilla chips is enough?" Sophie asked, inching herself through my front door, both arms carrying two overflowing paper bags of groceries. Her chin kept one of the bags balanced. "I didn't want to go overboard."

I laughed as I took a cantaloupe from the top of one bag, letting her relax her chin.

"Overboard?" I exclaimed. "Honey, I don't think one more bag of chips would matter at this rate. How much stuff do we need?"

"Dang it, so I should have gotten three, huh?" I took one shopping bag from her as she followed me into the kitchen. "I knew it. Should have gotten more than two."

"I'm not hitting any crazy cravings, yet, Sophie. I think two bags will be plenty." I started sifting through my bag's contents. "What on earth did you get?" I pulled out a bottle of Bloody Mary cocktail mix. Wouldn't be riding that boat for a while. "And what'd you get for me? Some a-ma-zing Ginkgo biloba, gluten-free, lactose-free, tasteless vegetable shake?"

"Don't be such a goof," she said. "Ginkgo biloba isn't allowed for pregnant women. Not enough scientific research about it. And it could affect insulin and blood sugar levels. Don't take it."

"God, someone's really been doing their homework. You sure you aren't pregnant?"

"Ha-ha. You're reading that book, right?" She was starting to sound like a mother. That was Lara's role, generally. Lara, perhaps because she had been our camp counselor back in our first year of college, was always considered *the* maternal friend. I appreciated her looking out for us, and she couldn't help her personality or the role she was placed in when we all met one another. But one mom-like friend in the group was enough.

I told Sophie that relaxing reading in bed meant picking up a Jennifer Weiner book, not *Baby Expectations* or *Expecting the Unexpected* or whatever that baby book of mine was called.

We chatted about work and about how Claire and Conner were doing while we prepared homemade guacamole. The two recently had an ongoing argument about getting married, and about a possible move to Conner's hometown of Los Angeles. Claire wanted to get married and stay in Seattle, where she had her friends and a great job as a social worker working with elderly and disabled patients. She even made their adorable rented home over in nearby Madison Park a real home for the two of them and their dog, Schnickerdoodle...plus Sophie now.

Conner didn't want to talk about marriage, insisting that he could still be true to Claire and love her with all of his heart without bringing up the dreaded 'M' word. But the 'M' word, as in "moving," was something he *did* want to talk about. He had some great friends in Seattle; after all he, like all us girls, was a graduate of the University of Washington, so most of his best friends lived in town. However, he was itching, for some reason, to make a move to California. Apparently he wanted a change. (I could tell him that change isn't necessarily all it's cracked up to be. Next thing he knows, he won't be allowed to drink caffeinated beverages. Or something equally annoying like that.) Last I'd heard, Claire and Conner both agreed that they wouldn't be leaving their Madison Park home, nor would they be tying the knot any time soon.

"You think they'll *ever* get married?" I asked Sophie, as I passed the rest of the guacamole duty off to her and started opening up the chip bags. A girl's got to do a little taste-testing beforehand.

"Oh sure. At some point."

"They've been together, like, forever. What's the big wait?"

"Seven years. And Claire doesn't let him forget it. Think we can start the quesadillas already?"

I checked my watch and told her to go ahead. The rest would be arriving any minute.

"Why's he so slow on the uptake? Does he not realize Claire's a catch and that there's absolutely no reason they should wait to get married?"

Sophie shrugged her shoulders as she warmed the griddle.

"They both have solid jobs," I said. "They've got a nice place. I don't get it."

"Claire thinks *Chad's* not exactly the best influence—" Sophie started, but was halted by the loud pounding on my front door. The girls!

"Robin!" Claire cried out, wrapping me into a warm hug the moment I swung open the door.

"Hey, Robin," Lara said, giving me a big squeeze right after Claire, a bottle of vodka in one hand and a bag of fruit in the other.

"Hey girls, come on in."

"What's up, bitches!" Jackie shrieked, giving me the tightest of hugs before charging into the living room. Jackie: always the life of the party.

"You off to a hot date tonight?" I asked Jackie, taking note of her slinky, tightly fitted black mini, paired with her four- or five-inch black heels. "You look like you're ready to rock the town."

She gave me another big hug, then slipped out of her shoes, instantly shrinking to her endearing height of five feet.

"I got a hostess job at one of those swanky jazz bars," Jackie said, winking. "Hey, Sophie!"

"Hey, Jack!"

"A job?" I asked. "Since when?"

"Oh just this week."

Jackie could never hold down a job longer than a few shifts. Luckily, she didn't have to worry much about a roof over her head or making ends meet. She had Lara, who would always (and I mean *always*) be there for her in a pinch. Whether it was extra cash or a shoulder to cry on, Lara and Jackie were best buds, and Lara's trusty maternal side could never disappoint Jackie.

Jackie also had Emily's apartment to crash at, since Emily was usually trekking the globe doing some volunteer project or excavating some unknown site, and had a small apartment that was often vacant over in Fremont. And if her friends weren't fending for her, Jackie usually found herself in the temporary arms of some jackass "gentleman." Jackie couldn't pick (or keep) a decent job, just like she couldn't pick (or keep) a man. Her spirits and attitude were usually high and positive, however. She didn't want to let anything get her down, and since her last relationship with some forty-something bar owner tanked, she'd picked herself up (with some help from the girls) and went out and found herself a job.

"Well, good for you, Jackie," I said. "And it's going well?"

"Eh…it's a job," she said, as we all ambled towards the kitchen. "I'm hoping to meet an eligible bachelor at this place. That's what

I'm counting on. Some rich dude who enjoys jazz, going out, blah-blah-blah, and is looking for the love of his life."

"Oh, Jackie, don't get into another shitty relationship," Claire said, starting to help Sophie with the quesadillas.

"Yeah, that last guy was a real winner," Lara added. "Next time you pick a guy, make sure he has some integrity."

"Please," I interrupted. "Let's not open up the wounds. He's history and Jackie's moving on."

"That's right," Sophie resounded.

"Yeah," Claire said. "But next time definitely find someone with a little more integrity."

"And someone with a bigger you-know-what," Jackie said, licking a large dollop of guacamole from her finger. She swirled her tongue playfully around it while doing a voluptuous dance with her hips.

"Oh, gross," Sophie said. "Gross. Gross."

"Hey, it's Bloody Mary time," Lara said. She started to gather the necessary ingredients.

"Wait a minute," Claire said. "We're going Mexican. Why didn't we do margaritas?"

Lara: "Marys are easier."

Jackie: "Yeah, and just as good!"

Sophie: "They get the same job done."

"Well we're not out to get drunk, ladies," Claire said. "We do have to work tomorrow."

"Yeah, yeah," Jackie said. "Some even have to work tonight, but that ain't stoppin' me!"

We started giggling, like we were all back in college and getting hyped up over some fraternity party that would end up being just as lame as the one the week before. But it didn't matter so long as we had one another's company. And some giggling. And a little buzz was always fun—for those who could still get one.

"Here you go," Lara said, handing me a cocktail. Suddenly the aroma of the tomato juice was so overpowering I felt an instant urge to vomit. I tried my best to suppress it, but to no avail. I rushed to the kitchen sink, shoving Sophie out of the way, and hurled.

"Damn, does it look that bad?" Lara kidded.

Sophie rubbed my back and handed me a paper towel. "Girls, Robin's—"

I waved the paper towel behind me, flushing my mouth with water. I did not want them to find out I was pregnant while I was bent over the kitchen sink spewing forth bits and pieces of my midday snack.

"I'm fine," I shouted, patting down my mouth and face. "Was feeling a bit woozy at work today, but I'm fine. I think the smell of all of that Tabasco sauce tipped me off or something. No worries."

"Well, if you're sure you're okay..." Lara said.

"Positive." I put on my best fake smile and encouraged everyone to get the fun started.

Lara brought over the documentary film *Babies*, which I thought was about as ironic as it got. She figured it was a relaxing film we could have on in the background since she'd heard it was pretty much a silent film. We didn't even get past the DVD's menu when I decided it was time to share the real reason behind why I called a sudden and urgent girls' night.

"Come on, the movie's supposed to be great," Lara said, motioning to press play.

"No, I'm sure it's great," I said. "I want to tell you all something before, though."

The room fell silent save for the munches and crunches of tortilla chips smothered in guacamole and salsa.

"Oh my goodness!" Claire said loudly. "You got that promotion you've been wanting at work? That...that...that PM position? Huh?"

I sighed. No, no promotion. And no, no pay raise yet, either.

"I won't know about that until the spring or something," I said dismissively. "And it's not even a sure thing—if we'll even get the client or—"

"The raise!" Claire exclaimed. "That's coming up, right? Did you get that?"

I shook my head.

"Well what is it?" Jackie asked.

"Yeah, why the sudden command of the room?" Lara asked. "Found a love interest or something juicy?"

"Oooo," Claire cooed. "Is that it? Met someone?"

"That's it!" Jackie stated. "That's definitely it. Robin found herself a new piece of meat."

"Is he hot?"

"Where'd you meet him?"

"Have you shagged yet?"

"What's his name?"

"Is he a lot older than you? Older guys can be really great lovers."

"Come on, who is it? Is it serious?"

I looked to Sophie, tuning out the drones of questions and exclamations. She gave me a sympathetic look and then a short nod of her head. It was time to spill it.

"I'm pregnant," I said without warning.

Silence.

Not even a single chip was munched.

"You're kidding," Jackie finally said. "You. Are. Kidding."

"No, I'm serious," I said. "It's all very real and it's all happening."

"Is this new guy the baby's dad?" Jackie asked.

"Jackie, there is no new guy." I was tired of even considering a new romantic interest in my life.

"Then it's..." Lara said.

"Yeah, it's Brandon's."

And more silence.

Thankfully Sophie broke in. "We've been trying to tell him. We tried calling him but he didn't answer. He still hasn't answered, right?" I shook my head. "Typical piece of shit," Sophie said colorfully.

"How long have you known, Robin? Sophie?" Lara asked, still shocked. Her face was long, her eyes wide.

I told them everything I knew and everything that had happened up until that point. It was certainly no secret that I'd done the unthinkable and slipped up with Sophie's boyfriend at the time. It had been inconceivable up until a couple of days ago that I was actually pregnant with his baby.

"No," Lara interjected at one point, when we were discussing how I'd go about getting a hold of Brandon. "It's not *his* baby. It's *your* baby, Robin. You can tell him that you're pregnant, you can work out whatever financial deals you want to, but this is *your* baby. Ultimately it is your child and if you don't want him in your life—"

"Yeah and *he* won't want to be in *your* life," Jackie added. She didn't mean to sound hurtful—bad choice of words.

"Well—" I started.

"It's your baby and you're going to make the decisions for *you* and *your* baby. No one else. You don't need him," Lara said fervently.

"I want to give him the chance," I said timidly. "At least see what he has to say..." I looked to Sophie for help in convincing the suddenly enraged girls that telling Brandon of the news, and maybe even having him play some form of a role in the baby's life, wasn't such a wretched idea. He *was* the father, after all.

Sophie came to my rescue. "Girls, she's going to tell him. She has to."

A few objections, to which Sophie replied, "Look, if I of all people can look beyond the shallow reasons for not wanting Brandon to have anything to do with any of this, then we all can. Right?" She gave me an effusive look.

They nodded collectively. Lara came towards me and enveloped me in a hug. "No matter what happens, we're going to help you through this," she said.

Everyone nodded and piped in with, "Definitely!" and "Absolutely!" and "Duh!"

I looked from Sophie, who was smiling sweetly, to Lara, who had tears forming, to Claire, who was hugging her knees to her chest and glowing, as if she herself were pregnant, and then to Jackie, who was taking a gulp of her Bloody Mary. She smacked her lips. "Girl—" She took another gulp. "You bet your ass we're here for you. But boy am I glad I can drink. That part's going to suck for you."

I laughed. "Yeah, I haven't even managed my caffeine withdrawal yet. I don't even want to think about kissing my cocktails goodbye for the next seven months."

"Uh," Sophie interrupted, snagging two double-chocolate cookies from the tray nearby. "Try seven months plus breastfeeding time." She handed me one of the cookies as I let out a stiff moan and the girls howled in laughter. "Just eat the cookies and don't think about what you *can't* have," she said, giving me a wink.

"That's right," Lara said. "Think about what you *can* have. I'm sure there are lots of things."

"Yeah," Jackie said, a questioning look suddenly glazing over her face. Then, "You can still have sex, right?"

More fits of laughter. "Jackie," I said. "I think it's fair to say that that's the *last* thing I want to think about right now."

"But if the right man comes along..." She stirred her celery stick around in her cocktail.

"How's this: If the right man actually comes along, you'll be the first to know, and I'll be sure to make an appointment with my doctor to see if it's all right to have sex. Sound good?"

"*Got* to be prepared."

Before we called it a night, the *Babies* film watched intently once everyone knew the topic hit closer to home, I quietly pulled Lara aside. I wanted to see if she wanted to go to my ultrasound appointment with me. I was awfully nervous and didn't want to go by myself —and I wanted my best friend to join me. So that following Thursday we had a date to go see my baby, in pictures, for the first time. I was ecstatic, and grateful that, even though I didn't have a partner with whom I could share the baby's first photo moment, I had my best friend—*all* of my girlfriends—right there beside me.

As the hour approached midnight, I decided to call it a night and close my sketchbook. It felt good to break in the new pencils and charcoals that I'd picked up at the art supply store earlier. It felt even better to spend some time with the creative muse and play around with some sketches I'd yet to finish, including one particular sketch that I started and left unfinished a few weeks ago—a fruit bowl, filled only with oranges. I'd watched *The Godfather* with Lara not too long ago, and I wanted to run with the whole orange symbolism thing, whatever that was about. I ended up with a sketch of a large bowl of oranges, as opposed to my original plan of the classic bowl of fruit, with a lone orange set off in the background...or maybe the foreground. Not my greatest work, but something to keep me sketching.

I curled up in bed, and before I turned out the lights, I remembered that I needed to share my news with the one friend whom I had not yet told.

Emily! Remember to send Emily an email tomorrow, I told myself. Though still in Ghana and without regular access to the internet, Emily had to be in on the big baby news. She may have always been roaming about somewhere foreign, but she managed to get to her email account in some way, shape, or form at some point. *Don't forget.* Then I let myself drift off to sleep, restfully thinking of oranges, and Emily's small African village, and my baby.

4

A whole week! And no word from Brandon! He was quickly becoming an even bigger asshole than I had assumed. One entire week had passed by and not a single call back or even a shallow text message. Nothing. How could he be so careless about his own flesh and blood? All right, so it wasn't like he knew he was going to be a dad, but still. I'd left a voicemail that hinted at some amount of seriousness; you'd think he'd be curious or at least have a shred of dignity and do me the kindness of calling me back. And shouldn't my calling him be alarm enough that something strange was going on?

Maybe that's why he doesn't call back. Ignorance is bliss...

"Morning, Robin," Bobby said, strolling casually into the break room.

"Hey, Bobby. How's things?" I methodically dunked my tea bag into my hot mug of water.

"They're going. And you?"

"Feeling a bit sluggish this morning."

"So, Miss Sinclair's suddenly a tea-drinking kind of lady now?" he said, sidling up to me. I caught a whiff of his cologne. It was intoxicating that morning, rather than the usual intriguing or delightful.

"Why the big change? I thought coffee was the lifeblood. The secret serum behind all of those brilliant book cover designs."

I flashed him an ironic glance and continued steeping my tea, hoping and praying this decaf blend Sophie gave me would grant the pick-me-up I certainly needed that morning. I'd been behind my desk for a good hour already, and the mystery novel cover was still missing that special something I couldn't quite put my finger on.

"Oh, thought I'd try out this new blend that my friend gave me."

He picked up the package of tea and looked at it with a discerning eye. "It says 'decaf' here, Robin." He held it out so I could see for myself.

"Silly me," I said, pretending that I had no idea the tea was without the "secret serum."

"No wonder you're feeling sluggish. You funny lady." He gave my arm a light, playful shove, then started to open the cupboards over-head. "I'm sure there's some juiced up tea in here somewhere, if tea's your new preference."

"That's all right," I said, throwing away my tea bag and making my way towards the break room doorway. "This blend is growing on me. I'm fond of it, actually."

He kept rifling through the cupboards.

"I'm really quite fine. Thanks, Bobby," I said, although his persistence made me smile. Sophie went out of her way to make sure I had a quality beverage. But Bobby? Since when did a man—not even a friend, a co-worker—become insistent on helping me find my morning lifeblood? Maybe my pregnancy glow and charm were starting to show already. I'd read about that the other night in my baby book, which had actually become my new book of choice after hours.

The book mentioned that as an expecting mother, your partner and even strangers of the male sex (in my case, we'll just go with random men) will show a more willingness to help you with things, like taking your groceries to your car, or opening doors. Kind of nice in an age where I swear chivalry is nearly dead. They'll ask if they can help with the most minor of tasks, such as pulling out your seat or offering an extra pillow for back or feet support. Although these gestures are more common during the second and final trimesters, when the mother is clearly showing she's about to drop, over-the-top helpful gestures by men are commonplace during pregnancy. Not to mention the extra attraction males will have towards the mother-to-be. Apparently a pregnant woman's lips and cheeks become rosier. Her skin becomes so clear she wonders if she's back in elementary school, before the plague of pimples attacked. I had noticed that my lips were a brighter shade of pink. And while I'm not one for globs of makeup to begin with—nothing more than a dab of powder and blush, and perhaps light applications of eyeliner, mascara, and lip gloss work for me—I had discovered that I didn't need any blush or lip color lately. Sometimes I felt I could even do without the light dusting of powder. Maybe I was working some momma charm, and Bobby was being so helpful because of the bun in the oven, even if he had no clue I was a-bakin'.

"If you're sure," he said. He leaned against the counter, his thick chest standing out ever so slightly behind his jet black dress shirt, the top two buttons open, giving way to a hint of casualness. I caught another whiff of Bobby's cologne, and I wasn't particularly fond of what it was doing for my hormones. Was it sudden attraction I was feeling towards Bobby? My goodness! Or were my pregnancy hormones out of whack?

Damn. Stop that, sister!

"You let me know if I can bring you coffee after all," he offered.

I tittered as I began to make my way back to my office. Back to the mystery novel cover that awaited my stroke of genius. "I'll be sure to come to you if I want some coffee, Bobby," I called out. "You do know how I take it."

"A spoonful of cream and a cube of sugar."

Pregnancy charm? Maybe. Or maybe *I* was just the tiniest bit charmed by Mr. Bobby Holman. I'd never really thought of it before, but then again he'd never gone out of his way to be so kind to me. He was always civil and nice, but never a bring-me-my-coffee kind of guy. And to actually know just how I took it? That *was* really peculiar. Maybe my "pregnant aura," as *You're Going to Be a Mother* called it, was the reason for Bobby's gentility. And maybe my fondness of it was not hormonal, but the result of a small office crush.

The weeklong wait with no word from Brandon was eating me up. I couldn't work properly; my head was clouded with too many what-ifs and how-comes. I knew there was only one thing I could do to alleviate at least a portion of the distraction—it was time to call Brandon again. Lunch break would be the perfect opportunity, because the time crunch would encourage me to buck up and make the call, and, if he answered, keep it short and to the point.

But first, I had to call Sophie.

"It's been a whole week and no word," I said once more to Sophie from inside my car. I had driven a few minutes to one of the nearby parks to eat lunch. I needed complete solace, save for Sophie's encouragement. "I have to try again. Something could have happened to my voicemail and he never got it. Or something happened to his phone. Or...I don't know. It doesn't matter. I need to try again." There was no stopping me.

"Go for it," Sophie said. "You plan on leaving another message if he doesn't pick up?"

I sighed. "Yeah, probably. I really hope he picks up."

"You and me both."

"Well, thanks for the quick chat. I think I'll give it a go now."

"Good luck."

I didn't allow myself one more moment of hesitation. I scrolled down to my list of recently placed calls and selected Brandon's number.

You better pick up.

After the longest five rings of my life, I was once again directed to the damned voicemail.

"Brandon." I took a quick swallow. "It's Robin. Again. I *really* have to speak with you. I don't want to talk anymore than you do, but I don't have a choice. All I'm asking for are a few minutes of your time. *Please.* Please call me back. Or text me that you got this message. Just...just something so I know you hear me."

I started up my car engine, crumpled up my empty paper lunch sack, and turned up the car radio. Some NPR repartee sounded. "Please call me back," I whispered to myself. "Please let me put this behind me and move on." I sent Sophie a text message letting her know I was still not any further in our grand plan to drop the bomb on Brandon. Her fast response made me smile, and kept me smiling the whole drive back to the office: *Fuck him. Oh, wait...bad advice. ;) Gotta keep our sense of humor, right? XOXO*

One week after my initial call to Brandon, I hadn't heard back from him, and the day after I gave him a second voicemail, I *still* hadn't heard back. I didn't know Brandon that well, but I knew him well enough to know that he was practically married to his career as an IT consultant with some big firm in Downtown. He always had his cell phone on him and was ready to take any incoming call, work-related or otherwise. He had gotten each and every one of my calls and voicemails. He was choosing to ignore me.

After a repeat performance during lunch break just twenty-four hours later—same park, same sack lunch, same voicemail that would never be answered—I thought back to how I had landed myself in this whole mess. How foolish I was, on so many levels and for so many reasons. Why, oh why, can a girl so easily make stupid-ass mistakes in life?

It was a spring evening in March, the night of one of my colleague's parties—some random celebration he'd hosted after landing a big account or something. It didn't matter. I was there with my friends, and Sophie had brought along Brandon. It was a huge party with all the usual party trimmings: alcohol, music, and either dull conversation about work, or a small dance "contest" going on in the living room. As the party became too slow-moving, and the liquor was being consumed at much too fast a pace, Sophie and the girls headed out to continue the party at a bar or club, while I stayed behind. I vaguely remember, under the hazy stupor of five-too-many cocktails, that I felt I should stay behind to show party support for my colleague. Apparently, Brandon felt I needed a chaperone.

Before I knew it, Brandon and I were sharing a cab home. I remember droning on about how I was no longer with Joseph, my previous boyfriend with whom I had the longest running relationship of my life—fourteen months I think it was. Ta-frickin'-da. Brandon started to talk about problems at home with Sophie and how he wasn't feeling the connection anymore or something like that. It was all very hazy, but before I knew it the cab had stopped at Brandon's place, and *only* at Brandon's place.

I'd like to say we sat around in his living room for a while, talking about failed and failing relationships before we jumped into bed (not that that makes the situation any better). However, I think we started kissing in the cab and took it right into his bedroom from there. His bedroom. The bedroom he shared with my best friend, Sophie.

A few hours later I came to, and in a hell of a hung-over state I realized the grand calamity I had created.

Breaking my trek down memory lane, I rested my hands on my stomach and smiled. At least there were still some good things that could come from such a mess. I did have Sophie back. And all of my good friends were back on speaking terms. (God knows the kind of rift I created was unpleasant for everyone involved.) *And,* I had my baby. My little baby who I was going to see for the first time in only a couple of days.

As I'd done the day before after I called Brandon during my lunch break, I sent Sophie a brief text message, telling her that I'd taken another stab at contacting Brandon and was crossing my fingers. If he didn't reach me during any point before the end of the day, I'd be calling him back. Again. And again. And again.

Come half past seven that evening, as I expected, Brandon still hadn't returned my calls. No text message. Nothing. I'd already completed my *Godfather*-inspired sketch, and had started on a new one of a misguided seagull flying over vast expanses of a Grand Canyon-like landscape. My creative muse seemed to have returned, and I was already thinking of some watercolor ideas that I planned on testing out later that week. But I couldn't shirk the frustrating fact that Brandon was ignoring my calls.

I picked up my cell phone and speed-dialed Lara.

"Hey, Robin," she answered.

"Can I come over?" I asked bluntly. "Brandon's not calling me back. I'm feeling a little lonely. And I don't know... Can I come over?"

"Like a sleepover?"

"Yeah, like a sleepover," I said energetically. "And let's go all out, sleepover-style. What do you say to some TV, maybe some pedicures, some girl time?"

"I say we're long past due for one-on-one time together. Definitely! Pack your stuff up for the night and come on over. I'll make sure your bed's ready." Lara's second bedroom was convenient for a sleepover—a great solution to those long and lonely sleepless nights.

As fast as a flash I packed up my overnight bag and headed to the adjacent neighborhood of Wallingford, to Lara's quaint two-bed and two-bath apartment she'd rented since she graduated grad school three years ago. As I made my way up her small brick walkway, I noticed the smell of the freshly cut grass, and how it tickled my nose and made me feel warm and happy. Summer was around the corner, and with it always came picnics in the park, pool parties at someone's apartment pool, and, of course, weekend getaways to one of the nearby island towns for some sun, sand, and surf. Being pregnant might change all of that, though.

"We seriously should have done this a lot sooner," Lara said, shaking a bottle of Paint the Town Red nail polish. "Especially now that you've got the baby on the way. You need supervision."

I laughed, painting my toes a light shade called Tickle Me Pink. "I don't need *supervision*. I'm just lonely."

"Well, whatever you want to call it, you shouldn't be alone so much. Look, whenever you feel you need some girl time or some socializing, or don't want to be home alone, then give me a ring. You know you always can."

I usually did take Lara up on her open-door offers, but since the craziness of the past couple of weeks began, I'd tried to become more resourceful and independent—tried to keep from unloading my problems on everyone else's doorstep. God knows I had a lot of them, and the offer to unload was tempting; and I felt I'd already done plenty of that when I had confided in Lara initially about my betraying Sophie. Lara's doors and arms were a twenty-four-hour convenience store during that period. Poor thing.

"You're always welcome here," Lara continued. "I was there for you before, and I'm here now. Don't forget about me. Little old date-less, man-less me."

"Hey, you're not alone. We can be date-less and man-less together," I said. I took a sip of the warm tea with honey that Lara prepared. "Any news on that front, speaking of which?"

"What, me? Dating?" Lara laughed. "Nothing serious."

"Oh, so there is *some*one then? Looks like we aren't date-less together, eh?"

"No, we're definitely date-less together." She took a sip of her tea before continuing with what I was sure would be some juicy gossip. "But there is this guy."

"Oh-oh-oh. 'This guy.'"

"It's not like that."

"From work?" I pried.

She nodded and blew at a loose strand of her short, dark hair, which was slowly falling out of its ponytail.

"And?"

"And...it's only harmless flirting right now—I think." She looked confused, but continued. "Anyway, it's just some guy at work who is unusually nice to me now...and he's attractive and...well, I've been doing a little flirting with him. Shameless stuff, you know? But I'm not sure if he's really flirting with me or if that's just how he is. Although, he's never been that way before..." She looked at me, as if for answers.

"I think I know what you mean," I said. "There's a guy at my office, too."

She pointed her finger at me and bellowed. "*Who's* calling the kettle black now?"

"I'm not saying that there *is* flirting going on," I said, trying to correct her. "But I think I know what you mean by him treating you especially nice all of a sudden...or something. Right?"

"Exactly. Like, we've been civil with each other in the past. Nothing unusual. But lately he seems to be upping the charm. And I'm doing the same, too." She finished painting her last toe. "I don't know. We talk almost every day in the break room. He even asked me to join him for lunch one day—with him *only*—but I turned him down because I had a report I had to finish." Lara could read my doubting face. "And that was the truth, Robin."

"Had you not had the report, would you have gone to lunch with him?"

She thought for a brief moment before answering with, "Probably."

"So there's attraction on your end?"

"Hell yes!" Her response was quicker than anticipated.

"Whoa," I said. "So you've got it bad for this guy. What's his name?"

"Paul." Lara's blue eyes, no joke, started to look a little dreamy.

"Do you think you and this *Paul* will go out soon?"

"Go out?" she asked, surprised. "Oh, heavens no! Oh no. No!"

I asked her why the proposition seemed so appalling, and all she could say was that she was sure he didn't feel anything like *that* about her, even if there may or may not have been some flirting going on. She said she needed to be sensible and come to terms with the fact that she was destined to be, like me, unlucky in love. I found the whole thing rather confusing.

"You know me, Robin. Always Mr. Wrong, never Mr. Right. That's the story of my life."

"Tell me about it," I said, taking the lead to share my own office romance, or crush, or whatever was going on (if anything at all). "This guy at my office, Bobby, I think I'm making myself crush on him just because he's offering me coffee and making sure he says 'hi' to me every morning. As always, I'm blowing it out of proportion I'm sure. Thinking he's actually interested in me..." I chuckled. "Oh well. He's got a girlfriend anyway. And it seems pretty serious."

Lara shook her head, then changed the subject. "What do you say to some *90210*? Think that's coming on soon. Or would you rather I pop in an old *Sex and the City* episode? Or we could watch *Pretty Woman*. Oldie but goodie." She pulled her hair back into a neat and small ponytail.

"We need the inspiration; unlucky in love over here. Put in *Pretty Woman*."

There we sat that night, cuddled together under a big blanket on the sofa, watching Julia Roberts work the screen. Our nails freshly painted, the Brandon dilemma left for another day, and my ultrasound appointment on the horizon. Lara and I may have been unlucky in love—on the constant, unsuccessful hunt for Mr. Right—but we were unlucky in love together. We were both concocting imaginative love affairs with our office boys, and we were all right with that, I suppose. At least we had each other...and Julia to give us some encouragement. Love can be found in the strangest of places, so perhaps there was hope for us after all.

5

"Comfortable bed?" Lara asked the next morning, while she poured some milk into her dry cereal topped with freshly cut peaches.

"Heavenly," I said, taking one last look at myself in the hallway mirror before I headed out for work. "Thank you so much."

"Any time, girl."

I started towards the front door and Lara called out, "Aren't you going to eat some breakfast? You've got to make sure you're eating right. You're eating for—"

"I know. I'm eating for two now." I gave her a smile and headed out the door. "I'm going to grab a muffin at a café. I'll call you later. And thank you again, Lara. I really enjoyed last night."

She waved goodbye, her cereal spoon in hand. "Later," she mumbled through a mouthful of cereal.

Before I pulled out of the apartment parking lot I stole a glance at my cell phone, hoping that Brandon had called or texted. Nothing.

That's it. Enough is enough.

Before I drove off, I rushed out a text to Brandon and typed,

Robin here. PLEASE call me!!! Maybe that would get his butt into gear. And if it didn't, I'd call again. Today during lunch. Same story, hopefully a different outcome.

The drive from Lara's apartment to my office was a breeze. Most certainly an improvement in time efficiency and mileage compared to when I drove my usual route from my apartment in the U District. The girls had been pestering me for years to move closer to them and out of the U District where we'd all gone to college. Since graduation they'd all moved into various areas of Seattle—Fremont, Queen Anne, Madison Park, and even wealthy men's upper class penthouses in Downtown and Waterfront, but that was usually Jackie's terrain as she was often on the move depending on Cupid's arrow. I, however, chose to stay in the familiar apartment at Pacific Green Hills near campus. It was still relatively close to work, but seeing how brisk a dash I'd made from Lara's apartment I started to second-guess my living arrangements.

Once the baby came I'd have to seriously consider a new living arrangement anyhow. A small one-bedroom and one-bathroom apartment in a rather loud part of town, college students all over the place, probably wasn't the ideal setup for a woman with a baby. I decided against even thinking about a move; the overwhelming stress of it was more than I needed on my plate at the moment.

"In early today," a colleague said to me as I walked through the office's front doors a good hour earlier than my usual time.

"Lots of work to do," I said cheerfully, charging off to my office. My creative muse was back and doing well, I had a great night's sleep under my belt, and I'd figured out last night while shaving my legs what special touch the mystery novel cover needed.

I was cruising like a rock star at work, getting many small to-dos off my list, returning a few phone calls, even sending off my first draft of the mystery novel cover to the editor. The title's font needed to be changed from burgundy to eggplant, and some added depth and shadows across the moon in the background needed to be created, and shifted slightly more behind the novel's bold and enticing title. The changes got my approval. Now it was up to the editor. I was hopeful that the adjustments (if there were to be any) would be minor and easy to fix.

"Want to join us for lunch?" Bobby asked, peering his head around the corner and through my office door as he'd been doing quite often lately.

"No," came Janet's curt response.

Bobby made a contorted face at me, then grinned. "How about you, Robin?" He clearly had not invited Janet, but he was too much of a gentleman to bring attention to the fact.

Unlucky in love. Mr. Wrong. Mr. Right.

My mind went back to the conversation Lara and I had the night before. Was Bobby, like Lara's co-worker Paul, actually flirting with me? Or was he only bringing our acquaintanceship into a new realm —a very friends-only-ish realm? Or was it all my imagination? Or was I secretly pining away for Bobby? The entire scenario was so convoluted.

"I'm heading out to grab some Chinese with some of the gang from editing and reception. Want to come?"

Hmph. Not convoluted. I'm thinking things I shouldn't and I'm misreading everything. Bobby's just a nice co-worker.

I quickly thought about my lunch plans. I wanted to give Brandon another call, so I politely declined the invitation, but said, "Maybe next time."

"What is *that* all about?" Janet asked once Bobby left.

"What's what about?" Couldn't she mind her own business?

"You and Bobby seem to be awful closey-close lately."

I made an incredulous expression. "I don't know what you're ta—"

"I wasn't born yesterday, Robin." She rolled her eyes. "'Can I get you some coffee?' 'Here's your print out.' 'Want to grab lunch?'"

"So what?"

"You don't think it's peculiar that he's being ridiculously nice to you all of a sudden?"

"I don't follow." Honestly, what was she getting at?

"Don't be so blue-eyed. He's only being saccharine-sweet to you so you'll choose him to be a part of your team if you get the PM position next spring."

What was she talking about? Why would Bobby feel the need to butter me up if I got the PM position? And why wouldn't *he* try for the position himself?

"I don't know what you're talking about, Janet, but I think you've got your information twisted."

She walked up to my desk. "Don't play coy. You know very well he's not trying for the position. He wouldn't want to be the lead for some stupid, half-wit chick lit author's cover anyway. He'd rather play up to you now, sit right under you, Miss Big PM, then snag up all the credit he could on the job. Use that to take the next best thing." She paused. "That is *if* you get the position. And there's no guarantee of that."

How dare she! What nerve...

"Why wouldn't he be 'saccharine-sweet' with you, too, then?" I countered. "If his plan is to cozy up to the potential PM, why wouldn't he do the same to you? You're obviously pursuing it."

"He knows he can't get away with simple-minded shit like that with me. I'm the *real deal* here, honey."

I wanted to stand up and shout out, "Bitch!" But that's not me. That's what I dream of doing to pushy brats like Janet. I would never actually gather the nerve to stand up to her. I could lose my job if I did that. Well, maybe not lose my job, but you never know. I could probably kiss the PM position away, at least. And the raise. No, I'd let Janet think she was all that and then some and carry on my way.

Don't let her get to you. Don't let her get under your skin.

"Whatever, Janet. I've got work to do." I turned my attention back to my computer screen, momentarily pretending to be busy with my emails, scrolling through my inbox.

When Janet didn't leave and kept looming near my desk, I said, "Besides, there's no certainty I'll get the position. And there's no certainty that Bobby wouldn't get it or wouldn't try for it. There's not even a certainty that our firm will get the contract with this author. So we're only wasting our time making conjectures. We've got enough work to do as it is."

She pivoted on her long, nylon-clad legs, and resumed her seat at her own desk. "Only looking out for a fellow woman in the work-place," she said, the falsity of her statement oozing from her pores. Who was she kidding?

"Men will do anything to get to the top of their career," she said.

I wanted to retort with, "And women don't?", suggesting that she take a long, hard look in the mirror. But, of course, I didn't say such things. I never do. I went back to busying myself with my inbox before realizing there was indeed real work that needed my attention.

'Saccharine-sweet' with me? What nerve! Bobby wasn't doing anything slimy like that. What did Janet know? Just because she was a vindictive bitch, willing to do anything to claw her way to the top, didn't mean that the rest of us were. God, sometimes...

I was eating the sandwich that I'd picked up from a nearby café, once again choosing to dine in the solace of my parked car, when my cell phone rang.

Probably Sophie checking up on the old Brandon report.

My third lunch in my parked car, solo, was a habit that was getting really old really fast. I needed to contact Brandon ASAP before I lost my mind from this dull routine, or before I became that creep-o lady who drove to the park and watched its visitors from inside her car, eating her sandwiches, and making phone calls, always looking stressed or sad or angry.

The number on my cell phone was at first foreign. Perhaps the doctor reminding me of my appointment? Or needing to cancel it? Then I realized it was Brandon's number.

"Shit." I looked out my rearview mirror. Why? I don't know. For answers? Looking back hoping this was all a dream? That none of this was happening. Here. Alone. In my car with a half-eaten sandwich in my hand, the other half in my churning stomach. I looked down at my stomach, my cell phone still ringing.

I'm not alone. I've got you, sweet baby.

Then I gathered my thoughts and answered the call that I'd been waiting for for what seemed like an aching eternity.

"Hello," I squeaked.

"Hey," the voice on the other end replied. "Brandon here."

What the hell now? I had prepared as best I could for this moment, but really, there's no amount of preparation that could have truly prepared me for what I was about to do.

God, this is awful.

"You called," he said. So point-blank. So...emotionless.

"Yes. Like a dozen times."

Short. Keep it short and strong.

"Yeah, sorry about that. I've been crazy busy at work lately."

I fluttered my eyelids and stuck out my tongue. *Such a douche bag.*

"Well I'm glad you finally found the decency to call me back after nearly two weeks."

"Has it been that long?"

Another flutter, and this time I gave him the bird.

"Like I said, so busy at work—"

"That's nice and all," I cut him off. "Look, there's something I need to talk to you about." I tried my hardest to stay in control and direct.

"Shoot." He was cool right now. Just he wait.

And then I told him. I let it spill forth without giving him room to retort or deny.

"I've taken the tests. Several tests. Each one positive. I'm pregnant, Brandon. There's no doubt about it. And I've got an appointment already with a doctor. I'm going to see the baby for the first time. And don't think for a minute it's not yours. There isn't anyone else. There wasn't anyone before we shacked up that night...no one within any reasonable time, that's for sure. No one since. It's yours, Brandon. And I thought you should know." I could feel myself starting to lose my calm after the words fluidly poured forth without an ounce of hesitation. "And—and, well, I wanted you to know. To see—"

His words in response to becoming a father were ice: "I'll send you some money for an abortion."

"What? No. No. You didn't hear what I said. I'm having a baby. Brandon, I'm *keeping* the baby."

"And why are you calling me? You want money for this problem? Fine. I'll send you the money you need for an abortion."

"I'm not having an abortion, Brandon!" The words stung as I spoke them, and my lunch churned even more violently. "I'm calling because...because...because I figured you should know. It's your baby, too, and you have a ri—"

"It may be mine, but I didn't plan on having a baby at this point in my life, Robin. Not this way. Not with you. To be honest, I don't care what you do with it. Have it, give it up for adoption, go at it alone. I don't want to be involved."

"But—"

"Look," he continued. "You want help with this...situation—I'm helping you. I'll take responsibility, and your word, that it's mine, and I'll cough up whatever it costs for you to get rid of it."

"I'm not 'getting rid of it,' Brandon. How can you be so insensitive?"

"*I'm* not choosing to keep it, so you'll have to deal with the expenses on your own. You'll have to raise it on your own—"

"I fully intend on raising my baby on my own if that's how it's going to be. I don't want you involved if you want nothing to do with it. Sophie and I thou—"

"Sophie? She knows? Well, I'm glad you two made up." Despite the hurtful tone and words of the conversation up until that point, I knew that Brandon hadn't wanted our one-night stand to come between the friendship that Sophie and I had. He'd made it clear to me on several occasions, and, according to Sophie, it was one of the last things he told her before they said goodbye. Although at this moment in particular I'm sure he was elated Sophie and I were best friends again. That way I'd have someone to help me with the baby, since God knows he didn't want anything to do with it.

"Sophie and I are just as good as friends as ever. Better, even," I said proudly.

"Glad to hear it."

"That's not the discussion, though, Brandon. All I'm asking is that you please do your part and help where you can. If you don't want to play the dad role, then fine. But man up a bit. I know you're not penniless. Can you find it in your heart to want to help *feed* our child? *Clothe* it?"

"Look, Robin, congratulations, or whatever you want to hear. I've got to go. I'm swamped with work. Let me know how much the abortion costs and I'll send you the money. Until you have that information don't call me again."

"Bra—"

Click.

"What the hell?" I shouted, tossing my cell phone to the floor of the passenger seat.

That was not *how things were supposed to go!*

Brandon was allowed to be angry, that was fine. But he was supposed to understand—should understand—that the decision to keep the baby was my decision; and he had a duty, a *legal* duty, to uphold his end of the bargain. He was just as responsible and, hell, I wasn't even asking for him to man up and take full responsibility. All I asked for was a little cash to help me out, like Sophie and Lara and all the girls had said wouldn't be unreasonable.

I broke down into tears, gripping my steering wheel with all the strength I could summon, and let out a loud cry. It hurt so much. It hurt to be rejected. To be run over. It hurt that Brandon couldn't even have a shred of decency to help the mother of *his* baby. To help his own child.

"Why does this have to happen to me?" I cried out pitifully. "Why like this? Unlucky in love, knocked up, no care. I'm just a one-night stand after all." I wiped at my tears from under my foggy glasses, then gripped the wheel tightly again. "Why?" I glanced down at my cell phone. "Why?"

I was repeating the question over and over to myself when a bright blue car pulled up next to mine, and a young woman stepped out. I grabbed a tissue from my glove compartment and tried to clean up my tear-stained face. I watched the woman walk around to the back passenger door of her car and retrieve a small child from a car seat. The child couldn't have been more than a year old. A small thing, wearing a soft blue hat, and the cutest set of blue jean overalls with what looked like a duck embroidered on the chest. I managed to crack a smile through my tears as I watched the young mom gently bounce her baby on her hip, making him squeal with delight.

I rested a hand on my stomach, where my own baby was, and let wash over me the peace of knowing that I *could* manage this without any help from Brandon if I wanted to. The girls were right: I didn't need Brandon's help, his money, or anything. Though I was entitled to support from him, we all agreed that the worst case was that I went at it alone. And, like my friends said, I wouldn't even really be alone. Lara promised to go to my ultrasound appointment with me. Sophie said she wouldn't miss the birth for anything in the world. Claire and Jackie both swore they'd make sure I had the most smashing baby shower. Emily...I hadn't heard back from her since I'd sent the email letting her know of the baby...but she would undoubtedly give her word that she'd show this baby all the love in the world. And all of my girlfriends said they'd be there for me— from baby's first photo to high school diploma time. "And then of course he'll go to our alma mater, U Dub," Jackie had said proudly. "And get the finest sorority or fraternity house tips from Aunt Jackie."

As the mom and baby next to my car made their way to the park, their small dog now joining them, I proceeded back to my office. If that was how Brandon wanted to react, that was his business. I, however, had to get back to work. There was no more time for tears or self-pity today. The projects were piling up and I was determined to deserve, and receive, the raise. If I wasn't going to be getting any help from Brandon then this single mom needed to do what was right by her child. And I didn't need to waste my energy or let my mood turn sour because of some prick who wasn't worth a second thought. It was all about what was best for the baby. And Brandon was not going to play one single role in my child's life if he truly didn't want my baby. If he didn't want to love it as I did. He'd made his decision, and so had I.

6

I was nervous, enthusiastic, and curious all at the same time. Lara and I were on our way to the doctor's office for my first appointment and ultrasound. With the okay from my boss to arrive late to work, and with Lara by my side, I was ready for the big day. Lara was a doll, because she let me stay yet another night over at her place; it made perfect sense since we'd be carpooling today with the appointment first thing in the morning. She even insisted I pack an extra change of clothes in case I felt like crashing her place that night too.

The drama with Brandon yesterday was already old news. At least that's what I was telling myself. I spent a good portion last night telling the dreadful story to Lara, and then to Sophie and Claire who shared "oohs" and "ahs" and "ughs" together over the speaker phone, and then once more to Jackie, but in a quick-as-it-gets manner as she had to hop off to work. I was proud that she was holding down her gig as a hostess, even if her drive to show up for work on time and do her best was fueled by the hope of landing herself a man.

"Thanks again for going with me," I told Lara as we drove along I-5 towards the medical centers over in First Hill.

"Oh my gosh, don't think anything of it, Robin."

"I'm really glad we get to share this moment together."

"Me too. I hope I'll be the best company I can be. I'm not Mr. Dreamboat or Mr. Right."

I shrugged. "Well, of course it would be nice to be sharing this with my Mr. Right, but—"

"It'll happen some day." She made a cautious lane change before exiting the highway. "Don't fret your pretty little head. It'll happen. And look who's talking. I'm still a woman on the manhunt." She flashed me a smile.

"You're right. I'm just really excited that I'm not going at this alone. Even if the asshole wants nothing to do with all of this. It's great to have you with me, Lara."

"Looks like this is it," Lara said once we neared the medical center, signs filled with acronyms pointing in all different directions. "Yup, here we are. Dr. Jane Buschardi, OB-GYN. You ready?"

I nodded. I was as ready as I'd ever be. Nerves were in high gear, expectations non-existent, and curiosity and excitement rolled up together into one big ball. "Let's do this!"

Even though I absolutely knew that I was pregnant, standard procedure at Dr. Buschardi's office was to do a quick pee-on-the-stick test. (I was at a pro at this now.) No big surprises from those results. Now I was sitting in the cool, air-conditioned examination and ultrasound room, wearing nothing but my socks and a skimpy apron loosely tied at the neck. Though I was of average height at five-foot-five, my feet couldn't touch the floor from my position on the examination table. I oddly felt like a child about to get her back-to-school checkup, with a nasty little immunization about to prick the arm.

"How long do you think we have to wait?" I asked Lara. I was starting to get cold; no thanks to my less-than-stellar wardrobe. You'd think after decades of women delivering babies in hospitals, with all of the modern conveniences and pain-reducing medicines and what have you, they'd be able to supply you with a more appropriate dressing gown. The fluffy little sheep that spotted mine didn't make me feel any more comfortable (if that was their goal)—my butt barely covered and my breasts looking as unsupported as, well, they were.

"Hello," rang out a cheerful voice. In walked a tall, svelte woman in a stark white lab coat, a stethoscope hanging around her neck. "How are we today Ms...." She breezed over her files. "...Sinclair? I'm Dr. Jane Buschardi. How are you?"

I shook her hand and told her I was doing well.

"Pleasure to meet you. And you must be..." Dr. Buschardi looked at Lara, who was seated off to the right of my table.

"I'm Lara."

"Well, Robin and Lara, it's great to have you here today." Her words were cheerful and sweet, and a big, ruby red lipsticked smile was plastered across her face. "So Lara, you're...Robin's life partner?"

I tried my best to suppress the laughter. Lara, however, couldn't contain herself.

"Oh no," Lara said, still giggling. "We're not lovers. We're best friends."

Seattle was proudly a very welcoming gay and lesbian community; not too surprising, apparently, that Dr. Buschardi may have assisted in a handful of same-sex couple pregnancies.

"Well isn't that neat? To have your best friend here to show her support. Let's get started then, shall we?" The doctor wanted to get down to business, asking me lots of questions about when I thought (ah-hem, *knew*) I'd conceived, if and what I'd been reading about pregnancy, nutrition, vitamin supplements, and the like. Finally, after Lara was handed a million and one pamphlets that apparently held the information about what I could and could not do, and should and should not do, throughout my pregnancy, it was time for the ultrasound.

"Oh, wow," I said. "I didn't expect this gel to be warm." Dr. Buschardi started to spread the warm gel around my stomach with the ultrasound scanning instrument.

"Such a simple thing so many doctors neglect to consider," Dr. Buschardi said. "We've come quite a long way in the obstetrics field.

Why some doctors still can't figure out that a woman doesn't want to be squirted with ice cold gel still gets me."

Could the medical world possibly take another step forward and get proper dressing gowns while they're at it?

"All right," the doctor said. She tapped a few keys on the keyboard below the monitor, then made some clicks with the mouse, the pointer set at grey voids on the screen that told me nothing.

A few more turns of the instrument and she said, "You're definitely at the end of your first trimester...your calculations are spot on with your date of conception..."

No advanced medical breakthroughs needed to find out that one.

"...You're definitely at about your twelve-week mark, Robin, so I'll calculate your due date in a sec..." She squinted behind her small, rimless glasses, tapping a few more keys.

I looked over at Lara, who was also squinting at the screen behind her reading glasses. "See anything?" I asked both of them. Lara gave me a big smile, then went back to squinting at the black and white screen.

A few more clicks and taps, then, "Okay, it looks like there's only one baby in there."

"Well good!"

Dr. Buschardi let out a small laugh. "We always want to make sure."

God, twins? I don't think I could have handled that kind of news.

"Is it a boy or a girl?" Lara blurted out.

"Oh, we won't be able to tell that for another ten weeks or so. Okay...the size of the baby is right on schedule. Looking healthy, too." Dr. Buschardi looked over at me and gave a nod of "all things look great," then said, "Ready for the heartbeat?"

"Oh yeah!" Lara and I said in unison. And within seconds I heard the strong thumping of my baby's heartbeat interwoven with my own.

"Wow," Lara breathed out.

"Wow. That's my baby?"

"That sure is," Dr. Buschardi said. She moved the instrument

69

around my belly. "Can you see the head here?" She tapped another key and pointed at a white, oval figure. "And in a couple of months we can do another ultrasound..." A few more keys. "...And then we can find out the sex of the baby if you want. Do you think you want to know?" Some more taps and clicks, then she pulled back the instrument.

"Oh, definitely! I couldn't imagine the suspense. I definitely want to know."

Dr. Buschardi told me to make an appointment with reception about nine or ten weeks from now, as she was sure she'd be able to do a gender test then.

"And you don't want to forget these," she said, tearing out the print she'd made with the machine. "Baby's first pictures."

I stared, mouth wide open, at the roll of three black and white photos of my baby. I'd never in my life felt how I did at that very moment. It was more special and unique than the feeling I'd had when I first learned that I was pregnant, and stronger than when I actually realized that my life was going to change in drastic ways because a baby was, no doubt, going to come into my life. Right then and there—with the faint remnants of gel cooling my stomach, my butt probably hanging out on the examination table, still looking somewhat like a child with a scant apron on and white socks scrunched around my ankles, my best friend to my right, and across from me the doctor who would help me bring my baby into this world—I felt like nothing else in the universe mattered but my baby and its health. All I could think about was how I would make sure my baby was given everything and anything it needed to grow into a healthy newborn. I wanted to give him or her the world. I was absolutely enamored of the small life that I was growing. That I had helped create.

"It's beautiful," I gasped.

Lara was by my side the instant Dr. Buschardi had handed me my photos. "So beautiful."

"Congratulations, Robin. And what a wonderful friend you have here to support you."

"Oh, Lara's the best," I gushed. "I don't know what I'd do without her."

Dr. Buschardi smiled, hands folded in her lap. "Well I'll let you get dressed," she said. "And then be sure to make your next appointment up at the front. The nurses will also supply you with all of the pre-natal vitamins and information you need. Oh, and before I forget—your due date." She scribbled on my file. "We're going to plan on your little bundle coming around...the seventh of December. Congratulations!"

Before Dr. Buschardi left the room she said, "If you have any questions, don't hesitate a moment about calling me. You have my card. If for any reason I'm not available to take your call, I have a very reliable and wonderful team. You'll be taken care of, Robin. Now, you've got some big news to share. Got to call up all the friends, mom, dad, the whole family!"

Mom. Dad. The whole family. I appreciated that Dr. Buschardi left out "and the daddy," as my bringing along Lara probably tipped her off that there was no father. But my parents? In the frantic activity of everything I hadn't even thought about breaking the news to my parents. Telling my dad wasn't really a consideration, anyhow. I didn't even have his phone number—only his office email address. He ran out on his fatherly duties when I was a pre-teen, so I doubted he'd give a flying flip that he was going to be a grandfather.

My mom, however, was another story. I was on some form of speaking terms with her, but they were terms of few words. My mom was rather aloof and seemed to think that now that her children were grown and out of the house, her motherly duties were over. That meant she didn't feel the need to keep in regular touch with any of us.

My older sister, Kaitlyn, was married, had two kids, and lived out in the 'burbs. My kid brother, Alex, younger by almost two years, was a Notre Dame graduate living in Atlanta now. Or maybe it was Maryland. Or Connecticut? Needless to say, Alex and I didn't keep in touch outside of the occasional Christmas greeting card. Kaitlyn and I had a relationship that was a wee step up; we called each other on all major holidays and on each other's birthday, and maybe we'd manage a visit one fleeting Memorial Day weekend or Thanksgiving, but nothing more.

No one in my family was very close. We had all gone our separate ways, with a father who was practically estranged, and a mother who was the last person I considered talking to just to shoot the breeze. Even considering contacting either of them about my being pregnant was a joke.

"You don't have to tell your mom or your family any time soon," Lara said on the drive from the doctor's office to Forster & Banks. She could read my mind. She knew that Dr. Buschardi's casual mention of sharing the exciting news with my mom and dad was preoccupying my thoughts.

"You don't ever have to tell them, but I'm sure your sister would like to know," she said. "And sooner or later your mom, and I guess dad, will find out. Might as well do it on your grounds and get it over with." I looked over at her. "Whenever you're ready," she added.

Yeah, whenever I'm ready. I'd much rather think about anything else. Yeah, I'd rather think about my baby. About how exciting it will be to actually see it with my own eyes!

"Anyway," Lara said after a brief silence. "I think a dinner out is in order, don't you? We need to celebrate baby's first pictures! I'll plan something out for all of us, okay?"

That sounded great. A nice dinner out with all the girls, celebrating, would be a lot of fun.

"Can we go to Lucky Lee's?" I asked. It was a favorite all-American mixed cuisine restaurant not too far from Lara's apartment.

"Lucky Lee's it is."

"And Lara?" Perhaps because of my slightly solemn attitude towards the whole parental/family thing, my voice was low. "Is it okay if I sleep at your place again tonight?"

She pulled up in front of Forster & Banks, patted my leg, and said, "You never have to ask."

"Show us already!" Jackie squealed from the opposite end of our table at Lucky Lee's restaurant that Friday night. "I want to see this baby already!"

"Patience, patience," I said, bringing the ultrasound photos out from the large, bright yellow and blue patterned Vera Bradley handbag that Lara surprised me with that morning. She said it was a "congrats on the first doctor's appointment and baby photos" gift, and that of course I could expect many more spoils as time went on, especially when the baby shower came.

I made a dramatic reveal of the small black and white photos, shouting out, "Ta da!" loud enough for more than our table to hear.

"Oh my God!"

"It's so tiny!"

"What am I looking at?"

"Is it a boy or a girl?"

"A girl maybe?"

"No, definitely a boy."

I laughed as the reel made its way around the table. "It's too early to tell. I have another appointment in August. They'll tell me then."

"This is freaking surreal!" Jackie said. "I can't believe this little thing is actually inside you."

"Yeah, can you feel it move around yet?" Claire asked.

"Sometimes I think I do, but it's probably only digestion. The doctor said I'd be able to feel it in about a month or so. Maybe sooner."

"And the baby's healthy?" Sophie asked. "Everything's Grade A?"

"Yup. I'm going into my second trimester in a couple of days and the baby's right where it should be in terms of growth. Healthy. It'll really start growing noticeably larger soon. Which means—"

"Shopping!" Claire said. "We get to go out and get you maternity clothes!"

"Yeah, and baby clothes, too. Maybe?" I looked around the table at each girl, making sure my excitement about shopping for cute bonnets, tiny shoes, and the most adorable outfits wasn't lost on any of them.

"Shopping trip, for sure!" Sophie said, eliciting emphatic yes's from everyone.

Our meals arrived and everyone started diving in, all the while chatting about the best boutiques to find the cutest baby outfits and hippest maternity clothes. About the must-visit stores for baby items and furniture. About plans for a baby shower.

"I want to host the baby shower, if I may," Claire offered. "At my house. I'll kick Conner out and we'll have a really fun, girly baby shower. Oh please let me do this for you, Robin."

"All right," I said, chuckling. "If you want to, go for it."

Claire bounced up and down and started throwing out ideas for baby-themed games we could play, the decorations we'd have, the kind of food we could eat—"Sophie, you can make the desserts!" It was an all-out baby-talk dinner. And the best part was that once we feasted on our various plates of food, we all headed back to Lara's apartment to continue the evening's fanfare with some movies, dessert, and, of course, girl talk.

Sophie came out of Lara's kitchen with a square, pink cardboard box and a handful of small, paper dessert plates and napkins.

"Dessert time!" Claire said, hot on her heels with the plastic forks and spoons in one hand, and a half-gallon of ice cream in the other.

"Oh you guys did not," I said, not expecting an official dessert. I figured we'd snack on some Chips Ahoy from the pantry, or maybe pick at the box of leftover doughnuts and assorted pastries that Lara had brought home from work earlier that day.

"Girlfriend," Sophie said. "This is a big-ass occasion here. You're going to have a baby! Of course we need to celebrate appropriately."

"Yeah," Jackie added. "And since you're off the drinking train until this baby comes out—"

"Once it's weaned from the boob," Sophie corrected.

"Yeah," Jackie said. "Since you're off that train, we still wanted to celebrate in style. Just because we can't go out and drink doesn't mean we can't have a kickass time. So bring on the cake!"

"And the ice cream," Claire said.

Sophie said she hadn't found the time to make me a homemade cake or one that she whipped up while at work, but she did pick up the next best thing from a delicious all-local-ingredients bakery near Waterfront.

"My word, this is amazing," I said in between bites of the red velvet and cream cake.

"Your new craving now, huh?" Lara asked, smiling.

"You know, it's the strangest thing, but it's like the baby book says: The foods that make me nauseous aren't really *so* bad anymore, and I *am* finding some new cravings."

"Or maybe red velvet cake and ice cream always taste good," Sophie said.

That was probably more like it, but I'd forgotten that earlier that day for lunch I'd had spaghetti and wasn't made ill by the tomato sauce. And I'd sneaked in a cookie that had some cinnamon, and I wasn't sick to my stomach.

"So, Lara," Sophie said while flipping mindlessly through the satellite menu's channels. She stopped the cursor on an episode of HGTV's *House Hunters*. "What's new in your neck of the woods?"

"Work's going well; boring, but going well."

Lara was an advertising associate for a big agency in Downtown, and before long she was going to become an executive. We all knew it. She was the MBA-holding, very driven, and successful career woman. Total Type-A when it came to business. And sometimes her personal life too. Her ad agency kept her well compensated (hence the sexy little Audi she'd recently purchased), her colleagues loved working with her (Paul, too, though perhaps a little more than the rest of them?), and she was on a great path to becoming a woman with a lot of power in her branding strategies department.

"Might be traveling again soon," Lara said. "The last trip I took to Spokane went really well with the client. We might have to go back there again and make some more big decisions and exciting deals."

"We?" Sophie asked.

"Well, yeah..." Lara said. "Like...yeah, me, we...we as in the team. The whole team. My team and me. You know."

I wondered if Lara would bring up the topic of Paul in the middle of her stammering (perhaps he was part of the "we" team?) and how he was making things a bit more interesting at work. Was there a potential love affair, or was Lara misconstruing things as I may have done with Bobby? Lara dropped the topic of work, saying there was nothing exciting to share other than another possible trip to Spokane, so I forgot about it and turned my attention to Sophie as she was catching everyone up on her life's events.

"The café plans are going slowly right now because it's major wedding season. I've got so many cake and catering orders going Katie needs my full attention at work."

"But you're still going to try to set up your own shop?" I asked. Sophie had a lot of potential. I'd hate to see her give up on it.

"Oh, of course. I'm still doing some small things like market research and even scoping out possible storefronts. But...I've got enough on my plate right now at *Katie's Kitchen. And*, my brother John is going to London before the end of the year!"

"Ah, I've always wanted to visit London," Lara said dreamily. "You're going to visit him, aren't you?"

"Hell yeah! Not until after the baby's here, of course," Sophie said, catching my furrowed brow at the mention of "before the end of the year." "I'm hoping for a trip in the spring, perhaps. Well after Robin's little bundle of joy arrives."

"That'll be a fun trip," Lara said. "But don't give up on these bakery dreams. You have the potential, and the opportunity is there. You really need to give it a try."

"I know." Sophie casually waved a hand at Lara. "I'm still figuring things out. And I *am* still bumming off of Claire." Sophie rolled her eyes.

Claire gave Sophie a shove and told her that she wasn't bumming off her at all. Rather, she liked having Sophie back as a roommate.

"All right, so 'bumming' isn't the right word," Sophie said. "I wouldn't feel right opening up a shop and still unable to get on with my life...get a place of my own..."

Lara nodded and added, "Well, I still think you should seriously pursue the shop. And soon."

"I will. But I've *got* to go to London." Sophie was trying to dismiss the topic. "*Ob*viously."

"God, think of the men there in London!" Jackie said. "Men with sexy accents. Oh, yummy. I want to come along."

"All right, all right," Sophie said. "Fill us in on the new man, Jack. Who is he? What does he do? There must be a new one. Am I right?"

Jackie filled everyone in on her new job, making it clear, contrary to Sophie's assumptions, that so far her hopes about finding a man to snag were fairly dashed.

"I am beginning to wonder when the supposed jackpot of hot and available men will appear," Jackie said. "All the girls I work with say that that jazz bar is a goldmine of hot bachelors, but I haven't found a soul yet. They're either young and obviously attached, or they're way too old with nothing to offer to make dating someone my dad's age even worth it."

"No money, no looks...no good, eh?" I said. I hit it on the head.

"But the job pays a little and it's steady work. And I'm optimistic. That reminds me!" Jackie looked at Lara, who didn't need more than a second to catch her drift.

"Some cash?" Lara asked indifferently.

"My cell bill's way larger than I could have imagined," Jackie explained. She puffed out her bottom lip, like a small child begging for that teddy bear in the toy aisle, then broke out into a large grin when Lara conceded, as a parent occasionally does. "Thank you so much!"

Lara gave me a sheepish smile then typed a reminder into her BlackBerry to deposit funds into Jackie's account.

"All those late-night call boy centers racking up your bill?" Claire teased.

"Ha. Ha." Jackie tossed a crumpled napkin at her.

After a few of us tried to hint to Jackie that she should drop the search for a man as her reason for keeping up employment (our efforts clearly flying over her head), Claire struck up a conversation about the baby shower. "When do you think we should plan it?"

"We'll want to wait until after we find out the sex, right?"

"Oh, for sure. We need to make sure we know whether to buy blue or pink."

"That's right. Definitely after we find out. That's when? August?"

"Yes, then. After August."

"August is much too hot," I said, interrupting the flow of banter. "And if Claire is wanting the shower to be outside in her backyard..."

"You're right. Okay. September? Does September work for everyone? Early or mid-September?" Claire looked around the room. "A Saturday's probably best. How about..." She promptly looked over her cell phone's calendar. "...September fifteenth? Or we could do the twenty-second? Let's leave those two dates open and see what works best for everyone. I'll make sure Conner is out of the house and goes somewhere with Chad or something. Speaking of Conner!"

"Easy on the sugar there, peppy," I said, chuckling. Claire was usually bouncy and positive—a real stereotypical ball of sunshine. But one too many bites of cake and spoonfuls of ice cream had her going a little overboard. All eyes were on Claire as she commanded the room with her burst of excitement.

"Yeah, yeah," she dismissed. "But *speaking* of Conner!"

"He didn't propose, did he?" Sophie asked, looking immediately at Claire's left hand.

"*Puh-lease!* As if he'll ever propose this century. That's exactly what I'm talking about. Conner!" Claire rolled her eyes and took a big bite of cake. "Sometimes I could just choke him." A small piece of cake flew from her mouth and Sophie joked that so long as she spit food out while talking he'd never propose.

"Oh, shut it," Claire said. "I'm serious. I could choke him. I hinted, just *hinted*, at getting married again the other day and he was all, 'We're not talking about this, Claire. Case closed. We said we weren't going to talk about it.' Isn't that so stupid?"

"Claire," Sophie said. "I thought you guys agreed that *you* wouldn't talk about marriage and *he* wouldn't talk about moving to L.A.."

"Yeah, well, still. I barely mentioned it and he made a big stink about it. I tell you, girls," she roughly stabbed at the small remaining pieces of now ice-cream-soaked cake on her plate, "it's all Chad. He's the rotten influence here. *He's* the one who's been discouraging Conner about making a move and being a man. I know it's all his doing. Chad's so...anti-marriage or something fucked up like that."

Chad was Conner's best friend; best buds since the beginning of college when the two pledged their fraternity; roommates for years. Chad was a real player, I always thought, and I could see how Claire figured him an influence in Conner's anti-marriage stance.

"Chad can be so obnoxious sometimes," Claire said.

I stole a quick peek at Sophie to see how she reacted to the mention of Chad. Sophie actually had a one-time-only fling with him several years ago, and swore to us that it was the most rebellious and stupid thing she'd ever done. Sometimes we kidded her about it when Chad was around or brought up in the conversation. Usually we let it pass, though, since she always seemed uncomfortable or weary about it. At the moment she looked uncomfortable.

"We all know Chad can be a little somethin'-somethin' sometimes," Jackie cooed, nudging Sophie in the ribs playfully.

"Oh, shut up." Sophie nudged her back, hard. "Forget about it already."

"You don't still feel, like, *something*, for him, do you?" Lara asked.

Sophie was quick to deny any feelings, or ever having had any feelings from the onset.

"Then what's the big deal?" Jackie asked. "Sometimes we get it on and then it's over. Forget about it. No big deal. It's not like you guys should be all weirded out with each other. You're still friends, right? Friends who shag. Not a bad thing."

"Acquaintances, I guess," Sophie said. "And we're not friends who *shag*. It was one time." Sophie stuffed a piece of cake into her mouth. "But he's Conner's friend and isn't terribly awful to hang around so, whatever. I tolerate."

"Yeah," Claire added. "He's not that bad, I guess. Not bad at all, really—just this influence of anti-commitment or something. I don't like it and it grates on my nerves."

"Well, I wouldn't worry about it, Claire," Jackie said. "Conner's his own man, and when he's ready he'll propose and then you two can get married, have a million babies, and live happily ever after."

Claire smiled. "Thanks, Jack. I know it'll happen. At some point. Until then, whatevs. Things between Conner and me are still great, don't get me wrong."

"Sex still good?"

"Jack, what is it with you and sex all the time?" Lara asked, laughing.

"What? They say that those who tend to talk about it all time are the ones who aren't necessarily getting it all that much. And...I'm not exactly getting any lately, so there."

"That's no excuse. You talk about it all the time even when you *are* getting it," Sophie said.

Jackie laughed. "I know, right? God, I just love sex. Could you imagine life without it? Man, there'd be no point in living."

"Suicidal are you, now that you're going through a dry spell?" I kidded. Jackie just nodded in agreement, her plastic fork sticking out of her mouth as she leaned forward to get another sliver of cake.

"Bummed Emily can't make it to the shower," Sophie said. "Anyone heard from her lately?"

"Actually, Lara and I emailed her last night," I said. "We even sent scanned copies of the baby pictures. She's sure to respond to that one soon!"

"And hopefully she'll be back in time for the baby's birth," Jackie said. "When *is* she supposed to come home?"

"Last I heard it was some time in September."

"Then that means maybe she could make it to the shower?"

How wonderful would it be for all the girls to be back together again, under one roof? For one big celebration!

"Well, it's getting late, so I guess we should be heading out," Sophie said, looking at Claire. "Claire's making me go for a jog with her and Schnickerdoodle tomorrow bright and early. That damn dog needs his exercise before the sun rises, apparently."

Claire defended her little mutt of a dog as we prepared to head out, with Jackie not far behind.

"You heading out, too, Robin?" Sophie asked.

"No, I'm staying here tonight. Have been for a while, actually."

"Now there's an idea!" Claire said in her chipper voice. "Why don't you two move in together? It totally makes sense."

Lara and I looked at each other, perplexed expressions on our faces.

"I *have* been staying here a lot lately," I said after a pause. "Lara's been nice to let me stay a few nights but I—"

"That *is* a good idea, actually!" Lara said. Her response took me by surprise. "How come we didn't think of that before? Like the moment we found out you were pregnant?"

In what seemed like a matter of a couple of minutes, my living situation was all figured out. Lara and I agreed that it was a solid idea that I move in with her. There was no point in me living in a cramped apartment with a baby on the way when my best friend had a spare bedroom and bathroom, and was willing and eager to live with me. To help me out. Like the good old college days!

"It's probably best if I move before it gets too hot. I don't want to be well into my second trimester and moving all my stuff."

"How about next week?" Lara said excitedly. "And I'm sure Conner, even Chad, can come help with your stuff. And all of us can band together. Let's do this! Next weekend?"

"Next weekend it is!"

7

I pushed my stomach out as far as I could manage. When was I going to start showing? I thought I could see the slightest of bumps developing; sometimes I wasn't sure if that was the regular tummy tire that I never seemed to shed no matter how many miles I jogged. (Not that I'd been jogging that much since I found out I was pregnant.)

My baby book said that it was perfectly fine for me to keep up my routine jogs. I ran track throughout college, and didn't completely lose the habit once those years were over. But to say I became lax in my jogging routine, especially since becoming pregnant, would be a gross understatement, and I was somewhat fearful that starting up routinely again would harm the baby.

"Ugh," I groaned, pinching my sides. "Just regular fat and no baby bump."

Well, that's not so terrible. I'm not really ready to show and have to tell everyone at work. To tell my mom. Or my sister.

I grumbled some more, pushing my glasses further up the bridge of my nose, then taking them off, trying to decide which look better suited me. I tied my long hair up into a messy bun, and when that look didn't suit, I let it fall back down to the middle of my back. It hung there, listlessly, and I pinched at my sides again.

"A real looker here, Robin." I put my glasses back on and stuck out my bottom lip.

No pregnant charm today.

I checked the time on my cell phone to make sure I was still ahead of schedule. I wanted to get to work a good hour early, since I had some great ideas brewing for another mystery novel cover that I was recently assigned. The more time I had in the office without glory-hog Janet the better. I still had a few more minutes before I wanted to head out, so I kept looking at my bare belly in the mirror. I kept pinching my sides, running my hand over where I imagined a bump was forming, and thinking about when I'd call my mom and sister.

Emailing my dad was a cinch. I had actually already written him a quick and dull email letting him know (if he cared) that he'd soon be a grandpa, but the letter was still sitting in my draft folder. I may not have been particularly close to either of my parents, but they needed to know, and such news was owed to my mom first. She may have been detached and in her own world, but she wasn't the one who tore our family apart by leaving us for another partner.

How would I approach her? I thought about the hows, the whens, and all of the imaginable what ifs, much like I'd done with Brandon. There wouldn't be any easy way about it as every girl, no matter how distant a relationship she may have with her mother, still wants to feel her mother's approval, her mother's support, and her mother's pride. Her mother's love. I didn't expect to wow my mom in any positive light with the news, but I hoped that over time, once she learned that her little girl was having a baby of her own, she would be proud of my choices to raise my child, and proud to have a daughter who wasn't too afraid to go at it solo.

I got close to picking up the phone the previous night to call my mom, but eventually I decided against it. The watercolors were much more appealing, so aside went mom, and on came a field of purple- and peach-colored tulips. Somehow, at one angle the tulips looked more like bubble gum balls, and at another like splotchy blobs of paint atop thin green sticks. So I was a little out of my watercolor practice. I was looking forward to setting up a small workspace in Lara's apartment's alcove, right near her desk, where I could dabble with my watercolors. The lighting was fantastic, and since Lara didn't spend great deals of time working at her desk, as most of her overtime hours for work were spent at the office, she said the space was practically mine. And the treadmill that was adjacent to the spot where I'd plant my easel would be handy too. Maybe, once I got settled into Lara's place—my new home—this weekend, I might gather the nerve to try a small jog. Just a small one to make sure baby approves. I needed to do something about my belly tire, anyhow.

I checked my phone's clock once more and realized my daydreaming had zapped up a few more minutes than I'd anticipated. "Off to work, off to work," I chanted, making a mad dash out of my apartment.

My baby's first photos were always in my purse, and sometimes at work I'd sneak a look at them, a small and heartwarming reminder that something amazing was happening in my life. Every time I looked at those photos I couldn't care less about a raise or a promotion at work. Brandon didn't matter. My not wanting (and needing) to tell my family seemed like a minor detail. Everything superfluous in life melted away and felt, well, superfluous. Nothing else mattered. Then, when my mind floated back to thoughts of a raise or a promotion, the images of my little bean sprout of a growing baby staring up at me, I figured that some things still mattered, obviously. So I'd tuck the photos discretely back into my purse and get back to work.

That morning, in the middle of my private cooing session over my photos, Janet charged into the office a good ten minutes late.

Surprise, surprise. Look who's not perfect after all.

I bid her good morning, immediately stashing my photos.

"Please. You're probably delighted I'm late," Janet said, more grumpy than usual. She practically threw her briefcase onto her desk, then slammed herself into her seat without taking off her blazer.

"That's not true." My voice was almost inaudible over her heavy huffing and puffing from what I'm sure was a sprint from the parking lot to her desk.

"Whatever. You'd think my own sister would understand how important my career is and how I am *never* late to the office." She turned towards me. I thought I detected a small bead of sweat on her brow, which was all squished up in anger. "I am *never* late, isn't that right?"

I nodded my head, too afraid to contradict, though I honestly couldn't think of a single time in all of Janet's existence at Forster & Banks when she was even a minute late.

"Sometimes my sister can be such a bitch."

"You all right?"

"No, I'm not *all right*, Robin! My careless sister decided to call me *before* work to tell me the news that, ohmigod, she's pregnant."

The small hairs on the nape of my neck started to prick up. *This is an odd coincidence...*

"*Before* work, Robin. Can you believe that? So bitchy and inconsiderate."

It took me a few seconds to try to see the situation from Janet's point of view, but I couldn't. I was a new mother and I could see the merit in breaking such news to your loved ones as soon as you could. Who cared if Janet was on her way to work?

"I don't think there's anything wrong with that, Janet."

"Of course you wouldn't. You make doctor's appointments before work rather than on Saturdays or after hours, or during lunch break, like a serious career woman would do." She opened and slammed various desk drawers. "What, are you going to waste more of my morning, too, by telling me you're knocked up?"

How does she know?

I felt my face go pale and all I could do was stare at her, speechless.

"What?" she asked, nearly shouting. "I'm just joking. God, don't take me so seriously."

Phew. Close one.

"Anyway, enough of my morning has been taken up by crazy baby talk. Time to get to work. Like a *real* modern woman. I'm going to be taking charge on those edits for the mock-up we did together."

Was that a question or a statement? Knowing Janet...

"All right?" she demanded.

I didn't want to deal with Hurricane Janet a second longer, so I quietly told her that was fine by me, even though it wasn't. I'd worked just as hard, if not harder, on those mock-ups. Why was she the one who had all the say on the edits? And why were there edits that needed to be made in the first place? I thought we did a smash-up job and nailed every point our boss wanted us to hit.

Forget about it. Let Janet deal with it.

When Janet left for the editing department I stole another look at my sweet angel's photos. "You're not going to be a punk brat, are you, honey? No you're not. You're going to be so loved and you'll have lots of friends and you'll be sweet..." I looked over at Janet's now empty desk and snarled. "Not like some people your mom must unfortunately tolerate."

I was exhausted after the past few days of work. Janet's bitch mode was up a good seven notches. Bobby hadn't been making any gestures lately that I could at least misconstrue as flirty to give me something fun to dream about and blow out of proportion. Sophie was still pestering me about figuring out the Brandon thing, though I wanted to put his abortion advice and our phone call out of my mind. On top of it all, I was overwhelmed with moving everything I owned from my apartment and over into Lara's in a couple of days. Boxes littered every room of my apartment. Half the time I couldn't find the things I had already packed, and the things I thought I had packed were actually misplaced. Oh, and did I mention I was pregnant and had started having cravings for dried blueberries and kettle popcorn? A very tasty combination, I might add.

Just when I thought I'd found some equanimity with nothing but a cool glass of lemonade and a blank piece of paper awaiting its first drop of paint, Sophie called. My first guess (and I'd only need one) was that she'd want to talk about how I *had* to talk to Brandon. Emergency. Code Blue.

Sure enough, nearly the first thing out of Sophie's mouth was, "We're figuring the Brandon thing out tonight."

"Sophie, I don't want to."

"We're beyond what you want and don't want to do, Robin. It's about doing what needs to be done. Brandon's going to give you what you want, or else."

"He *is* giving me what I want." I took a long pull on my iced drink, then came the quick brain freeze.

"You're sounding absurd. This isn't what you want. You want him to do what's right. He owes you."

I shook away the brief albeit painful freeze. "Sophie, this *is* what I want. I want him to stay out of my life if he's going to view his baby as something that needs to be 'gotten rid of.' And he doesn't seem to have any problems staying out."

She groaned. "Forget it. I'm coming over there right now and you're coming with me."

"What?" I nearly choked on my next sip. "Where are we going?"

"We're going to see Brandon. We're settling this once and for all." Before I could object, or so much as whimper a response or a simple sound, Sophie was off the line, and on her way over.

With not a minute to spare Sophie arrived and demanded we drive to Brandon's immediately. I angrily grabbed my new Vera Bradley handbag from the dining table and followed Sophie out to her awaiting Prius. She hadn't even turned off the engine; her parking job wasn't much to speak of, either.

"Sophie, this is ridiculous!"

"Not another word. Get in the car," she demanded. Clad in yoga gear, she jogged to her car door and leapt over the parking block like a determined gazelle. "I'm sick of what he's doing to you. We're going to his place right now and we're finishing this. Once and for all!"

There was no stopping her. I certainly couldn't. It would have been interesting to see Jackie or Lara in this situation. They'd protest once, maybe twice, and put Sophie in her place. I wasn't going to do that; it was much too frightening and forward a move. No, no. Besides, I didn't want to make Sophie feel like I didn't appreciate her help. She was, after all, only doing what she felt was best, and I was grateful for that. Her approach of dragging me out of the house and forcing me to stand Brandon down, face-to-face, wasn't exactly the method I preferred, but it was Sophie's way or the highway once we crossed Lake Union and were entering the high end part of the Queen Anne district. Billionaires lived in the area and had pretentious mansions overlooking the rest of Seattle society. I suddenly felt insignificantly small...very out of place. I gently tried to protest Sophie's actions, but there was no turning back as we descended down the sloping hills into Lower Queen Anne, some short blocks from Brandon's modest brownstone apartment.

"Sophie, I can't do this," I cried, gripping her right arm. "Please, let's go back home. I don't want to do this."

"Too late," she said. "You could have just not come."

"Yeah, right. Like that was an option. You barreled into my place demanding we go, or else. Like I had a choice."

We were only a street or two away and my stomach was in knots. I wanted to retch. What would happen? Would there be yelling? Punches? Cursing? Slammed doors? How about unanswered doors? The precariousness was too much to handle.

"I'm not getting out of the car," I told her. "I don't want to see him." She tried to persuade me to join her while she planned to have it out with him, face-on, but I stood firm.

Then we arrived. There it was. The familiar apartment. The front room light was on. The street was silent save for some very light cricket chirping and the occasional dog barking. There wasn't a single pedestrian or neighbor in sight.

Great. No witnesses.

I looked over at Sophie, her neck veins looking as if they were starting to throb. "You sure you want to do this?" I asked.

"You sure you don't?" Her eyes were wide; game-on. I nodded my certainty, and without a hiccough she got out of the car. "Your photos." She held her hand out, her eyes begging for them.

"Oh, Sophie..." I groaned. "Not the drama."

"Please, Robin."

I reluctantly conceded. The situation was already high on drama. Why not add some fuel to the fire?

I watched intently (and in terror) as Sophie stormed up the steps of her old apartment, the fluttering reel of my baby's photos in her hand. Breath held, window narrowly cracked so I could spy on what was sure to become an all out war, I tensely watched and waited.

Please don't be home. Please don't be home. Please don't be—

A small movement of the front door, but no figure on the other side. Was it my imagination or was the front door actually opening? Sophie still stood stoically at the top step, both hands, made into fists, planted firmly on her hips. Then the door pried open slowly, slowly, still slowly, and then—there he was. Brandon. The door now wide open, Brandon standing there, a shocked expression covering his face, and Sophie still standing as stoically as ever.

I heard some muffled voices but couldn't make out a single word.

I thought of cracking the window some more, but I didn't want to draw any attention to myself. If I was lucky, Brandon would never know I was in the car.

Well, there goes that plan. Sophie was suddenly pointing at me, abruptly shaking her finger in my direction. Brandon looked over and our eyes locked. I couldn't help but quickly turn away.

Become invisible. You're not here. This is not happening.

I could finally make out their words. Sophie was screaming at Brandon that he needed to grow up and do what was right by me. Brandon, whose voice wasn't quite as shrill or loud, seemed to be making his case. I stole a swift glance, mad curiosity getting the best of me. Brandon had his hands jammed deep into his jean pockets and was rocking back and forth on his bare heels, calmly speaking inaudible words to Sophie. But Sophie wouldn't hear it. She started flailing her hands about, a few curse words cropping up here and there, still shouting at him that all of this was his fault. He started shaking his head over and over and over, then he ran his fingers through his wavy brown hair, head cocked to one side, mouth slightly open. Sophie shoved my baby's photos at him and his mouth fell agape.

"Take a look!" I heard her yell. "This is *your* baby!"

He had the pictures gripped in his fingers. He brought the reel up closer, furrowing his brow and shaking his head in what I knew to be denial. The pictures were handed back to Sophie.

A sudden urge to defend my unborn baby sprang forth, and I bolted out of the car. I didn't like the fact that Sophie was showing him my baby's photos, but what had I expected when she asked for them? With this mysterious newfound aplomb, my hands shaking and heart rate quickening with each step I took closer to Brandon, I forced myself to be brave and defend my baby.

Stand up for yourself, Robin. Stand up for your baby. You can do it. Be brave.

"Robin," Brandon said, sending my thought pattern askew.

My steps had started out briskly. I was overpowered by a sense of urgency and courage. Then, when Brandon called my name, I came to realize how displaced I felt by standing up and taking charge of the situation. What was I doing? I slowed my pace. Was I out of my mind? I became timid, asking myself why the hell I'd gotten out of the car. It seemed like a bold move at the time—but this wasn't my style. What was I going to do now?

So stupid, Robin. Stupid. Stupid. What now?

Sophie came over to me and linked her arm in mine. She asked if I was all right and told me she'd take care of things, as if reading my mind, or perhaps my body language. I was going to crack at any moment. Run back to the car, tearing up, telling myself how foolish I was trying to stand down Brandon. Trying to stand up for myself and my baby. Doing this over the phone was one thing; attempting it in-person was social suicide for me. I just couldn't do it.

But then, when I looked up at Brandon—his hands once again deeply sunk into his pockets, rocking on his bare heels, a smirk growing on his face—I summoned that boost of courage once more and told myself I could do this. If not for me, then for my unborn baby.

So I said, "Listen."

Be as courageous as you were when you talked to him on the phone, Robin.

"I don't want you to have anything to do with my baby," I said. "It is my decision to have and raise this child and I want to do so without you. Sophie, here," I looked at her and gave a very small but knowing smile, "is only doing what she thinks is best. She's a bigger person than you'll ever be. And...and...and so am I." My hands were trembling, knees practically knocking; I persevered. "I'm never going to get rid of this baby. I never considered it. You wanting me to abort it tells me all I need to know about you, Brandon. I don't want someone like you in my baby's life."

Sophie squeezed me close to her, giving me that extra vote of confidence I needed right then.

I continued. "She only thought I—*we* only thought you could have some decency and help out with some of the expenses at least." I swallowed deeply, the frog in my throat abating. "I know I could take this to court and have you forced into paying child support. But to be quite frank with you, this is supposed to be an exciting and new time in my life. I don't want to spend any of it in court, dealing with custody or support battles or any of that shit. I want to leave now and get on with my life. And I don't want you to be a part of it." I looked long and hard at him, his smirk gone, leaving him with nothing but an expressionless face.

Wow! Courage from nowhere...kind of nice.

I took my baby's photos from Sophie and turned back towards the car, my hands and knees noticeably shaking and my heart pounding so loud and so hard and so fast I could feel it pulsate deep in my ears. I was nearly back at the car when Brandon spoke.

"I'll send you what cash I can. When I can." His response took me by surprise. I pivoted on my tottering legs. "I'm not a total dick," he added, looking hard at Sophie. "And I promise I'll stay out of your life, Robin. If that's what you want."

"If you don't want to love and care for this baby, then yes, I want you to stay out of our lives."

"Consider it done."

I muttered a "thank you" for whatever reason, and as I was about to get into the car he said, "I'm sorry about this. You know, I never imagined something like this would happen."

"My baby isn't anything to be sorry about. But if you're apologizing for—"

"I'm sorry things turned out like this for everyone," he said. "And I'm sorry you're going at this alone. I just don't—"

"I know, I know. You don't want this," I said, the deafening pounding of my heartbeat in my ears starting to recede. I took in a shaky breath, then exhaled, closing my eyes briefly. "I'm okay with that now," I said. "Come on, Sophie. I'm tired. Oh, and Brandon." I looked at him one last time. "I'm not alone. Never was." I looked to Sophie and said, "Let's go home now."

Sophie gave Brandon Lara's address for where he could send his checks (I'd be surprised if anything ever arrived), and I shut myself into the car. It was time to leave. Sophie had come to do what she felt was necessary. I'd said everything I'd needed to say to Brandon. It was time to go home.

I watched as Sophie said something low and brief to Brandon up close, then came some inaudible response from him, followed by a swift slap across his face. Sophie shouted some more obscenities, probably rightly deserved, before jogging her way back to the car.

"And I mean it!" Sophie shouted, right before she got in and started to roll out of the neighborhood.

After a painstakingly long silence, I said, "Thanks, Sophie."

She blurted out, "Why thank me? You didn't want any part of this scene I made."

"Thank you for your support. For your friendship. It's really admirable how you're trying to help."

"Yeah, well," she said gruffly. She turned on her window wipers as a light rain developed. "He deserved it. And I think I needed it, too. Selfish bastard."

"You did what you had to for both of us. For all three of us." I rubbed my nonexistent bump of a belly. "And we should both be over him. Through with him. He's gone and out of our lives now, save for a few checks that I *doubt* I'll ever see...he's gone now, Sophie."

She nodded emphatically and added, "That's for sure. He's moving to New York. Before the end of the year. Says he found a new and better job and is moving. No looking back kind of thing, I guess." She looked at me. "Probably for the better, huh?"

"Definitely," I said, still rubbing my stomach. "Definitely for the best here. So, what did you tell him?" I was madly curious. "And what a slap! What ever for?" I'd nearly forgotten the last-minute blow she sailed his way.

She laughed a loud, solid sound. "He said a few choice words. Called you something I didn't appreciate. Anyway, I told him that if he ever came near you or any of us, *especially* your baby, that I'd come after him and tear him apart."

"What, with some mobsters you've befriended?" It did sound kind of funny.

"Oh, I'd find a way to hit him where it hurt. We were together for three years, Robin. I'd figure something out. I don't think any of us have to worry about him, though. He's leaving for New York and he's getting out of our lives completely. Like you said, he's gone now."

"Fresh start."

"Yeah, fresh start for everyone."

I found myself smiling slightly, and not because Brandon was not only steering clear of our lives and moving across the country, as far as he could possibly go within the continental US. I smiled because

Sophie was right. It was a fresh start for everyone. A new chapter. And I was actually looking forward to it. Really looking forward to it, as daunting as parts of it might be.

"What do you say to a gelato and a brief shopping run downtown?" Sophie said, upbeat. "There's a new baby store I saw open up a few weeks ago. I bet we could find little Robin Junior something super cute. My treat."

8

Moving day had arrived, and it was all hands on deck! I didn't have that much to begin with, as my apartment was as small as they come, so packing my personal effects was no great task. Lara helped orchestrate an online sale of most of the furniture that I no longer wanted and didn't need. A lot of the stuff was pretty shabby—stuff I'd never replaced from my college days. Lara's apartment was exquisitely furnished, and her hardwood floors and immaculate kitchen with granite countertops and all stainless steel appliances, didn't need a ratty coffee table like mine around. We did keep a few things that I didn't want to let go of or that we actually found a use for, but most of my furniture had either been sold or donated and was in the process of being hauled on out. Slowly the apartment I'd called home for four years was emptying out. A small wave of nostalgia overcame me as I stared at the area where my bed had once been, the carpet beneath a brighter (and cleaner) shade.

God, how many nights did I spend in that bed cramming for tests? Or how many nights did the girls and I spend in this room together...in this apartment together...

"You sure this is everything?" Claire asked, picking up a small box from my bedroom and snapping me out of my nostalgia. "Doesn't look like all that much."

"Lara's helped me get rid of a ton of stuff. Just personal things are left, really. Clothes, shoes, books..." I did a sweeping three-sixty of the bedroom. "Not that much stuff, nope."

Claire wiped some sweat from her brow with her shoulder. "It's effing hot. I'm glad we've got the boys to help with the heavy stuff."

Seattle graced us with a particularly warm June day, and no level on the air conditioning unit could keep any of us cool enough with all the moving going on. And no matter what I tried, I couldn't keep from having what I swore were hot flashes. I took a sip of the lemonade I'd whipped up (four gallons worth) before the helpful crew of movers arrived.

"Ow," I moaned, rubbing at my forehead. "Damn brain freeze." I read somewhere either online or in my baby book that sometimes pregnant women would experience bouts of strange bodily reactions, such as night sweats, a sudden outbreak of goose bumps, and, yes, brain freezes. "It's not even that cold." The heat was melting the ice fast.

Sophie came in to retrieve yet another box as Claire made her way out with another.

"And you're sure this is all you have?" Sophie asked, surveying the room and its few remaining boxes.

"My goodness, yes," I said, chuckling. "I don't have all that much."

Sophie shrugged, now holding a box that contained many of my paintbrushes, watercolors, and various other art supplies.

"Careful with that one, doll. That one's got my treasures."

Sophie read the label *ART SUPPLIES* written in bold, black letters on its side and said, "So how's that going? Still painting and sketching like your usual self? Any masterpieces yet?"

"Yeah, yeah, don't think so." I followed Sophie out to one of the cars, carrying a very small box myself. The girls, and Conner and Chad, who had also offered to help me move, insisted that I not carry anything that weighed more than ten pounds. And even then,

Sophie said that I should consider making my weight limit five pounds "to be safe." I told them they were overreacting. It wasn't like I was about to burst or anything. I still wasn't even showing. But then Lara popped in with a stern warning that Dr. Buschardi had told us that the first trimester was the most dicey of times in a pregnancy. "You could miscarry if you're not careful," the doctor had said. "When you clear your first trimester your rate of miscarrying decreases significantly."

"Well I'm pretty much done with my first trimester," I'd told Sophie. "Actually this weekend marks my moving on into the second one. And boy have the cravings already hit!"

It didn't matter, though. I was not to lift anything more than five pounds, and my friends would make sure of it.

"Looks like this is the last one for this car," Conner said, taking the box from Claire and arranging it in her Corolla.

"And that's the last for this baby," Chad said, taking the box from Sophie's clutch and setting it in the trunk of her compact car.

Everyone had pitched in, bringing over their cars and trucks, and spending their entire Saturday helping me move to Lara's.

"Thanks, guys," I said, stretching out my back. "I don't know what I'd do without your help."

Jackie came up beside me and started to massage my lower back. "You didn't lift something too heavy, did you?" Her tone was scolding, and I told her not to overreact. It was the expected cramping and general discomfort that comes with being pregnant.

We finished loading Lara's car with some more boxes, and utilized every inch of space in both Conner's and Chad's large trucks. Then we made our way for the second time from my old University District neighborhood to the adjacent neighborhood of Wallingford, where Lara lived. Where my new home was!

Wallingford was an old working-class part of town that is now a very pleasant district. It has some interesting bookstores, DIY-style and thrift stores, coffee shops, and inexpensive eateries. Wallingford is as much a "real" neighborhood as you can get. It still has some old-fashioned hardware and handy and supply stores, even some ruggedly handsome and quaint pubs and espresso shops. It's mostly a residential part of Seattle, much like Claire and Conner's neighborhood of Madison Park, and is very quiet and serene with next to no traffic. It would be the perfect location to have a newborn and start raising a baby. And Lara's snazzy apartment would be like high living. Granted we'd soon be three living under one roof best suited for two and Lara's cat, but we'd make it work. It'd be a substantial improvement from my place.

"Who's up for some burgers?" Chad asked, getting out of his massive truck once we arrived at my new home. "We could unload Sophie's roller skate and then you girls could go for a burger run?" He looked over at Sophie, who was rolling her eyes.

"It's an *economically-* and *ecologically*-sized car," Sophie defended. "Unlike that monster of a gas guzzler you have. Who needs such a big truck like that anyway? Overcompensating for something, are we?"

Sophie had asked for it; she should have known better. Naturally, Chad had a smooth one coming: "You of all people should know that's not true, Sophie baby."

Conner made a low and drawn out groan, followed by a whistle that said, "Burn! He got you good!" He clapped Chad on the back.

"Whatever," Sophie said, tossing her silky, long, brunette ponytail behind her. "It's still a ridiculous vehicle."

"Hey, that truck's helping make this move go quickly," I reminded her. If it weren't for Chad's large truck, and Conner's, too, we would be looking at a few more carloads. And in this heat I didn't even want to consider such a possibility.

"Got a point there," Jackie added, lighting up a cigarette and making sure she stood several yards away and downwind from me. The first time she'd lit up around me post-pregnancy news all of the girls had practically screamed admonitions at her. Jackie made a motion with her hand, silently asking me if she was far enough away. I gave her a smile and a thumbs up that she was fine.

"Oh, you know you like it," Chad teased Sophie, who was looking in the opposite direction, clearly not wanting to carry on a discussion with him. "Besides, it comes in handy when I need to transport a big canvas. Not to mention it hauls mom and dad's boat, the kayaks... Which I *know* you enjoy riding."

"Big canvases, eh?" Sophie said. "I didn't know you were selling your art literally by the truckload."

Here we go. A Sophie-Chad banter session. All out this time.

Sometimes, you could practically cut the sexual tension, or the "I really can't stand you" attitude, with a knife. I wasn't sure which way the discussion was trending, but the lot of us watched and snickered as it unfolded.

"Actually, yeah," Chad defended. "I *did* sell a painting the other week. And it *was* a large canvas, thank you very much."

Chad was an aspiring artist, but not like myself. I enjoyed painting and sketching as a hobby, and nothing more. Any so-called masterpieces that I created were for my and my close friends' pleasure alone. I had no desire to try to make it big with my art, and I didn't even care to sell a piece. It was strictly a hobby for me; that is, unless it was graphic art and I was designing book covers. That was a different medium entirely, though.

Chad, however, worked in the marketing field in some ritzy Downtown office building by day, and by night and all other spare hours he was a fledgling artist. Actually, he was quite good, so fledgling is probably the wrong word; he was *aspiring*. And his work had promise. Real promise. He'd sold a few paintings over the years and seemed eager to make a full-time go at it at some point. I didn't understand why he didn't quit his day job and try it out, seeing how his dad was some IT big shot millionaire who obviously had enough to go around. If I were Chad, I'd probably bounce on the whole trust fund baby way of life.

Hmm, spend most of my time working a job when I could spend all of my time painting and doing what I love...

"How about those burgers?" Conner interrupted the ribbing. He, like the rest of us, didn't want to stand under the blazing sun watching a back-and-forth between Sophie and Chad all afternoon.

"Fine, unload my *car* then, Chad, and we'll go pick something up," Sophie said, opening her trunk.

"God. Someone needs to get laid," Jackie said to me after she stamped out her cigarette and started to tote a blanket and some pillows off to Lara's apartment.

"Yeah," I said, helping her out. "You, right?"

Lara's apartment was slowly beginning to look like a bomb had gone off, with everything disorganized and boxes haphazardly placed in my new room. Lara's poor little cat, Beebee, took cover under Lara's bed when we had started lugging in the boxes, and she hadn't moved since. Once the last box had been set on the kitchen counter, the boys decided it was time to head out.

"We're going to hit a few balls," Conner said to Claire, motioning towards Chad, "before it gets dark. Meet you back at the house later tonight?" Conner and Claire kissed each other goodbye, and I thanked the guys again for all of their help.

"Think nothing of it," Chad called out before he left. "Oh, and congratulations, Robin. You'll make a great mom."

Out of the corner of my eye I saw Sophie shake her head. Apparently a little of Chad could go a long way.

"Thank you, all of you, for the help," I said when the guys were gone. "And thank you, Lara, for letting me do this."

"Are you kidding?" she exclaimed. "This is going to be awesome. We're going to have so much fun raising little baby X together. And how fun will it be to set up the baby's stuff in your room? It'll be a little cramped but—"

"It'll be perfect," I said. "There's plenty of room for a crib. And even a rocking chair over in the corner by the window."

"Oh my gosh, girls!" Claire said. "That's right! We still have to get the baby's room all set up."

"One step at a time," I said. "Let's organize Mom's part of the room first."

"She's right, Robin," Sophie said. "We definitely need to get the baby's area of the room going, at some point. And getting more clothes for it and—"

"*More* clothes?" Jackie asked. "You already bought some stuff for the little bubby?"

That reminded me. The girls hadn't seen what Sophie and I picked up the other night during our little to-hell-with-Brandon celebration. I ushered them into my new room so they could see what we'd picked up.

"We got a little carried away, but aren't they adorable?" I showed off the dainty cream and yellow bonnet, the tiniest (and softest) socks they'd ever seen, and the cute and totally gender neutral onesies in shades of green, yellow, and basic all-white.

"And look at *this* one!" I dug through the shopping bag I'd thrown onto my bed and withdrew the cutest little yellow t-shirt, which had a bright teal and pink cupcake on it. "Sophie said I just had to have this, even if it ends up being a boy."

"Kid could be a baker. You never know." Sophie gave a wink.

"Okay. I'm jealous," Jackie said. "You get all this cool and freaking adorable stuff."

"Jealous, yeah," Claire piped in, "that you guys already did some shopping! When's the next outing? We definitely all have to go shopping now."

We went back and forth for a while figuring out what we should do first—shop for more baby clothes, or some of the essentials like Sophie suggested? Bottles, blankets, pacifiers, rattles and baby toys, and something called a Boppy, whatever that was (Lara insisted I needed one). Or shop for the baby furnishings? Or the "you can't forget the safety things," that Claire brought to our attention? "Babies get into all sorts of trouble, I've heard. Electrical outlets. Toilets. Slamming their fingers in doors. Trashcans. Under the kitchen sink."

Suddenly the idea of shopping for adorable baby bonnets and shoes and all-things-baby seemed a daunting task. Wherever to begin? And what was that about trashcans and electrical outlets?

"Girls," Lara said, trying to calm everyone down. Some of us were heading down tangents about completely safeguarding and baby-proofing an apartment, while others were saying that a baby needed so much stuff there certainly wouldn't be enough space for everything in this apartment.

"Chill a sec," Lara said. "We're not baby-proofing any outlets just yet or putting clips on the toilets. We need to focus on getting this baby the bare necessities and some clothes for starters. A little bit at a time, okay? No need to overwhelm poor Robin. She's got enough to deal with." She gave my forearm a little rub. "And we're going to need to get her some maternity clothes soon. Before any of us know it, she won't have a thing to wear."

"Thanks, Lara. Way to make me feel good," I kidded.

"But first. What we absolutely *must* do before anything else—"

"More baby clothes shopping?" Claire asked.

"Nope. First, we need to make a toast. A toast to Robin's big move and the two of us living together again!"

"Like the college days," I said, thinking back to the many fond memories of Lara and I sharing an apartment together.

"Yeah, like the college days," Lara said, producing a bottle of champagne from the refrigerator.

"Except that now you're pregnant," Jackie said in a tone that slightly hinted at jealousy. I knew Jackie wasn't riding cloud nine over my move in with Lara, but at some point she'd have to grow up. Lara would still be as great a friend and support system as ever to her, and would continue to bend over backward when she was in need. But Lara was also *my* good friend, and she was there when I needed her, too. And I needed her now more than ever.

"To life as roomies, with a little one on the way!" Sophie cheered, raising her glass. Everyone else followed suit, their glasses filled with champagne, mine with some sparkling water.

"Cheers!"

That first night in my new home, boxes still spread out over my bedroom, I turned on my low-lit bedside lamp, pulled the blankets up snuggly around my waist, and propped up my knees as I got comfortable in my bed. I started working on a new sketch that evening. It was of the five of us—myself, Sophie, Claire, Jackie, and Lara—all darkly shaded figures toasting glasses of bubbly, with a sixth figure on the far left of the half-moon grouping of girls: Emily, lightly shaded, representing that she was there with us in spirit.

I still hadn't heard from her, and imagined that the native village children either had her caught up in a fun game, or the village elders were teaching her how to properly weave or grind something. What an adventurous life Emily led. Too bad she didn't live in the world of modern communication half the time. I was dying to hear back from her since Lara and I had sent her the ultrasound photos. *Maybe tomorrow...*

I set down my pencil and looked around the crowded room. Where would I decide to set up the baby's crib? The rocking chair I knew I wanted to buy (because *You're Going to Be a Mother* highly suggested a rocking chair for Mommy and Baby during nursing time) would work ideally in the corner. Perhaps the crib could be situated right next to it. Or I could move my bed around. Lara said she didn't mind if I moved the furniture. She even suggested that if I wanted to move some of the pieces out we could put them in a storage unit.

"I'll figure something out," I said to myself. I decided against continuing work on my sketch of the girls for the night and chose to work on a room plan for the furniture I'd soon be collecting for the baby. "Let's see I'll put the rocker here...then maybe move my bed here..." I madly began sketching out room plan after room plan, excited about my new home and the room that I'd soon be sharing with my little baby.

9

I was more than fifteen weeks pregnant, and it showed. My bump had officially arrived. My cravings were developing further, adding to the list fresh cherries, melted Swiss cheese, baked beans, and salt and vinegar potato chips. The chips were a horrible guilty pleasure and nasty craving that I sometimes suspected were the cause of the bump. But as the bump grew and grew I was convinced it was the little pea pod. No great consumption of potato chips could morph my body overnight. And besides, I'd successfully taken up light jogging for a few minutes five mornings a week on the very handy treadmill that Lara had set up in her alcove.

Take that, potato chips!

I fished for a dried cherry from the bag I kept stocked in my desk at the office and popped one of the succulent treats into my mouth.

Nope, it was official: my baby bump was here.

"It's here," I had told Lara that morning before work, the two of us staring at my naked upper half, save for my lone white bra that would also soon need replacing as my breasts were becoming fuller. (Not a bad side effect of being pregnant.)

"The bump is officially here," I said, trying to suck in my stomach.

Nothing. Still a bump. We looked at each other and agreed that the coming weekend we would have to go maternity clothes shopping, so we made it a date (more like an emergency) with some of the girls.

But before the fun of a shopping weekend, I had a heavy load of work waiting for me at the office. I made sure that I wore the baggiest shirt I could find that morning, and managed to zip (I didn't say button—just zip) a pair of somewhat loosely fitted dress slacks. I hadn't told anyone at work yet about my being pregnant, and, as Lara insisted, it was probably something I'd need to do sooner rather than later if I wanted to make my maternity leave plans well in advance. I didn't want to draw any attention to myself at work, though, and I didn't want to deal with anything of the sort before my possible raise.

The timing wouldn't work out, however. There was simply no way around keeping my pregnancy a secret until my review at work was scheduled. "I'll break the news next week," I told Lara, halfway lying. I *planned* on telling my boss and colleagues next week, but *actually* doing it was another thing entirely. I figured I'd wait until next week and see how I felt (and looked). If the bump was still somewhat of a covert subject, then why press the matter? From the looks of it, though, my bump seemed to be on the rise and every morning I could swear I was getting bigger and bigger. Absolutely no denying the inevitable.

Mmm, why are you so good?

I snagged another handful of cherries from the bag, then made a silent promise to close the drawer (and keep it closed) and get back to work on the finishing touches of the mystery novel cover. I was sure I could have it finished before the weekend. At least the preliminary draft.

Janet had already made some off-color remark about my clothes earlier that morning when she caught sight of even what I considered a hideous and baggy ensemble. Since then I tried to stay put behind my desk as much as possible, not wanting to attract any further attention (or insults) towards me or my choice of wardrobe

styling. So when I thought all was clear and most everyone was already at lunch, I made a dash for the restroom.

"Miss Sinclair!" It was Bobby.

I spun around. "Bobby, hey." I made sure I didn't cross my arms over my chest, no matter how uncomfortable I may have been, because that was a sure-fire way to attract a glance at my ever-growing stomach.

"Haven't chatted with you in a while." He sidled up to me—a little too closely for my taste given my predicament.

Please don't think it odd I'm dressed like someone at Wal-Mart on a Tuesday night.

Honestly, the way I was swimming in my large shirt made me feel like all I needed was a pair of sweatpants and jogging shoes, and then a shopping basket full of salt and vinegar potato chips, and I'd fit right in at Wal-Mart.

"Well, you know how it goes. Busy, busy." I tried to inch towards the bathroom, but Bobby inched along with me.

"How's things?" he asked.

"Oh, same old. You know. Busy."

"Yeah, yeah." He rubbed at his jaw, and I caught a tantalizing hint of his cologne. There it was again—that wonderful aroma that I could never peg. "Been wanting to ask you about something," he said.

Oh no. What? He thinks I'm pregnant?

"The, uh, project manager position that's been the buzz around here. In the spring, you know?"

I nodded, slowly registering the topic up for conversation and becoming relieved he wasn't addressing my wardrobe disaster...or growing girth.

"So, uh, you thinking of going for it?" he asked.

I wasn't sure what to say. Would it be, "Absolutely. The position's got my name on it, so hands off!" or, "Oh, I don't know...maybe."

Strong, coy, strong, coy, strong, c—

"Because I definitely think you should try for it. You have a shot. I'm sure of it."

I was taken aback. Someone at this firm was actually on my side about becoming a PM? And wait a minute, Bobby wasn't vying for it? Why didn't he want the position?

Maybe Janet's right...

"I seriously think you should consider it," he said. "If you haven't already."

"Yeah, actually, I am considering it." I tried to sound confident. "Don't know if I'll get it." And there goes that confidence.

"I think you'd make a great PM. And I bet you'd be a rock star working in the—oh, what are they calling it? The chick lit genre? Probably a fun change from the usual mystery or action novel."

"We'll see," was all I could say. Janet's words were running through my mind.

Was Bobby really going to play the suck up game with me, the potential PM, so he could be my number one guy? Then take advantage, somehow one-up me? Get an "in" with the bosses... No, that's ridiculous. Or is it?

"Try for it, Robin," he said. "For what it's worth, I'll be rooting for you."

I smiled weakly and tried to inch on to the bathroom.

"I saw your work on that mystery book you did recently," he said, still keeping me. "Some solid stuff there, Sinclair." He made a pumping fist action with his hand. "Saw the print proof and it looks really awesome. Nice work."

I thanked him coolly and wished him a good lunch break before finally escaping into the bathroom. A second longer and I was afraid he'd take notice of my unusual, baggy clothes, and I was afraid I'd say something stupid like, "Of course I want the position! I'd die for it." Or, worse, "Is Janet right about you?" Then I'd look like a total fool. And, shoot, why didn't I ask him if he was going to try for the position?

What a lost opportunity.

Even though the office was nearly cleared out for lunch, I still wanted to ensure my privacy as I planned on giving my mother a call during my lunch break. I drove to the familiar park where I'd

already spent many-an-awkward lunch break. I'd decided to break the baby news to my mother the same way I had with Brandon. I wanted to do it when I was pressed for time, where I could easily end the call and tell her it was time to get back to work.

The weather was warm and filled with sunshine, so I opted to plant myself on one of the park benches while I enjoyed a sandwich, with a very large bag of those salt and vinegar chips on the side. Lara suggested I take a sandwich bag-size of chips for lunch, but I insisted the entire party size bag was a better option.

I tentatively listened to the ringing on the other line as I waited for my mother to pick up her phone.

"Hello," she answered.

"Hey, Mom," I said, reminding myself to be strong and go through with the call as planned.

"Kaitlyn?"

"No, Mom."

"Robin?" She sounded surprised, and I couldn't blame her. I think it was Christmas the last time I'd talked to her.

"Robin! What's new with you?"

We made small talk, and I learned that she was currently dating a very successful architect who was going to take her to the Florida Keys this winter, since he'd gotten a big project down there.

"I'm going to be there the whole season! Christmas and New Years too, isn't that wonderful and so exciting for me?"

Nothing had changed. It was still all about Mom, but I couldn't care less. Years ago, I'd let myself get over the fact that I didn't have that traditional "mom figure."

"That's nice, Mom. I'm happy for you. Listen, I wanted to share some good news with you."

"Oh, you met an architect too, honey? Or a successful business-man? Oh, architects make such great lovers. So in tune..." She rambled on. She sounded like she'd returned from one of her feel-good, do-good, and be-good retreats, incense burning around the clock, and meditation teachers and people called "life guides" helping her find her aura or color or something voodoo-hokey like

that. She'd become very New Age a year or so ago. I wasn't in the mood to hear about it, though, much less entertain the notion.

"Mom, no, nothing like that. I, uh..." I decided I'd come right out and say it. "I'm going to have a baby."

She was speechless. I couldn't coax a response out of her until I said, "Can you please say something? Anything?"

"Robin Elaine Sinclair, are you telling me you're pregnant?"

Just now coming out of a hypnotic state? In denial? Bad phone connection?

"Yes, Mother. I'm going to have a baby. I wanted to let you know you're going to be a grandma."

"What? This and no architect?"

"Forget the architect."

"No businessman?"

"Drop the businessman, architect thing, Mom. That's *your* life. *I'm* having a baby."

When she asked who the father was and I vaguely told her that it was some guy who's out of the picture now, that it didn't matter, her response was curt and loud. "Don't come to me looking for a handout!"

"I'm not asking for a handout, Mom!" I was appalled at the assumption. I'd made it through college without ever asking for help except once, only for a little gas money. I'd be damned if I was going to ask her to help out with a baby.

"Then why are you calling me?"

"To tell you the news. God, Mom, I thought you'd want to know that your daughter is having a baby."

"If she were married or in a committed relationship, sure. Not knocked up with some bum's baby."

"Mom—"

"Robin Elaine, you disappoint me. How could you do this to me?"

As always, the conversation went right back to her. Could she ever get off her damn throne and realize that there was more to life than what happened in her multi-colored, hazy-dazy world?

"Well, I thought you should know." I didn't know what else to say. So far the only people who seemed to give a damn about my being pregnant were my girlfriends and the couple of guys who were connected to our tight-knit group. No support from family. Not even the baby's father.

"And I was hoping that you'd find some joy in this. But, well, I guess you're just as bad as the father," I said, surprising myself with my bold choice of words.

"What is that supposed to mean, young lady?"

"I thought you'd be able to find some excitement. Be *somehow* happy for your daughter. I'm doing this all on my own, you know? No man. Evidently no family. Of course, I have my friends. And I'm living with Lara."

"Lara? Who's Lara?"

"God, Mom, you really don't know anything about my life, do you? No care for anyone but yourself."

"You watch your tongue young lady."

Here we go, a lecture. Just what I need.

"You better grow up if you're going to be a mom yourself."

You're one to talk!

"I've got to go, Mom," I said, finished with the phone call a good five minutes ago. "Lunch break is over. Got to get back to work if I'm going to schlep it as a single mom, you know?"

"Have you told your father?"

I sighed. "Going to email him tonight. You know I don't talk to him. He won't care, much less notice, that I'm pregnant."

"He won't be any more thrilled about the news than I am."

"I'll talk to you later, Mom." I was much too drained to deal with her antics any longer.

"I owe you some congratulations, I suppose...before you go." She sounded forlorn or preoccupied. "So, there you have it."

"Thanks, Mom." *Thanks for nothing.* "Gotta go now."

The call, unlike the one with Brandon, went pretty much according to expectations. I didn't expect my mother to be thrilled with the news. I didn't expect her to give me votes of confidence or even heartfelt congratulations. However, I didn't expect her to completely shut me out. I suppose in her own little way she *did* congratulate me and keep the lines of communication open. But I couldn't turn to her for any form of support, least of all emotional. My mother had checked out from the family gig a long time ago and now it was all about the men, the vacations, Vive le whatever floated her boat, and nothing difficult or demanding. She'd said repeatedly that she was in the "highlight of her life" and didn't want to be "bothered with the shitty things." I guess my news was categorized as the shit. Oh well. Another one bites the dust.

10

If there's one thing that can turn a frown upside down, it's a shopping spree. Granted, shopping for maternity clothes, or what I occasionally like to call "glorified muumuus," does not necessarily qualify as a *real* shopping spree. But when you're four months pregnant and seem to be growing larger by the day, a shopping spree not only helps alleviate random and totally unexpected mood swings, it becomes absolutely critical. I could barely zip my jeans anymore. Many of my dress shirts couldn't be buttoned completely, and what still managed to zip, button, or close up pulled unattractively (and uncomfortably) taut against my skin.

"Shopping emergency, indeed!" Lara said, as we walked into what looked like a hip, modern, and no doubt slightly pricey maternity clothing store in Downtown.

"Thanks for this, guys," I said. "I'm lucky I found what I'm wearing as it is. I've been getting so used to wearing ridiculously baggy clothes to work all I have left is the stuff that barely fits."

"Yeah, and the packed like a sausage look is very unbecoming," Claire kidded, giving me a gentle shove.

Claire, Lara, and I were on a maternity mission that Saturday. I couldn't stand one more day without some appropriate clothing hanging in my closet.

"I'm not wearing that," I told Claire, who was holding up a bright yellow knee-length dress that was covered in small black polka dots. "It looks like a test pattern. Are you crazy?"

"Claire, that's pretty hideous," Lara said, stifling a laugh.

"Just because I'm preggo doesn't mean I need to look like 1995 computer desktop wallpaper."

Claire grabbed a light pink dress, also knee-length, but pattern-less and only sporting a small ribbon around the waistline, with a small bow set off to the left. "How about this?" she said. "This is way cute. And I'm sure this ribbon will come right at the top of the little baby bump. It'd look way cute."

"Well it *does* lack a hideous pattern." I took the dress from her, keeping it for consideration.

"What size are you, anyway?" Lara asked. She was rifling through the racks of dresses and skirts.

"How the heck should I know?"

A sales associate walked up at precisely the most opportune time. She offered her help, and Lara took the lead.

"Our friend here," Lara pointed to me, "is about four months along, and we have no idea what size she needs. We're looking for some semi-formal-like clothes for the office." I nodded when she shot me a questioning look. "And some everyday kind of clothes too."

"Basically a whole new wardrobe," Claire said.

I softly poked Claire in the ribs when the sales associate wasn't looking.

"Ow, what was that for?"

"Have you seen these prices?" I whispered while the sales associate was speaking with Lara. "I can't get a whole new wardrobe from here."

"Come with me, ladies," the associate said, taking the pink dress from me, and saying, "This will look fantastic with your blonde hair. Natural?"

"Of course," I said, lying through my teeth. I knew it, the girls knew it, my hair dresser certainly knew it. I hadn't been naturally blonde since I was in grade school, but I insisted, like the "natural" red headed Lucille Ball, that my blonde hair was anything but artificial. I don't know why I kept up the lie, but I used it one day, too embarrassed as a teenager to tell the world I was unhappy with what God gave me, and the lie just stuck.

"So beautiful," the associate said. "Well, follow me and we'll get a dressing room started and get Mommy here on her way to a whole new, fabulous wardrobe."

I glared at Claire, and she glared right back.

"See, a whole new, *expensive* wardrobe," I said.

"Ha," she laughed teasingly. "And you're a natural blonde."

I gave her one more playful poke in the ribs before Lara ushered us along like a mother duck.

"How many more must I try?" I said brusquely. Lara was zipping up the back of a cream summer dress that I thought was much too short. Claire had her hands at my waist, tugging the dress down.

"Too short," I sighed. Claire nodded.

"Now wait a minute," Lara said, standing back as far as she could in the narrow dressing room. "It's super cute."

"It's ridiculous."

"It's adorable, Robin."

I looked in the mirror. The dress came halfway between my knees and my woohoo. *Way* too short.

"Hell no," I said, making a motion for someone to start unzipping me. "Uh-uh. Take it off."

It'd been like this the past four or five outfits, each one seeming to look worse than the previous.

"I don't get it," Claire said. "This stuff is supposed to be high end and everything's either too short or too tight in all the wrong places. And we have the correct sizes."

"At least most of the office clothes worked," Lara pointed out. "Those black and grey slacks and those pastel dress shirts we found are really nice."

Lara was trying to keep the situation upbeat as my face said it all: I wasn't happy. I didn't love any of my new clothes, even though the office clothes *would* be nice, but those were for work. Then what? Schlep around the house in ragged muumuus or sweats? That'd be a great confidence booster. Sure to rally the men with that ensemble.

"How about we get these work clothes and then try a new store? There are tons around here."

"Good idea, Lara. What do you say, Robin?"

I shrugged, starting to lose my luster.

"Come on, it'll get better. And this stop wasn't a total lost cause," Lara said.

"Can we at least find a place that doesn't have such high price tags?" I asked. I flipped over one of the dress slacks' tags. "Not that these prices are all *that* bad. For these office clothes, at least." The tag read $59.99. "I don't know what normal maternity prices are, but those dresses! That disgusting yellow thing you showed me, Claire, was like a hundred and fifty bucks or something."

"Hey, it wasn't *that* disgusting." Claire made a pouting face as Lara picked up the clothes we decided I'd purchase, then led us out of the dressing room.

"I'm sure we can find something else," Lara said.

When it came time to pay for the clothes, Lara surprised me and beat me to it. She whipped out her American Express and said, "I've got this one." I insisted on our way out of the store that she should not have picked up the tab, and that I owed her. I wasn't exactly broke, but she insisted that there would be plenty more expenses headed my way. And if she could afford to help, she wanted to.

"Besides," she said, opening a door to another maternity clothing store a few doors down. "Brandon might not send some cash your way like he said he would, and you don't need financial stress on top of everything else. And it's fun for me. Don't worry about it."

Lara was already giving me a bargain on rent. At first, she suggested I only pick up a utility bill or two, but I demanded that she let me pay for things fifty-fifty. After several minutes of back-and-forth, we had agreed that we'd go fifty-fifty on the utility bills and rent. Then she quickly added, and refused a rebuttal, that she pay for my parking permit and groceries. Case closed; there was no arguing. And now she was picking up the tab on my maternity clothes.

By the end of our shopping spree, we'd accumulated more outfits and accessories than I thought possible. I figured we'd be lucky if we found a small number of outfits that I could make work for the office, and perhaps a new pair of pants or a couple of shirts that I could use for all non-office hours. But we made out like bandits!

"I'm beat," I said, rubbing my lower back. "And I've been having some lower back cramps lately."

"That's normal, right?" Lara asked, breezing over the lunch menu at a sidewalk café near Pike Place Market.

"Yeah, but not so painful until I really get bigger, when I've got all that weight to carry around."

"Maybe it's the jogging. Maybe you're doing too much or it's too strenuous," Claire posed.

"No," Lara said. "I think it's just normal baby stuff. Maybe what you need is a massage. We should book you a prenatal massage."

"Oh yeah! I've heard they're really amazing."

"Me, too. What do you say, Robin?"

"Please." I held up one hand. "Let's let my credit cards cool down a minute. I'm not a pampered princess who can book massages spontaneously."

"Well—"

"And don't offer to pay for it," I cut Lara off. "You've done enough. I'm *already* a pampered woman."

The waiter came by and took our orders. I ordered a club sandwich with extra chips on the side—obviously.

"And she means extra," Claire added. The waiter looked at us with raised eyebrows and scrawled on his notepad.

"So I think I'm going to have a talk with my boss on Monday," I said randomly in the middle of our lunch. I threw down a couple of salty, delicious potato chips. The scent of the vinegar lingered, mixing with the humid air coming in off the water and making its snaking way through the small alleys and passageways off the waterfront. It made the experience of eating my favorite craving all the more enjoyable. I munched on a couple more before saying, "Decided enough's enough already. I've got my nice new clothes for work now. No sense in trying to hide the baby bump anymore. And I can't stand wearing those baggy old clothes anyway. Time to tell the boss I'm preggers."

Claire and Lara were happy to hear I'd come to my senses and reminded me to make sure I followed the doctor's orders about the timing of my maternity leave. I would want to make sure I had a good week or two before my due date to be at home and do something called "nesting."

Really, I need to put the paintbrush and pencil down and pick up that baby book again.

I made a mental note to look up what a "Boppy" was as soon as I was finished Googling "nesting."

"And we've got holiday vacation time coming up too," Lara said excitedly. "Totally forgot about the Fourth of July. Any plans?"

Claire waved her hands about frantically, finishing a bite of her sandwich. "Don't make any. We've already got them. I totally forgot to mention it." She swallowed. "So Chad's parents are going away for the holiday. Somewhere in Victoria or something. Somewhere Canadian. I don't know. Go celebrate an American holiday abroad, whatever. So Conner said that Chad invited us all to his parents' place up over in Green Lake. How cool is that?"

How exciting! I was game for a party at Chad's place. His parents were beyond wealthy, and their mansion-like, tudor-style lake home was gorgeous. An ideal place to relax in the sun by the water or the pool, and feel like that pampered princess after all.

"What do you say?" Claire looked eagerly at the both of us.

"I'm game!" I didn't need any persuading.

"Sounds like an awesome plan," Lara added.

"Perfect, then I'll call Jackie and let her know. Sophie's already game too."

"Sophie's coming?" It shouldn't have surprised me like it did. Sophie and Chad could be tolerant of each other, and it wasn't like there was *always* tension. Given the last Chad and Sophie interaction, however, I was surprised that she was willing to see him again so soon.

"Who'd pass up on a party at the Harris mansion? Of course Sophie's coming." Claire was right. No one in her right mind would pass up such an opportunity. "And besides, we can have the house for the entire holiday weekend. Conner said he and Chad are taking off early Friday so they can make one huge ass holiday of it."

"Then Friday night consider me there!" I said.

"Yeah," Lara said. "Friday night sounds great. What a *fantastic* weekend that's going to be!"

Our holiday plans were set, and this year's Fourth of July, despite my being pregnant, was going to be just as fun as any other year. We'd had a few parties at Chad's parents' place before and always had a smashing time. But how can you not when you have an outdoor, poolside kitchen that's packed with everything you could want? Windsurf boards, kayaks, and a speedboat at your constant disposal. Even a sailboat if you wanted to be adventurous. And an entertainment room that could rival Scorsese's. And, to top it all off, you get to share it all with your best friends.

"Should we swing by another shop real quick and find you a bathing suit?" Claire asked.

Great, I totally forgot that a summer holiday poolside or lakeside was synonymous with sporting a bathing suit.

"I'm sure she doesn't need a new one just yet," Lara said. "Unless you want one?"

"Please," I said. "I don't think my current bikini or a new one will make one ounce of difference. A pregnant chick is a pregnant chick no matter what kind of bathing suit you put her in. There's no hiding it."

I dabbed at my face with the hand towel resting on top of the treadmill screen.

"It's not like I didn't expect things to go that way," I huffed, turning the treadmill off. "What else should I have expected?" I walked into the kitchen where Lara was pouring herself a piping cup of tea. She offered me one and I declined, favoring my water bottle after a good twenty-minute jog.

I lifted open one of the alcove windows. "It's my mother, after all. She's not exactly Super Woman." I'd tried to put the whole conversation with my mother behind me; however, I had to keep Lara up to speed on the baby drama.

"You'd still think she'd have class enough to at least *feign* excitement, right? Didn't she at least congratulate you? I mean, having a baby's a pretty friggin' big deal."

"Yeah. She *feigned* that one."

"And your dad?" Lara joined me in the dining room, pulling up a chair beside me as I stretched my calves using one of the chair's legs for support.

"Oh, please. I don't anticipate I'll hear from him. Like, ever. I did finally email him."

Lara blew on her hot beverage, shrugging. "You do what you can."

"Oh! That reminds me!" I exclaimed, dashing into my bedroom to retrieve my laptop. "I totally forgot to tell you! Emily wrote back."

Lara scooted in close as I opened my email inbox and clicked on Emily's message.

"I can't believe I forgot to tell you. I got her email late last night."

"Read it out loud. I don't have my reading glasses."

I tried to catch my breath; the jog's effects still had hold of me.

"*Dear Robin and Lara,*" I read. "*It's so good to hop onto the internet when I can manage and see your names pop up in my inbox. Oh how I miss you girls! Robin, congratulations!!! That is some very big news. I'm still in shock, but I'm so happy for you! And the photos are amazing. That little guy (or girl) is going to be gorgeous, just like its momma. I am not sure when I'll be heading back home, but you can bet I'll be home in time for the birth. What an unforgettable Christmas it'll be this year!*

"*All is well in Ghana. The village has decided to adopt me and never*

let me return home. Ha Ha. Their way of life is so back-to-basics it's
refreshing. (Although 24/7 wireless service would be nice.) They're very
kind and hospitable—even learned how to braid my hair just like the
locals (pic attached). I've been helping build a small school in between my
town and the nearest one about thirty miles from here. It's really crazy to
see how two communities have to share one school, unlike at home where
we have how many per district? Crazy! It's also interesting, and endearing,
to see the kids' faces light up when a shipment of books and chalk and
crayons comes in. Really puts things into perspective.

"Well, it's time I head home to help herd the animals. It's getting to be
that time of day again. Congrats again, Robin. I am so very, VERY proud
of you. And can't wait to see you soon and give you a hug. Lara, keep
taking care of our girl and I'll see you both soon. P.S. Send my love to all of
the ladies and tell Jackie to keep out of trouble. God knows what's
happening at my apartment when I'm not there. LOL

"Hugs and Kisses, Emily

"And I forwarded it to the rest of the girls already."

Lara blinked away one lone tear. "God, I miss her. She's off seeing
the world, herding animals and braiding hair..." She laughed and
wiped at her eyes. "Look at me. All goofy and emotional. Like *I'm* the
pregnant one."

"Aw, Lara, it's been a while. We all miss her. But she'll be back in
the fall!"

Just then, as if on cue, Beebee leapt onto Lara's lap and immediately started purring. Lara rubbed her behind her ears and hugged
her tight.

"Before we know it Emily will be back in Seattle, regaling us with
all sorts of adventurous stories and sharing tons of fun photos,"
I said.

I especially loved it when Emily, the hobby photographer, shared
the pictures she took on various trips. She was lucky that she was
getting to do what she loved without really having to worry about
who would foot the bill. She was that trust fund baby I was talking
about, much like Chad. Emily's parents were well to do, too, and
encouraged her to travel the globe and chase her dreams. She could

always get a "real job" when she wanted to explore that side of life. Until then, the world was her oyster, pearl and all.

None of us really understood how she did it. We all would love to take off and hit the open road, sure. Some of us, like Jackie, would naturally tire of the on-the-road lifestyle eventually, but many of us would keep on trekking and throwing ourselves into this culture and that without thinking twice. At some point, though, we'd all worry about how long we could sustain such habits. I guess that's for all us non-trust fund babies to contend with while the Emilies and Chads of the world can come from wealthy stock and do pretty much whatever the hell they want. At least, through it all, given the endless opportunities and no-questions-asked, Emily and Chad hadn't become like the Paris Hiltons of the world; having everything handed to them on a silver platter, and feeding off of everyone and everything and never giving a damn thing back.

"Well, I'm bushed," I said, closing my laptop. "I'm going to shower and cash in early tonight."

"Another early day at the office tomorrow?" Lara asked, still cuddling Beebee.

"Yeah. I want to get in early so I can talk with my boss about maternity leave. Whoopee." I meandered back to the bathroom.

"At least you'll look smoking hot doing it. You with all your fancy new clothes."

11

The following Monday I arrived at the office at a quarter to eight, confident that I would be there at least fifteen minutes before my boss. I was dressed in new clothes head to toe. I pulled my hair in a high pony-tail, covering the rubber band with a strand of what I still and will probably always insist is my naturally blonde hair. The pale blue, collared dress shirt was simple but attractively pleated in the back, making the contours of my now ever-present baby bump look just the way Claire said it should: small 'n' sweet. And the charcoal grey dress pants with the widened waistband done discretely and comfortably were the perfect match. With the slightest sweep of mascara, finished off with an application of pale pink lip gloss, I admit I looked like one hot momma who *also* rocked her career. Looking good in my new clothes, I felt bolstered with confidence.

On schedule, my boss, Mr. Lober, charged into his office, a Venti size Starbucks cup in one hand, his briefcase in the other. I quit my peering around the corner and tidied up the countertops of the break room where I'd been preparing my own morning beverage.

You can do this. Go in there and get it done.

"Mr. Lober?" I asked, knocking on his open door.

"Yes, Miss Sinclair. Do come in," he said, sounding rather scatterbrained. He'd opened his briefcase and was digging through papers, setting aside books, files, folders. "I got your email. You wanted to make some time to chat this morning? Glad to see we can do it before the rush-rush of the day, eh?"

I thanked him for his time and took a seat while he continued busying himself with the contents of his briefcase.

"So what's this all about? You're not leaving us for greener pastures, are you?" Still sorting through his case.

I reassured him it was nothing of the sort, that such an idea was the farthest thing from my mind.

Finally, he closed his briefcase and took a seat himself. "Then what can I do you for?" He folded his hands on his desk and smiled at me.

Here goes...

"I wanted to let you know that I'm expecting."

He raised one eyebrow.

"I'm expecting a baby," I clarified.

Both eyebrows suddenly rose and then an, "Oh, wow! Golly! Well congratulations, Miss Sinclair!"

"Thank you."

"Well, this is indeed a surprise." I caught him giving me a quick once-over, trying to see if his usual scatterbrained behavior had caused him to completely oversee that one of his employees was obviously pregnant. "Well you must have *just* found out. I'd never tell." I started to blush. "Congratulations. How wonderful. So we need to chat about maternity leave then, eh?"

A wave of relief washed over me—this was a completely relaxed, worry-free, and much more easy-going situation than I'd expected.

In a matter of only a few minutes, before anyone else sauntered into work on the usual manic Monday, Mr. Lober and I had my maternity leave all worked out, in addition to the vacation time I wanted to use. I was going to take the entire months of December and January off, and play it by ear when it came to February. I wanted to be accountable at work, while at the same time I wanted to be a good mother, and there for my baby when it needed me most.

One step at a time, I had to keep reminding myself. The maternity leave was squared away and didn't seem like it'd be too troublesome if I wanted to switch a few things around, when and if the time came. What a relief to have that one taken care of. Of course, there was still the matter of the entire office finding out, Janet and Bobby in particular, whose reactions weren't easy to predict. Although I was sure Janet would play her usual bitch card.

That's going to be fun.

"And we're still having your review in August, correct, Miss Sinclair?" Mr. Lober said, as I was heading out of his office.

I turned towards him, my heart skipping a beat at the prospect of receiving that raise. "Oh, absolutely. I'm looking forward to it."

He nodded his head and began fiddling with the mountain of papers, files, and books that he'd unloaded onto his desk when he arrived, returning to his scatterbrained world.

"Well, well, well, look what the new Ann Taylor LOFT cat dragged in," Janet said from behind me, causing me to jump. I spilled a small amount of hot tea onto my office floor, but only cursed the accident in my mind. Luckily I missed my hand and new outfit. Tea stains wouldn't go with the sophisticated career woman look I was going for.

"You startled me, Janet," I said. I set my mug on a stack of papers on my desk.

"What's with the new clothes?"

Why does she even notice? Or care? I thought her world revolved around her.

As I turned towards her, I watched her eyes grow to the approximate size of golf balls. I withheld my laughter.

"I needed some maternity clothes." Simple and concise. And shocking.

"What? Wha— When? Who? Huh?"

I couldn't hold in my laughter anymore. "Baby's due December seventh. Exciting, huh?"

"Wow. Well, uh…"

"Yeah, I know. I was a bit surprised myself, too. But, sometimes these things happen." I took my seat and started up my computer. "Sometimes little surprises show up and whatcha gonna do, huh?" I flashed her a bright smile, remaining unexpectedly upbeat and nonchalant about the whole thing.

When the shock finally subsided Janet returned to her usual, predictable vindictive self. She let out a forced guffaw. "I don't know whether to say congratulations or I'm sorry."

Wow, she and Brandon could hit it off.

I wanted to tell her, "Then don't say anything at all," but I decided against it. Seriously, did *anyone* watch *Bambi* when they were kids? All I replied with was, "I'll take congratulations. Thank you."

Janet shook her head roughly and started to get to work. "I guess some women have their priorities. Looks like I *will* be the one getting that PM position. The Board would be nuts to hire a woman who *obviously* has other priorities in life. Not that there was ever any doubt. Anyone can see I'm clearly the right woman for the job."

I had so many things I wanted to say to Janet the Bitch right then, but nothing would come out. I couldn't form the words properly nor bring myself to say anything—anything at all. And then, while my hands were balled up into fists and my mouth was drawn tight, glaring at the back of her tiny pinhead, I heard Lara's voice running through my mind, "You need to keep your stress level low. Think of the baby."

So I yanked open my desk drawers and took out my bag of cherries, and the reel of ultrasound photos from my purse. I then slammed my drawers closed as the best response to Janet I could muster. I cut one of the photos from the reel—the one where you could clearly see my baby's profile—and taped it to the bottom of my computer monitor.

Looking beautiful, baby!

"I really hate her," I told Lara over the phone while I waited in line at the nearby Quiznos during lunch break. "She says the most asinine things sometimes. No. All the time. She's a bitch. I can't stand her." I caught some harsh looks from the other customers in line, so I lowered my voice.

"Don't get yourself worked up over her," Lara replied. "She's just a stupid co-worker who sounds miserable in her own life and wants to make everyone else around her just as miserable. Forget about it."

"I guess."

"You should be excited that your meeting with your boss went so well. And that you're getting some nice time off later." She was right. "And remember, keep that stress low. It's not healthy, pregnant or not." Right again. "And when you find yourself getting all worked up over her, look at your baby picture and know that you're doing all of this for her...or him. Never mind the assholes in life."

There was only one more customer ahead of me in line; I needed to wrap up the call soon, because there's nothing I hate more (aside from Janet) than people who talk on their cell phones when ordering or paying for their food or groceries. Just talking away and ignoring the person behind the counter who is trying to offer customer *service*.

"And, don't forget that in a couple weeks' time we'll be enjoying the high life for the Fourth of July. Nothing to worry about *at all*."

Yeah, except for how I'll probably look like a disaster in my bathing suit.

It was my turn to order. "Got to go, hon. Love ya. See you after work." I slipped my cell phone into my purse and proceeded to order. I was about to add an iced tea to my order when I heard Sophie's voice, this time ringing through my head reminding me to steer clear of caffeinated beverages. "And a water, please," I ordered. Surprisingly, the no-caffeine rule wasn't too tough to live by, and I was feeling fine without it by then. At first, my withdrawals were a little painful—a couple of splitting headaches that I simply had to ride out since I (surprise, surprise) couldn't take over-the-counter pain medication as a pregnant woman.

"Whoa, feeding an army there, Robin?" a familiar voice asked. I picked up my large tray of food. It was Bobby Holman.

Crap, I hope he didn't hear me talking about Janet.

"Bobby!" I said, taking note that he was at the end of the current line, meaning he must have recently walked in, so there was no chance he could have heard my phone call.

Phew.

"Can I join once I order really quick?"

"Uh, sure."

Not that I planned on eating lunch with anyone today...but...all right.

"Congratulations, Robin," Bobby said, taking a seat at my table for two. "Was teasing you back there. You know, since you're feeding two now."

"Aw, so the word is out, huh?" I'd spent most of the morning on the phone and hadn't meandered about the office halls. Whether anyone other than Mr. Lober, myself, and the Bitch with whom I regrettably shared an office knew of my pregnancy was unknown. Looks like word travels fast.

"I didn't know you were planning on having kids yet."

"Well, it wasn't exactly *planned.*"

Awkward. Shaping out to be a very awkward lunch here.

"Congratulations just the same. And congratulations to the proud papa, too."

"Just me," I said, nibbling on my chips.

He looked confused.

"No father. Just me." I gave him a weak smile.

"Ah, sorry about that." He looked uncomfortable, probably wondering if there was no father because we split up, or he croaked, or something dramatic like that. Probably wouldn't peg Miss Robin Sinclair to be the kind who'd get knocked up from a one-night stand.

"Don't be. Nothing to be sorry about. It's in the past. From here on out it's me and baby." I sat up a little taller in my seat, showing that I was fine with there not being a father in the picture. "Me, baby, and my girls, of course."

We chatted for a few minutes, on a personal level, me dishing about my girlfriends—how they were the only supportive team I had, and how I wouldn't know what I'd do without them. Even if I had a supportive family and the baby's father was in the picture, I still wouldn't know what I'd do without Lara, Claire, Sophie, Jackie, and Emily. We shot the breeze about work, too, even shared a few cracks about Janet and her much too serious demeanor. That was rather refreshing, seeing how I wondered half the time if I was the only one who could see Janet for what she truly was—a self-righteous, hell-on-wheels Medusa of a woman.

Bobby and I didn't talk about the project management position, which was sort of a relief. I thought of asking if he'd try for the position, seeing how I was curious and missed the opportunity to ask last time we had a chat. But what did it really matter? Whether or not Bobby tried for the position should have no bearing on my chances. Or on my decision to I try for it or not.

And if Bobby *did* get it, great for him. Besides, I was growing more and more confident over the course of our lunch that if he did become the PM, he'd certainly choose to have me on his team. And I kind of liked that idea. I wouldn't mind working alongside Bobby. He was intelligent, easy-going, kind, and very personable. He'd make a great team leader, not to mention wouldn't be bad eye candy. That wavy, auburn hair, those piercing blue eyes that I could take a bath in, that determined chin, and that ass. Not bad. But what was I thinking? Bobby Holman had a girlfriend, and he clearly wasn't interested in being any form of partner with me other than a project teammate or co-worker. *And,* I was four months pregnant with some guy's baby. For all Bobby knew, I was in the middle of a messy breakup. Or in the midst of a vicious custody battle. Who knows what he thought of Miss *pregnant* Sinclair.

I can't deny it, though; that lunch turned out to be really enjoyable. It was as if we'd known each other for years, as if we shot the breeze together all the time. What I was sure at first would be an awkward situation, having to explain how I was single and pregnant, turned out to be a pleasant lunch with a nice co-worker. No flirting, not *too* much personal talk; just an easygoing lunch at a Quiznos on a random Monday afternoon. *Strictly business*, I had reminded myself repeatedly. And just because Bobby said we should do it again some time didn't imply that this time, or the next time, or any other time for that matter, would be for pleasure.

Strictly business, Robin. Strictly business with a nice co-worker. Even if it does oddly feel like he's been your friend for a long time. Remember: He has a girlfriend. A girlfriend. And you're pregnant, pregnant, pregnant.

"How about next week?" Bobby asked, opening the door for me.

"Next week? For what?" I clicked the car unlock button on my key ring.

"For lunch. Next Monday sound good? Or are you taking some vacation for the holiday?"

I rattled my brain, trying to remember if I had anything planned for Monday.

"I think that should work. Sounds great," I said somewhat nervously. Maybe this "strictly business" thing wasn't as strict as I'd thought. He did seem eager to make sure we had another lunch planned. This one had happened by chance, and I didn't think he'd enjoyed it *that* much that he'd really want to do an official repeat. So soon. I mean, don't get me wrong—I could easily stare at him and breathe in his cologne over another lunch.

"Then next Monday. Noon. It's a date," he said, shutting my car door for me and giving me a small wave. "See you back at the office," I heard him say through my closed door.

Date? It's a 'date'?

I didn't like the sound of that. I'd been that girl who stepped in between a relationship before. There was no way in hell I was about to make a repeat mistake like that again. I quickly started my car engine and rolled down the window.

"Monday. The date's the ninth?" I sounded like a moron, but I was trying to squirm my way out of believing, or agreeing, to anything that connoted a "date."

He chuckled. "Last I checked my calendar. See you back at the office, Robin." He got into his own car, still laughing.

Well, you may have made yourself look like a babbling moron, Robin, but at least you feel better about this "date" thing. I do feel better. Don't I?

Though I wasn't keen on the mere mention of a date (whatever that was supposed to imply), I did like the idea of having another lunch with Bobby. I didn't need to be the cause of a potential breakup, however, or any relationship discord with Bobby and his apparent girlfriend. Sure, we could do a lunch together. A planned lunch. A business lunch...

I started to pull out of the driveway. Enough time spent at Quiznos that afternoon; enough time being tortured by images of that sweet, curly-haired blondie standing in Trafalgar Square, cuddled up close to Bobby, clawing my eyes out and choking the life out of me for stealing her boyfriend.

I needed a vacation, and I needed one fast. Things were already strange in my personal life. Work didn't need to become awkward too.

12

"I s this exciting or what?" Jackie screeched from the front passenger seat of Lara's luxurious Audi. Even the back seats were lavish and comfortable. I stretched out my legs and leaned my head back on the soft pillow of a headrest. Friday had finally arrived and in all its fabulous glory brought with it a holiday weekend filled with nothing but R & R—*stylish* R & R.

Lara wound her way through the nearly endless turns and picturesque streets as we made our way into the Green Lake district, mere minutes from Chad's parents' home. I watched the vivid green clumps of the trees pass by, thinking not only of how surreal it was that in only a handful of months I was going to have a baby, but also about the simply stated fact that I *was* going to be doing *just* that—having a baby! Was I really ready? I don't think anyone is ever fully prepared to have a baby—to go into labor, to bring into this world another person, to be responsible for it in every way imaginable. Yet prepared to love it? Absolutely!

As the weeks had passed, I continued reading *You're Going to Be a Mother* and learning of my baby's size each week ("approximately the size of a kidney bean," "just about the size of a pearl onion now," "Wow! The size of an apple!"). And as time went on, the love and adoration for my baby only grew. Yet with love, excitement, and sheer joy at the idea of finally meeting my son or daughter came naturally the overwhelming fear and uncertainty. I'd never done this before. I had never fathomed I'd be doing it so soon in life. And without the father here. When a girl dreams of her love life, of her happily ever after, and of having her first baby, she usually doesn't picture my whole scenario.

But hey, the past is the past and there's nothing I can do about it. Like Lara had told me: The future is yours and it will be whatever you choose to make of it. Whenever I grew weary thinking about going into labor and facing motherhood straight-on so soon, I'd remind myself of Lara's prudent advice. So simple but oh-so-true.

So, little baby. I rubbed at my stomach, wondering if its head was on the right side of my womb right now, or maybe the left. Was he doing somersaults? Was she stretching her little arms or moving her tiny fingers? *Well, your mommy will do the best that she can.*

I sighed and looked out the window, the vibrancy of Seattle's landscape (positively breathtaking in the summer season!) continuing to whoosh on by as Lara made her way closer to the house.

"I'm so glad Chad invited us all up here this year," Lara said. "It feels like it's been a while since we were all up here together, just chilling."

"This is it!" Jackie practically screamed, pointing at the home that was undoubtedly the Harris's. Its opulent brick columns on either side of the privacy gate, complete with a key-pad and intercom, displayed the home address in sleek metal numbering on one, and a giant, ornate 'H' emblazoned on the other.

We waited for the gate to open once Lara buzzed the speaker, and as it rolled away a voice sounded over the intercom. "Where the fuck have you been?" Conner. And tipsy, from the sound of it. The loud thumping of bass could be heard in the background, accompanied by a tinny rapping voice. "The party's started, ladies. Get the hell up here. The par—"

Claire's voice came on. "Sorry girls. Gate's open. Park wherever."

Jackie turned in her seat and gave me a huge grin. "Are you excited or what? Oh, I can't wait to get my drink on!"

I laughed. "Oh, definitely. That's what I'm most excited about."

Lara peeked at me in the rearview mirror. "We don't have to drink to have a great time, Jack," Lara said, more to me than to Jackie.

"Speak for yourself, sister! I'm partying like there's no tomorrow."

"Do you party any other way, Jackie?"

No sooner had we gotten out of the car than Claire ran out of the house, a beer bottle in-hand, screaming. "This weekend is going to rock. I am so excited you're all here!"

Once we unloaded the car (and after Claire yelled from the top of her lungs, over the pounding music, for the boys to make use of themselves and "carry their crap already!") we made a beeline for the pool.

"You girls hungry?" Chad asked. He strode into the outdoor, poolside kitchen and tossed his empty bottle of beer into the recycling bin. "Mom likes to keep this place stocked when I'm home and have friends over." He helped himself to another drink from the refrigerator.

Though the rest of the girls said they were all right, I had other plans. "I'm starved." I found a bowl of fruit and immediately went to town.

"Hey, beer me already, will ya, man?" Conner called out from his floating lounge chair in the pool. His tan chest was oiled up like he came out of a tin of sardines.

"Conner getting his sexy man tan on for you?" I asked Claire, who was helping herself to an ice-cold beverage.

"Oh, I don't know what he's doing," she said with a flip of her tight, blond curls. "He bought this oil when we stopped at Walgreens on the way up. He's going to fry his ass." She yelled to Conner, "Hey! Boyfriend! Don't burn yourself to a crisp, all right?"

He tossed a carefree wave at her.

"I'm serious! We just got here. Last thing you want is to be all crisped out this whole weekend. And I'm *not* going to spend my vacation putting aloe all over your sorry ass."

"You want something else to drink, sugar?" Chad asked Sophie.

Sophie swayed up to the kitchen bar wearing the most adorable bright pink sari wrapped loosely around her hips, her long legs already looking as if they'd gotten some sun. She was wearing one of my favorite bikinis of hers: a white, very James Bond/Ursula Andress-style number, minus the whole knife-on-the-hip thing.

"Don't call me sugar," Sophie replied curtly. (Although Sophie probably wished she had the knife right about now...)

Chad flashed a toothy grin as he sauntered off.

Perhaps in an effort to avoid another possible Sophie and Chad incident, or perhaps to simply strike up conversation, I said to the girls, "Did you all read Emily's email that I forwarded you?"

As dusk disappeared and as the poolside activities continued, even after a hardy picnic dinner, everyone tossing back cocktails or chilled beverages, lounging around, cranking up the music, and enjoying, well, *youth*, I started to wonder about what life would be like once my baby was born. Life had already taken a strong turn for me; it wasn't going to become any more "normal," nor were things going to return to "as usual" once I had my baby.

None of my friends were married and none of them had children. Even though Conner and Claire were practically married, they still technically weren't, and the topic of children, as far as I knew, was not in near sight for them. Sophie, Chad, and Lara were single, and Jackie, too, although who knew how long that would last. *Certainly* none of them were even conceiving of having children in the near future. And Emily. She may have frequently been in and out of relationships that often became long distance or eventually fizzled, but she wasn't going to get hitched or pop out a baby anytime soon, either.

And then, there was me. All right, so I wasn't going to be hitched

anytime soon, either, and that part of my life wouldn't be changing drastically. But I *was* going to have a baby. The dynamics were going to change considerably. Would I still be able to randomly drive over to one friend's place and hang out for the heck of it? Still be able to hit the clubs and the bars with the girls like I used to? Okay, so we didn't go out all that much when I really thought about it. We all had careers that kept us busy, and in the few years that had gone by since we all graduated from college, we had found ourselves going out less and less often. But we still managed our girls' nights, wherever they led us and whenever they happened. We could still put everything on hold for a night or a weekend and hang out, just us girls.

Now everything was going to change. I was going to be a mom and that whole young and fancy free lifestyle would no longer be what it was. Could my friendships withstand such a test once my baby actually came? Or would all of my friends still go out, still party, while I'd be left at home taking care of the baby? What would happen to me? To my friendships? To my life? Even thinking a few minutes about this made me feel awful, like I didn't want or care about my baby. The contrary. It's only natural, though, that these kinds of thoughts creep up. Would *everything* as I knew it really change? Could I really manage it? And would my girlfriends honestly be there for me? What would life be like after December seventh?

I suddenly felt extremely depressed. Sitting there, poolside, staying for a weekend in one of the most palatial homes I'd ever seen, among my best girlfriends, and I oddly enough felt terribly depressed. On the one hand I adored my baby and was thrilled that something so special and important was happening to me. On the other, I was terrified and a little sad about the things that I liked in my life that would most likely change.

"I want to go windsurfing!" Jackie said from her seat at the edge of the deep end of the pool, running one foot along the water's edge and smoking a cigarette. I forced myself to crack a smile at her enthusiasm, trying to abate my sudden bout of depression.

"We can do that tomorrow afternoon," Chad said. He flicked his

lip ring with his tongue a couple of times, then stretched his arms overhead, yawning heavily. "By the time we get the gear out now it'll be dark. And tomorrow we should have some nice breeze. Perfect for windsurfing."

"I say we hang out by the pool, crank up the tunes, get in the Jacuzzi later..." Lara suggested.

"Yeah, get in your suit already!" Chad said, tossing a beach ball at Jackie's pixie-styled, bleach blonde head.

As much as I wanted to protest slipping into my suit (like *that* was going to help my mood), I knew the girls wouldn't hear of me being a grouch. And I was among friends; no one was going to cast judgment on my ever-growing belly, my newly-arrived stretch marks, and my misshapen bathing suit form.

"Now, *you* look adorable!" Lara gushed at me. I emerged mopey-faced from the guest bedroom Lara and I were sharing on the first floor. I'd slipped into my favorite bikini, a navy blue number with large white polka dots. The bikini top fit tube-style, with a small knotted half-bow tied in the center. Simple and somewhat classic, but it was certainly more attractive when I wasn't busting at the middle.

"Save it," I said.

"You do look really cute," Jackie said. "The preggers look suits you. Now come on, let's get into the Jacuzzi."

"I can't," I replied glumly. "Remember? Pregnant?" I made a drawn out face and pointed at my stomach.

Lara gave me a hug from the side and rubbed my arm, trying to cheer me up. "Come on, Robin," she encouraged. "You look beautiful. Enjoy yourself. Don't be bummed."

Jackie plopped down on my bed and curled her legs up tightly into her chest. "Yeah, don't be saddsy-waddsy, Robin."

I dabbed at my unexpected forming tears. "I'm fine."

Lara gave me another hug before pulling me over to the bed. I sat down next to Jackie, who immediately started to rub my back and asked what was wrong.

"Oh, these stupid hormones, I think." I sniffled. "I don't want to ruin anyone's time. Can't be a grouch. We're on vacation, after all."

"Oh, bullshit," Jackie said with a floppy flick of the wrist. "Babe, troubles come before vaca. What's wrong?"

"Well," I started. I looked from Jackie, to Lara, then down at my lap. "I was thinking about how things will be totally different once the baby comes. That's all."

"Things will be different, yeah," Lara said. "Of course they will be. But it's nothing you can't handle. And nothing we can't help you with."

Jackie: "Yeah! We're here for you!"

Lara: "What would make you think differently?"

"I—" I sniffled back the rest of the tears and stuffiness from my sudden crying spell. "I know things will be different. There's no escaping that. I don't want to lose you guys, though. You know?"

"You're talking crazy talk!" Jackie said.

"Things will be very different with the baby and I guess…I guess…I don't want to be left behind. That's all. I don't want to be that boring girlfriend who has the whining baby and can't meet up for a drink or go to the movies or come and hang out randomly. And I know that sounds totally selfish."

"It's natural," Lara said.

"Yeah. I figured that." I pulled my hair into a sloppy bun. "I was only getting to thinking. That's all. About how things will change."

"Listen," Lara said. She looked me straight in the eyes. "Listen to me. We know things are going to be very different for you. Different for all of us. But that doesn't mean we're bailing on you." She pulled herself further up onto the bed. "We're not going anywhere, whether you have a baby, two babies, a whole slew of babies. And Mr. Dreamboat down the road, too." I let out a subdued laugh.

"What do you think our friendship is like?" Lara asked. "We're only friends when we can all meet up at the bar, stay out all night, act like we're still back in college or something?" Jackie was nodding vehemently. I think the cocktails were starting to get to her. "Anyway," Lara

continued. "We're best friends for a reason. Our friendship will stand the test of time, and that means when we all get married, have kids, and grow old, we'll always be friends. We'll always be in each other's lives."

I smiled, feeling the awful heaviness of my depression start to peel away. "I suppose it's only normal that things change."

Lara nodded, her head cocked to the side. "Of course they do." She pushed a loose strand of hair from my face and tried to stick it in my messy bun. "Now, let's get you to the pool. Just because you can't use the Jacuzzi and or have a cocktail doesn't mean you can't hop in the pool and have a smoothie or something. Come on. Let's have fun."

Jackie hopped off the bed. "Yeah! Come on!"

"Even though I don't look super hot?" I guffawed and looked down at my figure. It wasn't horrible, but I still hadn't gotten used to being pregnant and carrying around the extra weight.

"*Puh-lease*," Lara said, exasperated. "I'm pushing thirty, babe, and I've got hips and an ass that refuse to quit."

I laughed loudly. "What are you talking about?"

"Look at this!" Lara smacked her rear end. "What they say about the big three-oh approaching is all true, sadly. I can't run enough to shed this unattractive poundage."

"Whatever," I said. "Come on. You're right. To the pool. And girls." Jackie and Lara turned to me as they were about to head out the door. "Thanks for cheering me up."

Lara grabbed my hand, pulling me out of the room with them, and said, "That's one of the many things we girlfriends are good at."

She looked to Jackie, who was doing a small, childish dance on her toes, itching to get back to the party, "Duh!" she said. "Besides, did Carrie and Samantha blow off Miranda and Charlotte when they got preggers? *No!*"

———

"Cocktails, my ladies?" Chad asked, as Jackie tiptoed over to the kitchen's bar in a much too sexy and playful manner.

I grabbed an inner tube and waded into the pool water—a perfect temperature on a perfectly tepid evening. Conner then burst out of nowhere and made a cannonball dive, splashing everyone within a good ten feet of the pool, and tidal-waving everyone in it.

"Oh, Conner!" Claire screeched, spitting out a large mouthful of water.

"Dude! That was awesome!" Chad and Conner could sometimes be mistaken for sixteen-year-old pubescent boys.

"Honestly!" Claire started splashing Conner, and he scooped her up and started to dunk her.

"Aww, lovebirds at play," Sophie kidded from the Jacuzzi.

I twirled around with the tube around my chest and watched Jackie coquettishly order her cocktail while Chad shook together some forbidden beverage.

"Hey, Robin!" Chad shouted. "Want a virgin daiquiri? I make a mean one. Fresh strawberries too!"

"How could I deny such an offer?"

Chad handed two blue beverages to Jackie, each with a colorful umbrella on top, and she passed them out to Sophie and Lara, then took two more over to Claire and Conner. I hopped out of the pool to join Jackie and Chad at the bar.

"You make amazing cocktails," Jackie said to Chad, drawing out the word "amazing." I sat my soaking butt down on a barstool. "Robin, Chad makes *amazing* cocktails. Virgin too." She gave a small smirk in Chad's direction, then took a sip of her own blue cocktail in between drags on her cigarette. Chad gave a shrug as he blended my fruity virgin daiquiri.

"So, have you given any thought to baby names yet?" Jackie asked. She put her cigarette out and blew the smoke opposite my direction. Her question caught me off guard. My head wasn't in baby land. Quite the contrary. I found it curious that Jackie was suddenly flirting with Chad. Jackie was always the overtly flirtatious type. She was a man magnet and completely comfortable in her glowing skin. Flirty, and with an attitude that she could get any man she wanted. But she'd never really flirted with Chad before. Not that I knew of.

We were always somewhat good friends with Chad and Conner, seeing how Conner and Claire had been together since freshman year and now lived together. And Chad and Conner were best buds. The group often came together in some form, but Jackie had never flirted so intensely with Chad. So obviously. Maybe her prospects at the jazz bar weren't what she thought and she was...desperate? We still teased Sophie now and then for stooping so low as to have a fling with Chad. He wasn't a bad guy. But...it was just...weird. It was *Chad.* That dopey, greasy-haired guy who tag-teamed it with Conner —nice guy, but more into chasing booty, it seemed, than chasing, well, anything else.

"Baby names?" Jackie asked, waving her hand in front of my glazed face.

"Oh, no." I said. "Haven't really given any thought to it, actually."

"Probably makes more sense once you know if it's a boy or a girl."

I nodded my head as Chad handed me my drink. He put some fresh strawberries on the rim of the glass. It was delicious. I thanked him then hopped off the barstool and made my way back to the pool once Jackie started to give all of her attention—her flirty attention —to Chad.

"We are *not* watching *Scarface*," Sophie protested late that evening when we were all dry from the pool and in comfortable clothes— some of us in pajamas—ready to watch a film in the impressive entertainment room.

"And *not The Fast and the Furious*," Claire chimed in. "Or any stupid souped-up man movie."

I cuddled up under my blanket and reclined slightly in my chair. Lara and Sophie did the same on either side of me, while Claire and Conner shared the reclining love seat for two. Jackie was passing around bags of popcorn and bottles of beer, while Chad fiddled with the entertainment system.

"I've got something I think we'll all like," Chad said. "And once it starts there's no going back. No complaining."

"Better be some porn, dude," Conner said, snickering. Claire gave him a solid whack on the head and told him he could sleep by himself tonight if he didn't behave.

"A little something the ladies and gents will enjoy." Chad took a seat a couple recliners down from Lara, and Jackie took one right next to him. Just then the screen flashed the usual FBI warning and the room became silent, everyone intent to find out what Conner was going to make us sit through for a good two or three hours.

"*Out of Africa!*" Conner shouted once the opening credits rolled on.

"Come on, man, it's a classic," Chad said. "And one we can all enjoy."

I had to give it to Chad. *Out of Africa* was the farthest choice from *Scarface* or *Casino* or any gangster thug film I was expecting we'd have to watch. And I was always down for anything starring Meryl Streep.

13

The next morning, bright and early around nine o'clock, we all staggered into the large and immaculate kitchen.

Chad removed a pitcher of hand-squeezed orange juice. He poured Lara and me a glass, then one for Sophie as she came around the corner. "Sleep well, ladies? Pillows and beds soft enough?"

"Oh, amazing," Lara said. "Thanks again for inviting us, Chad."

"Think nothing of it. Totally my pleasure."

Sophie threw back some aspirin with her orange juice and offered Lara the bottle, who also threw some back.

"A little too much drinking, girls?" Chad teased. He started to pull out various breakfast foods.

"What's on the plan for today?" I asked. Claire and Conner made their way from their upstairs guest bedroom, still dressed in their pajamas.

We discussed whether we wanted to try out windsurfing first, or save that for the afternoon, when the wind would probably pick up. Or if we wanted to go kayaking, hang by the pool, even take out the speedboat. It was decided, and without much debate, that we'd first take out the speedboat since drinking and operating a vehicle aren't exactly the wisest of combinations. And, since we'd be taking Chad's

truck to the water with the speedboat in tow, why not throw on the windsurfing gear and make it a whole "day at the lake" trip?

Green Lake was always packed with locals in the summer, and the Fourth of July was no exception. But with a speedboat and not having to resort to beachside lounging only, we didn't have to worry much about the crowds.

"Now *this* is vacation," Sophie said, laying out on one of the many red and white striped, monogrammed beach towels with which the speedboat was equipped. The sun was shining brightly at only half past ten, and the sky was a stunning blue with not a cloud in sight. A breeze was starting to pick up, and Chad assured us that come three or four in the afternoon we'd have enough of a breeze to make the windsurfing worth our time.

"Brilliant Fourth of July plans," Claire said, also laying out on a beach towel, her forehead resting on her hands, her bikini top untied, letting her back get some strap-free sun.

"Hey, Robin!" Jackie called out. "Want to take a dip with me?" In all her near-orange, faux-tanned glory, she was standing at the stern of the boat, looking like she was ready to jump right into the water. "Come on, let's take a dip and swim around a bit. Laze it up. Last one in the water's a rotten egg!" Jackie didn't even give me a second to respond as she jumped off the boat's edge.

"I'm coming, too!" Lara was a split second behind, only a flash of her bright red bikini and then—*Splash!* Eventually the rest of the girls dove in, followed by the guys, who brought along a few kick boards, tubes, and other flotation devices so we could relax and lounge in the cool lake water.

———

Windsurfing ended up being a lot of fun. I'd only done it once or twice before, but when I got up on the board and took it easy, one step at a time, it became less and less difficult. I caught a few good runs and enjoyed the wind blowing through my hair, careening over the glassy water, not a care in the world. Having fun and letting the wind physically take me wherever it wished. Of course, I had the entire crew of friends keep an extra careful eye out for me. They were insistent that I not take a run too long or too far. And they pressed the matter that I was pregnant and needed to be extra cautious of *everything*. As grating as it could be, I knew they were only doing what they thought was best.

By the end of the afternoon I was finally feeling like I was on vacation, and I wanted to soak up as much of it as I could. The day had been filled with plenty of swimming, some great windsurfing runs, and some much needed lounging on the speedboat in the sun. Tomorrow night we'd all be heading back home, back to the grind. But before then we were hitting up a local bar, or "pseudo club," as Chad called it, that night.

"Maybe you'll get lucky," Sophie said to me while we were getting ready in the bathroom.

"Please," I said. I ran a brush through my slightly wet blonde hair.

"I mean as in 'lucky' with dancing with some really hot guys," she corrected.

From the sound of it, this local bar would be crawling with old fishermen, or forty-something townies, or married couples. I doubted it would have the dance or date material that a club like Vogue or the jazz bar where Jackie worked had. Although, if well-to-do, forty-something men were what Jackie was in the market for, then perhaps our pseudo club for the evening would be right up her alley.

"Don't be a downer," Sophie said in response to my negative reply of most likely not finding anything more than some gramps and cheezers at the club.

"Men can sense when you're not confident and then that's a total turnoff," Lara said, straightening her hair with a hot iron. She'd already put on her "going out makeup" and looked fantastic. Maybe she'd catch herself a fish and tackle man.

"She's right, Robin. Men can *totally* tell if you're down on yourself. You need to *ooze* that confidence, baby. Ooze it!"

Neither of them knew about Bobby. *He* didn't detect my lack of confidence. At least I don't think he did. *He* was nice to me, and, I think it's safe to say, purposely flirted with me. He seemed somehow interested in me...or at least interested in a repeat lunch date. Even if it was business. Still, I didn't lack *that* much self-confidence. I was in a precarious situation. It wasn't exactly easy-going for me, yet I was trying. Pregnant chicks still know how to dance and have a good time.

I applied a smooth layer of peach-colored lipstick and smacked my lips. "I'm confident." My tone was more whiney than brassy.

"'I'm confident,'" Sophie mimicked in an exaggerated, whiney tone.

I gave her a playful nudge, then gave my loosely iron-curled hair a spritz of hairspray. "Oh shut it. Some guys find me and my confidence to be just fine."

Sophie's jaw dropped. "Do tell, girl! What are you hiding from us?"

I told her it was nothing serious—that there was a co-worker of mine, and we weren't really flirting, but we weren't exactly on our regular business or co-worker terms.

"It's weird, that's all it is," I told Sophie dismissively. "Not awkward-weird like I'm uncomfortable, per se..."

"Just weird since it's different now." Lara finished my sentence perfectly. "Weird since things used to be one way—simpatico, really —and now they're turning towards flirtation. Am I right?"

"Basically Bobby's super nice to me now, and I don't know what to think of it since he obviously has a girlfriend, and I'm, well..." I motioned to my stomach. "And your co-worker, Lara! What's his name? Paul?" I looked at Sophie. "Paul is also nicey-nice now with her, too." I looked back at Lara. "Kind of random all of a sudden and it's..."

"Weird," Lara said. "But anyway."

Sophie was shaking her head and hemming and hawing. "So this Paul guy ordeal is the exact same thing as Bobby, Lara?" she asked.

"He's flirting with you all of a sudden and you're not sure how to take it? And you obviously like him too?"

I opened my mouth to protest that I didn't necessarily *like* like Bobby that way, but Sophie put up her hand to stop me from spouting such ludicrous things. It was extremely apparent that I was developing some kind of romantic feelings for Bobby. I couldn't hide it, or fight it.

"Oh, no!" Lara suddenly protested. "It's not the same thing. Definitely not the same thing."

"How so?" Sophie asked.

"Paul and I don't have anything going on. He's definitely not 'into me' and I wouldn't say I'm really all that 'into him.' Not really... No, not the same thing."

I shot Lara a confused look. Earlier she told me she was into Paul, and that he was acting like he was interested in her. Now a different story? Was she as much in denial as I was? Probably.

Lara replied to my quizzical look with, "Well it's not really *that* different, I guess. If all this stuff with Bobby is only in Robin's head—making mountains out of molehills—then sure, it's probably the same thing. But there's nothing that *can* or ever *will* become of Paul and me. That *is* all in my head."

"Uh huh." Sophie blew her bangs away.

"It's true," Lara continued. "Nothing serious will come of it. He's acting a little flirty, but I'm blowing it out of proportion. No bigs. And I don't really like him all that much anyhow."

I still couldn't believe her, but if that's how Lara felt now, that's how she felt. I shrugged my shoulders and said, "So Paul's *not* the same as Bobby. I admit it, girls. I think I do have a tiny thing brewing for Bobby. But he *does* have a girlfriend, and I'm not going there." I looked to Sophie. "I'm not going there."

I put my makeup back into the cosmetic bag, trying to tidy up to some degree the mess on the counter, and walked into the bedroom to slip on my pair of black, strappy sandals. "Not going there, ladies. Unless Bobby gets rid of his girlfriend—and he *won't*—there's nothing to discuss. Latent romance on my part; probably just blowing things out of proportion. Forget about it. And maybe Sophie's right. Maybe I'll find my dream man at this club tonight. Or at least someone I can have a fun time dancing with."

"Latent, well..." Sophie said. "So you're saying if this guy, this Bobby, didn't have a girlfriend—"

"Forget about it."

"But if he *didn't*, you'd be interested, wouldn't you? You'd pounce on this guy?"

"Gosh, pounce is a little...suggestive."

Lara giggled, slipping on her own pair of summer sandals. They looked great with her simple, dark purple, cotton halter dress. "But you would, wouldn't you?" Lara added in.

I grabbed my cell phone and wallet and headed out the bedroom door, pausing in the doorway. "In the right circumstance. If he was in fact single. And available. And looking. And *interested*. Interested in dating a woman with a baby on the way, mind you. Then..." I briefly looked over in the direction of the foyer, watching as our group started to gather and filter out the front door, ready for a night out. "Then yes. I'd try my damnedest to make Bobby Holman mine." With a turn on the heel, and a flick of my hair, I made my way to the foyer where I joined Conner and Claire. Behind me I could hear a small duo of giggles from Sophie and Lara.

The following morning we decided to take the kayaks out for a while. The previous night was fun, and, as expected, no real luck was found in the male department, but we still had a great night out. Today's late morning weather and conditions were ideal for kayaking: not much of a breeze, the water still and not as congested, because most of the holiday goers were making their way home, and the sun wasn't blazing as badly as it had the day before. The relief from a few passing clouds was refreshing, and the juxtaposition it created overhead on parts of the water were idyllic.

Kayaking is something I've loved doing since I was a kid. It's as much a second-nature sport among locals in Seattle as windsurfing. You can paddle around, solo or in a group, and be one with nature. Paddle into small coves or a beach briefly to take a break in a quiet patch of grass, or have a picnic. Even paddle as far out as the lake or the sound will allow, alone and in peace.

I ventured out a ways on my own, heading towards a jutting piece of land. It looked like the perfect spot to temporarily beach and stretch my legs. My endurance in a kayak wasn't what it used to be, being four months pregnant and all. I cautiously maneuvered my watercraft up the pebbly beach, careful not to strain my back or make any difficult movements that might prove harmful for the baby.

I'd brought along my sketchbook, and I managed to fit it snugly between the inside of my life vest (that I had a heck of a time snapping closed) and my back. It would be a peaceful treat to do a little sketching out in nature, by myself and with no clock reminding me it was time to get to bed.

I took up the patch of wildflowers and grass off to my near right as composition, and started to make sweeping motions and brushing lines with my pencil. Then my mind started to wander to the conversation I'd had with the girls about Bobby last night. About how under the right circumstance I *would* be interested in pursuing a relationship with him.

I'd smelled Bobby Holman's cologne and been swept off my feet by the intoxicating scent for years. I'd caught myself taking sporadic peeks of him at his desk when I made my way from my office to the break room. Recently, I'd been getting butterflies in my stomach when he came up to talk to me, and I was sure it was partly due to being worried about what I *thought* I was feeling for him (and wondering if he felt for me), and partly due to actually feeling something for him. And, Bobby had recently started to play a prolific role in my daydreaming...in my thoughts. Bobby definitely had a hold on me, but I couldn't let that hold become tight, and I couldn't let it grow into something that it wasn't. I knew how I felt. I conjectured how he felt. He had a girlfriend. I had a baby on the way. I was only being absurd.

I finished with a couple of flower heads, and made a few more brushes and a small amount of erasing in one of the grass sections I sketched, then decided to call it a day. Enough daydreaming about the man who had suddenly become the object of my desire. Seriously, since when did that happen? Why must everything sneak up on you?

Such fantasies...only fantasies. Putting them out of my head now. Reality here, Robin.

I got into my kayak, securing my sketchbook one last time to make sure it was intact, and paddled my way back to home shore.

Under different circumstances, sure. But this is reality. In reality the pregnant girl can fall in love with the co-worker who has a beautiful girlfriend. It is only in dreams, though, that the co-worker would reciprocate the feelings and fall in love with a woman and her fatherless baby. There are dreams, there is reality, and sadly the two don't tell the same story.

"The fish is really good," Sophie said, taking another bite of her fresh salmon, straight from the grill compliments of Chef Chad.

"And the chicken is amazing," Lara said, enjoying the succulent lemon pepper chicken that I was also eating, again, compliments of Chef Chad.

"Hey, what can I say? I'm the master of the grill."

Sophie rolled her eyes, then said, "Totally random subject, but guess what?" We all looked at her. What was the sudden news?

"Claire and I were talking today. And..." Sophie looked to Claire, who was seated right next to her around the enormous table by the pool. "...And we decided that it's about time I get my own place."

"Decided to kick her out," Claire joked.

"No, it's time. I've been living there for, what? Like three and half months or something? It's time I pick up my feet and get going. Get myself my own place and get out of Claire and Conner's hair."

"You haven't had a place of your own in forever," Jackie said.

"Thanks for reminding me." Sophie smiled slyly at her. Sophie hadn't lived more than a few weeks in her own apartment right after college when she moved in with Brandon. And now she was with Claire.

"It's finally time. Time I get on out of there and let Claire and Conner have their home back."

"You know you're always welcome," Conner said.

"Yeah, and, you know," Chad said, taking a hearty bite of chicken. "You're always welcome to move in with me."

Sophie only gave a snarling look.

"I'm serious, babe," he said, taking yet another hearty bite as Conner started to roar with laughter. "My roomies wouldn't mind. They'd love to shack up with you." Sophie dropped her knife and fork, causing a loud clanging noise. "We've got plenty of room," Chad added.

"You're disgusting," Sophie said, picking up her utensils.

Chad laughed and continued teasing. "Aw, come on, babe. You know my door is always open."

"Stop it."

Jackie was looking from Chad, to Sophie, to Chad...then she looked at me and sighed heavily.

All right then...

"I think it's a great idea that Sophie goes and looks for a place of her own," Lara said, trying to break up whatever it was that was going on at the table now. "While the offer is nice, Chad, I don't think Sophie sees herself living on Lake Union. In a houseboat. With some guys."

"Hey, the pad's super comfy. Really sweet place. Lots of room. Got a kitchen so you can bake your little cakes."

Sophie was about to say something most likely inappropriate and offensive, but Lara stopped her. "Nope. No houseboat for Sophie. Thank you, Chad. I think a nice apartment near work is probably what she's thinking. Yeah? Somewhere in Belltown? They've got a lot of nice new apartments and condos going in over there." Lara finally pulled Sophie's attention in her direction, and she nodded in agreement.

"Well, like I said. My door's always open," Chad said, slinking down in his chair, satisfied with his meal...and with his usual round of teasing.

"As it always is," Jackie said. She stood up, as did Sophie and Claire, and started to clear the table.

14

It'd been three weeks. Three whole long and somewhat excruciating weeks since I was supposed to have had my lunch "date" with Bobby. I was feeling under the weather when I woke up on the day we had lunch planned and couldn't so much as drag myself out of bed to brush my teeth until after noon. I thought the worst of the morning sickness had passed with the onset of the second trimester. Lara thought it was the large amounts of food I'd had over the holiday at Chad's, and the excessive amounts of sun were probably not in my favor.

Yet three weeks later and there was still no new "date" set with Bobby. In fact, he wasn't acting his usual, somewhat flirtatious self with me. Don't get me wrong; he was still very civil and nice—opening doors for me, bringing me forgotten copies on the copier, and saying the kosher "good morning" and "see you tomorrow." But no more shared coffee (or tea) moments in the break room. No more checking to see if I wanted to join him and some of the gang for lunch. And no more random popping his head around the corner to say "hi" or to see if I needed a refill. Initially, I didn't think my breaking off our lunch due to illness rubbed Bobby the wrong way. But after three weeks, when he still hadn't even attempted to make new plans, I started to wonder if maybe Bobby *was* upset with me and thought I'd blown off our lunch on purpose.

I tried not to get too upset about it or work myself up into a tizzy thinking about the what-ifs. Lara told me to ride it out and keep cool on my end, as if there was nothing wrong, and to let Bobby do his own thing. After all, as she pointed out, he was only a co-worker with a girlfriend, and I only had a small office crush on him. No need to blow anything out of proportion or borrow trouble.

In the meantime, while my love life was pitiful, or rather, nonexistent, Jackie had finally landed herself a man. It happened precisely as she had planned. She was working a late night shift at the jazz bar, and some swanky-looking, forty something-and-single man walked in, asked her for the best seat in the house—asked her where she, the "lovely lady, would find herself seated on a fine night like this if she weren't working." (Really smooth.) Half an hour later he arranged with the manager on duty to let Jackie off her shift (which I'm sure cost a pretty penny). He then asked her to join him for drinks and oh, about two weeks later, Jackie was hauling her crap out of Emily's apartment and into his swanky place in Downtown.

"It sounds like this guy's more of a winner than the last one," Lara said to me one night when we were rearranging my bedroom furniture. I'd sketched out a few more ideas for the setup of my bedroom for when I bought the baby's stuff. I found the ideal, simple yet sleek crib and matching furniture while flipping through IKEA's latest catalog. With the measurements squared away, I wanted to test out different arrangements of my bed and furniture.

"Jackie has never had a penchant for picking out winners. We all know that." I tried to push as little weight as I could, but my bed was quite light, so Lara could easily manage the majority of the moving on her own. "Not that this guy really needs to be all that better than the last one in order to be 'more of a winner.'"

"She says she's happy. Even though she always says she's happy."

"That's how it is at first," I said. "She meets a guy. Her expectations are wild. He seems to fulfill them. Then he turns into a complete jackass. She's lost without him. Starts drinking more when she's all depressed. They fight, he leaves. Or they fight, she leaves. Somehow it always ends in disaster and heartbreak. Always a crap load of drama."

Lara pushed the nightstand closer to the bed and said, "Same story. Let's hope different results this time."

"Oh, did you hear Sophie's all moved in to her new place now?" I changed topics.

"Damn, that was quick."

"Apparently she'd been looking at places for a while. Found just what she was looking for—in Belltown, I think it is—and she's all moved in. And she's planning on having a small housewarming party."

"When's that planned?" Lara asked. She sprawled out on my bed, looking exhausted, and stuffed a fluffy white pillow under her head.

"She didn't say exactly. But she mentioned some time after she gets furniture. I suggested we do an IKEA run at the same time." Lara's eyes lit up. I knew she loved shopping at IKEA. And, who were any of us kidding? We all loved shopping there.

"That's a great idea!"

"That way I can get some of the baby furniture then, too," I said. "We were thinking this weekend maybe?"

My cell phone started to ring. After I searched around the fairly messy bedroom, I hastily answered the call without even glancing at the caller ID.

"Robin, is this an okay time?" It was my sister Kaitlyn.

"Uh...sure. Hey, Kaitlyn. What's up?" Lara got up at the sound of the name Kaitlyn, as she knew the chances of my sister randomly calling me was slim to none, so it must have been serious. She closed my bedroom door behind her.

"You feeling all right?" Kaitlyn asked me.

Why are you calling? This is peculiar...

"Of course I'm feeling all right. Why wouldn't I be fee—"

Ah hah. Mom must have tipped her off about the pregnancy.

"I'm feeling great, actually," I said. "So mom told you the big news, am I right?"

She confirmed, saying that she wished I had called her too.

"Don't get me wrong, Kaitlyn, but it's not like we're all that close. We're not exactly the best of friends. Or close siblings..." I didn't mean for my words to sound as callous as they may have come off. "I mean, I had a hard enough time telling mom. And finally emailing dad. I honestly didn't think of calling the whole family—mom, dad, sister, brother, aunts, uncles—"

"Don't be silly," Kaitlyn said. "I'm your sister. Of course I'd want to know. We may not exactly be close, but I still want to know."

I didn't know what to say. Then came one of those awkward silences that I'd experienced more than a few times with Kaitlyn.

"Anyway, that's neither here nor there," she finally said, her voice sounding chipper. "So do tell. How far along are you? What are you having? When's the due date?"

"I take it mom didn't fill you in on much?"

"Well, she told me that the father is some random guy who's not in the picture. But I don't think you really want to talk about that."

I sighed. "Yeah, not exactly."

"So, do tell me—the due date, the first ultrasound. You've had that, right?"

Once we'd gotten beyond the initial uneasiness of the call—the fact that we hadn't spoken in more than half a year—we carried on in a way we hadn't since I was, well...in high school. Kaitlyn's mood was cheerful and welcoming. I could hear that she was actually interested in my life and had a genuine care for me and her soon-to-be niece or nephew.

Perhaps Kaitlyn could understand where I was coming from with the newly pregnant thing and all. She herself had two young children and could relate to the ups and downs of becoming a new mom. One day you feel great in your skin, then next not so hot. And then the worries about being a good parent and a good enough caretaker for your baby...whether you'll be able to give it everything it needs and everything you want to provide for it...

"You'll make an outstanding mom, Robin," she said sweetly after nearly two hours of conversing. "There's no doubt about it. You're going to be a super mom!"

"Hey, uh, Kaitlyn. You think you want to come to the baby shower?" It was worth asking. We'd been getting along so well on the phone, and I was comforted by the fact that at least *someone* in my family seemed to care about me and my baby.

"I'd love to," she said, sounding taken by surprise. "I would absolutely love to make it. Well, I guess I should let you go. You need to get your rest now that you've got the little one on the way. Congratulations again, Robin."

"Thanks, Kaitlyn. You have a good night yourself. I'll get in touch with you about the shower as it nears."

"Yeah, and keep in touch. You know, call me anytime. I'm here for you."

I smiled. I don't think I'd ever heard those words from my big sister before, not even when we were speaking more regularly than twice a year.

I went to bed that night feeling so good about the unexpected reconnection I'd made with my sister. And the girls' words kept resounding in my head: *You're not alone, Robin. You are not alone.*

That weekend, the girls and I, minus Jackie, who was out of town with her new boy toy, made a trip to IKEA, with plans to meet up with Chad and Conner afterward so they could haul off the hoards of furniture that Sophie and I would no doubt be buying. I felt as if I'd cleaned out the store, although that's impossible; I did have nearly everything an expecting mother could imagine she might need. The all-white and very simple yet adorable crib that I wanted was in stock, so I added that to my list of purchases, as well as a dresser, a diaper changing station, a relatively small but storage-laden wardrobe, and some shelving units.

Sophie purchased more items than I did. She was shopping for everything from bedroom furniture to a dining set. And both of our carts were stuffed with every sort of knickknack imaginable—vases, candles, picture frames and poster boards, toss pillows, small rugs, and of course a variety of baby toys and decorative items—all very colorful and gender neutral. I was elated that I could possibly find out if I was having a boy or a girl in only a few days! Yet, though I was still unsure of the baby's sex and would know soon enough, nothing could keep me from shopping with my friends.

"You guys really outdid yourselves this time," Conner said, securing the various boxes into the back of his truck.

"Who's going to build all this stuff?" Chad asked, running a hand through his sun-bleached, ever so slightly greasy hair. He then rubbed at his face, which was covered in at least two or three day's worth of stubble. "There's a ton of crap here."

Sophie pointed to the both of the guys and said, "Here's fifty bucks." She handed Conner the cash. "Go buy yourself some lunch and take my stuff to my place pretty please." She tossed Conner her keys and quickly told them how to get to her new apartment. "And help yourself to whatever you want in the fridge. There's a fresh batch of homemade cream puffs in there. All yours if you boys don't mind dropping off these boxes. Maybe doing a little building." She exaggeratedly batted her eyes, oddly enough at Conner, not Chad. Although Sophie probably wouldn't dream of provoking Chad. Not after his relentless teasing her over the holiday.

"Score!" Conner said. He hopped in his truck after giving Claire a kiss goodbye, after which she complained he was too close for comfort—too sweaty, dirty, and in dire need of a shave.

"Have at it, boys," Claire said, wiping Conner's sweat from her cheek.

"Let's go, Chad!" Conner said excitedly. "We'll drop your stuff off at your place, Robin. Then we're going to Sophie's."

Claire rolled her eyes at us. "Any time Conner gets to build something and pretend he's frickin' Tim the Toolman Taylor he's all over it like white on rice. You're in luck, Sophie."

The boys peeled out of the warehouse garage, and we proceeded to our cars.

"You don't want to make sure they don't screw things up?" I asked Sophie, as she jumped into my car with me; Claire rode off with Lara.

"Oh, please. And pass up on the opportunity to help you build the baby furniture? I'd much rather help you out. And I'd never pass on some girl time."

"Claire, I honestly don't think that piece goes there," Lara said. She was becoming agitated and started to read over the tri-fold instruction sheet for the diaper changing station for the third time. "Look at the diagram. You're doing it all wrong."

Claire heaved a sigh and roughly laid down the Allen wrench. "Then you try it. One of you is telling me one thing, the other another. I've never built a damn diaper changing station before."

Sophie picked up the wrench and had a go at one of the legs. Lara warned that she, too, was doing it incorrectly.

"I know what I'm doing," Sophie said. "It's common sense. Any idiot can figure it out."

"Hey, thanks a lot!" Claire crossed her arms and pouted like a child.

"Oh, quit it." Sophie twisted tightly at the leg. I suddenly imagined the shiny white leg splintering in all directions, then cracking right in half.

"Stop, stop!" Lara said, putting her hand over Sophie's. "That's *not* how you're supposed to do it."

"Talk about common sense," Claire said, sticking out her tongue. Sophie stuck hers right back out at her.

"Girls," I said, leaning against my bed. "We should really make sure we're going about this the right way. After all, this *is* a diaper changing station. I *am* going to be laying my baby on it. I really don't want this thing to come crashing down."

"I don't think we should have sent the boys to your place, Sophie," Claire said. "We need them here."

"We don't need the boys' help with this." I ripped the instruction sheet from Lara's hands. "We're four intelligent and educated women. I'm sure we can handle this on our own."

"There's so much crap in here," Lara muttered. "You bought way too much, Robin. There's no way this will all fit."

I tossed the instruction sheet aside and gruffly responded, "What the hell am I supposed to do?"

Sophie's and Claire's eyes widened. Lara and I didn't argue often, but between my hormones and her sudden life change, with a new roommate and a second soon on the way, the two of us had it coming at some point.

"What am I supposed to do?" I repeated. "The baby needs a crib. It needs a diaper changing thing. It needs a closet. It needs all this stuff!"

"Yeah, yeah," Lara said. She roughly snatched back the instruction sheet. "I know you need all this." Her tone then became softer, and I instantly felt horrible for having exploded like that all of the sudden. "Sorry, Robin," she apologized.

"Me, too." I handed her the Allen wrench. "I know my crap's all over the place. I don't want to be a pain."

"Oh, you're fine." Lara gave me a smile and started to tinker with the screws. "We're fine. Hey, Sophie?" Lara looked up at Sophie. "Can you turn up the air conditioner? And Claire?" Claire had started fidgeting with a plastic bag of screws. "How about you turn on some music. Let's get serious about this *and* have some fun at the same time."

The girls hopped off as Lara suggested, and she, once again, gave me a smile. "Sorry. Not easy for either of us, huh?"

I nodded. "So true."

The sweet, melodic sound of The Beatles poured from the living room's entertainment system, down the hall, and into my bedroom, where it looked like furniture mart had exploded, boxes strewn all over the place and pieces of fiberboard to the left and right. Once the music started playing and all of us decided to take deep breaths and have fun assembling the furniture properly, we really got the hang of things and the quasi-bedroom, quasi-baby room was starting to look up.

"Robin, you picked out some great pieces," Claire said, surveying the room, which now contained a completed crib and diaper changing station, and a half-assembled wardrobe not far behind.

"Yeah," Sophie said. "It's really coming together. It looks great. And that rocker that you ordered online is going to go perfectly in that corner."

"Things really are a surprising fit in here. When I first moved in and started rearranging I admit I was a little worried, but everything's working out."

"Of course everything's working out. Here, take some photos and send them to Jack," Lara said, handing me my cell phone.

"She's out of town with that stupid new guy of hers, hah?" Claire asked. "What's his name?"

"Andrew," I said, snapping photos of the room in its current state—somewhat disarrayed and somewhat complete. "Looks like we're back on track with Jackie making girl functions only when it's convenient and doesn't disagree with her flavor of the month's schedule."

"Now, girls," Lara scolded. "We haven't even met the man yet. As far as Jackie's told us, he's a really nice guy. We shouldn't be so quick to judge, even if her past *can* be telling..."

"A real doll," Claire said, giggling. "Jackie says he's the best thing she's ever had."

Sophie: "In the bedroom."

Claire: "In *and* out of the bedroom."

Me: "Ohh. The real deal now."

"Whatever 'deal' he is, I'm glad Jackie's happy," Lara said. "And I'm glad she seems to have met a really good guy."

"Don't hold your breath just yet, Lara," I said. "You know she has a history of picking less than upstanding gentlemen."

"Let's at least give her the benefit of the doubt. He's offered to let her move in—"

"And you don't think *that* says anything? Two frickin' weeks!" I was surprised. Wasn't anyone else mystified by the whole Jackie and Andrew thing?

"Okay, that *is* a little fast. But who are we to judge?" Lara said.

"You're right," I conceded. I sent the series of photos off to Jackie, with a little note attached that we hoped she'd make it when it came time to pick out some baby clothes. "I do hope he turns out to be a good guy after all. I hate seeing Jackie hurt...*all* the time."

Everyone voiced their agreement. We'd all been there, done that. More times than we could count on both hands we'd carried a drunken Jackie back to her dorm room. Or consoled her as she cried over some frat guy who was two-timing her. Or tried to cheer her up when she turned out to be wrong about the guy who worked the midnight to five o' clock shift at the corner mini mart. Or took the cigarette out of her hand or pried the cocktail from her fingers, and drove her to our place to nurse her back to health. And, always, always, we'd tell her that she was much better than she treated herself, and that she deserved more. She needed direction, and not by way of a sleazy man or on the way to the bar.

"I hear Andrew's helping her out financially," Claire said. "Jack told me he gave her two different credit cards just last week. Both in her name. *His* accounts."

"And he *is* letting her drive his BMW or Mercedes or whatever she said it was when he's not in town," Sophie added.

"Seen all that before," I sighed.

"Maybe this time he's not a bad apple." Lara, always positive and encouraging. "She *is* with him on some island nearby for a relaxing weekend getaway. She's being pampered and it doesn't seem precarious or anything."

"Hey," Sophie said, putting the final screws in place in the wardrobe. "If we can't all be treated like royalty, let's at least live vicariously through Jackie, who *does* get fed from a golden spoon now and then."

We continued building and moving into place the remaining baby furniture. Each and every piece came together without too much of a hitch—save for a few protests of "not there!" and "don't turn it like that!" All the while we chatted about Jackie and her new life of luxury.

"Oh and his townhouse! Jack says it's amazing!"

"What does Andrew do? Do any of us know?"

"She says some kind of a banker. Travels a lot. Or maybe it's a broker? It starts with a 'b' and he makes a lot of cash."

"Something that definitely pays the big bucks. Apparently he drives a *couple* of blinged out cars."

"Jackie's even talking about quitting her job."

"He *is* keeping her lifestyle nice and cushy."

"He's like forty-something, right?"

"Never been married? Isn't that peculiar?"

"He must have some serious Freudian issues."

"You never can tell, can you?"

15

The summer heat of August was stifling. Poor Lara was nearly chilled to the bone in the apartment, because I had to crank the air conditioning to the max in order to stay somewhat comfortable. My hormones were out of sorts, and the heat and sticky humidity only exasperated the problem. Fortunately for her, Lara wasn't around the apartment much lately, as she'd had a lot to do back at the office dealing with the big Spokane client; she'd even pulled a few late-nighters.

With the heavy workload, Lara wasn't able to come to my second and last ultrasound that day, but Claire pounced on the invitation. She'd never seen an ultrasound before, and she didn't have a problem getting off work an hour or two early to accompany me.

"This is going to be so much fun!" Claire said as I drove to the familiar medical center, parking at a sign very near Dr. Buschardi's front doors, which read, *For Expectant Mothers Only*.

"Oh my gosh—and you get your own private little parking space. How cute!"

I tried to make myself as comfortable as I could with the dressing gown barely covering my bare butt; there was no real way to feel at ease during these kinds of appointments. The only saving grace was the fact that I would most likely find out in a matter of minutes if I was having a boy or a girl.

"So this is the funny little thing that reads the baby?" Claire asked, pointing at the instrument that did, indeed, do just what she said.

Before I could answer, in came the ever-svelte Dr. Jane Buschardi. "Hello, my dear Robin!" Dr. Buschardi shook my hand and smiled brightly.

"Nice to see you again, doctor."

The doctor turned towards Claire, hand outstretched, and when formalities were exchanged Dr. Buschardi commented on what an amazing and supportive team of girlfriends I had.

"Don't know what I'd do without them," I said.

Claire clapped her hands excitedly and said, "I'm so happy to see the baby! We can find out if it's a boy or a girl today, right doctor?"

"If that's what Robin wants I'm ninety-nine percent sure we'll get to find out today. So long as Baby isn't shy and doesn't want to hide."

God, please don't be a self-conscious thing like your momma, little baby.

I mentally scorned myself for such thoughts. How silly of me. I know kids inherit traits—physical and otherwise—from their parents. But how obviously self-conscious was it to worry about your child being self-conscious?

Don't be silly, Robin. But come on, baby, don't be shy. Be bold and show us your stuff today. Please.

Some warm gel, some clicks and taps of the mouse and keyboard, a few revolutions with the instrument and then...the heartbeat. This time much louder and stronger than the first ultrasound. And then an image popped up on screen!

"That's its head!" I said, delighted it was so defined (and so much larger), and that I could see it without any assistance from Dr. Buschardi.

"That's right. And here," the doctor moved the instrument some more, this time pushing against parts of my stomach with her free hand. She then pushed gently with the instrument, saying, "We get

Baby to turn a little towards us...wiggle around little baby...ah...there we go." Click, tap, and then, "Robin is going to have a little girl!"

Claire screeched and I let out a tearful but joyful cry. I was having a girl. A baby girl!

"Congratulations, Robin. It definitely looks like you're going to have a little sugar and spice and everything nice." Dr. Buschardi took some photos, made more clicks and taps, then ran the printer so I could have my baby's new ultrasound photos. My baby *girl's* ultrasound photos.

"Your daughter looks healthy and fabulous."

My daughter. My daughter!

"She's right on schedule, growth-wise. December seventh still looks like a solid due date. Of course, you never can tell for sure. These little babies have their own schedules." Dr. Buschardi handed me my photos and Claire and I gawked at them. "Keep on doing the same things you've been instructed to in the books and pamphlets I sent you home with. And I'll give you some more today."

I smiled at the photos, trying to take in everything Dr. Buschardi was saying, but so overwhelmed with joy and disbelief that I was really going to have a daughter. A baby girl. All my own!

"Congratulations, Robin. Any questions at all, you know how to reach me. Until then, keep up what you're doing. It looks like you're doing everything right." Dr. Buschardi looked to Claire. "With great friends like yours, that's probably unavoidable."

I felt as if I were actually glowing during the car ride from the doctor's office. Everything seemed so surreal, yet so...*real*. The first ultrasound revealed that I was, without a shadow of a doubt, having a baby. This ultrasound reiterated that point, but *loudly!* When you're told that you're having a boy or a girl it seems to make the baby even *more* real, if that makes any sense.

"You know what we have to do now?" Claire asked, offering to drive, since I was still in such shock over the news.

"What do we have to do now?" I asked, glowing as I stared at the three new photos of my baby daughter.

"Baby clothes shopping time!"

"You're right!"

"Now that you know you're having a girl we *obviously* have to go pick out some adorable pink and lacy things."

"Yeah, and we can pick up a Boppy. In pink."

I discovered that this thing called a Boppy was Mom's best friend. With the Boppy, I could better nurse and bottle-feed my baby, not to mention let her rest comfortably and near me on the sofa, or even on the floor. It provided head and body support and would be just the piece of baby gear I could use for several months as my little girl grew from infancy to pre-crawling stage. And, when she wasn't using it, *I* could, apparently. A little back support? Pillow? I didn't need to read much more about the Boppy to know that I needed one.

"Obviously, we'll have to do another baby clothes shopping run with the rest of the girls," Claire said, as she pulled into the parking lot of one of our favorite local shopping centers. "We can't have *all* the fun."

Whoever said five best friends was better than one must have been a shopper—and a mommy in the making.

Almost the instant Claire learned that I was going to have a girl she went to work on the baby shower invitations—pink from top-to-bottom. The theme, we decided, would be all things "sugar and spice and everything nice," since the phrase stuck when Dr. Buschardi mentioned it during the ultrasound. That meant the grand theme of the baby shower was sweet pastries, cupcakes with cherries on top, little bows, cinnamon sticks, sugar cookies painted in pastel colors and dotted with white sprinkles, and anything that could fit under the heading "and everything nice" (and feminine). Wherever to start planning such a theme as that?

The shower was up to the girls to figure out, thank goodness. Claire was gung-ho about planning the affair and that was fine by me. I didn't have a knack for throwing parties or organizing fun get-togethers. I could do nachos and TV-on-DVD at home, or a girls' night at the movies. Or I could coordinate a group trip to a local art gallery. A full-scale party, especially a baby shower, was not my forte. "Martha Claire Stewart" was the queen of handmade crafts, themed parties, anything to which you needed to *répondez s'il vous plaît*. She agreed that I stay out of the planning details, my only requirements being that I show up and that I give her the addresses of any of the women I wanted at my shower. So I gave her only two, as I wanted an intimate shower with my best girlfriends. One address was that of my sister Kaitlyn, which I gave happily. The other, my mother's, and whether or not she'd come was another issue. I'd chosen to invite her out of civility, and actually had a brief discussion about it with Kaitlyn one morning before work.

"I invited her, but I don't know if she'll bother coming," I told Kaitlyn over my cell phone's speaker phone system as I French braided my hair. The Seattle summer heat and humidity were really getting to me, and the only way I could function having long hair was by braiding it.

"You're the bigger woman. You invited her and now the ball's in her court," Kaitlyn said. I had called Kaitlyn that morning because I wanted to share the news that she was expecting a niece. It was rather odd to be reconnecting with my sister after all these years— ten plus at least—and I'd never imagined it would have taken children to bring us together. We agreed that it was nice to have that reconnection nevertheless.

"She won't see it that way," I said. "You know Mom. She always finds something to bitch and blame about."

"You invited her; I'd leave it at that. She knows how to get a hold of you. Until she does, or doesn't, carry on and go about your business. You know she'll show up in the end."

"She better not bring her latest love interest. She tell you about that?"

"The Florida architect thing? Yeah. Who knows how long that'll last. At least she seems happy. Until her aura changes, that is." Kaitlyn giggled, and I couldn't hold back either.

I tied off my French braid and grabbed my cell phone and purse.

"Hey," I said. "I've got to run to work. Thanks for gabbing. I'll see you September twenty-second?"

"I wouldn't miss your baby shower for the world. See you later, sis."

I grabbed a travel-size bottle of orange juice and the muffin that Sophie had brought over the other night when she came to watch some television with me. I was getting lonely with Lara not home by dinnertime every night. The past couple of weeks she'd been tied up at the office, working late hours that went well past the time when we'd usually eat dinner. After a while, the dinners in by myself in front of the TV grew old, even with Beebee occasionally coming out from her various hiding places to sit next to me on the sofa. I knew Lara had her own life and things to keep her busy, however I didn't imagine I'd be alone at night so often once I became her roommate.

Work was demanding, though, and, as Lara said one night in passing, "I don't get to live in a nice apartment and drive a fancy car by sitting on my hands and clocking out at five every day." A couple times, I'd neglected to hide my frustration with her late nights at the office. I wasn't sure if I was reacting rationally since her behavior was, in fact, a little grating, or if I was going through hot and cold mood swings and simply didn't know how to handle things on Lara's end. (One can never really tell when they're pregnant.) Not having Lara home until eleven, twelve, even one in the morning some nights was beyond frustrating. I'd lash out occasionally, then apologize, then she'd apologize and come home earlier the next day; it went like this now and then but we always made amends and carried on as usual.

I walked into work that morning with only the slightest of waddles to my step. I was already past my halfway mark with my baby girl, and I was most definitely pregnant by the looks of it. Everyone around the office was generally nice and helpful, me being the only pregnant woman there—and the only one in quite some years. Doors were always held open, many times people waiting there in the doorway until my slower-moving self could make my way along. Some of the ladies brought in a small, pink-iced cake when they found out I was having a girl. I was invited out to lunch and for coffee or tea runs by nearly everyone, but not individually by Bobby. Not by the co-worker I was crushing on and couldn't shake from my thoughts.

More and more time was drawing out since Bobby and I had talked about having lunch together. He was still his genuinely kind self, but no more so than the rest of the men in the office who held open the door for me. No special treatment. Whether the flirtation was real or a figment of my imagination was still up in the air. Bobby *still* didn't address the overdue lunch topic. He didn't mention my having missed it because I was, in fact, sick, nor did he try to schedule it for another day. Nothing. Nada. It was as if we never even had a lunch planned!

I couldn't stare any longer at the image on my computer screen —an imposing and pompous mock up of Napoleon's traditional battle hat. I'd finally caught a break from mystery novel covers, and now I was charged with a period romance novel cover. But Napoleon's hat was grating on my nerves, since the arching shape wouldn't look right no matter how much I toyed with it; and I was hungry; and I wanted my owed lunch with Bobby already!

"Hey, how about we grab that lunch we were supposed to have, like, *ages* ago?" I stood at Bobby's desk, my hands resting on my lower back. I was nervous and surprised I had the gall to approach him point-blank, but there I was, waiting and ready. "That is, if you're not too embarrassed to eat with a pregnant girl who'll order more than a salad, no dressing." Humor never hurt a fraught situation.

He turned around in his swivel chair, tapping his pen on his chin.

"What do you say? Go to the little corner café over here?" I pointed in a vague direction to where I knew of a gourmet sandwich shop a short walking distance away from the office.

He didn't say anything for a while, then a small smile played upon his lips. He took his wallet and keys out of a desk drawer and led the way, waiting and holding open the door for me. As I turned to follow him out the door, always having to catch up on other's steps, I noticed that the photo of Bobby and his girlfriend in Trafalgar Square was missing from his desk.

That's odd.

I didn't think anything more of it as I made my way to the door, eager to enjoy a long overdue lunch with my office crush.

"Nice choice," Bobby said, as I took a big bite of my sandwich.

"Some of the best gourmet sandwiches in town," I said, continuing the small talk we had going on for the past ten minutes. We'd beaten the rush and were lucky to have found seats outside the quaint café on the corner of a peaceful, tree-lined street, where soccer moms were walking their pet poodles and coffeehouse purveyors were getting their afternoon fix in one of the many aromatic cafés that filled the area.

I sorely wanted to delve into deeper topics than the tastes of our sandwiches, or the beautiful sunshine, or how we thought the Sonics needed to return home from the middle of nowhere USA. I wanted to talk about *why* we'd let so much time pass before we finally had our lunch date. And why he never asked again. I wanted to tell him that I was having a little girl. And that I had no idea what to name her. I wanted to talk about...personal things. I didn't want to talk about work, actually, even if that was the initial reason we made a "business lunch date."

Fortunately, I didn't have to wait long to talk about deeper (and far more fascinating) topics than profit margins and potential losses in the traditional publishing world. Bobby opened the floodgates when he said, "I've been meaning to apologize to you for not making another lunch date. That was really immature of me and I apologize."

"Oh, don't worry about it." I tried to play the part of the carefree co-worker, not the role of the woman who would say what she felt: Why *didn't* you?

"It was rude, and I'm sorry. I'm glad we could finally do this."

I nodded, happy to hear that he was sorry we'd let so much awkward time pass between the last lunch and this one.

"Things have been going rough for me, personally." He cleared his throat uncomfortably. "I haven't exactly been myself lately—not at home, not at work." He looked into my eyes, arousing butterflies (certainly not baby flutters) in my stomach. "Not myself with you. You see...I broke up with my girlfriend of five years a couple of weeks ago."

I told him I was sorry and mindlessly put my hand on top of his.

"I don't want to go all into it, bore you with pointless details. But it's been rough."

"Being dumped is never easy," I said, wondering after the thought if my word choice was poor.

"I broke it off with her."

I nodded slowly, then noticed my hand on top of his and removed it.

He shifted in his seat. "It was a long time coming. We wanted different things. I want a serious relationship...like forever kind of stuff." I noticed an ever so slight blush to his cheeks. "And she's not ready for anything *too* serious. She doesn't want any kids, either. *I* do. And there just weren't any sparks anymore. You know what I mean?" He leaned back in his chair. "Sparks. Passion. That *real* love. It wasn't there."

I'd like to say that I was right on board with what he was saying. That those sparks two people could have were amazing and definitely worth finding, and keeping when found. I'd never had those shared sparks, though, even with my longest lasting relationship; I never felt crazy, over-the-moon-for-you kind of sparks with Joseph. And he sure as hell didn't have any with me. I wondered at that moment what it was like to experience earth-moving sparks for someone. *With* someone...

"We didn't have the sparks anymore. I guess our relationship ran its course and that was that." He paused. "Not that it makes it any easier."

"Oh, of course not," I agreed.

Breaking up, whether you're the dumper or the dumpee, is never an easy thing. No matter how many or few sparks there are, or were, or never were.

"But you know...it's not necessarily realistic to think you'd feel sparks for someone *all* the time," I said.

Of that I was sure. Even in the cheesiest of chick flicks and romance novels, couples eventually come across some rough moments, or even spark-free times. Claire and Conner were a prime, real-life example. They loved each other, and they both knew they did, and there were plenty of sparks. But there were also plenty of times when Claire wanted Conner to spend the night on the sofa, and when Conner grew tired of Claire's nagging.

"I know that," Bobby said. "Sparks aren't there *all* the time, that's true. It's that connection, though, that I'm talking about. That—that —*passion*. Where you know, even in the heat of an argument or when you're bummed out and want to be left alone...you know that you still love that person so much. That you still want to spend the rest of your life with them and grow old together. *That's* the passion, the *sparks*, that I'm talking about, Robin."

His small speech gave me goose bumps. I wasn't sure what to say after such dramatic and passionate words. All I could manage was, "I completely understand. That's what we all want, isn't it?"

It was all I wanted, that was for sure. I wanted sparks. I wanted passion. I wanted love. And I wanted everything that came with it: the hugs and the arguments, the laughter and tears and moments of passion, the kindness and compassion and support. I wanted it all. And I think I wanted it with Bobby.

"Anyway," he said, sounding deflated. "I didn't have that with Chrissy. Didn't want to waste her time or mine so I called it off. The worst part was that she didn't seem all that bothered."

I considered asking him if he thought she was seeing someone else, however I didn't want to impose.

"For all I know, she's already got someone else. Been with him for a while. How should I know?" He then rested his hand on top of mine, and I softly gasped. *I* may have been thinking about sparks and passion with Bobby, but he couldn't be coming on to me. No.

Fantasies are one thing. Fantasies are my playing grounds. Reality was, well, supposed to be a strictly "all business" kind of thing here, wasn't it?

I was worried about what Bobby would say next, but was a tiny bit relieved when he said, "Thanks for listening. It helps to have a friend to talk to."

"A friend?" I uttered the word faster than I could think.

Is that truly what this is? Friendship?

I wasn't sure if it was friendship or something else bordering...more.

"I'd like to think we're friends," he said. "I know I haven't exactly been all chatty-chatty with you recently, like a friend would be." He tried to catch my gaze; my eyes were transfixed on the floor. "I'd like to think we're friends, though, Robin."

I looked up at him and answered. "Yeah. Friends."

"Good." He smiled, removed his hand from mine, and continued with his meal. He apologized again for delaying our lunch for so long, and for spilling his thoughts on love, during what was supposed to be, and I quote, "a casual, fun break from work."

"It's fine," I said sheepishly. "No problem."

"I don't get it!" I shouted, slamming the utensil drawer shut in the kitchen. Lara and I were emptying the dishwasher that evening. I was pleased, to say the least, that she was finally home before dinnertime, *and* before the sun was well past set. "'Friends.' 'Date.' What the hell does it all mean?"

"Stress levels," Lara warned, drying off the bottoms of the mugs still wet with dishwasher water. "Not healthy for you or the baby."

"Yeah, yeah. I'd like to know what the *hell* Bobby and I are. What the *hell* he thinks we are."

"Apparently friends, Robin." Her tone was so calm it angered me even more.

"Bull. He's driving me crazy!"

Lara cracked a small smile, and I defensively asked her what she thought was so funny.

"You're making this out to be a lot more than it should be. It's an office romance...in your *head*. You've said it plenty of times before, Robin. You don't know what to make out of his 'flirting,' and you're fantasizing about things. Let it go. Don't invest too many of your emotions or too much of your time in this whole thing. And...keep riding it out."

"Keep riding it out? You mean, see where it goes? *If* it even goes anywhere?"

"Exactly. Don't get all strung out about it and overdramatize things. Just...ride it out. Let things be. And, when all is said and done, Bobby might only see you as a friend. Is that such a bad thing? He *does* want to be friends."

"If I'm fantasizing about him in my shower, yeah, it's kind of a problem when we're trying to go over graphic art design concepts."

Lara laughed. "Well *try* to put those fantasies away and just be friends. You never know. Things could develop from here. Lots of great relationships start out as friendships. Some of the best ones, in fact."

I had read plenty of love stories in women's magazines about best friends from grade school who were celebrating their thirtieth and fortieth wedding anniversaries. Hip-hip-hooray for them. What about me? All my grade school male friends picked their noses, gave my arms snakebites, and laughed at me when I wore what I assumed were fashionable *Little Mermaid* leggings. There was never going to be a budding romance there.

"Fine," I conceded. "I'll stop fretting over it and try to keep things professional. *And* I'll 'be friends' with Bobby, whatever that means. Really, Lara, what *does* that mean?"

She put away the last of the dishes and turned out the kitchen lights, leaving me in the dark until I made my way into the living room with her.

"I think it could mean that you're just that—friends. And that could be a really beautiful beginning to something special."

"Special friends? As in friends with benefits?"

"Ha! Mind out of the gutter, Miss Cynical. No, I mean...you never know what could develop. Bobby reaches out to you with this whole dramatic story about losing a girlfriend of four, five, however many years...he obviously enjoys talking to you, and values your opinion. And trusts you with that information."

"And?"

"Well," she said in a playful tone, petting Beebee, who instantly jumped on her lap the moment her butt hit the sofa. "This could be the start of something special. Something that becomes more than friends. *Not* friends with benefits. But something serious. I don't know. Something special. You'll have to wait it out. Let the chips fall where they may kind of thing."

She'd piqued my interest. Could Bobby Holman be laying the brickwork for a possible relationship with me? Could there be sparks in the works somewhere in the future?

"Until then, my suggestion, missy, is that you keep your focus on your work. Keep doing a great job on your cover art. And focus on your little girl. You're going to have a baby!"

I rubbed at my stomach, which was about the size of a volleyball, but more oblong.

"I *am* going to have a baby. A baby *girl!* Oh, and you know what?" I said, plopping down in the recliner opposite Lara. "Bobby mentioned he wanted kids. His ex doesn't. He does." I twirled a lock of hair around my index finger.

"Mind out of the gutter, girlfriend!" She then turned on probably the only thing that could actually get my mind out of the gutter...and into a different one: *Beverly Hills: 90210.* "I can't believe we're still watching this," Lara sighed. "We've seen the reruns like a hundred times."

"And each time gets better," I said as I turned up the volume, the theme music ringing its familiar tune.

16

As it turns out, Lara was right about keeping my cool and letting things ride out. Not having grandiose (or any) expectations about my relationship with Bobby made me feel relaxed and worry-free when I spent time with him, even when we simply crossed paths at the copier or in the break room. Bobby had made it clear that he viewed me as a friend; and I had gladly accepted his friendship. If something more blossomed from that, so be it. If not, then I suppose that's the way of things. No point in trying to clutch at straws. It wasn't like I didn't have enough going on in life to keep me preoccupied.

Since the afternoon Bobby and I shared our second lunch, we'd gone out and grabbed a bite to eat, or taken a break at a neighboring coffee shop several times. Sometimes we'd have "just us moments" twice in one day. I really enjoyed his company, and as it appeared, he enjoyed mine. Being with Bobby felt so natural and relaxed. Granted, we'd been working together for a few years and weren't complete strangers to begin with, but our new friendship evolved quickly, yet organically.

And when we spent time together at work, we weren't only talking about preferred title fonts among sci-fi readers or the development of our current works-in-progress. We chatted about me having a little girl. About how I was getting to know my sister after all these years. About how nervous I was about my upcoming review at work. About Bobby's long time zeal for his favorite writer, whom he called "Stephen *the* King." Even about Bobby's fear of squids and his ironic dream of someday scuba diving. And we discussed Bobby's plans to advance as much as he could at Forster & Banks, because he liked the firm and preferred working with a smaller-sized company as opposed to the large publishing houses he'd familiarized himself with back in New York, before he made his way out to Seattle. We talked about all sorts of things—personal and work-related. The whole "letting the chips fall where they may" that Lara referenced the other night was giving way to a newly born and rewarding friendship.

"See, I told you," Lara said, as we cooked dinner together one night. "Be patient. Don't blow things out of proportion, and see where it goes."

"Yeah," I said. "This friendship we're forming is really cool. Bobby's a nice guy. A *really* great guy."

"So...when do I get to meet him?"

I let out one loud, exaggerated laugh. "Slow down a minute. Who's been the one telling me to take it slow? Now you want to meet him? It's not like we're *serious* about each other or something. It's not like he's my boyfriend and I need to show him off to all the girls. Get the approval or something."

"You know what I mean. As a *friend*. That's not strange. Maybe you can invite him to Sophie's housewarming party this weekend. Or is that too forward?"

"That's too forward for me *and* too much to impose upon Sophie. Besides, only the girls are coming and one new guy in the group would be way awkward."

"I thought the boys were coming?"

"Evidently Chad and Conner already had tickets for some monster truck something or other. Anyway, that means no Bobby. At all."

"Well, at some point I'd like to meet this charming friend of yours."

I started to set the table, shooing Beebee off Lara's chair. "Maybe. No promises. If the right situation presents itself...*maybe*." I turned the topic of conversation to something I'd been meaning to comment on earlier. "So it's nice to have you home at a decent hour again. Work's been pretty brutal lately, huh?"

Lara let out a heavy sigh. "You have no idea. Up to my eyeballs in work. This Tacoma case is really getting me."

"I thought it was Spokane?"

"Oh, yeah. I meant Spokane. See? Perfect example. I'm so swamped I don't know who's who and what's what anymore. You want to pour your own sauce?" She held up the saucepan over the stove and I told her to go ahead with it.

"Well, I'm just glad you're not coming home at God-awful hours of the night anymore. They work you to the bone over there."

"Like I said, cushy life...got to work for it."

I told her I could relate. While my workload wasn't nearly as stressful or heavy as hers, I was still busting tail and only barely meeting deadlines and personal project goals. My boss and I figured we'd push my maternity leave up a few days, seeing how the Thanksgiving holiday fell so closely before the third of December, when I planned my leave. And I might as well get as much of my work turned in as I could before Thanksgiving, then call it a time-out and go into full-on baby mode.

All of the prep to make that transition smoother beforehand meant there was a lot of work to be done. And with Bobby still hot on my mind, despite my convincing myself to keep things on a purely platonic level, keeping my focus on "all-things-business" when at the office was proving to be very difficult. See, as much as I enjoyed my growing friendship with Bobby, and as often as I told myself that I needed to focus on the friendship aspect of our relationship and not try to distort anything that would meet my fantasies, I couldn't help myself. I think I was falling in love with Bobby. How much longer could I hide that fact? I couldn't hide my baby bump longer than a couple of weeks. Could I keep burying my feelings for Bobby?

———

Sophie's housewarming get-together could not have fallen on a more beautiful summer day, especially considering it was August. The sun wasn't beaming intolerable heat, and the humidity levels were surprisingly low. It was the perfect day to lounge by or in the pool, or simply relax in the shade. And all of that was exactly what the girls and I spent much of our time doing that Sunday afternoon by Sophie's new apartment pool.

Her new, modernly designed and freshly furnished one-bedroom, one-bathroom apartment in the very gentrified neighborhood of Belltown, a very short distance from her job, was a perfect fit for Sophie and this new step in her life. She'd crossed her fingers she'd get the fourth floor apartment—the one that had the best sliver of a view of Elliot Bay from a small balcony—as opposed to the only other vacant apartment in the complex, which was on the first floor. Luck would have it the other interested party bailed out at the last minute, leaving Sophie to claim her fourth floor home. She couldn't have been happier, and we all couldn't have been happier for her. This was a big step for Sophie. Finally breaking free from the comfort and reliability that came with living with her best friend, Claire, Sophie was stepping out on her own; said she was adamant about starting fresh and keeping her chin up. I could totally relate.

"And look at all the closet space," Sophie gushed, opening up her built-in, and somewhat walk-in-sized bedroom closet. "And there's tons of random storage space in this place, too. Like for all the pots and pans and coats and cleaning supplies and all that random stuff. Lots of closet space!" Sophie was beaming with pride and excitement over her domain as she concluded her tour.

"Nice pad," Jackie said, taking a seat on the sofa. "You scored here."

"Yeah, and everything looks so new," Claire said. "The paint job, the wood floors, the kitchen. Not bad, girl. Not bad at all."

"This building used to be run-down office space, but some architect came in and wanted to flip it. Apparently he's flipped a few of the buildings around here—mostly into apartments and townhouses and such." Sophie passed around a bowl of fruit.

"And it looks like the boys managed to put together all of the furniture for you," I said.

"Those boys. Give them pizza and beer and they'll do anything."

"Or a little weed," Jackie said, tossing her head back dramatically and laughing.

The rest of us exchanged quizzical looks while Jackie ate some grapes.

"What?" she asked.

"You're not doing that as much anymore, are you, Jack?" Sophie asked, herself munching on some of the tasty fruit. "The pot. You really should kick the habit."

"Oh, only once in a blue moon."

"Like what, once a month?" Sophie's voice was harsh. We all disapproved of Jackie's smoking habits, not to mention her cigarette-smoking habits, but Sophie, in particular, never felt the need to hide even a fraction of her disapproval of Jackie's less-than-savory behavior. "Once a week? A day? What's 'once in a blue moon' to you?" Sophie pressed.

"Don't be such a drama queen," Jackie said lightheartedly. "I haven't smoked in forever. Not since I've started going with Andrew." She looked proud of herself, as if withholding the urge to smoke a whole month was something to toot your horn about.

"Wow, a whole month, Jack," I said, half-joking.

"Actually, for your information, and if you *must* know," Jackie threw back a few more grapes, "it was more than a month ago since I last smoked. And *I* wasn't carrying any on me. I just accepted."

"Well that's something," Claire said, with an obvious hint of sarcasm that Jackie totally missed. "A real step up there."

"Thanks!" Jackie smiled brightly and continued snacking.

Sophie told her she shouldn't hang out with losers like that. She could get into real trouble. Jackie replied with an "Andrew will help me, then," and took us all by surprise when she added, "Besides, we're all one to talk about 'associations.'" She motioned quotation marks with her fingers on her last word. "For your information, it was *Chad* who offered me a little smoke. Up at his parents' place. For the Fourth of July."

We all groaned, threw up our hands in surprise and dismay, telling her how immature that was of the two of them.

"Hey," Jackie said defensively, "he had some on him, asked me if I wanted to share one and...well...let me just say that we shared more than a little smoke."

Claire: "What?"

Lara: "What the hell does that mean?"

"Oh my God, Jackie," I said. "What happened between you two?"

Jackie was so nonchalant, munching on fruit and waving the topic off with a flick of her manicured hand. "It was no big deal."

"Like hell it's no big deal!" Claire said, eyes wide. She kneed her way across the living room rug, getting closer to Jackie, practically right in her face. "Are you saying you actually *did* something with Chad?"

Jackie only smiled.

"Jackie Anderson, you big ho!" Lara said, giving her a light slap on the thigh. "You did *not* sleep with Chad Harris."

Jackie put a purple grape between her lips and made a fish face.

I glanced at Sophie, whose expression was without. She even looked slightly pale.

"Tell us! Tell us!" Claire urged.

"It wasn't a big deal or anything. We were smoking a little...you know...getting the buzz on. We'd had a few drinks already—"

"Wait, when *was* this? Where were we all?" Claire interrupted.

"Oh, you know...when you all went out kayaking. When Sophie was out at the market. We figured why not strike up the doobie and have some fun? And, well...one thing led to another...and..."

"You *big* ho!" Lara said. "I cannot believe you, Jack. Chad? My God." Despite Lara's shock, a slight smile played her lips.

"Hey, I'm not the only one who's had a fling with Chad," Jackie deflected, looking straight at Sophie, whose face still lacked any expression or color.

"Still," Claire said. "That was Sophie in rebellion. And that was *years* ago. Sophie and Chad...with alcohol. In the past. But *this!* Jackie, you crazy girl."

"What?" Jackie asked. "How's it any different? That was Sophie and Chad, this was Jackie and Chad. With some dope and a few drinks and...what? Don't look at me like that. We were horny. What can I say? I was unattached and, girls, let me tell you, I'd been without for *much* too long. Thank *God* Andrew finally showed up."

"So Chad, what, tied you over until then?" I asked, perplexed about the whole matter, regardless of how Chad seemed to be simple fling material for more than one of us.

"You could say that," Jackie giggled. "It's not a big deal, guys. Come on."

"Well, *I* think it's a big deal. And I'm surprised," Claire said.

"I'm not," Jackie said. "Chad'll do it with anything that walks. And, sometimes, girls, so will I." She started into a personal fit of laughter.

"You people have the scruples of farm animals," Sophie said in a stern voice, and the rest of us were thrown into a fit of unintended laughter. "I'm serious!" she proclaimed. "What is with you people? It's not funny."

Jackie stopped laughing and tried her best to turn on her most staid face. "No need to get your panties in a twist over it, Sophie."

"At least I *wear* panties."

That's it—this whole exchange was too much to bear. Sophie and Jackie had us rolling on the floor.

"Hey, I wear panties!" Jackie said.

"Yeah, crotch-less ones." I couldn't help myself.

"Oh, good one, Robin!" Claire cried.

"Come on, Sophie, what's the big problem?" Jackie said. "It was just a quick and lousy lay. Who cares?"

"It was lousy?" Lara asked, surprised.

Jackie popped another grape into her mouth. "Although I must say all those tats he's been collecting were a bit of a turn on. Definitely has that whole bad boy vibe going. It made me a feel a little naughty. And naughty can be good sometimes." She ate a few more grapes, then said with a full mouth, "He is ripped. Has a body to die for. Ain't bad there, right Sophie?"

"But lousy? You said lousy?" Claire asked. She looked stunned.

"Kind of. I mean, I was tripped out of my mind so it's not like I'm really the best Judge. But I guess lousy, yeah."

"Sophie said Chad was the best she's ever had," Claire said.

Sophie's face finally had color—bright red with anger.

"Claire!" Sophie shouted, the first word she'd said in a while. The room grew quiet.

"Look, Sophie," Jackie said. "I didn't mean to get your feathers all ruffled. Chill. It's not like Chad or I were in relationships with anyone. He was free; I was free. We had some dope. We had some fun. That's all. Casual sex. No harm done. God, don't have a cow over it. What? Do you have some underlying affection for Chad?"

I didn't think it was possible, but Sophie's face grew a darker shade of red. "No!" she said, squinting her eyes and shaking her head dramatically. "Don't be ridiculous. I don't feel *anything* for that guy. That pig! He really will sleep with *any*thing."

"Hey, that's not nice," Lara said, ready to disarm two girls about to break out in battle. "Break it up already."

Sophie's face started to cool. "Sorry, Jackie," she said, quickly. "You didn't deserve that. I'm shocked, that's all."

Jackie didn't take much offense, and ended the conversation with, "It's in the past. And I guess it wasn't *that* lousy. He did have some good moves. Not bad rhythm. But then again, it was hard to judge."

"From the high?" Claire asked, her lips curled.

"Well that, and we were in the laundry room riding the washing machine."

And another burst of uproarious laughter; even a tiny smile at the corner of Sophie's mouth.

Jackie, Jackie...what could any of us say? Always up for a quick romp, always able to get us squealing. Always something out of this world.

"Onto a less *dirty* topic," Lara said after the Jackie and Chad memories that had been conjured up were laid to rest, and once we had all meandered out to the pool to relax, oiled up or coated in sunscreen. "How are those bakery plans going, Sophie? Now that you're more independent...have your own apartment now. You seriously going to take those next steps finally?"

"You know, I've been doing a lot of thinking lately," Sophie said. "I still definitely want to open up my own shop, but with the baby coming and all...and with my brother moving to London for a year..." She propped herself up on her elbows and shaded her eyes with one hand. With her hair done up in a tall twist, her large pearl earrings still on, and her cat-eye sunglasses over her eyes, she was a dead ringer for Audrey Hepburn. Too freaking adorable. Although I'd have to say I didn't look half bad myself; this very large (and still growing larger by the day) tummy of mine actually suited my bikini. I was kind of digging the pregnant chick in a bathing suit look.

"I feel maybe now's not the best time to aggressively work on the café, you know?" Sophie said. "So much is going on right now. And I'm not saying all of this because I'm trying to make excuses. I think waiting awhile is the best thing for me right now. I'm getting back on my feet after Brandon—after *I* have a new place of my own after how many years?" She pushed her sunglasses further up onto her nose. "And I want to be able to spend my free time helping you out with the baby, Robin. I can't run off to London for a few weeks in the middle of trying to open up a shop. *And* I'm obviously not missing out on the opportunity to visit my big brother because I have a new store to manage."

"I think that's a wise choice," I said. "When you're good and ready to open up your bakery, you will."

"Yeah," Claire said cheerfully. She started to reapply another layer of sunscreen. I think this was her third application in under an hour. Silly girl. She probably recently read an article in *Reader's Digest* about the top ten preventative measures everyone should take against skin cancer, and took it to an exaggerated length. "And in the meantime you can keep practicing your recipes on us."

We got to talking about how things were going for Jackie and Andrew (apparently he was still just as sweet and dreamy now as Jackie made him out to be when she started seeing him). Good news on that front. I shared the news that Kaitlyn and I were still keeping in touch and actually having a sisterly relationship; that was something new and exciting for sure! And I even brought up Bobby, about how we were forming a nice friendship and how I hoped something along the lines of romance would stem from it. But I wasn't going to hold my breath. Remember, let the chips fall where they may.

17

I was so anxious I couldn't stop chewing on my nails, and my cuticles, and my lips. It was a dreadful habit when I was extremely nervous that I'd tried to beat time and again. When the going got tough, though, like when my future at Forster & Banks was held in the balance, I couldn't stop myself. My long-awaited review with Mr. Lober had arrived and I not only wanted that raise and a glowing review, I needed it. Brandon's promised child support checks had yet to come floating my way (big surprise there). My wages would suffice, and sure Lara would be there for me if I were in a pinch, but I wanted to be able to support myself and my baby without always having my hand held out. I could do it. I had the college degree. I had the experience. I *did* have a great reputation at the firm. Why shouldn't I get the raise?

Ugh. No pep talk is going to help today.

I stopped chewing on my nails for a second and resorted to mindlessly scrolling through my email's inbox. No new message.

Of course there wouldn't be. You checked only thirty seconds ago. Wait! How about my personal email?

I typed in the Gmail address and logged in to my personal

account. My scheduled review with Mr. Lober was already five minutes overdue. His previous meeting with another employee who also happened to be up for review was taking longer than expected.

Oh this anticipation is eating at me!

Once my Gmail loaded my eyes noticed without a second's hesitation that I had a new message from Emily.

Oh yay! I wonder what she has to say.

The email was addressed to all of the girls—one mass message that we usually expected from Emily on a monthly or bi-monthly basis.

Hey all my chicas!

How are things back at home?

Sophie: You still planning on a trip to London to visit John? Do it. That city's filled with history! I'll so join you!

Claire: Conner pop the question yet? (Sorry to bring it up if he hasn't. Trust me though, he will!!)

Robin: A girl? (Thanks for sharing the latest ultrasound pics, BTW). Congrats! So you're going to name her Emily, right? ;-)

Jackie: Have you burned my place down yet? Or have you found your lover man, leaving my home to fill with dust? Seriously, email me back, girly!!!

Lara: Hope work is treating you well. I say you need to take a sabbatical from the grind and come join me in Ghana. It'll change your life!

And speaking of Ghana. Girls...don't get upset. I've decided to prolong my stay here. The village really needs me. The school's nowhere near complete. (Lax construction deadlines aren't any different over here than they are in Seattle.) Anyway, the school still needs work and I'm spiritually not ready to leave. Much too much to do. But I promise I'll be home in time for baby Emily's (wink-wink) birth. I promise you, Robin! I'll be home after Thanksgiving.

Got to go. Getting a shipment of two-by-fours in so we can get some more progress underway with the school. Always exciting! Kisses and hugs all around.

XOXO

Emily

I contemplated sending her a reply, uncertain of when Mr. Lober would conclude his current meeting and commence mine, but before I could make a decision, my phone rang. It was time for my review.

"Good luck," Bobby whispered, as I passed by his desk, on the way to Mr. Lober's office.

"Thanks."

"We're still on for lunch afterward?"

"Yeah. Either celebratory or mournful."

"Congratulations, Robin!"

Bobby and I clinked our soda and water glasses over what was fortunately a celebratory lunch together. Mr. Lober sang only praises about my past year's worth of work during my review, and he was sure that I'd continue to "impress the Board, and inspire colleagues" (his words, not mine) for many years to come. He awarded me the attractive raise I had hoped for, and added a small lift in my annual bonus package. And the best part of the review was that he said I should consider the project management position in the event the author in question signed on with Forster & Banks. No promises, although I should certainly consider the position and leave my options open.

"It couldn't have gone any better!" I said to Bobby. "Couldn't have asked for a better review. I'm so happy."

"You're a shoo-in for the PM position then." He took a big bite of his salad.

"I wish. I know the opportunity is there, but no promises. The boss even said 'no promises.' At least I've got a shot, though."

"I bet you'll get it. I *hope* you get it."

I finished chewing, then said, "Aren't you interested in the position?"

Bobby shook his head.

"Why not? It'd be a big promotion. It's not every day we sign a new author. And you want a long-term career at the firm. Why not try for it?"

"This is how I see it," he started, leaning in closer to me, his fork in his hand. "I may be wanting to move my way up—get the promotions and the fancy titles and all that jazz. Obviously moving my way up the corporate ladder and whatnot is ideal, especially since I want to keep at this firm for a long time to come. But I want to go about it the right way, you know what I mean?"

"What? Not sleep your way to the top?" I joked, tapping my fork with his in a frisky way.

"The new author...she's contemporary women's fiction—"

"Chick lit, yeah," I cut in.

"That doesn't rub you the wrong way? As a woman? An empowered, career woman? 'Chick lit' doesn't bother you?"

I laughed. "Why should it? It's not any different than references to chick flicks, and I don't see a problem with that. People whine that it's all anti-feminist and derogatory. I don't buy it. Let's call it what it is: literature that chicks...dig."

He smiled, his bright blue eyes twinkling playfully. "All right... chick lit, then."

"We can be high-powered, women's lib, and corporate wonder women and all that and *still* enjoy a good book filled with all-things-female," I added. "But we're off topic. So this new author is a *chick lit* author and...?"

"And I'm no chick lit man," he said, resuming eating his lunch. "I appreciate all genres and all forms of cover art, but I don't see myself as being the best PM for an author of that genre. And I don't think it'd be in the firm's best interest and longevity to hire on to the project someone who doesn't have their heart in it...someone who can't give their all and their best. That's what the firm needs. I don't think putting me in charge of making the calls for a pink book cover with stilettos and champagne and hearts is the best move. For anyone."

"Not *all* chick lit covers are covered in pink and hearts."

He gave me a cunning look, letting me know that he'd won this case; and I commended him for his stance. I liked the way Bobby thought about the firm's best interest, not only his own. It was kind of sexy, yet *so* not what I needed to add to my Bobby Holman fantasies. Not to mention, it undeniably made Janet's take on the PM position clear for what it was: a selfish move with only herself in mind. No care for the firm or those involved in the project. Not even the author.

Bobby and I talked briefly about Janet and her outlook on the position. We'd gotten very comfortable in our new relationship; Bobby and I knew that what we shared with each other about Janet and other colleagues stayed between us. He agreed that Janet was a selfish bitch with an ego the size of Texas, but he assured me I had nothing to worry about because "what goes around comes around; Robin will come out on top and Janet will be another bottom feeder."

"She'll move on at some point, anyhow," Bobby said, finishing his salad. "She'll get tired of us tiny people and ship on out."

I nodded in agreement.

Tell me about it. It can't happen soon enough.

Only that morning Janet had made some snide remark about how my feet were starting to push out like puff pastries in my ballet flats. I kindly told her that that was an unavoidable side effect of pregnancy. And that I didn't mind, because I was doing something bigger than myself—and my feet. I was going to have a baby! Her response was only a cold, "I know. My sister's feet look like sausages."

"Shall we get a move on?" I asked Bobby. "Get back to work so we can get out of here on time? Nothing I hate more than staying late on a Friday."

Bobby looked a little discombobulated. Was the food not settling well with him? Had I said something wrong?

"Robin," he said, shifting in his seat.

"Yes?"

"There's something I've been meaning to ask you."

"What is it, Bobby?" I asked, nervously playing with my straw wrapper.

"Will you have dinner with me?"

"Uh..." His question came out of nowhere.

"You don't have to if you don't want to." He was so fast to respond to my one utterance of a light sound.

"No, I, uh...yes. I mean, yes. Yes I'll have dinner with you."

"You sure?" he asked.

"Of course. I, uh..."

Was this a date? As in a date-date? Or was this another "business lunch" kind of thing?

I wanted to be clear before I put on my best perfume and (secretly) got my blonde touched up. Before I blew things way out of proportion and ended up looking like a lovesick fool.

"Like, dinner instead of lunch?" I asked.

He smiled. "Dinner as in a date. A real date."

I was speechless, and I don't know why, since a large part of me assumed that's what he meant when he suggested we go out for dinner, but still....I'd been dreaming of this kind of thing. Only in my wildest fantasies did Bobby Holman ask me out on a date. All right, my *wildest* fantasies included some Tarzan loincloth thing for him and some I'm-stranded-and-helpless Jane thing going on with me. This was reality, though, and in reality Bobby didn't ask out Robin.

Except he *did*. For a date! For a dinner date!

Seeing how I hadn't responded, he continued. "I don't want to ruin anything we have going on between us, Robin. I'm really enjoying getting to know you and getting to talk with you. I really like...being around you." He fumbled with his napkin. "I can't hide my feelings anymore, though. I've been feeling some *crazy*, amazing things for you. All this time we've been going out for coffees or lunches or all those little breaks together in the break room...I know it all seems so fast. But, er, well..." He continued to fumble with his napkin, and I couldn't help but grin. He looked adorable all nervous and frazzled. "Well, I've been attracted to you for a while," he said. "And when I'm around you I'm always happy. I feel good. I feel like myself. Completely like myself. I know it might sound absurd, all so fa—"

"Bobby," I said. He pulled the crumpled napkin into his lap and looked into my eyes. "I thought I was making our flirtation out to be something that it wasn't. See..." I broke our gaze for a moment, suddenly nervous about the entire discussion. "See...I really like you."

God, I sound like a teenager. Get it together, Robin.

I straightened up in my chair and looked back at Bobby. "I've enjoyed getting to know you, too, and if I can be completely straight up with you, I am *elated* that you want to go on a date with me. But, I can't help but have some reservations—"

"It's too fast, isn't it?" Bobby said quickly. "Too fast, too soon. We may have worked together for years but we haven't *really* known each other that lo—"

"No, no. Yeah, I mean, yes, it's all happening really fast; that's true. But that's not it." I stole Bobby's napkin that he'd returned to the table, the edges threadbare from his nervous habit. "It's just that...it's..."

"What?" Bobby rested his hands softly on top of mine, and I decided to tell him exactly how I felt. I'd fantasized more than enough times about having a relationship with Bobby, but I'd be a liar if I didn't admit to some misgivings about Bobby striking up a relationship with a soon-to-be-mom.

"I'm pregnant, Bobby." I searched his facial expression for any sign of discomfort, or understanding, or even bewilderment. So far, nothing. "And right now my baby is my priority. Don't get me wrong, I would absolutely *love* to go out with you. See where things take us. But, well...I'm in a very sensitive situation. It's *honestly* not every day some amazing and attractive and just...well...unbelievable man wants to date me. But a pregnant me? You understand if I'm a little, well, shaky about it all? No..." I corrected. "No, that's not the right word." I removed my hands from under Bobby's and rubbed at my forehead.

What am I trying to say?

Bobby leaned in over the table and said in a low voice, "Robin, I completely understand that you're in a difficult position right now. I can respect that. And if you're not ready to date—"

"I want to take things really slow." My response was sudden. It was honest. I couldn't let myself get hurt. I couldn't put myself or my baby in a tough spot.

"Slow it is, then. Absolutely."

"You really want to go out with a pregnant woman? You do realize that it's not just me you're dating? Wait, that sounds kind of strange." I twisted my mouth for a second, then said, "You know what I mean? With me comes a baby. And even, and God forbid, the baby's father. I come with...well I'm more than just a single woman you work with."

Bobby smiled, then said, "I like you just the way you are, Robin. I liked you before I knew you were pregnant. And, well, your daughter is a part of you now."

I sighed in relief. I figured Bobby still wanted to date me even though I was pregnant; obviously he was asking a *pregnant* me out. Hearing it from his own mouth, though, was comforting.

"I still want to take you out on a real date, Robin. Get to know you more beyond the usual office lunch break. And *I* have no reservations about dating a beautiful and brilliant woman who is going to have a baby. Now come on. Let's finish work up. We've got a date tomorrow night. Sound all right?"

"Sounds perfect."

I sucked in a deep breath of relief and excitement as Bobby and I sat there, looking into each other's eyes. I wondered if the chips were falling in a way that meant we'd share a kiss. At that very moment? Perhaps tomorrow? I was nervous and excited and full of anticipation at the sheer thought of Bobby's lips meeting mine. How romantic and sweeping the moment would be. And how romantic it was, in its own crazy sort of way, that Bobby wanted to take me, pregnant *me*, out on a date!

Oh! Such a thing from my fantasies! Was this really happening?

He pushed his chair back and stood up, and I followed suit. The anticipation of a kiss would have to keep stirring until tomorrow night, when maybe, just maybe, I'd get to share a beautiful kiss with the man of—quite clichéd but quite possibly true—my dreams.

The evening of our date, I was so nervous I couldn't keep my hand from shaking long enough to apply my eyeliner properly.

"Lara, I need your help!" I called out.

Lara rushed to my side. She was all sweaty, wearing gym shorts and a ratty U Dub t-shirt she'd had for nearly a decade.

"Something wrong with the baby? You all right?" she huffed, arming away some sweat from her brow. She must have been getting some time in with the treadmill.

"No, nothing like that. I can't put my darn eyeliner on, I'm so nervous. Can you help?"

Like a trooper, she applied the perfect thin black line all around, just how I liked it.

"I'm really happy for you, Robin," she said.

"Aww, thanks. I can't believe it's actually happening. It seems like yesterday when I was bitching about this day never coming. And now...wow! Hey, do you think my new black dress will look fine?"

Last night after work, Lara and I dashed over to buy a new dress for my big date. It looked lovely in the dressing room, covering the extra two dozen or so pounds of me I'd put on since I became pregnant. Although I wasn't so sure now, with only minutes before Bobby was to pick me up.

"Of course it'll look fine. Better than fine!" She blew away any excess powder on my face. "And he's going out with *you*, not your dress. I'm sure he couldn't care less about what you're wearing."

I gave myself one last look-over in the mirror once I was ready.

The gold heart pendant necklace that Lara lent me looked stunning with my solid black dress. And the dress itself really was both beautiful and comfortable. Probably my favorite maternity dress I owned, actually. It had t-shirt-like sleeves, and the neckline scooped down into a crescent-shape. Below the breast line it had a black ruche ribbon, giving way to an A-line skirt that fell right to the knees. The fabric was of high quality (for nearly two hundred big ones it ought to be), and it draped perfectly over my six-month pregnant tummy. I even managed to slip into a pair of my favorite statement-making ruby-red high heels. Special heels for a special occasion. I couldn't last long in them with all of the extra baby weight and the water I was retaining (and since my feet were so swollen), but for a date with Bobby I'd make it work.

I don't know why I doubted the dress. It was beautiful, and I thought I looked really nice in it. I wanted to look my best for Bobby without noticeably overdoing it, like I wasn't trying too hard. I'll admit, whenever I was around Bobby my self-esteem sort of got a boost. I felt beautiful, and more confident than usual. I felt, like he'd said at lunch the other day, really good around him. I felt like myself. And I was comfortable feeling like myself, and being simply Robin around him, even when six months pregnant.

Now I couldn't blow it. This was a big step in our relationship. The chips were falling, and I wanted them to fall in my favor, naturally. One side of my brain reminded me to take things slow. To think of my little girl, of the big changes going on in life. The other side was shouting out vociferously, "Land the man!"

"You're sure I look my best?" I asked Lara. I nervously picked at the hem of my dress. "Not over the top like I'm trying too hard, but I look...confident? Right? Comfy in my own shoes?"

"He won't be able to resist you," she said, looking at me fondly as I sat on the sofa, eagerly awaiting Bobby's arrival. "Now try not to be nervous, Robin. Think of this as another fun and easy-going lunch with him. Remember: Let the chips fall where they may. And have a good time!"

When Bobby arrived and I saw him standing at the door, his

auburn hair slightly slicked back with gel, a few stray locks freeing themselves and lying limply to one side, and his bright blue eyes, seeming to shine the moment he laid his eyes on me, I was positively smitten.

When he smiled and took my hand in his, telling me that I looked "exactly like an angel," I knew I was falling in love.

So much for taking things slow.

Bobby had made reservations at one of the finest restaurants in Seattle, located in one of the ritzy hotels downtown. It was the place to dine for many of the city's literati, well-to-do, and up-and-coming businessmen and artists. The price of the food nearly made me choke, but the taste was worth every heavy dollar. He insisted I order anything and everything I wanted from the menu, since we were both celebrating my stellar review at work (for a second time), and our first *official* date. Even though he made it clear that night that he considered most all of our lunches together dates. And the coffee runs, too.

"What?" I said, taking a sip of my sparkling water. "So those were all *secret* dates?"

"You know what I mean. No two co-workers go out together for lunch—just the two of them—*that* often. We definitely had some dates in there." He gave me a wink. "This one's only *official* because I finally worked up the nerve to ask you out, on a *date*, outside of work, for dinner. A real date."

"Been wanting to ask me out for a while, have you?" I was enjoying our lighthearted and flirtatious banter—this time without the pretense of a strict business lunch.

"You have no idea. I don't know if I should say this or not..."

I was madly curious; I urged him to share.

"Part of the reason I'd split up with Chrissy was because I'd been wanting to ask you out for a while. Things were already going sour with that relationship, but after you and I'd spent a little more time together...and I got to know you better...well...you charmed me, Robin."

"I don't want to be the cause of a breakup," I said, hoping to God that wasn't the case.

"No, no. That's not what I meant. That's why I wasn't sure if I should say anything or not." His voice was a tad hushed. "That's not it at all. It's only that you made me realize that sparks...that—that passion really *can* exist. I know that us dating is still very new. Obviously there are sparks." He smiled softly. "Being with you feels so natural. So right. I enjoy being with you."

"I enjoy being with you, too."

"I'm twenty-nine years old." He took a sip of wine. "I know what I want now. And that relationship wasn't it." He cupped my hand in his, his touch gentle, yet strong. "I'm really fond of you and I hope we can keep seeing each other."

"The date's not over yet, Bobby. You could run away screaming by the end of the night." I infused some humor into the conversation.

"What's that supposed to mean?" he said in response to my poor attempt at a joke.

"I'm only saying that, well, I come with a lot of baggage, as you know." I pointed to my stomach. I again reminded myself to listen to the rational side of my brain, arguing for moving slowly with Bobby, no matter how attracted to him I was, no matter how much I really did want a happily every after scenario. I told myself not to be cynical and expect all relationships to wind up in the gutter, however, but to still be reasonable and take things slowly, because I was living and planning for two now. My situation wasn't that of a typical single, twenty-five-year-old woman. I'd had a rough year, and there was a lot going on. Bobby could be a welcome addition to my life, but we'd have to move slowly. That's right, slowly. I couldn't take any heartbreak, if it came to that. And that's not being cynical. That's only being prepared. Being realistic. And life's a reality, not a fantasy, after all.

"I hope you understand," I added.

"Robin, we went over this yesterday." His voice was serious, yet still kind and warm. "I'm well aware that you're going to have a baby. That doesn't change anything for me. I told you: I'm twenty-nine; I know what I want in life, and I know what I don't want. How's this? Would it be too forward to ask for another date?"

"Wow," I said, surprised. I took a quick drink of my water. "This one's not even over yet, and you want another one? I'm flattered."

"Just trying to prove how serious I am about you. Is that too forward of me?"

"Not too forward at all," I said, and smiled. "I suppose I *was* waiting a long time for this first date."

"So was I." He leaned in closer to me across the small table that we shared. Then ever so slowly he pressed his lips softly against mine. He lingered for only a brief moment before he pressed them a bit further, still maintaining a balance between a soft and sweet kiss, and one filled with a pressing, fiery passion and desire.

When he pulled back we were both grinning.

"And I've been waiting to do *that* for a long time," he whispered.

Fast, slow, fast, slow. Oh, it's all so much for me to take in! So many emotions. So many changes. But, you know what? I feel happy. I feel really, really happy and all lit up inside. Maybe—slow and steady, of course—that whole happily ever after scenario isn't that unrealistic...

The enchanting evening came to a close shortly after midnight. Our date was magical, complete with dancing and even a horse-drawn carriage ride around Downtown. The sweet summer evening air coming off the water and breezing by, the secure touch of Bobby's arm wrapped around me tightly, and the unmistakable scent of Bobby's cologne were all like heavenly gifts on Earth. I thought that perhaps, only perhaps, this was where reality and fantasy could collide. I rested my head on Bobby's shoulder while he lightly rubbed my arm and pulled me close during the carriage ride. Being with Bobby like this, in a romantic and intimate way, the two of us outside of the constraints of the office, felt so natural and so right and so comfortable.

"Bobby?" I asked, trying to keep my eyes open and stay awake in the calming atmosphere.

"Yeah?"

"What's your cologne called?"

"Calvin Klein's Eternity." He squeezed me tight and kissed the top of my head.

"Eternity," I whispered, dancing my fingers on his chest as I closed my eyes and buried myself in the rapturous moment.

Eternity—precisely how long I want to stay like this, together, wrapped in each other's arms.

18

I was nearing my third trimester, and I was on top of the world! Work was going fantastic. Bobby and I were dating, going out for dinner and a movie, or for coffee, or even the old-fashioned lunch dates a few times a week. My baby shower was almost here, to which my mom and my sister had actually R.S.V.P.'d. All of the baby's furniture for the room was put together and set up, then moved out of my room, then back in again.

See, Lara decided my room had to be made into more of a nursery than a bedroom/nursery, and insisted she paint the walls pink. So she charged herself and Jackie with the task one very long (and loud) night, and ordered that I take the time to steer clear of the paint fumes by way of the shopping mall. So Sophie and Claire took me shopping for some new, larger, and much-needed maternity clothes. And, since we couldn't resist, we did some shopping for the baby, too.

I think if Lara had known what a lousy sleeper I had become since I became pregnant, she wouldn't have chosen to paint my room and claim me as her new bed mate for the next couple of nights. No matter which way I lay down, how I propped up my pillow, situated my blankets, or curled up my knees, I couldn't lie still for very long.

It seemed like the baby was sitting on my chest, making it extremely difficult to breathe when lying down. And I couldn't very well sleep sitting up. The nights were long, back-achingly sore, and very distracting for poor Lara. By the third and final night that we anticipated I'd need to keep clear of sleeping in my freshly painted room, I slept on the sofa so Lara could finally get a good night's rest.

Problem was, I couldn't get any more comfortable on the sofa. And the distracting noise of Beebee's cacophonous purr was driving me batty.

"What's the use?" I said, flipping the television on and instantly turning the volume to a hair above mute. I mindlessly flipped through the program guide, noncommittally settling on some HBO film I knew I'd seen before.

In the wee hours of the morning I found myself doing some sketching, shooting Emily a friendly email, and eventually, around four in the morning or so, falling asleep.

It was the strong aroma of freshly brewed coffee that stirred me from my peaceful slumber, only to be slightly disappointed that I couldn't partake in the drinking of the delightful morning beverage.

"Morning, sleepy head," Lara said, dressed and ready for yet another day at the office. "Why'd you sleep on the sofa?"

I rubbed at my sleep-crusted eyes and stole a glance at the clock on the wall. Luckily I still had another hour before work—plenty of time for me to throw something on and head out.

"I've bothered you enough. I'm always tossing and turning. Can't have you head off to work all exhausted." I yawned, louder than expected. "Man, will *I* be exhausted at work today."

"What are you talking about, you goofball?" Lara pulled a box of cereal from the cupboard. "Since when did you work Saturdays?"

"What? Are you serious?" I racked my brain and realized it was, in fact, Saturday. "Thank goodness! I'm exhausted! I don't know how I would've managed work today."

I took Lara's advice and crashed in her bed for a good three hours or so. The baby shower was planned for that afternoon, but not until midday (I nearly forgot about it with all the chaos of painting the room), so I had plenty of time to catch up on my much-needed zzzs.

Before I situated myself in the most appealing position I could find (wedged between two body pillows, and one thick, down pillow propped under my head), my cell phone vibrated. I snagged it from the nightstand. A text message from Bobby. In spite of my exhaustion, I opened his message.

Hey beautiful. Have a great baby shower. Been thinking about you. See you on Mon. PS-looking forward to lunch. The best part of work now. :)

Bobby. What a catch, I thought. I tossed my cell phone to the end of the bed and snuggled tightly to my pillow.

What a lucky, lucky girl I am. To have someone so sweet want to be with me...to have someone so special...

And I slowly drifted back to sleep, dreaming not of fantasies of Bobby as Tarzan, and I as Jane, or some other flighty fantasy. But of the possible reality that Bobby could be that Mr. Right that Lara and I were always talking about. Life had thrown me stranger things; why couldn't that be a possibility? Even a probability?

"Hey, Lara," I said, turning off the blow dryer. I was in the middle of getting ready for my baby shower. My long morning nap and bath afterward had left me feeling refreshed.

"What's up, babe?" she answered from my bedroom. She'd been scurrying about gathering all sorts of things and reorganizing furniture, I gathered from the sounds coming from her hitting the walls with God knows what. She insisted that I see my completed bedroom/nursery before we headed to Claire's for the baby shower.

"You want to be my Lamaze partner?" I asked.

I read in *You're Going to Be a Mother* that all first-time moms should sign up for a Lamaze training class so they'd be as prepared as possible for labor. There were a lot of natural child labor instructional classes around town, led by people called doulas, who were these really cool childbirth coaches—very popular all over Seattle, apparently. I'd seen a couple of advertisements at coffee shops and grocery stores recently. There was a four-week-long Lamaze workshop offered throughout the month of October at one of labor centers next door in Fremont.

"Oh my gosh, I totally forgot about Lamaze," Lara said, passing by my bathroom on her way back out to the living room. "Of course I'll be your partner." She dashed by again, carrying something into my room.

"Classes are every Saturday in October, nine to noon. Can you make it?"

"Definitely!" She popped her head around the corner. "All right. You can come in now."

"*Oooh.* I'm finally allowed to enter my bedroom. After, like, three days?"

Lara impatiently grabbed hold of my arm and led me into my bedroom, instructing me to close my eyes until she said I could open them.

"Mmm. It doesn't smell like paint. That's good."

"Okay. One...two...three...open!"

The bedroom's walls were the daintiest shade of soft pink—not overdone as I was afraid it might be with wall-to-wall paint. The intricate crown molding up top separated the pink nicely from the white ceiling, easing the transition of color. And the new chair rail molding that was recently installed looked beautiful. And! Oh! The darker shade of pink right below the white molding! Lara and Jackie really outdid themselves.

"It's beautiful!" I cried, clasping my hands to my mouth. "It really is beautiful."

"You like it?"

"Are you kidding? Lara, I *love* it."

I walked towards the crib, which had been set up in the corner opposite my bed, adorned with the cutest pink and cream bedding that I picked up at Pottery Barn recently, not caring one iota about the steep price tag. It was exactly what I imagined my baby girl sleeping in the day I brought her home.

"And the rocking chair! Oh it looks perfect in the corner." I took a seat in the vintage rocking chair that I had refurbished a soft cream color, then distressed slightly. It may not have matched the rest of the very modern furniture all that well, but I saw a version of it one day when I was wasting time on Pinterest and knew I had to have something just like it for my nursery. It seemed like the ideal piece you could hand down to your children some day, something you'd keep in the family and always find a use for.

"Lara, you guys really outdid yourselves."

"Jackie did nearly all the chair rail molding herself," Lara said, impressed.

"Wow! Who would have thought our little Jack was a carpenter?"

I didn't want to tear myself from the room; it was so breathtaking, and more than I could have ever wished for. All of the furniture was assembled, the paint was on the walls, the decorative touches were up—and it had my girlfriends written all over it. We'd all come together to help make Baby's room positively perfect. Now all we needed was for Baby to arrive!

"Come on, we don't want to miss out on your special day." Lara ushered me to the bathroom, assisting with the finishing touches of makeup and helping me put on my shoes since I was pretty much helpless in that department now. Bending over was a thing of the past.

"You look fan-damn-tastic!" Lara said, spritzing me one time with a quick shot of Ralph Lauren's Romance, my signature scent since sophomore year in college.

"I feel fan-damn-tastic!" I looked at myself in the mirror, feeling like a genuine princess.

Since the theme was "sugar and spice and everything nice," and pink would no doubt be *the* color of the afternoon, I picked out (with the girls' help, naturally) the most beautiful pink dress. It was more of a hot pink or a watermelon pink than the typical pastel baby shade. It was a long and flowing chiffon dress, with thin spaghetti straps and an adorable ruche in the bra area where the folds of the fabric came together in a twist, then splayed out to the back of the dress. A loose bow draped from below the back waist and spilled on downward. Sophie had found the most befitting walnut-colored gladiator-style sandals with small gold snaps. September was still seeing some very warm weather, so I jumped at the opportunity to wear one more fabulous summer ensemble before my baby arrived.

"Let's get the woman of the hour to her party already!" Lara said, grabbing our handbags and leading the way to her car.

Everything about the baby shower was absolute perfection. The girls outdid themselves, transforming Claire's backyard into a paradise of pink. There were pink balloons, streamers, and a banner over the deck reading "Congratulations! It's a Girl!" One long picnic table covered in lace and a pink tablecloth was set up in the yard, leaving an expanse of freshly cut grass set up for a round of croquette. Small table and chair groupings were arranged around the yard, too, all decorated to match the pretty-in-pink-style decor. It was all so very shabby-chic, like something you'd see in one of those design or DIY craft magazines. It had the handiwork of Claire written all over it, especially the miniature cloth diapers, no bigger than the size of coasters, which were embroidered with the guests' names and used as place settings. As it turned out, Claire had made those herself, insisting the hankies-disguised-as-diapers were the cutest take-me-home gifts for everyone. Right on theme, of course.

It was, in every sense of the words, "sugar and spice and everything nice." Pieces of assorted pink candies and treats were arranged in tea cups. Heart-shaped confetti and glitter littered the buffet table, on which, per my wishes, was a three-tier cupcake stand, holding miniature marzipan and strawberry cupcakes.

"Guys!" I cried. I was so overjoyed and touched. "This is all amazing!"

Lara gave me a big squeeze before taking my handbag and wrap from me.

"So happy you love it," Claire said, giving me a hug and a kiss on the cheek. Her Jack Russell Terrier mix, Schnickerdoodle, jumped repeatedly in excitement up against her, wanting in on the festivities and fun, too.

"Congratulations!" Sophie said. She started passing around pink lemonade, served in mason jars that were tied at the lip with pink ribbons.

"You look *great*, sis," Kaitlyn said, giving me a hug. "Congratulations."

"Mom," I said, as my mother came up from behind Kaitlyn, lemonade in-hand, her arms loosely crossed. "Mom, I'm so glad you could come."

"Congratulations, Robin," she said timidly, her face telling me she didn't want to impose.

"This is going to be a *fun* time!" I said aloud, although more as a warning to my mother than as an exclamation. I wanted to make it clear to her that there was to be no drama at this party, although I was sure she wouldn't pull any wayward antics or razz me in front of everyone. She nodded her head obligingly and took a long pull on her drink.

"So," Claire said, once everyone had greeted each other and was working on their second helpings of lemonade. "Buffet-style finger foods for lunch. Cupcakes for dessert. For starters, though, we have some fun games planned. The first one you've all probably heard of. It's kind of gross, but it's really fun."

Jackie came out onto the deck from inside the house balancing two TV trays holding what looked like baby diapers.

"You have to guess the melted candy bars that are in the diapers," Claire said. "Most correct guesses wins a prize!"

Laughter and whispering commenced; it was the classic (and rather disgusting) baby shower game of candy bar baby poo.

The game, and the similar and equally entertaining ones that followed, were great icebreakers for my mom and Kaitlyn. Get me and all my friends together and we could start up a party like nothing. The games were a smooth and cute way to get things going, get everyone comfortable, and get into the spirit of the baby-themed party.

Then came gift time, and, I won't lie, I was *really* looking forward to it. I'd already received so many baby and maternity clothes from the girls, not to mention help with a dreamy nursery, but let's face it—who doesn't adore the gift-giving that comes with birthdays and Christmases and anniversaries, and now, for me, baby showers? When I caught sight of the table covered in pink bags and boxes, I couldn't wait to find out what my little girl was getting!

"This one's from the both of us. A together, team-effort gift," Sophie said, motioning to her and Claire and handing me an envelope.

"A day at the spa!" I exclaimed, reading quickly over the pamphlet that accompanied the gift certificate, which was made out to "Robin, the Mom-to-Be." My eyes scanned over the words: *Full-body prenatal massage...Aromatherapy...Paraffin treatment...Mani and Pedi...Facial...*

"Girls," I exclaimed. "This is *amazing!* Thank you."

"And I don't know if it says it on there or not, or if you saw it," Sophie said, "but a chauffeured town car will pick you up and take you home, too. It's a full-on relaxation treatment. All about the mom-to-be."

"Thank you." I gave them each a hug, then passed the pamphlet around for everyone to see.

I reached over to the next gift, a very large box wrapped in solid, bright pink paper, with a gigantic bow on top. Terribly curious what surprise lay in wait, I ripped apart the paper rapaciously.

"Oh my God!" I shrieked, bouncing in my chair. "I can't believe you got this! Who got this?"

It was the mechanical and musical baby swing that I wanted the moment I'd laid eyes on it in this really chic and high-priced boutique over in Belltown.

"It was my pleasure," Jackie said, grinning shyly.

"Jack!" I gasped. "You didn't need to get me *this* expensive thing. This *exact* one. Any swing would have been fine." I knew the price tag of this deluxe swing. The tag was the very reason I didn't snatch it up the day I'd seen it in the store during one afternoon when Sophie, Jackie and I had been doing some window-shopping.

"*Now* you tell me," Jackie kidded. "No, honestly, it was my pleasure. You and your baby deserve that awesome swing."

"Did—"

"No!" she retorted, knowing at exactly what I was hinting. "Andrew did *not* buy it. I actually bought this with my *own* cash."

"Robin," Lara said to me in a scolding tone. I suppose I'd forgotten it wasn't our usual group of girls together. When it was just us, we'd casually poke fun and joked with one another—really no topic was off-limits. I could imagine what my mother must have been thinking.

"Sorry, Jackie. I didn't mean anything by—"

"Forget it. Andrew may wine and dine me and buy me, well, everything I want. But when it comes to my friends *I'm* the one doing the shopping." I pulled her into a hug and whispered in her ear that I loved her.

Jackie and I didn't always see eye-to-eye, that was obvious. It was no secret to me that she wasn't always fond of the way Lara and I palled around together, especially now that Lara and I were roommates. Jackie was bigger than the petty things, though, even if I sometimes thought she wanted to catfight with me when she heard that Lara and I had gone out for dinner together, or that we had decided to check out the newest romcom on our own. Our friendship was bigger than the tiniest, and the heaviest, of problems.

"I love ya, too, Robin," Jackie whispered back. She gave me a light spank. "Now get back to opening the rest of your gifts already!"

The girls spoiled me and my little one rotten. By the time I was finished unwrapping all of the presents, I was up a deluxe baby swing, a Baby Bjorn carrier, dozens of baby clothes in all sorts of colors, with different patterns, and some Winnie the Pooh characters —onesies, dresses, tiny t-shirts, even blue jeans and overalls. I'd gained more socks in sizes from newborn to twenty-four months than I thought I'd ever need, and plenty of burp rags, pacifiers, newborn baby bottles, one-year-old baby bottles, even two-year-old baby bottles, and some sippy-cups. I'd gotten everything from rattles and teething trinkets, to *Baby Einstein* DVDs, teddy bears, and chunky cardboard books teaching Baby the 1-2-3s and A-B-Cs. Claire even knitted me a baby blanket, saying she tried to match the yarn to the pink shade of my crib decor as best she could. And, I couldn't forget the all-inclusive prenatal spa day. Make out like a bandit? I think so!

"I don't know what to say." I looked at the gifts that littered the table and spilled all around it. "You guys all rock. Thank you. And thank you for coming! This party is more...much more...than I imagined!"

"And, that's not all," Kaitlyn said, walking towards the deck and disappearing into the house, my mom hot on her heels.

I looked around at everyone, asking if they knew what was going on.

More gifts? Some extra surprise?

No one said a word; they smiled and waited.

"Surprise!" Kaitlyn shouted, my mom pushing a grey Schwinn jogger stroller out onto the deck. "Something for you *and* the baby."

Mom pushed over the stroller, encouraging me to try out the smooth handgrips. "It's perfect, since you're a runner. It's supposed to be top-of-the-line." Her voice started out chipper and kind, then, as if she realized she was showing her soft side, she firmed up and said, "That's what they say anyway. What the sales clerk said. What your sister says."

"Mom," I said, peeling my eyes away from what I figured was the most impressive stroller on the market. I couldn't believe I had such a stroller. And from my mom. "That's too much. On top of every-thing else you got me?"

She waved her hand in front of my mouth and told me to hush. "Well, Grandma can't be a complete ass. Needs to do some of that usual grandmother spoiling stuff. And plus, you'll be needing to get back into shape once that baby comes out. Run off all that baby weight."

Good God, here we go. Can a gift just ever be a gift? A kind gesture

SAVANNAH PAGE

remain a kind gesture? A sentiment be only a sentiment?

Kaitlyn stepped in. "I think it was a great choice, Mom. It's perfect for Robin." She gave a weak smile, bobbing her head as if to say, "Let's change the subject. Sorry!"

"So does this mean my little girl can call you Grandma?" I asked. I know she was never fond of being called Grandma, having Kaitlyn's two children refer to her as Nanny.

Mom laughed her high-pitched cackle. "Yeah, right. I'm Nanny to your little girl. Make sure she knows that. No one's going to be calling me Grandma."

"Cupcakes, anyone?" Claire and Lara asked in unison, Lara holding up a pot of coffee that appeared seemingly from nowhere.

"I think it's dessert time," Sophie said. She was stuffing the wrapping paper, bows, and ribbons into a large trash sack. "Definitely time for some dessert."

"I agree," Kaitlyn said. She nudged Mom's back as they made their way to the buffet table.

I mouthed a "thank you" to my sister and she mouthed back a "no problem."

"I love you, Mom," I said, sighing and following them over to the picnic table. "Thanks again for the stroller. It's really cool."

She responded with a simple grin and a nod of the head as she held up her teacup for Lara to pour her coffee.

Can't win them all.

I glanced up at the large oak tree. Its leaves and new branches were swaying considerably with the light breeze. A grey cloud, looking heavy with rain, passed slowly in front of the sun, casting interesting shadows over the grass and the flowerbeds that lined all three sides of the backyard. The chatter was resuming once again. Spontaneous giggling and story-swapping circulated the tables, along with some news updates. Ironically enough, a robin, of all birds, landed for only an instant on the handle bars of my new stroller and gave a few tweets, as if chirping her own well-wishes, before flying off over the oak tree, and swooping down into the adjacent yard.

210

19

"Are you sure we're doing this right?" I asked, my knees drawn up to what felt like my chin, the weight of my upper body clumsily burying into Lara's upper body as she sat with me on the yoga mat. She was supporting the weight of us both with her hands splayed behind her, an angled (and very uncomfortable) position.

"It's what everyone else is doing," she muttered.

"Well it doesn't feel very good."

"It's not supposed to. That's not the purpose of the exercise."

I blew out a quick puff of air. It felt like a twenty-pound brick was resting underneath my breasts.

"Now, this position is supposed to be very calming. Very *relaaaxing*," the Lamaze instructor cooed, walking around the room of yoga mats, inspecting the couples seated on them.

"See," I said to Lara, trying to keep my voice low. We'd already been asked once by the instructor, Sky, to keep to our library voices. "I told you it's supposed to be a comfy position. And I am *not* comfy."

"That makes two of us." Lara tried to heave herself further up, pushing me right with her.

"Ow, ow. Stop moving."

"Ladies?" Sky asked, bending down to us. "Is everything all right?"

"I think we're doing this all wrong. This is anything but comfortable and soothing," I said.

Sky helped me up into a seated position; Lara readjusted her position on the mat. Sky said we could give it another go when I was ready. This time Sky helped ease me back, trying to help me find the right way to fall into Lara's chest. My chin was smashed on my own chest, and what I thought was belabored breathing earlier, was even more so this time around.

"No, no," I whined, my arms flailing as I tried to pull myself up out of the position. "Not going to happen. I can barely breathe."

Sky rubbed at her jaw, poised in thought. "Baby's still sitting up high. Feels like a ton of pressure sitting on your chest, correct?"

I nodded, wincing.

"Baby hasn't dropped yet."

"Dropped?"

Sky explained that at some point during the last trimester, as the due date neared, the baby would turn and drop, getting ready for that "thrilling rite of passage, the ride through the birthing canal," as Sky so romantically described it.

"Yeah, think I read about that somewhere," I said casually. I made a motion to Lara to not bother with another try at the position. No one in hell could make me sit like that again so long as I was carrying around a watermelon on my chest.

"We like it when our mommies have dropped babies during Lamaze. Makes it easier for exercises like these." Sky walked to the front of the class and fished for a piece of paper on the table.

Lara and I giggled like children at Sky's choice of words: "dropped babies." She returned with a diagram of a couple doing a modified exercise. She told us to try it out for ourselves and see if it helped with the breathing and pressure.

Turns out this modified exercise worked out well, and it actually did help relieve the backaches, like the original exercise intended. Lara and I decided we'd try it out one night when we were sitting in front of the TV watching yet another episode of *90210*. Lara joked that show had become a preggo craving just like my food cravings. (Little did she know I anticipated still having that "craving" long after the baby was born. Had she truly forgotten what it was like living with me during college? Some things never change.)

"How'd you think we did? B plus? Minus?" I asked as Lara unlocked the front door of our apartment. She flicked on the overhead lights, a slow-burning, golden glow cast across the living room, the eco-friendly power-saving bulbs creeping to life. Beebee, obviously startled, made a fast dash from the recliner and into Lara's bedroom.

Lara tossed her keys onto the coffee table, careful not to walk any further into the apartment with her soaked and muddy shoes. Summer was disappearing, autumn swooping down upon us with a hellish thunderstorm and dark downpour hitting us, no joke, the *instant* we left our first Lamaze class. "Minus. For sure! Definitely a B minus for that course."

"It *was* pretty awful." I took off my shoes and tiptoed, soggy socks and all, into the kitchen so I could set down the bags of burgers and fries we picked up for lunch. "Of course the super healthy doughnuts we had for breakfast probably didn't help us out."

"And our greasy burgers aren't going to do us any better," Lara said with a laugh.

"Got to live a little." Now and then a woman, even a pregnant woman (maybe even *especially* a pregnant woman), deserved to splurge on something that didn't follow the strict and healthy guidelines of the dietary rulebook.

"We'll do better next week. And we weren't *that* bad. Besides, it was tough for you; your baby hasn't dropped yet, or whatever Aura called it."

"Sky. Not Aura. Sky."

"Aura, Sky, whatever," Lara dismissed. "Some hippie name."

I carried our plates of greasy food into the living room, actually excited to pop in the birthing tutorial DVD Sky sent home with us. A good two minutes in on the section "Delivery," however, and I was ready to find some *92010* re-runs, or some HBO film I'd already seen a dozen times, or even a CNN World Report. Anything but a preview of what I was to experience firsthand in, oh, T-minus two months and counting.

"No way. No how," I said, shutting the production down. "No way in hell am I watching that."

"Robin, don't you at least want to know what you're in for?"

I gave Lara a blank stare. "What for? There's no going back. If I absolutely have to do that—and I *do* have to give birth—then I'll find out when that day arrives. It's not like I can prepare for that kind of trauma anyway."

"That's what Lamaze is, goober. Preparation."

"No. Forget it. Lamaze can teach me to breathe and count and remain calm. When it comes to *that*," I pointed at the blank screen, "forget about it." I headed into my bathroom, overdue for a shower and a change out of the confining yoga clothes. I had a coffee date with Kaitlyn in a few hours and I didn't want to go looking like I was minutes away from labor and delivery.

"Would you say it's serious?" Kaitlyn asked, sipping on her mocha frappé-style drink. I stole a finger swipe of her whipped cream topping.

God, I'm really sucking it up with my preggo diet today.

"I think it's definitely heading in that direction," I said. "Bobby and I seem to have a real connection. It's indescribable, really."

Kaitlyn and I met at Randy's, a friendly bookstore and café that I'd been frequenting since the college days. She stole a few hours away from the kids, leaving them with Dad, and we were finally enjoying the sister date we'd been trying to plan for months.

"He's a special guy, Robin? Like, 'the One' material, you think?"

I bashfully stirred my nearly cooled mug of tea. "Well...I don't want to jump the gun or anything. And we're taking things really slow. I told him I wanted it that way. You know, with the baby and all. With all these big changes and everything, slow is good."

"Things can still be slow but serious."

"Oh they're definitely serious." A smile spread across my face; I couldn't hold it back. Simply thinking about Bobby, about the way he dramatically draws his hand out when he holds the door open for me, saying in the cutest way, "After you, my Lady." Or the way he absentmindedly scratches at the back of his neck when he's deep in thought, or runs his fingers through his hair when he's answering a question of which he isn't sure the answer. Or that endearing way he presses one hand on the small of my back, and draws my chin near his, kissing me tenderly, at first slowly, supplely, and then with a steady increase of depth and pressure, yet still gracefully.

"Robin," Kaitlyn said, waving a few fingers in front of me. "Hel-loooo. Ran off to dream world there?"

"Exactly. I'm seeing stars with this one, Kaitlyn. Having those sparks. And *he* is, too."

"It sounds like you two have something. Something pretty special."

Like a love-struck teenager, I rested my chin in my palms and stared up at the ceiling, sighing deeply. "I'm falling in love with him, Katilyn." I looked in her eyes. "And it scares the crap out of me."

"Naturally it's scary. It's *love.* It's new, it's exciting, it's *real.* It's normal to be a little scared."

"I don't want to ruin things between us. Like I'm scared that I'll give up my hopes and he'll leave. Or that me having a baby will eventually scare him off. He says he knows what he wants...even told me he, unlike his last girlfriend, wants children. But...wanting mine? It's hard to believe, I guess."

"You've talked about it, though?" Katilyn took a drink.

"Yeah. Of course we've discussed it. He told me he knows what he wants and what he doesn't want." I slightly grinned. "He said he wants to keep seeing me. That he knows I come with a baby and he's completely fine with it."

"But you're not sure?"

SAVANNAH PAGE

"Exactly. I'm scared. No, I'm terrified. Robin? Find true love? And while *pregnant*? Pardon my language, but what the fuck?"

Kaitlyn guffawed loudly then took another pull on her drink.

"I'm serious!" I said, lowering my voice when I noticed there were several people within earshot who probably didn't appreciate my word choice. "What if things don't end up working out? They're great now, but what about when the baby's actually here? Will Bobby be ready for that? Can he really commit to a relationship with a woman who has a newborn?" I shook my head, as if in disbelief that such a fantasy—that Bobby would almost act as the adoptive father to my daughter—could become a reality.

"Time will tell, huh?"

"Yeah," I sighed. "Time will tell. I'm scared that time will tell me what I don't want to hear. And then I'll be alone. *Again*. I'm terrified of being alone, Kaitlyn."

"You're not alone," she said. "You're never alone." Those familiar words that my girlfriends told me time and again. They were right; I needed to remember that—play those words over and over.

"If things end up really working out with you and Bobby," Kaitlyn said, wiping a touch of cream from her lips, "you definitely won't be alone. And even if things don't work out with him...you still won't be alone. You've got a lot of support and love, Robin. Come on. Let's finish our drinks and then I'll show you some of the books I was talking about that have all sorts of neat and helpful information about infants."

The following evening, while I was skimming through the three new infant care books Kaitlyn recommended I read, I received a call from Bobby. It was nearly ten o'clock, rather late for him to be calling since he knew I was a stickler about getting to bed at a decent hour when I had work the next morning.

"How's my beautiful woman?" Bobby asked.

"Hey, Bobby. I'm doing great. What are you up to so late?"

"Yeah, I know it's late, but I wanted to hear your voice."

Such a charmer.

"Here it is, sweetie," I said softly. It still felt odd to be calling each

216

other pet names, and I blamed the start of it entirely on Bobby. One day he called me "sugar" and then over a sack lunch one day in the break room he called me "honey," so I went along with it.

Who am I kidding? I was on cloud nine whenever Bobby called me one of his adoring pet names. Even him saying my name was nice, knowing that I was no longer "Miss Sinclair, the co-worker."

"I'm bummed we didn't get to see each other this weekend. A whole weekend without you was rough."

"Well I had my first Lamaze class yesterday. Then coffee with Kaitlyn, which, by the way, went really well."

"Awesome. I'm happy to hear that. Glad you guys are reconnecting."

"And then of course I had the most *a-ma-zing* spa day today. The best day, ever." The pre-natal spa date Sophie and Claire gave me was pure heaven. By far one of the most exorbitant gifts I'd ever received.

"Your girls one-upped our first date, huh?"

"Ohhh, I'd say maybe an even tie."

"Is that so? Maybe I need to up the ante then."

"I'd like to see that."

"Well, Miss Thing wants to take things slow. I've got to be an upstanding gentleman and all..." I rolled my eyes, seeing that one coming a mile away. "But once a gentleman, always a gentleman. If that's the way my girlfriend wants things, that's how she'll have them."

It was the first time Bobby referred to me as his girlfriend. Were we, in fact, exclusive? I honestly hadn't given much thought to it, but considering how we were spending a lot of time together, going out on romantic dates, sharing our lunch hour together at work every day...I suppose we were an item. I suppose we *were* boyfriend and girlfriend. I wasn't seeing anyone else. (And I didn't want to or plan on it.) I was certain Bobby wasn't seeing anyone else. Where would either of us find the time, anyway? When we weren't sleeping (or having baby showers and luxurious spa days), we were together—at work, on dates, you name it.

"Girlfriend, huh?" I kept my voice as playful as his.

"I assume so. Did I assume wrong? Seeing another Prince Charming?"

"Of course not." I bit down on my bottom lip, unsure of what to say next. I was relieved when he took the liberty.

"I've told the boys at work that my girlfriend is the amazing graphic artist, and determined-to-be project manager of the new *chick lit* author our firm *has* to get. The one and only Miss Robin Sinclair."

"People at work know?" I asked, somewhat astonished.

"Uh-oh. Should we keep it under wraps? Someone ashamed to call me her boyfriend?"

"Ha. Ha. I didn't think about it, that's all. But we are official. We have been going out for a while...I *am* falling for you...*fallen* for you, I should say." I left room with my pauses for kittenish remarks. "I guess all of those lunches together would leave people talking around the office. And the kisses, too. Not too good at hiding those..."

"Aw, Robin, you're amazing," he sighed. "I've fallen *hard* for you and I'm enjoying every minute of it. I'll let you get some sleep now."

"Goodnight, Bobby," I said softly.

"Goodnight, honey."

Since Bobby and I had made it "official" a few days earlier, I wanted to lay something out on the table that'd been bothering me for a while. Complete honesty. Janet's vindictive mention about Bobby buttering me up for the promotion, so he could squeeze by, become my best right-hand man, then say, "See ya!" and move on to greener pastures—I couldn't shake it from my mind. I know it was a ridiculous thought, "totally absurd," as Lara had put it. However, I wasn't completely convinced. I needed to do what my gut was telling me and put it out there. If Bobby and I were an official pair, now, he'd have to get used to listening to my thoughts, no matter how obscure they were. And as secure as I felt around him, as comfortable as I felt being me and feeling confident when I was with him, I couldn't help but hear the nagging voice in my head warning me that something would spoil this fantasy-turned-reality. Maybe Bobby *was* only with me for the stupid reasons Janet said. Sure, he'd said he didn't want the PM position in the interest of the firm and his own career goals, but what about going at it from a different angle? Going through me somehow? What if Bobby did have an angle, and I was the pathetic pawn in it all?

I unwrapped the sandwich I'd hastily packed for lunch that morning. My mind was buzzing with thoughts of how I'd delicately tell Bobby what was on my mind. I didn't want to hurt him or accuse him of something I hoped to God was false, yet I needed to dispel the thoughts and ill feelings by laying it out there.

"Come on, Robin. What is it?" Bobby urged, caressing my forearm. The weather had surprised us with a tepid day with more sunshine than rainclouds, so we took our sack lunches out on the bistro table on the sidewalk outside the office.

I glanced up at a co-worker who passed by on his way to his car in the parking lot. I made sure the co-worker was in his car, door shut, and no one else was around. When all was clear, I told Bobby not to think that I was stupid or childish or petty. Sometimes I could be irrational—a trait enhanced by being pregnant, but also what came with my unfortunate general lack of confidence. I told him Janet's stupid theory about why he was suddenly interested in me, why she thought he turned on the charm and, as she said that morning, that "Bobby's only using you by making you his girlfriend now. *How* convenient."

"That couldn't be further from the truth," he said, his face turned down, the veins in his neck starting to push forward. "That's deplorable. Nothing could be further from the truth!"

I told him to calm down, that I was sorry for bringing it up.

"No," he said, trying to relax. "Don't be sorry. It was on your mind and I want you to feel like you can talk to me about anything. You need to follow your heart, though." He took my hands in his. "Ignore what Janet, a miserable woman with no one to love, thinks about us. You know none of that's true."

"But why now? Why me and now?" I asked, still wanting to press the matter, not because I actually believed Janet's stupid theory, but because why on Earth would someone like Bobby, such an amazing man who could probably have a handful of women out there, want to be with me? And at eight months pregnant!

"Robin," he said, his voice stern. "I'm going to tell you something."

I nodded my head slowly.

Dear God, what is he going to say?

"I've said it before. I'll say it again. Your being pregnant has no bearing, *whatsoever*, on the situation. I would have asked you out whether or not you were pregnant. Whether you were caught up in some custody battle with the father...even having to split time with the baby, seeing him. So long as we were both single, I would have asked. Hell, I probably would have asked you even if you *were* seeing someone. *Not* that I condone sweeping a girl off her feet and out of the arms of another dude. Not cool." He pulled in closer to me, leaning over the table, my hands still tightly clenched in his. "But knowing what I know now. Knowing you. Knowing how I feel about you. About what I feel when I see you walk into a room. When I'm around you—I couldn't imagine life without you now, Robin.

"So I'll say it again, once more. I'm not trying to sabotage your career or advance mine by making you my girlfriend. I'm not trying to weasel my way into anything. I'm not with you because you're pregnant and single and I feel sorry for you or anything ridiculous like that. In fact, if I had my head on straight, I would have asked you out years ago." He glanced down at the table, then looked back up at me, straight into my eyes. "I've fallen for you, Robin. Fallen hard. I'm with you simply because...because I've fallen in love with you."

I swallowed the lump that had been forming in my throat the instant he said he had something to tell me. My feelings for Bobby were, without a hint of doubt, reciprocated.

I felt my stomach flip, and I thought they were butterflies, until I recognized the peculiar movement. I was feeling my little girl kicking, rolling around.

"Oh my goodness," I said, clutching my stomach.

Bobby jumped forward out of his chair slightly, alarmed. "You all right?"

"Yes," I said, grinning widely. "Yes, yes. Here, feel." I grabbed his hand and placed it on my stomach as my baby girl continued kicking and moving.

"I think she's celebrating!" I laughed, tears springing to my eyes. "She liked your little speech there, Bobby." She kept fluttering about, a small nub apparent to the naked eye, right there through my shirt, skirting across my stomach. "My God! Look! You can see her!" I gently touched the moving button, Bobby's hand moving with mine.

I looked up at him, wiped a strain of tears from my cheek, and said, "I've never felt her move so much. This is amazing. This is incredible! I think she really is celebrating, Bobby."

With one hand still on my stomach, feeling the constant kicks and movements of my baby, he brushed away the last tears from my cheek with a soft swipe of his thumb. His ocean blue eyes looked deeply into mine, lightening up to an even bluer shade, as he smiled, and said, "I love you, Robin."

"I love you, too, Bobby." I sniffed back my tears and met him halfway for the most passionate, most beautiful, and most meaningful kiss I'd ever had.

20

The final Lamaze class went very well. Lara and I were confident we knew all the proper breathing and relaxing exercises. We knew more than we wanted to about things that can tear, needed to be stretched, massaged—the works. We were well-prepared for when the baby would arrive. I was approaching my last full month of pregnancy and couldn't wait to meet my little girl. She'd been doing a lot of moving in recent weeks, and Sky said she had dropped. I was well on my way to delivering very soon.

Naturally, when the girls heard that my baby was getting into position for birth, they agreed we were in need of one final girls' night before the big moment. Location: not a bar or a club or the usual spot with loud music and dancing. Jackie and Claire had originally suggested we go to The Clubhouse, a converted warehouse-turned-bar that was, in spite of its rowdily suggestive name, a low-key, but high-on-fun bar in Capitol Hill. But Lara chimed in with me when I suggested that it was probably best I put my club-visits on hold for a while. And, as they reassured me, there'd be plenty of time in the future to toast with a cosmo and hit the dance floor, all the girls together again going out for a night. This time, however, with my daughter's due date right around the corner, we decided to head over to Josephine's and Josie's, a very laid-back coffeehouse that often hosted poetry readings, book signings, and the occasional weekend evening piano or guitar performance.

All of us, save for Sophie, who was spending the weekend at her parents' in Santa Barbara saying goodbye to her brother before he left for London, got dolled up for the special acoustical guitar duo performance that night. Although I'd found myself the designated driver in a few situations since I became preggers, I could no longer fit behind the wheel. So Jackie did what Jackie does best, and she called for a stretch limo, saying that Andrew wouldn't mind. "We have to go in *style* for your last night out before the baby's here," Jackie had insisted.

It was a bummer that we couldn't manage to gather everyone together, but lately it was a miracle we could find a weekend when Jackie was free. As great as Andrew was (and Jackie reminded us on several occasions how fabulous and generous he was), he did demand a lot of Jackie's attention and time. He traveled a lot, but when he *was* in town he wanted Jackie by his side, no questions. When she said she was free this weekend we pounced; not like I had that many free weekends left before it would be all about midnight feedings, diaper changes, and possibly something I recently read in my new infant books called colic. Sometimes I was really nervous about the big delivery day, then I'd think about finally getting to meet my daughter and I'd get excited. Still so very unreal, yet somehow, at the same time, it all felt very real.

Things were going spectacularly with Bobby. I still couldn't believe I was in love with the most incredible man. I mean, these kinds of stories exist in fantasy only! The stuff fairy tales are made of. (Even though Snow White and Sleeping Beauty weren't knocked up, single, and *then* swept off their feet by the knight on the white horse. Different stories, same happily ever after, I hoped.)

My whole office learned really fast that Bobby and I were an item. Janet continued making underhanded remarks and I did my best to ignore them, brush them off and not let her get under my skin. Damn was that difficult. Back on our one-week anniversary (so cute!), Bobby had brought me a colorful bouquet of roses, with a handmade card: a simple heart cutout on pink card stock, that read, *Roses for my Rose. XO, The Man Who Loves You.*

Janet had exaggeratedly rolled her eyes and told me that such public displays of affection were immature and that we should keep our personal lives to ourselves. She repeated this antic in her usual distasteful manner whenever Bobby brought me a drink, or left a sweet Post-It on my desk, or shared lunch with me in the break room. I got used to tuning her out, admiring my gifts and enjoying Bobby's attention, and then getting right back to work. Bobby and I were affectionate towards one another in public, but not to a revolting level, and certainly not to the point where our job performance suffered. I don't think we kissed more than once a day when at work—usually reserved for lunchtime. We were a solid item, but we weren't, contrary to my wretched officemate's opinion, behaving like "love sick middle schoolers."

On the way to the coffeehouse, the girls sipped champagne in the back of a snazzy limousine that had extremely comfortable seats, really taking the strain off my lower back, which had been killing me in recent days.

I'd finished filling them in on the Janet saga, and about how over-the-moon I was for Bobby, gushing over the story of how Bobby brought me a gift for just a one-week anniversary awhile ago.

"And that's when I finally found the perfect name for my baby," I said to them.

"When Bobby gave you your one week anniversary present?" Jackie asked, her face squished in confusion.

"Which is totally sweet, by the way. I honestly don't think Conner ever did that," Claire added. She threw back the rest of her champagne. "One year, yeah. Not a week."

"Tell us the name already!" Lara urged.

"Rose," I said. "'Roses for my Rose.' It hit me when I read Bobby's little card. Isn't it the sweetest name?"

"I love it," Claire said.

"Do you have a middle name picked out?" Lara asked.

"No. Just Rose. She only needs one. Who needs two names anyway?"

Lara moved her head in contemplation.

"True," Claire said. "Sophie hates her parents sometimes for naming her Anna-Sophia. Says she feels like she should be a Catholic nun or something. That's just her first name and she doesn't even use both of them. I wonder why we do have middle names..."

"Rose, I like that," Jackie said. "I like that a lot. And just 'Rose.' It's like just 'Madonna' or 'Pink' or 'Adele.' A good move, Robin."

"Yeah, because I definitely chose my baby's name keeping in mind popular pop star names."

We pulled up in front of the coffeehouse.

"Let's check this joint out!" Jackie shrieked, stepping quickly to the house's open patio doors.

"Find us some seats together, Jack. If you can," Claire called out. Claire tittered at the energetic Jackie, who had insisted that she slip into a hot pink dress for the night. We told her we were going to a coffeehouse, with some light acoustical guitar music, and not a bouncing bar, but no matter.

"Think they're serving drinks?" Jackie asked, before disappearing into the house.

"I'll go find us some seats," Claire groaned, high-stepping it after Jackie.

"It's been too long since we went out like this," Lara said. She took her seat next to me near the back of the coffeehouse. It was just about packed, the music not yet underway, but the chatting and sounds of the espresso machines and milk foamers filled the cozy room.

"And it's probably going to be a long while until the next time we get to do this," I said, a little somber.

"It'll be worth it. You're going to gush all over Rose once she's here. You know it," Lara encouraged. "I really love that name, by the way."

"Hey," Jackie interrupted. "I'm going to take a quick smoke before the music gets started." She dashed off to the patio.

"So, are things with Bobby *still* spectacular as ever?" Claire asked me. "Still as great after his romantic first week anniversary move?" She blew at her fresh mug of coffee.

"Oh my goodness. Better than ever. It's still so unbelievable." I blew on my own hot beverage.

"I'm really happy for you, Robin," Lara said. "Of course I'm going to miss my partner in crime when I need to bitch about the single life, but it's worth it." She gave me a wink.

The girls had all met Bobby, and they all gave their ten-score approval for both looks and charm. Lara had been hosting a *Will and Grace* marathon and cocktail night at our apartment not too long ago when Bobby came by to pick me up for a date at the folk festival going on at the Seattle Center. It was one of our dress-down, cotton candy and torn jeans kind of dates—my favorite. When I returned home, the girls all still planted in the living room, Will, Grace, and the gang razzing the audience (and the girls) into fits of comedic laughter, they gushed over how handsome Bobby was, and how sweet he was, and what a sexy voice he had. You know, typical girl raving and gossiping about men, love, our lives, and how amazing it is when they intersect.

"No new developments with Paul?" I asked Lara.

"Oh, no. Not a shot in hell. All in my head." Lara inattentively took a sip of her coffee. "Know what I mean? All blown out of proportion. Nope. No love life here."

"Hey!" Jackie said, quickly rushing back over to us. She pulled down her dress, holding her small breasts as she tugged so as not to accidentally pull the whole thing down and give everyone a peep show. "Some guys out there were talking about how one of these guitarists is pretty famous or something."

Jackie turned her back to Claire and asked, "Claire, my ass hanging out?"

"Nope, all's clear."

"Good." Jackie held out her hand to Lara, doing a dance with her fingers like a child who's begging for a sip of whatever Mom is drinking. "Let me taste." Lara gave in. "Not wearing any underwear tonight," Jackie said. She took a speedy sip, returned the mug to Lara, and gave a thumbs up. "With this skimpy dress I have to be careful not to show my business to the world. That tastes good by the way."

"Ooo. That's disgusting," Lara said, contorting her face. "Why the hell are you not wearing any?"

"Underwear does *not* go with this dress, Lara. Fashion one-oh-one, honey." She made a swooping motion from her shoulder down her side. "Thong line and tight tube dress are *not* a match. I don't care what *Redbook* says about seamless panties. No such thing. Best answer is panty-free. What's that drink anyway?"

Lara responded, to which Jackie said, "I want one."

Lara gave her mug to Jackie, looked at me, and said after a sigh, "I'll be back. You guys want anything else?"

The guitar duo performed a few of their own songs, one of which I swore I'd heard before; one of the guys probably *was* someone famous, but not one of us figured it out, even after learning of the duo's name.

After a couple of cover songs there was a brief pause, enough time to refill our beverages and mix, mingle, and chat.

"So are you and Bobby going to move in together now or what?" Jackie asked me over the raucous chatter and whirring coffee machines.

"Are you kidding?" I said. The thought of living with Bobby had yet to cross my mind. I had recently moved in with Lara. We finally got the baby's room complete. Goodness, my last moving box was unpacked (all thanks to needless procrastination) only last week. Move in with Bobby? No way.

"It's not such a crazy idea," Jackie said. "All right, so maybe Andrew and I move faster than the average couple, but are you saying it's out of the picture?"

"Of course not. I haven't given it any thought, though. We're keeping things paced. Not making any rash decisions. And we see each other all the time. And...I like my set up now." I set my empty mug on the side table. "I really like the way things are. I've got the best roomie." I smiled at Lara. "I've got the most beautiful nursery, which, by the way, Jack, looks *amazing* with that chair rail. You're quite the handy woman." Jackie made a mock motion of fluffing her hair. "I love my set up, and I don't think I should go gallivanting off in search of a new place with my dreamboat right now."

"What are we talking about, ladies?" Claire said, returning from the bathroom.

"How Robin here is going to run away with hot-lips Bobby," Jackie kidded. "Move in with him, get married, make more baby Roses."

"Oh my God! I will *kill* myself if you get married before I do, Robin. I mean, you're already having babies before Conner and me. Oh my God. You can't do this to me."

I calmed Claire down while trying to contain my outburst of laughter. "Honey, we are *not* going to run off and get married any time soon. Do *not* worry about that. And more babies? Don't be ridiculous."

"I mean, you know I'm not totally serious," Claire said. "I wouldn't actually *kill* myself. Or be all angry or something stupid like that. It would just...you know, be like, *what the hell?* Conner still won't get off his ass and propose. I'm going to be forty before he finally works up the nerve. Honestly."

"Don't be so dramatic; you know that's not true," I told her. "And Bobby and I are not even talking about marriage. Jackie asked if she thought we'd move in together, but that's not happening, either. Things are staying the way they are. I need stability. Rose needs stability."

"Well, have you at least done it yet?" Jackie asked.

"'Done it?' What are we, in high school?" Lara asked.

"Are you joking? Look at me, Jack. I'm pregnant. I can't even put on my socks and shoes by myself anymore."

"You know," she said, pragmatically. "I read somewhere that you can do it right up until labor."

"Enough," I said. "Not having this conversation. Not here, not now, not—"

"Not until you *do* do it, and then you'll spill the details?" She gave me a toothy, bleached white smile, nodding her blonde head.

"Yeah, not until then," I said, ending the discussion. The girls kept on chatting before the music recommenced, while I though about how much fun and how thrilling it would be when the day came for Jackie to be the expectant mother.

God save us all.

"Sent!" I said exuberantly, as I listened to the whooshing sound of the email making its virtual way to the editing department. I'd finished work on my recent book cover, and already had my initial mock-ups for the next one sent off, too. The long list of to-dos before I shortly took my maternity leave was shrinking.

"What are you so happy about?" Janet asked rudely.

As much as I was getting used to Janet's unnecessary and highly rude comments and quips about anything and everything under the sun, they weren't any less annoying. Sometimes I felt like bolting out of my seat and shouting, "Shut the hell up!" Other times I wanted to pull at her hair. Most of the time I wanted to wheel her on her swivel chair into the hallway and lock her out of the office. Hang a sign that read: *No Bitches Allowed!* My job security, and the fear of what would happen if I actually stood up to her, kept me from doing anything more severe than ignoring her.

"Hello?" Janet repeated, sounding just like that wretchedly dressed, redheaded chick from the film *Clueless*. Spoiled, snooty, and her words leaving a bad taste in your mind when you mentally repeated them. "Going to answer me? Or do you only talk to the people you sleep with around here?"

Oh she was crossing the line. That smarmy—

"Robin!" She was nearly shouting now.

"What?" I answered loudly. "What, Janet? I sent an email. That's all. No big deal."

"Well stop talking to yourself over there. It's distracting. *Highly* distracting. And you sound like a crazy person."

Speak for yourself. If you weren't such a busybody, then you wouldn't waste your time, or mine, asking about the slightest of pin drop noises around here.

I gruffly shoved away from my desk. Bobby and I weren't going to take lunch for another thirty minutes, but I needed fresh air. And a breath without Janet commenting I was breathing too loudly or something absurd.

"High strung, are we?" Bobby asked in between bites of his sack lunch.

"I don't want to talk about her," I said, not wanting to belabor the reason behind my flustered state.

"The bitch on wheels." He nodded, knowingly.

"Don't want to talk about her. Let's talk about happy things."

"All right," he said. "Let's talk about holiday plans. Anything special for Thanksgiving planned?"

"Not really. Lara doesn't usually go home for Thanksgiving. And I don't want to go anywhere being so near to my due date and all. You?"

"My family's spread out all over the country. Thought I'd stay home this year. Maybe spend it with you?" He raised his eyebrows, hopeful.

That'd make for a fun holiday. Easy-going, just the three of us— Lara, Bobby, and me—maybe we'd make a turkey this year. Neither Lara nor I were very traditional when it came to Thanksgiving. We'd spent it together last year, in fact, and I think the menu contained sushi and Saki.

"I warn you," I told him, "it'll be very low-key. Probably no big traditional feast. I'm doing my Thanksgiving *and* Christmas this year at home, with Lara. I have literally *no* idea what to expect from little Rose." I circularly rubbed my stomach. "I don't know for sure when she'll actually come. Early? Late? On time? It's getting closer and I'm getting kind of scared."

Bobby pulled me near, leading us for a walk through the park once we finished our food. He told me the clichéd and corny line that the only thing I had to fear was fear itself. That I'd be brave when it came time to give birth. I was prepared, after all. I'd been eating right, taking my vitamins, reading my how-to and what-to-expect books. I'd even managed four classes of Lamaze, which included a very hands-on tutorial on breastfeeding. Can you say, "awkward"? Poor Lara—the things that girl did for me. It's not every day your best friend will feel you up, cop a boob, and read the breast pump tutorial with you on an early Saturday morning.

"Would it be all right if I came to the hospital? When Rose is born?" Bobby's question sprang from nowhere. As with the idea of moving in with him some day, I'd never put any thought into Bobby being at the hospital when Rose was born. Those topics didn't really register under the heading *Moving Slow*.

I had already invited Kaitlyn, and all the girls (including Emily) to the hospital, and everyone said they wouldn't dream of missing Rose's birth. Lara would be the only one in the actual delivery room, though; everyone else would sit in the waiting room for God knew how long. I didn't think about that—the long and painful birth I'd have to endure—either. But Bobby? At the hospital? Why not?

"Sure," I said. "I don't know where my head's been. Should have asked you. Yes, yes, of course. All my friends will be there waiting... so if you're okay with sitting with a bunch of hyped-up, baby-crazy girls. They're more excited about all this than I am, I feel." I let out a thoughtless chortle. "But it's the fear of the unknown, and the pain, that I think has me worried."

"You'll do fine. And I'll be waiting there for you and baby Rose for as long as it takes."

"Hopefully not *too* long."

He wrapped me in a warm embrace, a comfort from the chilling breeze of the crisp November day, and he kissed me. He pulled back a short distance, told me he loved me, then dipped down for another passionate, deep kiss.

"You'll do a marvelous job, Robin. And you'll have your best friends, and your boyfriend who loves you madly, right there for you. You won't be alone. Not a thing to be scared about."

I gripped my fingers around his coat lapels and pulled myself up to his lips, stealing one more fiery kiss before we had to get back to work.

21

That weekend the thing that my baby books referred to as nesting kicked in, and that meant the baby was on its way. Tonight? Tomorrow? In a week or two? Who knew? I was still four weeks away from my due date, but what if Rose decided she was ready to come now? In a state of panic, I had called Dr. Jane Buschardi's office, thinking I was going to go into early labor. The nurse told me that nesting did not mean broken water was right around the corner. I needed to take it easy, keep on nesting—getting everything situated just right for Baby—but not panic. Unless I was having contractions or my water actually broke, there was no cause for alarm.

I'd given Bobby quite a scare that Friday night while I told him how I'd read all about nesting and all about false labor scares. And how I was worried I'd be one among the many women who went into early labor. Before I could reassure Bobby that the doctor's office told me I didn't have anything to worry about, he called to the waiter to bring our check and instantly started helping me out of my seat. "I'm prepared!" he'd said. "Completely prepared! I know the quickest route to the hospital. I've Googled it."

You can imagine the surprise on his face when all I could do was sit there in the middle of the restaurant and laugh while he urged me to get a move on to the hospital. At least I knew I was in good hands if I found myself going into labor with only Bobby around. He *had*, after all, searched for the quickest route to the hospital.

I knew I was in good hands, too, if it was just Lara and me at home when my water broke. I'd been choking on and hacking up a nut the other day when Lara practically had the car running and ready to go before she realized I was only acting too stupid to chew and swallow properly. Not even close to going into labor.

Jackie let Andrew know that she was on call with me and would dash off to the hospital whenever she got the go ahead.

Sophie and Claire already had Plans A, B, C, and D sketched out for when I'd go into labor, with Conner an integral part in Plans B and C...or D. I wasn't sure; I just knew they were locked, loaded, and ready for action when the time came. They even had a large drawing board set up in Claire's dining room mapping out the most convenient routes to the hospital depending on the current location and time of day. No messing around.

Emily must have been able to find herself an internet connection with more ease as of late, since we were messaging back and forth one to two times a week. She repeatedly said she'd be home in time for the birth. That particular plan I was unsettled about. With all my nesting going on, and plenty of thoughts of going into an early labor buzzing about, I was beginning to have my doubts that world-traveling-Emily would be able to make it in time.

We weren't sure when Rose would make her grand appearance, obviously, so each of us had to be ready to go from zero to sixty at all times. I was all about going one hundred percent natural with her birth, so that meant no planned Cesarean (unless medically necessary), no scheduled birthday, not even any pain relief treatments. Nope, I was going to try this rite of passage as nature intended it. And my Lamaze instructor Sky insisted that a natural birth was "the most holy and fulfilling of methods." Time would only tell.

We'll see what happens when I'm writhing in agony. One can only imagine...

The plus with nesting meant that the baby's room was finally complete, and the house was as baby-ready and baby-proof as it could be—electrical outlets stopped up, special locks on all of the lower cabinets and cupboards, and door stoppers that'd keep Rose from smashing her tiny fingers when she started crawling. Now all we needed was show time!

"The baby's room is done, at last," I said, cranking the musical mobile Bobby finished attaching to the crib.

"Look at this!" I said to Lara, who popped her head into my room. "Is this not the most precious gift ever?"

Lara squealed with delight when she saw the singing crib mobile.

"It's Bobby's gift for Rose. Custom made."

"This baby online shop lets you custom design these things," Bobby had said when he gave it to me, looking the slightest bit proud of his smart purchase. "The little hanging toy things. The music. Pretty neat idea to be able to customize it all."

The mobile was playing the original 1950s Bobby Day version of "Rockin' Robin," and five small, soft mobile charms hung suspended above the crib: a bird, a rose, a book, a painting palette, and a heart.

"That is *the* most adorable mobile I've ever seen. And 'Rockin' Robin.' For Robin?"

Bobby nodded. "Probably going to keep Rose up more than lull her to sleep, but I couldn't resist." He put his arm around my waist.

"And each little charm is something special," I pointed out. "Personal."

"Yeah, you never know," he said. "Rose may turn out to be a great artist, or cover designer or something, just like her mom."

I looked up at Bobby, into his trusting eyes, at his beautiful face, his one-day-plus five o'clock shadow balancing that look of suave and gruff positively perfectly. I gave him a light kiss and hugged him close.

How am I so lucky? And to put so much thought into a gift for a baby that he's never even met. For a baby that's not even his.

"Do you have any idea what you want to do for your birthday?" I asked Lara over dinner. "The big two-nine is *tomorrow*. You haven't told us what you want to do at all."

Lara shrugged nonchalantly, soaking up a piece of bread in olive oil. "I don't really care about it this year."

"It's your last year in your twenties! Some people think that's cause for celebration."

"Or mourning." She bit off a chunky bite of sopping bread.

"Talk about grim, sheesh. Maybe we *want* to do something for you."

The girls and I'd talked about doing something for Lara, in spite of her not so much as giving us a hint at what she wanted to do, or wanted as a gift. We ran the usual ideas by her: night out somewhere, dinner at her favorite restaurant, a movie, a ballet or a show, a spa date, gift card somewhere—all to no avail.

"It falls on a Tuesday this year; not ideal for going out and...I don't really feel like doing anything. I'll have more birthdays. We can do something fun next year."

I detected a slight indication of Lara's feeling down and out in the love department. Sometimes she'd get so focused on her being single, then she'd become transfixed on the ludicrous notion that she'd be single forever, then she'd indubitably spiral into a silent pit of somberness that I swore was a mild case of depression. Even Claire, who worked in the medical field and saw a fair share of disabled and elderly patients who were in need of medical attention for depression, thought that sometimes Lara might benefit from a little dose of pick-me-up via Zoloft. Whenever we brought this up, Lara would dismiss it as her simply being a normal, average person who got sad now and then—nothing she couldn't handle. Perhaps she was right, but I hated seeing her like this. And for the past few months, particularly once Bobby and I became more serious, I thought her brief bouts of depression were getting worse and more frequent.

"Are you getting down on yourself about your love life, Lara?" I didn't want to pry or upset her further. I was concerned.

"Lack thereof, you mean." She pushed her plate away, half its contents still uneaten. "I guess I didn't see myself turning the corner towards thirty and still being single. Don't get me wrong, I'm totally happy for *you*, Robin, even if I'm a little envious of what you have with Bobby. Please don't take it the wrong way. I just didn't think I'd be twenty-nine and single."

"It'll happen, Lara. Eventually, it'll happen." I reached out and stroked back her loose hair. "Don't worry, baby doll."

She immediately broke down, releasing what was probably a long-withheld dam of tears.

"I don't want to be that freaky cat lady who's alone, Robin. Thirty. Forty. Fucking *fifty* and alone!" She slammed her elbows down onto the table with such force the plates rattled and inched forward. "Alone, Robin! Me and Beebee. A freaky cat lady, shuffling about in her bathrobe and hair curlers, eating cheese balls and watching daytime dramas." She stuffed her face into her hands and continued her rant. "Living vicariously through those romances. Alone. Old and alone. And all dried up at fifty."

"Lara," I murmured, wrapping her in a hug. "Don't cry, honey. Shhh. Don't you worry. You know, at least you've got your sense of humor about you."

"Don't make jokes!" she cried out in half-laugh, half-tears. "I'm being serious."

"Oh come now. Cheese balls, daytime soaps, and hair curlers? Doesn't sound like my Lara. Have you forgotten who you are?" I rubbed her back. "You're Lara the camp counselor. The one who was there for three goofballs who didn't know their Sigma Chis from their libraries. Who didn't know the best bakery near campus when they needed a study boost." I pulled her chin towards me, looking her in her tearful, glassy blue eyes. "The one who's always been the leader of the pack. Who's been an inspiration to stay in school, go after our dreams, get kickass careers...be *strong* women!" I drew closer to her and said in earnest, "The woman who helped keep the glue between two best friends, who went to hell and back. You're an amazing and *beautiful* woman, Lara. I couldn't live without you. You stood by, full of hope and encouragement, making me see and making Sophie see that no jackass or stupid one-night stand is worth coming between us and tearing apart our friendship. You're our glue, Lara, and any man who can't see that—who can't see that you're a shining star with so much to offer, that he'd be lucky to have —is not worth it."

She cried more painful tears, pulling me close tightly. "Oh, Robin," she sobbed, her voice muffled against me. "It hurts. It hurts so much."

I let her cry, rubbing her back and holding her close, telling her, "Everything will be all right, dear. Everything will be all right."

Slowly she began to pull herself together, wiping back her tears, trying her damnedest to stave off another wash of them. "I just want to experience love. A real love like you have with Bobby. I want that for myself. Why am I the only one who can't seem to get her love life in order?"

I laughed in mirth. Was she kidding? "Lara," I started, wavering between feeling comedic and sorry. "You may think it's great and all —and it is, don't get me wrong—that I've fallen in love with Bobby. But don't forget that I *am* pregnant with one of our best friend's ex-boyfriend's baby. Not exactly a *Little House on the Prairie* quaint love story, all right?" She tittered. "And have you forgotten about Sophie? She's not riding the love express train, either. Emily? Well, who the hell knows there. And Jackie? Come on. That girl's always riding some express train, but it ain't the love line. Honestly, aside from Claire, are any of us in a long-standing, *healthy* relationship?" She shrugged and jutted out her bottom lip. "Actually, come to think of it, it's kind of depressing overall, isn't it? None of us are really hitting the jackpot of love, huh?"

She shared a small laugh again with me, and then I said, "A really wise friend once told me to let the chips fall where they may." She rolled her eyes as she cracked a smile. "And, what's that proverb?" I theatrically tapped my temple. "Ah, yes! Good things come to those who wait. That's how it goes, right? Your time will come, Lara." I grabbed her hands and squeezed them tightly. "Your time—your Prince Charming—*will* come."

She dried her tears with a napkin and pushed back her hair with an elastic headband, apologizing for her abrupt fit.

"We all have our tantrums," I said. "Now finish up your dinner. I saw that new Bradley Cooper film on Netflix. Should be good for a few laughs. And, cat lady, you could use a few of those."

She balled up a crumb of bread and tossed it at me. "Hey, watch it, preggers!"

I moved as fast as I could manage, clutching the underside of my bulging belly, trying to make it to the toilet before my bladder burst and released all over the hardwood floors.

Come on, Robin, move it, move it, move it.

Then a surge of pain kicked in, like the sharp pang I felt a minute earlier. It wasn't Rose doing her routine evening kickboxing, and it wasn't indigestion. Ow! There it was again. Then another, this one twice as sharp as the last. And then another...

"Uh!" I groused, shooting straight up, darkness enveloping me.

Where am I?

I looked to my left, my right, all around as I sat up, now wide-awake in bed. I was unable to focus on any light in the room; nothing but the ominous pitch black.

What time is it?

I slowly began to realize that I was in my bed, awaking from a nightmare.

11:03, the alarm clock read.

I threw my blankets off, feeling clammy. I noticed I soaked my nightshirt straight through.

What a nightmare.

I couldn't recall what I was dreaming. Then, as I climbed out of bed to make my way to the kitchen for a drink of water to replenish the likely gallon I'd sweated away in panic, the subject of the nightmare became clear. It became true!

I gripped my sides. A biting pang hit me and I drew in a quick breath. I took two or three paces towards the door, my eyes eventually adjusting to the darkness. I was able to see the outline of the door thanks to the green light cast by the alarm clock. Then another searing shot of pain. This one stopped me dead in my tracks.

Am I still dreaming?

A quick pinch of the wrist and I knew I wasn't dreaming.

I think I'm going into labor.

"Lara!" I cried, inching the rest of the way to my door, feeling the doorknob, then the light switch. "Lara!"

Before the next jolt of pain arrived, Lara was by my side.

"I think I'm going into labor," I cried, holding onto my stomach and trying to practice the breathing techniques I'd learned in Lamaze class. "It's too early but—" Another painful stab. "But...I think it's happening."

Fast as a flash, Lara darted about, gathering her things, my overnight bag, making sure (and double-checking) she had our cell phones. About mid-way through her rescue mission, I noticed the pain had stopped. It was the longest amount of time since the jabs had started that I didn't feel any sharp burns or aches.

Is that it? Is it over? Maybe this isn't labor after all.

"I think the contractions went away," I told Lara, not fully convinced of my own words. "Maybe it *was* indigestion."

"I don't think indigestion can be *that* painful. You looked like you were in a hell of a lot of pain, Robin. And you're all pale and sweaty. Are you sure?"

I wasn't sure, and that was the problem.

Is this labor? Am I going into labor prematurely? Oh no! Will Rose be all right? She's not supposed to come yet. Am I miscarrying? No. That can't be it. It's much too late in the game for that, isn't it? What do I do?

I looked to Lara, panic in my eyes, but I spoke even-tempered. Rose needed me to be confident and calm, so I told Lara to go ahead and call Dr. Jane Buschardi's office and let them know we were going to the hospital. I didn't want to risk anything. And, while Lara was at it, she might as well send out to the girls the prepared alert text she had saved, ready to hit the send button whenever the big moment arrived.

As we made our way to the car the pain started up again. "Okay, maybe this *is* for real," I said, picking up my pace. "Let's go. Get me to the hospital." Ouch! Another sharp pain. "*Now!*"

22

I'd been in the hospital for nearly thirty minutes, lying comfortably (surprisingly) in a bed in the maternity ward, hooked up to all sorts of monitors. The beeping of my heart rate monitor was beginning to grow irksome as a nurse came to check on me again (it had to be the fourth or fifth time already), making sure my vitals were good and my pain was diminishing. Luckily the pain *had* diminished, and significantly, once I was set up in the maternity ward. Funny how that happened. The pain was doubling me over in the car ride, then the moment I settled down into the hospital bed the pain decreased incrementally. Before I knew it I was back to feeling only the pain of the heavy pressure of "baby on the bladder" that's typical of nearly full-term moms-to-be.

"I can go ahead and let your friends in now if you want," the nurse told me, writing something on her clipboard of papers.

"Absolutely." I was wondering when my girls could come in.

"We'll keep you here for another half hour or so. Just to be sure everything's still all right."

I thanked her and as soon as she left the girls were by my side, asking a million questions a minute.

"I'm fine, I'm fine," I said, not wanting them to panic.

"So no baby tonight?" Sophie asked, incredulous.

"We don't get to meet Rose?" Claire said.

"Not tonight," I sighed, relieved. "Turns out I wasn't going into labor, only having very minor contractions."

"Uh, doesn't that mean you *are* going into labor?" Jackie asked.

"Apparently the contractions I was having were these things called Braxton Hicks. Long story short, it's false labor."

"Oh yeah, I read about that," Sophie said. "New moms especially can have them. I think I read that in your baby book, Robin."

"Yeah, well, guess I missed that chapter. Anyway, I'm glad it was only false labor."

"Why are they still keeping you here?" Jackie poked around at the wires that connected me to one of the machines that was still beeping aggravatingly.

"Precautionary. No biggie."

"Phew, well thank God everything's all right," Lara said. "It's too early for Rose to come." She patted my stomach lightly. "Too early, little baby. You stay in there a few more weeks."

I stole a glance at the clock on the opposing wall. It was five minutes past midnight.

"Girls!" I shrieked, alarming them. They immediately assumed I was in pain or about to deliver—a real ticking time bomb. "It's someone's birthday today!"

As if on cue, a gasping Sophie pulled from her large designer handbag a chilled bottle of Veuve Clicquot. "I come bearing sustenance, ladies!" She waved the easily recognizable orange-labeled bottle.

Jackie withdrew a handful of clear, plastic cups from her own handbag. "And *always* prepared for a party."

"Champagne is part of the emergency Operation: Labor equipment, so naturally we came prepared," Sophie said, popping the cork. She began to pour the bubbly. "As essential as baby's first outfit home, baby's car seat, the camera...you know."

"Just as essential," Jackie chimed in, starting to pass around the cups.

"Sorry," Claire said, making a sad, puppy dog face. "We'll get another bottle for Operation: Labor and you can have a sip then."

"Definitely. But tonight," Jackie said, raising her glass, everyone else following suit, me holding up the cup of water the nurse had brought me. "Tonight we toast to Lara. She's growin' up on us."

"Happy birthday, Lara!"

"Cheers, Lara! Happy birthday!"

"May the next twenty-nine be just as fabulous!"

Lara clinked cups with everyone. "That's so sweet."

"Worked out really well, actually," Sophie said, as the nurse walked in.

"Ladies, you can't have that in here," the nurse said, pointing at the chilled bottle of champagne in Sophie's hand.

"But it's her birthday," Jackie said, patting Lara on the back.

"I'm sorry, ladies, but you can't have that. There's no drinking allowed in here." The nurse unhooked me from the equipment and said that I could get dressed and be discharged, then she shook her head discouragingly at the girls as she exited the room, saying once more, "Hospital rules. *No* drinking."

The girls burst into laughter, throwing back the last of their small amounts of champagne.

"Happy birthday, Lara," I whispered under all the cackling.

Lara helped me tie back my hair, then took my overnight bag off my hands. "Now let's get you and little Rose home to get some sleep. You must be exhausted." She turned to the rest of the girls, who were trying to re-cork the champagne, desperate to take the bottle home. "Girls!" Lara's voice was stern. "Forget the bottle; let's go home."

"But it's a forty dollar bottle of champagne," Claire whined.

Lara couldn't help but laugh, and I tossed up my hands. "It's like junior year all over again," I said. "Whatcha' gonna' do?"

"Hey, this is a serious party foul," Claire protested.

"Then swig some back and let's go. Honestly," Lara said, looking from the girls, back to me. "They're like children."

Sophie, Claire, and Jackie shared last-minute swigs of the champagne, Sophie coughing and spraying champagne from her nose as she downed too much. The cackling became even more boisterous, and I tugged on Lara's hand, telling her to tell them they were going to be left behind and could call a cab home. Exhaustion was hitting me hard.

"Come *on*," Lara urged. Just then the nurse walked right up to me in the doorway.

"I said *no* drinking in here, ladies. Are you hard of hearing? Or am I going to have to call in security?" The upset nurse crossed her arms over her puffed out chest and tapped her foot.

"Come on!" I said. I made a strict motion with my hand for them to cut the crap and get a move on. "I still want to have my baby in this hospital. I don't want to have a warrant out for our arrest or something stupid."

Jackie took one last swig of the champagne before leaving the bottle on the bedside table. "Sorry, Robin." She ushered the rest of the girls towards the door.

"God," Claire moaned in a tone that sounded as if the champagne had already hit. Always the lightweight. "Nurse Ratched's sure got a pin in her ass." Claire hiccoughed loudly and she and Sophie fell into a fit of giggles.

"Good God," Lara moaned. She shoved the girls through the door and managed to get us all into her car without any more violations of hospital rules.

"Happy birthday, Lara!" Jackie cried from the backseat. Lara helped Claire, the last of them, get into the car. "We love you so much!"

"Yeah! Happy birthday, Lara," Sophie chimed in, then she, too, hiccoughed, and the backseat roared with mindless laughter.

I rubbed my stomach, relieved not to have any more false labor pains and contractions.

Welcome to the family, little Rose. Your aunties are crazy, but they're my sisters and I love them.

Thanksgiving was around the corner, I was nearly finished with work before my maternity leave, and, what was more, Emily was due home in only two weeks! Not to mention I hadn't had any more frightening Braxton Hicks scares since the girls and I had rushed to the hospital. Things were still as great as ever with Bobby. I couldn't wait to spend the Thanksgiving holiday with him and my best friend. And though I hadn't heard back from my dad (surprise) about my being pregnant, and although I still hadn't received any financial support from Brandon (even less of a surprise), the girls, Kaitlyn, and Bobby were all set to be there for me at the hospital when Rose would be born. What a great support group!

As well behaved as my mom had been at the baby shower, she didn't express an interest in meeting the baby at the hospital, and I didn't want to contemplate the possible melodrama that would ensue if she were there. Besides, she was busy working on her suntan and social status in Florida for the winter with architect Archie or whoever the hell he was. So my mother and I civilly agreed that she could meet baby Rose when she found the time. I wasn't going to hold my breath. And I was, honestly, all right with that.

Nearly every loose end at work was tied up, and I was looking at a nice, long, two-and-a-half month break from sharing an office with Janet. There was still no word about whether or not Forster & Banks signed the new author. Part of me really hoped I *did* get the PM position so the likelihood of me no longer needing to share an office with the co-worker from hell would be slim. With the new position, I imagined I would either move into a larger space, maybe even a more private space, or, what I really hoped would happen, Janet would grow discouraged and become enraged over me receiving the position as opposed to her, and she'd finally do everyone a favor and quit.

"Suppose I won't be seeing you around until February," I said to Janet as I packed up my things for the day.

"Yeah, suppose so," she said dismissively.

I bit my bottom lip, waiting for her to say something more. Nothing.

How about goodbye? See ya? Good luck with the baby?

"Have a nice Thanksgiving," I said. "And a nice vacation."

Janet was taking holiday before the firm officially let out for Thanksgiving. She was going up to Aspen to hobnob with the rich and the famous, I guess. She'd been rubbing it in my face for weeks that she was going to ski with some literary hotshots and that she would probably find her big break up there in the lodge and on the slopes with big-name authors and publishers. How she knew of them and, what was more, how she was able to hobnob with them, I'll never know. In all honesty, I couldn't care less. If being a snow bunny over Thanksgiving would get Janet out of my office, I say, "Hit the slopes already!"

"Oh, and I sent you the proofs you asked for," I told her. "For you to check out... You know, the proofs you asked for for the—"

"That I asked for yesterday?" she cut in curtly.

"Yeah. Well, they're in your inbox. And they should give you a good idea about the guidelines for your project. Similar styles and all—"

"If I need your help, I'll ask."

"Uh, sure," I said, not really wanting to be in contact with Janet during my maternity leave, but perhaps if she really needed my help... "I'll have my email."

She nodded her head in a patronizing fashion, then made a shooing motion with her hand. "I'll email if I need you. You can go now."

That was it!

I'd taken the abuse long enough. I didn't deserve to be treated like some underling or some lowly servant, at Janet's beck and call whenever she damn well pleased. She couldn't just shoo me away when I was no longer needed or wanted.

"Actually..." I said, pulling my shoulders back with a sudden and surprising air of confidence. I looked good. I felt good. And, you

know what? I *was* good. I did a damn fine job with my work. I was always kind and responsive and courteous to everyone at the office. Always keeping my mouth shut when Janet had something insulting to say. Always remaining kosher and keeping my temper at bay with every roll of Janet's eyes and flick of her hair and condescending gesture. Always being that meek, that insecure, that keep-to-herself and always-have-something-nice-to-say girl in her quiet corner behind her desk. Enough was enough already.

"Actually, no," I said.

Janet turned slowly—creepily—in her chair. She slightly squinted her eyes, creased her brow, and said, "Beg your pardon?"

"*I. Said. No.* Don't email me. Don't bother me. I don't want to hear from you while I'm gone. Until you can learn to treat me with respect and like a human being, don't ask for another damn thing from me. Got it?"

She couldn't speak. Her mouth just hung open, flabbergasted.

"And close your mouth, Janet. That look is *so* unbecoming." I turned on my heels and headed for the door, proud of the way I'd garnered attention, if not respect.

"Excuse me!" There was that defensive Janet I knew.

I abruptly turned back to her and before she could speak, I dramatically took a glance at my watch, looked her sharply in the eyes, then said, "It's after five. Looks like you're already on vacation, and I'm out the door. Don't forget—not a word from you. You can manage around here without me anyway, right? Miss, *Career Woman?*" I waved with my fingertips and said, in a childish voice, "Happy Thanksgiving. And have a *great* time in Aspen. I really hope you get some great job leads there."

I didn't take one look back. I didn't even stop to kiss Bobby goodbye for the day (he had to chase me out into the parking lot). I charged on out of there, proud of finally taking that stand to Janet I knew I'd owed myself long ago. Enough time spent being pushed around. Sometimes a girl had to keep her mouth shut. Other times she needed to take a stand. Today was my stand, and it felt great!

Before I knew it, Emily had returned to Seattle—and just under a week before Rose was due. The girls and I ran around like chickens with their heads cut off preparing for the reunion. I wasn't comfortable with the idea of staying the night at any place but home, so Lara and I were hosting the reunion: a big, celebratory sleepover with *all* the girls. Sophie, Claire, and Jackie would pick Emily up from the airport and bring her by our place "just to say hi after all this time." She wouldn't suspect a party in her honor.

"Okay, everything's set, right?" I asked Lara, taking a sweeping survey of the living room. "Balloons, the welcome home sign...and we'll shut off the lights and hide in the kitchen...you made sure the door's unlocked, didn't you?"

Lara nodded, opening up the last bag of chips and sneaking a taste. "And Sophie and Claire know to knock to warn us," she said. "We *won't* miss the chance to hide and shout 'surprise!'"

"This is going to knock her socks off!" I said, clapping my hands excitedly. "Oh! I can't believe we're finally going to get to see Emily after all this time. It's been almost a year!"

"The extra blankets and pillows Claire brought over are in your room?"

"Yup, everything we need is here. Plenty of food, drinks, extra blankets...all the makings we need for a sleepover." I flicked off the lights and we ambled into the kitchen.

"God, doesn't this take you back to our college days?" Lara asked fondly. "All those fun, late nights together. Super feminine times."

"Some things change." I touched my stomach. "But some things stay the same."

A sudden and loud knock at the door.

They're here!

The sound of the front doorknob turned, the door creaked, and then...

"Surprise!" Lara and I shouted simultaneously, flicking on the lights.

"Surprise! Surprise!"

"We fooled you!"

"Oh my goodness!" Emily screeched. She ran over to Lara and me, nearly knocking us down, embracing us in one gigantic hug. She planted a big kiss on each of our cheeks. "I'm so happy to see you girls again. Ohhh! Robin, look at you! You're *beautiful.* I can't believe you're having a baby." She touched my stomach. "Hi there, Rose. It's Auntie Emily."

Emily embraced Lara in another hug, and the two started crying, which then made me start to bawl. Before you knew it all six of us were hugging and crying, overwhelmed that we were finally, once again united after much too much time apart.

"That's so sweet of you to put this together for me," Emily said. She pressed her hand, bedazzled in unique wire and carved wooden rings, to her heart, taking in the party decorations. She gasped and repeated how excited she was to be back home and with all of us once again. "This is really amazing. Thank *you!*"

"I can't believe this is actually happening. It feels like it's been forever," Claire gasped.

"It *has* been forever," Jackie said. She curiously touched the tightly braided locks of Emily's long brown hair. "My God, look at you with your international fashion flair. Damn, girl." She seemed as fascinated as a child who first learns the joys of having a puppy.

"Oh, Jack," Emily said, giving her another squeeze. "Glad to see you haven't changed."

"Pssh! Not one bit."

"So, gush on all about this Andrew guy you were telling me about, Jack." Emily slumped down on the sofa. It was as if she hadn't been away longer than a day. "I want the scoop on all the big news, ladies."

"Uh, photos, too, Em. And stories," Lara said. "We want to hear all about Ghana."

"Definitely!"

"Oh yeah. We've set up the TV and everything so you can show your photos."

"You want news, you'll get news. Wait 'til you hear all about Bobby!"

"Oh the living end, eh? Bobby, Bobby, Bobby…"

"And! Guess what? Jackie slept with…Chad!"

"What? No!"

"Please, let's not talk about *that* again."

"It *has* been way too long since we've all gotten together."

"That's for sure," I said. "Too long, for sure."

It was wonderful to have all the girls back together again. Emily regaled us with some unbelievable stories from abroad, and, true to form, shared hundreds of photos from her time living in the village, day trips to neighboring villages, weekend trips to the capital, and even a two-week-long venture into the heart of the African wild. During this trip she'd explored the terrain and wildlife with a group of visiting Australian zoologists studying the current and developing state of the African elephant and its habitat. Sound far-fetched? That's Emily's life. She tooled around in a Jeep with some random strangers, snapped some amazing photographs of lion prides, African birds of prey, and herds of elephants on the move, grazing, you name it. Typical Emily: befriend complete strangers, make a connection, establish a friendship, and go out into the world together to explore, be adventurous, and then come back with some unbelievable photographs and stories to share. Her life was a true adventure; she definitely needs to write a book about it.

As it turns out (no surprise to any of us), Emily felt what she always referred to as "the great calling" to return back to Ghana after the new year. Despite her extended stay in Ghana this year, the children's school was not yet complete. She'd made a personal vow that she wouldn't give up on it. After baby Rose was here she'd head back to Africa for God knew how long. That was our adventurous Emily —always gone, but somehow, still, always here.

Naturally, we gave Emily the details of our personal lives and drama (funny how often those two words come together). She wasn't surprised in the slightest that Brandon had turned out to be a complete ass (yeah, still not a dime from him). And she wasn't surprised that Bobby was smitten with me. She said he sounded like the perfect match, and she couldn't wait to meet him for herself.

As for Lara and her long shot dreams of Paul, Emily had only, "Pish-posh. Forget about him," to say to her in her classic Bostonian accent that she never quite lost, despite having lived all her college years in Seattle and spending the majority of each year afterward in some foreign country. "If he doesn't see what a diamond you are, then pass," Emily wisely advised.

Emily rattled off to Sophie a long list of must-see London sights that were off-the-beaten-path. She also told her she should spend a few weeks there, then strap on a backpack, take the Eurostar to Paris, and explore Europe for a couple of months...or at the very least a few weeks. "Take advantage of having your brother in London," she told Sophie. "What an opportunity!" And, while she was at it, Claire should join in, too. That was Emily's response when Claire pouted about still being un-engaged.

Surprise news to all of us, Claire had recently gotten news that her older sister was engaged. And Claire was a bridesmaid. "She's a super hippie girl, too!" Claire said. "What the hell is she doing getting married? She's always been the anti-marriage feminist of the family. And making me a bridesmaid! It's just salt in the wound. Spinsterdom—that's what I'm headed for." Lara responded to this by giving her a high-five, then they toasted their glasses of chardonnay.

And Jackie. Good old Jackie. The close bond between Jackie and Emily was reignited as easily as a Bic lighter, swapping stories over cigarettes sitting half-in and half-out of the balcony doorway. Emily dispensed cautious advice about men and Jackie's proclivity to go after the salt-and-pepper flavor, who always somehow ended up more sweet-and-sour. Or was it sweet *then* sour?

"Girls, tell Emily Andrew treats me like a princess," Jackie called over from the doorway. We all resounded together, "A princess!" and "She does have his credit cards and his car, after all."

My best friends. All together again—the way it should always be. I drifted off to sleep that night happier than a June bug on a hot and steamy summer evening, cuddled next to Emily in my bed, knowing that Lara and Jackie were only one room away, and Sophie and Claire were snuggled up together in the living room, and that Bobby, my loving and handsome *boyfriend*, was only a quick phone call away. *And* knowing that my baby Rose was due in just five short days! I drifted off to sleep, a smile, I am sure, unmistakably playing on my lips.

23

"Emily!" I shrieked, clapping my hand to her side on top of the thick comforter. "Emily! Wake up! I think it's time. I think it's for real happening, right now for real. Real, really happening."

Emily lightly stirred, then slapped her arm across my chest.

"Emily!" I nudged her. She didn't respond. I nudged harder. "Emily! Wake. Up!"

She grumbled a few incoherent words and sat upright in bed. "Is it morning already?"

I turned on the bedside lamp. "No—no, not morning." I pulled out of bed and started to dress myself in the "going into labor ensemble" that Lara and I had, ironically, picked and laid out only yesterday. "I think this is it."

"This is what?" Emily rubbed at her eyes.

"The baby! I think I'm going into labor. It feels a lot like last time, but I'm sure it's for real now. I think I'm going to have this baby."

That's when it hit Emily like a truck. Her eyes widened and she sprang out of bed, digging madly through her large, backpack decorated with multiple airline tags.

"Okay, no panic. I'm going to get dressed. You're—" Emily looked at my half-dressed self. "Good. You're on your way to being ready. I'll throw on some pants and a shirt and...the girls! I'll wake them." She haphazardly threw on a wrinkled pair of jeans and an even more wrinkled t-shirt before running into the living room to stir everyone awake.

Okay. Stay calm. Remember what you learned in Lamaze. Breathe in. One, two, three. Exhale. One, two, three. Ow! Oh, dammit.

I clutched the underside of my stomach, feeling a light, warm trickle of water run down my leg.

My water broke!

Emily ran back into the room, eyes still wide. Then she gasped, "Your water! Holy shit. This is for real!" I stifled a laugh as she said, "At least you didn't already put your pants on."

"Okay, this is it!" Lara cried, bursting into the room. She grabbed my overnight bag, and Jackie, hot behind Lara, helped me put on my baggiest pair of grey sweat pants. She tried to wipe up the broken water with a spare blanket but I told her, "To hell with it. I don't even care if I'm dressed at this point. Just—*ow!*—just get me to the hospital. Hurry!"

Jackie and Emily helped me to Lara's car as the rest of them ran about the apartment askew (so much for the perfect plan), trying to make sure everyone was dressed, everyone had everything, and nothing was being forgotten. It wasn't exactly an easy task, seeing how it was three-something in the morning and we were all operating in zombie mode. I couldn't pay any attention to my sleep-blurred vision and my heavy head as the searing pains in my abdomen, all along the sides and even up top, were almost too painful to bear. Worse than the Braxton Hicks episode, by far.

I plopped into the front passenger seat and kept up the breathing techniques. However, they were becoming harder to practice, and taking in a breath for longer than the count of one was becoming more laborious with each inhalation.

"Here, I'll help you breathe," Lara said, rushing to me while Jackie ran back to the apartment to gather the rest of the gang. "Breathe in, try to breathe *sloooowly.* There we go. One, two, threeee..."

The pain kept coming, lasting longer, coming more frequently, and I was sweating. I was breathing and heaving as if I'd done a half-marathon.

"Okay, we're going now," Lara said. She yelled to Emily, who was now also back at the apartment, that it was now or never. "Show time!"

As another heavy contraction came, I let out a loud scream. Then the car doors slammed and Lara started up the engine.

"Wait!" Sophie shrieked. "The baby seat!"

"It's in the trunk," Lara said.

I gripped Lara's forearm as she was about to reverse from the parking spot. "No." I sucked in a deep breath, then exhaled in small bouts—one, two, three. "No, it's in *my* trunk. Remember?"

"Aw, shit," Claire said, jumping from the car. "Where are your keys?"

"Here! Here!" Sophie exclaimed. She dug through my purse. "They're probably in Robin's bag. Right?"

I shook my head.

"The overnight bag!" Lara said.

It was chaos. Pure and utter chaos. I remember actually contemplating the thought of having my baby right there in Lara's car, in the parking lot in the wee, dark and frozen hours of the morning.

"Hurry!" I screamed.

Claire dug through my overnight bag and Sophie asked if anyone had called my sister.

"She's on vacation," I managed. "Dammit. She won't be back for another two—*ow!*—two...two days!"

"I'm driving," Lara said, starting to back the car in reverse. "We've got to go. If we've forgotten something then too bad. This girl's going to give birth any second."

"Wait!" Claire said. She flew out of the rolling car with my keys finally in hand. "I've got to get the baby seat!" Her voice trailed as she ran across the lot to open my car's trunk.

"This is like a fucking movie!" Jackie exclaimed, pounding her hands on the shoulders of my seat. "This is awesome! Aren't you excited, Robin?"

I gave her a worried smile—distorted and forced.

I watched through the bright beam of Lara's headlights as Claire struggled to the slowly moving car, the large and awkward car seat with the pink, fluffy cushions bobbing in the night.

"Hurry!" Lara said, still motoring the car forward. "Throw the damn thing in the back with you. We don't have any time."

Claire all but threw herself into the back of the seat, landing on the laps of Sophie and Emily, the car seat thrown somewhere in the back with them. Jackie was crouched at the bottom of the car floor, her small head poking in between the two front seats.

"This is so freaking exciting, Robin!" She squeezed my hand and smiled brightly up at me. "I'm so proud of you. You're going to be a superstar!"

"Drive!" I shouted to Lara, squeezing Jackie's hand and making her face wince. "Drive as *fast* as you can!"

By the time I was wheeled into the maternity ward, the contractions were only two minutes apart. The nurses said it was a good thing I had such a great team of friends to help me get to the hospital so soon. I probably wasn't going to deliver for another hour or so, but that's the funny thing with babies. They come when they want, and had my contractions started to kick into an even higher gear I could have found myself in a real pickle.

"Two minutes apart, and coming up on a minute-and-a-half apart is really nice," the nurse told me. She finished hooking me to various machines, more machines than I'd used during my Braxton Hicks scare.

This is it. The time has come. It's really happening.

"If you like, you can have your friends come and visit," the nurse told me, her bedside manner already worlds better than the last nurse, who'd become quickly annoyed with our breaking of the hospital's alcohol rules. "Because once it's game time, that's it. Show's over and it's time to get started." She patted my arm and wrote Lara's name down on her clipboard after she'd asked who would be joining me in delivery. "I'll make sure Lara gets suited up when the time comes. For now I'll get you some more ice chips and let your friends come in. Beep if you need me." She patted my arm once more.

"We called your sister," Claire all but shouted, waving my cell phone at me when she strode into the room. "Left her a voicemail."

Sophie, Emily, Jackie, and Lara followed behind Claire, Lara bringing in my overnight bag, and Sophie the car seat.

"Thanks," I said. "Kaitlyn's up in the mountains somewhere on vaca. She's going to be so mad."

"Hey," Sophie said, "on the bright side, maybe this is just another one of those false labors."

"Yeah," Claire said. "One of those Brayson Wix things."

Sophie and I chuckled, and I told them that I didn't think so. This was probably the real deal. Rose would be here before we knew it.

"Oh!" I said.

"Another contraction?" Sophie asked.

"No, not for another..." I looked at the monitor. "Maybe thirty seconds. I mean, did anyone get a hold of Bobby?"

"Oh my God!" Jackie said. "We totally forgot. Man alert! Man alert! Call that boy, Claire!"

Claire searched my phone for Bobby's number and started talking to him, waking him from his peaceful sleep, I was sure, while my next contraction started up.

"Oh, God," I moaned. "Here it is. Oh no. *Ohhhh.*" This one was probably the most painful one I'd had yet.

Lara and Emily coached me through it, each holding one of my hands and telling me to focus on breathing. Nothing but breathing.

The contraction released and Claire said, "He's on his way. Poor guy sounded totally groggy."

"This is happening," Sophie said. She pushed back my sweat-soaked bangs. "This is really happening. Robin's going to be a mom!"

After thirty minutes, when the contractions were only a minute apart, Dr. Buschardi came in.

"Hello there, Robin," she said, much too smiley for four o'clock in the fucking morning.

Oh God, not another contraction. Oh, the pain...

This time Claire and Sophie had my hands, and Jackie was counting down the seconds to when the contraction would be over, intently focused on the beeps and lines of the monitor.

"Shit!" I screamed, squeezing their hands purple. The contraction receded, and I apologized for my language.

Dr. Buschardi laughed it off and said it sounded like and—as she glanced over the readouts printed out from underneath the contraction monitor—it looked like I was going to deliver before the sun rose.

"You're nearly fully dilated," Dr. Buschardi said. "Contractions are coming closer and closer together. I think your little girl is just about ready to make her big appearance."

I smiled brightly at the girls. "Did you hear that? *This* morning! My baby is coming *this* morning."

Another contraction, more painful, followed by another. I felt like I was going to die and be reborn at the same time. The pain was excruciating, but the joy that overfilled my heart was astonishing.

"I can do this. I can do this," I said to myself, and Emily repeated the encouragements.

"Um, Dr. Buschardi," a nurse said, stopping by my room a brief moment. "There's a Mr. Holman here."

I waved my hand as a sign for him to be let on through as I tightened my jaw and squeezed the girls' hands for another oncoming contraction.

"Is he the father?" the doctor asked, snapping on bright blue gloves and taking a seat on a stool that a nurse urgently wheeled over for her. My bed started to move forward and down, setting me in more of an upright position.

"No," I cried. Then the contraction receded, but I knew my thirty- or forty-second break wouldn't be enough to calm down and get back on my proper breathing track.

"He's her super hot boyfriend," Jackie told the doctor, wiping my forehead with a damp cloth.

"Super hot," Claire added.

"Well, Robin," Dr. Buschardi said, "you're still not fully dilated yet, but you're doing well with your contractions. Nearly thirty seconds apart. You comfortable?"

"You've got to be kidding me." I tried to readjust myself in my now upright bed.

Dr. Buschardi smiled. "With the bed—you comfortable with the bed? I want gravity on your side when you start to push, which I think is right around the corner." She smiled even more brightly. "But if you feel more comfortable laying down for a while, we can readjust."

"I don't care," I groaned, my lower back throbbing, my head pounding with what felt like a migraine, and my womb pulsating ten, maybe twenty times more painfully than the worst period cramps I'd ever had. "Can I have some drugs?"

"Robin," Lara said, shocked, "I thought you wanted to do this all natural?"

"Listen," I braced myself for what felt like another contraction. "I may have said that *before* I was in this bed with my legs strapped up and my stomach feeling like it's about to explode, but trust me— *screw* natural. This *hurts!*"

"Too late for those, honey," the doctor said. "Natural it is. Your daughter is on her way."

I thought another contraction was due, but I miscalculated. A nice little pause? Nope. Another one now, just as strong, just as painful.

"Okay, ladies," Dr. Buschardi said. "Looks like Robin's going to get ready to start pushing. We need some room in here."

As the girls were about to leave, Bobby rushed in. "Robin!" he exclaimed, charging to my side.

"Bobby!" He cupped my sweaty, clammy face in his hands and gave me a kiss.

"Oh, Robin, I came as fast as I could. As soon as I got the call. Are you all right?"

"As right as I can be. Rose is coming—today."

"Robin," the doctor said, a serious look covering her face. "We're getting very close."

"Okay," I said, knowing it was time for visitors to head out to the waiting room. Lara and I had a baby to welcome into the world, and soon enough everyone would be able to meet baby Rose. But first...

"Ow!" I screeched. Bobby grabbed my hand and I squeezed tightly throughout the duration of the quick contraction.

"Show time!" the doctor announced, as the contraction abated.

"I love you, Robin," Bobby whispered, wiping away my newly formed tears from under my fogging glasses. "And I'll be right out there with your friends when you and Rose are ready. You'll do a wonderful job. I'm so proud of you." He kissed me firmly, the taste of his mouth warm and sweet, familiar and enjoyable, even in such a remarkable moment.

"I love you, too, Bobby," I whispered. Another contraction was forming, and Lara took the helm, holding my hand and softly encouraging me as the gang filtered out of the room.

"Okay," Dr. Buschardi said. "Push, Robin."

I pushed. And I pushed. And I pushed some more.

A brief break, then more pushing.

I cursed a few more times, calling for pain medication.

Lara held my hand and kept telling me, "You can do it. You can do it."

She held my hand through the contractions. Through the pushing. Through what seemed like an eternity of pain and pushing and screaming. Through the moment Dr. Buschardi announced the baby's head was out. Through more contractions. Lara was there throughout the entire process. And she was there when baby Rose came out, screaming at the top of her powerful infant lungs; when the doctor rested her on my stomach and let me see my daughter for the first time.

"Congratulations," Dr. Buschardi said. "You successfully delivered your very healthy and beautiful baby girl."

Just then, a nurse took Rose away.

"What's going on?" I asked, utterly spent.

"Don't worry," Lara said. "I think they're just going to cut the umbilical cord, take her measurements, clean her up. I'm sure she's fine."

"She certainly is," the doctor said. "A few tests, clean her up, and then my nurses will help you with baby's first feeding. Congratulations, Robin. You did a wonderful job."

I looked to Lara, who was, like me, glowing. How exciting! It was all so very real; everything we'd prepared for and read about and talked about for months had finally happened. Rose was here.

"Where is that bundle of joy?" Sophie exclaimed, walking into the recovery room I was moved to once Rose and I were ready.

"There she is!" Claire said. She was carrying two large, foil balloons that wished *Congrats!* and *It's a Girl!*

Emily and Jackie crowded around my bed, *ooing* and *ahhing* at the sweet little bundle in my arms. Rose was wrapped tightly in a pink receiving blanket, eyes closed and fast sleep.

"She's adorable!" they cooed.

"Looks just like you."

"Aw, she's so precious."

"The *cutest* baby I've ever seen."

Bobby timidly walked in, a bouquet of pink and white roses in one hand, and a plush toy lamb in the other.

"Bobby," I cried, tears coming up the instant I laid eyes on the man I loved.

"Oh, Robin," he said, coming to my side. He placed the small lamb near Rose and gently touched her chubby cheek. "She's beautiful. Like her mother."

He looked into my eyes, his big blues still taking my breath away like the first time we shared a kiss. He pressed his lips to mine, kissing me gently. He whispered, "I love you so much, Robin," over my lips, his glance, his kiss, his words sweeping me into euphoria. "And I'm so proud of you." He kissed me once more, then, as if noticing he had a love-struck audience, sheepishly shied back and said, holding out the bouquet, "For you and Rose. The most appropriate bouquet, of course."

Lara kindly took the flowers to be placed in a vase of water, while everyone asked dozens of questions about the labor, the delivery, and, "Why does Rose have all that gooey stuff around her eyes?" or, also a favorite question of the day from Claire, "What do they do with the umbilical cord? Would they give it to you if you asked?"

"Welcome to the family, little Rose," I said, carefully rocking her. "Welcome to your crazy, fun, and very non-traditional family. We love you."

Surreptitiously, Jackie uncorked a fresh bottle of champagne. "Shhh," she said, looking mischievously over her shoulder. "Let's not get caught this time." She immediately started pouring rounds and we all, even a tiny sip for myself, toasted to the birth of Rose Sinclair. My daughter and, in all seriousness, the most beautiful little girl in the world.

"Robin?" Dr. Buschardi asked, startling us as we sipped on our celebratory bubbly.

"Yes?" I handed my cup to Lara, who tried her best to look inconspicuous.

"I've made sure your to-go bag is all ready for your discharge tomorrow. It's got all sorts of information and helpful infant items, like some diapers, emergency infant formula in case breastfeeding doesn't work, and such. Threw in some extra samples for you." She smiled and, once she took notice of our forbidden drink, gave me a wink. "I won't tell. Congratulations. And I'll be by again later this afternoon to make sure all is still well."

I stared at my gorgeous baby, still so in shock that I actually delivered this little creature—this bundle of perfection—and, while her family wasn't by common standards the "all-American family," it

was one filled with members who loved and adored her unconditionally. And that's what mattered. Rose may not have had a father,
but she had a mother who'd lay down her life for her. And five aunts
—no, six counting Aunt Kaitlyn—who would shower her with love
and spoil her with everything under the moon. And she had Bobby,
who had come into our lives at the most precarious of moments and
offered his love, his support, and his heart to a woman and her baby
who never thought such love could be found outside of fairytales.

The girls and Bobby continued their toasts, admiring Rose,
stroking her cheek, and kissing her small, bald head.

"I love you, Rosie," I whispered, kissing the tip of her button
nose. "I love you with all my heart. And I'm going to be the best
mom you could wish for."

Bobby massaged my right shoulder, sipping on his champagne
and looking fondly at the two of us. "My lovely leading ladies," he
said, giving me a soft peck on the forehead.

Two nurses returned to the room, one with a vase filled with
brightly colored garden flowers, a balloon bearing the word,
Congrats! attached, and the other nurse pushing a large cart carrying
a machine that looked like a breast pump.

"What's this?" Claire gasped. "More flowers?"

"Oh, these must be from Kaitlyn. Maybe she got your voicemail."
I reached out for the nurse to hand me the card.

"I'm sorry, dear," the nurse said. "No card attached. They came
directly from the hospital gift shop. By pre-order, I think."

"That's odd," I said. "Couldn't be Mom, could it? Or Dad?" I
looked from Bobby, to the girls, then back to Bobby. "Could you find
out for me, please?" I asked the nurse.

"While we find out the mystery delivery," the other nurse said,
"Robin and I need to get little Rose to breastfeed."

Bobby gave me one more kiss before following the rest of the
pack out of the room.

After what must have been a dozen failed attempts at getting
Rose to latch on and breastfeed, she finally did it! When the nurse
and I thought we'd give the breast pump a try so that way Rose

wouldn't have to have another feeding of formula, and so I could actually give a go at this whole breastfeeding thing, Rose figured it out.

"She's a smart baby," the nurse said.

"Robin?" the nurse who had come in with the mystery flowers asked, peeking her head into the door.

"Yes?"

"I called down to the gift shop and it seems that these flowers were on order since June. To be delivered to a Robin Sinclair whenever she gave birth."

I scratched my head, perplexed, and careful not to disturb Rose, who was suckling as best she should.

"That's so odd," I said. "Surely they're not from my mom...or my dad."

"Gift shop says they're from a...Mr. Brandon Crossley."

24

I didn't tell anyone what the nurse that day had told me—about who had sent me the mystery flowers. There was no card attached, and probably for good reason. Brandon didn't want me to know they were from him, or didn't want to be too obvious that... what? He actually had a sensitive and caring bone in his body? I didn't see the need to tell anyone about it and draw up some unnecessarily dramatic issue. They'd soon forgotten about the mystery flowers, and I figured if anyone asked I'd say they were from my dad or something.

And I didn't want to bring up the topic of Brandon with Bobby. Besides, Brandon wasn't a part of my life, or a part of Rose's. Why would I even mention the gifting of anonymous flowers only to possibly set Bobby off? Or maybe even cause a rift in our relationship or open the door to pointless questioning about Brandon. About that night I'd spent with him. About how I was without Brandon's help and support from the start. About how we agreed he'd be out of my and Rose's lives forever. Why start something that wasn't? I had a great thing going with Bobby, and nothing could spoil it, not even a meaningless vase of flowers from an anonymous man who never wanted Rose, or me, from the start.

I'm still curious as to why Brandon arranged for those flowers to be sent, though. Mad curiosity grips me whenever I'm up for a midnight feeding with Rose. I wondered where Brandon was. Already in New York? On the plane ride there? Already shacking up with some new chick? I thought about him not because I cared for him, or had some flighty hope of having him back in my life or in Rose's, but because, I guess, the flowers he had sent me must have meant *something*. But what? Why would he send them if his only interaction with Rose, and with me upon hearing I was pregnant with his child, was to offer me enough cash to terminate my pregnancy? Why would he even bother with flowers? Guilty conscience? Change of heart? An offering gift in hopes of cleaning his slate?

As it turns out, I think the gift of flowers, however nonchalantly scheduled, was a preview of what was to come. Two weeks after Rose's birth, a piece of mail arrived for me at the apartment, with a return address from New York, New York. It was a check from Brandon for a thousand dollars, and a handwritten note on a torn off piece of scratch paper, as if an afterthought, that read, *Will send more when I can. Brandon*

Still in shock, perhaps more in shock than I was over the mystery flowers, I opened up a bank account in my and Rose's name the day after the check arrived. Rose, like every girl, needed a little mad money...or college cash. Whatever she wanted to do with it when she became old enough was up to Rose. I didn't urgently need Brandon's handouts, but I'd be a fool if I didn't take them. If I didn't give Rose the least of what her birth father could do for her.

Kaitlyn came to the apartment to meet baby Rose as soon as she was back from vacation. And Mom even planned for a weeklong trip to Seattle at the end of January. Of course, I told Kaitlyn *she* would have to host Mom. Mom could come over when she wanted to help me out, see her grandchild, and fulfill the grandmotherly duties she said she should do. But she'd have to stay at Kaitlyn's place. A little of Mom can go a long way.

Dad finally emailed me back with congratulations, and that was that. Hey, oddly enough Brandon was actually turning out to be a better father than my own. But as soon as I saw Bobby (and we still made sure we managed a few date nights a week, even if that meant staying at home with baby Rose) I pushed any and all thoughts of Brandon from my mind. Bobby was the man in Rose's life. He may not have been her father, but he was my boyfriend, and with me came little Rose. Bobby told me he'd have it no other way.

Time flew by—having an infant who cries for a feeding every couple hours through the night makes time seem nonexistent. All my days blended into one and I was constantly tired, even though Bobby and the girls helped out as much as they could. Rose needed me for feedings at all times, though, so if I wasn't pumping breast milk in order to jet out for a quick dinner date with Bobby, I was feeding Rose. Or rocking her to sleep. Or singing to her, giving her sponge baths, reading to her, even going for short walks with her in the park.

Before I knew it, Christmas had come and gone (and my bedroom quickly seemed too small for the hoards of toys Rose received from Saint Nick and all her aunts), and New Years Eve was tonight! Bobby had put up a fight about the all-girls New Years Eve party we planned to have at the apartment. I promised him we'd share the next New Years Eve together, and he still gave the classic argument that the New Years holiday, once the clock struck midnight, was *the* night you had to receive your special kiss. It set the precedent for the year's romance.

"You plan on going somewhere next year?" I asked him. "Rose and I too much to handle?"

He caught my chiding. "Fine, then. You have your girls-only time this year. But *next* year you're mine. No arguments."

"I promise."

"Why are you doing an all-girls thing, anyway?"

I laid Rose gently down in the lace-covered bassinet I kept right next to my bed. She bunched her knees upward, then sprawled out and made the sweetest sigh as she drifted off to sleep.

"Because," I whispered, shooing Bobby out of the room. "We

promised one another last year that if any of us were single during New Years, we'd have a girls-only party. Sister support."

He grumbled as I closed the door behind me and turned on the baby monitor—my second cell phone.

"And since Lara and Sophie and Emily are single, we're having our party."

"You're not inviting strippers or anything like that?" Bobby raised an inquisitive eyebrow.

I gave him a soft slug in the shoulder and told him, "We save those kinds of things for bachelorette parties. Now come on. Go on home and I'll see you tomorrow. You're still coming over for a special New Years Day dinner?"

"I suppose..." He winked.

"Because you better. I'm really looking forward to my date with my super sweet and handsome boyfriend." I lured myself closer to Bobby, resting my hands on his waist, and leaning in for a kiss. He pulled me in to him and warmed my lips with a tantalizing kiss. I hadn't been kissed by Bobby like this in a while. Rose always demanded my attention; I was exhausted; the holidays left me even more scatterbrained...but this kiss. Wow. This kiss was...

"You okay?" he whispered, carefully drawing out of the tongue-twisted kiss that left me feeling listless.

"Oh, more than okay," I said, smiling ear-to-ear.

I heard Lara walk into the living room and brought myself down from heaven.

Definitely more than okay.

"I'll see you tomorrow then," he said, stealing one more kiss from me. "See ya, Lara. Have a happy New Year. And you girls don't have too much fun without me."

"To a *fabulous* and *fan-damn-tastic* new year, my ladies!" Jackie said, knocking back her martini. "And to a past year that, despite all the hurdles and drama and, well, *shit*, was a really kickass year."

"Ditto that one," Claire said, taking a sip of her cocktail.

"May next year be as equally amazing! And, you know, minus the crap." Sophie unofficially toasted. "And now our group of girls is *seven*."

"Rose is pretty awesome," Lara said, lightly tickling Rose's small belly. Rose kicked at her soft touch, making the cutest gurgling and bubbly noises.

"I can't believe she's going to be a month old in a few days," Claire said. "It seems like yesterday we were having the girls' night when you told us you were preggers."

"Yeah, and now look at her!" Jackie exclaimed. "Rose is the most perfect baby. She's beautiful and easygoing. She's definitely one of the girls already. Aren't you, little bubby?"

Rose made more bubbles.

"Hey, it's almost midnight!" Emily said, topping everyone's glass off with more champagne, mine with sparkling water.

"Em, why are you leaving us so soon?" I whined. Emily was already due to head back to Ghana the day after New Years. We'd all gotten accustomed to her being back in town and hanging out with us as much as possible; she'd been a huge help with Rose, coming to the apartment nearly every day.

"They need me over there," Emily said.

"We need you here, too," Claire said.

"I know, but you all have each other. And I'll be back soon enough. They really need my help there. I can't turn my back on them."

"No chance of us talking you into staying here?" Lara asked.

"Yeah. No chance?" I said in my baby voice, waving Rose's hands at Emily. "Pwease, Auntie. Stay."

"Oh, I'll be back soon. I always am. You know that."

"Midnight! We're almost there!" Sophie said, pointing a wagging finger at the TV. The ball in New York's Time Square had begun to drop, the countdown on. Ten, nine...

I started to think about New York, about who was there this busy night. I looked down at Rose, who was occasionally pulsing her legs and kicking her feet, as if in her own fit of holiday celebration. Then I thought, only fleetingly, about Brandon. In New York. New career. New life. Seattle becoming a distant memory. Everyone in Seattle forgotten.

"Six, five..." the girls chorused.

And I gave myself until the count of three to put all thoughts of Brandon behind me. A new year. A new start. A new life.

"Two! One! Happy New Year!"

We clinked glasses, the TV screen lit up with fireworks and sparklers. Baby Rose was looking up at me with her bright eyes. The muffled melody of "Auld Lang Syne" began to sound among the cheers and hollers from New York and Seattle, coursing around the walls of my new home—*our* home. The home that Lara and I made for Rose, and where six best friends and a baby rang in the new year, girl style.

EPILOGUE

"You got the candles, right?" I ask Lara as she sets the groceries on the kitchen counter. "Little pink ones?"

"Yup, little pink ones with white stripes."

"And Sophie's got the cake?"

"Cupcakes," Lara says, trying to catch her breath. She'd made it home less than thirty minutes before the crowd was supposed to arrive for Rose's party.

"Excellent!" I say. "Rose's one-month birthday is going to be so much fun. A great excuse for us all to get together. And I'm excited Chad and Conner and Bobby are coming, too! And Kaitlyn! It'll be so much fun." I add a smattering of lip gloss and rub at my cheeks to bring about a hint of color. "And Rose just needs her party dress on and we'll be good to go."

Lara puts the ice cream into the freezer, then follows me into my room where Rose has been taking her second nap of the day.

"Can we wake her?" Lara whispers. She peers over my shoulder as I open the bedroom door.

"If she's down for a good party like us, she'll be awake and ready to go," I say. I can't help but smile brightly as Lara and I step into the room and I see my daughter, wide-awake and gnawing on her tiny fist.

My daughter Rose is already one month old, and growing strong and healthy. She's beautiful and is going to grow up with some amazing female influences. Lara already said she'd make sure Rose knew the importance of establishing a firm presence in the office—make it known that at work she was all-business. Rose could be anyone and do anything she wanted in life, and no competitive rivalry or hotheaded boss could tell her otherwise. For the powerful career woman skills, Lara wanted to take charge.

Sophie said she'd teach Rose how to make the most succulent desserts and the flakiest croissants this side of the Atlantic, while Claire promised she would teach her all about proper puppy care and how to knit or DIY just about anything.

Emily promised she'd teach Rose all about geography, the various cultures of the world, and how to capture it all on camera. Jackie, God bless her, charged herself with the role of teaching Rose the art of landing a man "at any time, any place, any way. Guaranteed." I figure once Rose reaches the dating age we'll discuss Aunt Jackie's methods further—alterations may need to be applied.

And Bobby...well, he wanted to continue our relationship and be a part of Rose's life too. To be a strong male presence and care for her. He even said one night that he felt like Rose *was,* somehow, his. Of course when I told the girls this during a Thursday Netflix night they all asked if we were going to get married, to which I quickly responded, "Things are fine just the way they are. No wedding any time soon." Not to say I wouldn't like to be Mrs. Bobby Holman some day. Trust me, I think about it now and then. But I'm not really ready for that yet. As Lara always says, "The chips will fall as they may," so we'll see. Another story, another painting, another time.

Rose looks up at me and a smile spreads across her chubby-cheeked face. She pumps her slobbery fist about and I scoop her up into my arms.

"How's my little one?" I coo. I start to rock her, tickling her belly.

"This one here?" Lara asks. She's holding up the small pink and white dress that was resting on the diaper changing station.

"That's the one," I answer in a baby voice, directed more to Rose than to Lara. "Isn't that right? Your pretty pink dress, huh?"

Lara helps me dress Rose, and as we're finishing fastening her buttons, the doorbell rings.

"Party time!" Lara says. She gives Rose a light kiss on the forehead then jets to answer the door.

"Come on, little one," I say. I cradle Rose, who seems more content resting comfortably in my arms than moving about, curiously trying to take in her surroundings. She seems very at peace. As is her mom.

"Where's that birthday girl?" I hear Sophie's voice approach from down the hall. "There's the girl of honor!" Claire cries out.

I walk over to them and let them give her the usual kisses and tickles that are owed every time Rose is greeted. I'd heard that when you have a baby, she can command the room. They weren't kidding. Rose was always the center of attention.

"Hey, guys," I say calmly yet warmly, as Sophie, Claire, and I meander into the living room. Bobby, Conner, and Chad are already relaxing on the sofa, then Jackie bursts through the front door carrying a shopping bag, Kaitlyn following behind a second later.

"Baby!" Jackie screeches. She jogs up to me and after she gives Rose a kiss on her cheek, hands me her bag. "Didn't have time to wrap it, sorry," she says exhaustively. "Some cute outfits I found at Nordstrom's. From Uncle Andrew and me." She gives Rose another peck on the cheek, then scampers into the kitchen to help Lara with the party prep.

"Thanks for coming, sis," I tell Kaitlyn.

"Wouldn't miss this adorable bundle's party for anything," Kaitlyn says. She gently touches Rose's head.

"Hey, honey," Bobby says, getting up from his seat.

We share a kiss and he says hello to Rose, who is still peacefully resting in the cradle of my arms.

"This is awesome," I hear Sophie declare from the alcove. She's looking at my recently finished painting, which I'd forgotten to put away.

"Oh, thanks," I say. "Took forever, but it's finally done. Finished it just this morning. I feel good about it."

"It *is* awesome, Robin," Bobby says, taking a look for himself.

"You going to name this one? Or just shelve it like you have a bunch of them?" Lara asks from the kitchen. "I saw it. It's really great. Definitely deserves a name, don't you think?"

Bobby rubs at the back of his neck, deep in thought. "Should even have this one framed and displayed."

"It's basically a representation of my life—of life when Rose came along," I say.

Lara asks, "So *do* you have a name for it?"

"Yeah. What's the name?" Bobby asks.

"*Finding Rose*," I say, smiling, satisfied with the title that had *finally* arrived.

Bobby smiles, too, and says, "Then we best find *Finding Rose* a special place in the nursery."

"Perfect idea," Sophie adds in.

I look around and reflect on how fortunate I am. Funny how things seem to work out. Somehow, in some miraculous way, everything sort of fits together. The chips sort of fall and life goes on and everything comes together somehow. And, perhaps, fantasies and happily-ever-afters actually become realities.

"I think it should go right above Rose's crib," Bobby suggests.

"My thoughts, exactly," I say.

Bobby takes another long look at the painting, then leans over to give me a short but sweet kiss. His kiss, his love, my closest friends, my sister, and my baby girl...my family. They're everything I need, and everything I could ask for in this beautiful and unexpected life where I've found Rose, where I've found true friendship, and where I quite possibly have found true love.

THE END

ACKNOWLEDGMENTS

I would like to thank my dear family and friends for being the rockstars you are!

Many thanks to my super-awesome beta team and girlfriends, Ginger, Anne, Erin, and Jade, for the care and attention you paid to helping make this sequel the best possible. And to my childhood and forever-friend, Crystal, for helping me with all-things-baby.

Special thanks to my editor, Liam Carnahan of Invisible Ink Editing.

And endless thanks to my husband and teammate for never second-guessing my aspirations and abilities. *Ich liebe dich, Christian.*

ABOUT THE AUTHOR

Savannah Page is the author of *Everything the Heart Wants, A Sister's Place,* and the *When Girlfriends* series. Sprinkled with drama and humor, her women's fiction celebrates friendship, love, and life. A native Southern Californian, Savannah lives in Berlin, Germany, with her husband, their goldendoodle, and her collection of books. She enjoys board games, too much coffee, and, like Robin, adventures at IKEA.

Readers can visit her at:

www.SavannahPage.com

Made in United States
Troutdale, OR
11/08/2023